"From the electric, jazzy beginning to the startling climax, *Hot Plastic* is a funny, smart and compulsively readable joyride, peopled by characters as engaging as they are amoral. A real page-turner."

—**Richard North Patterson**, author of *Protect and Defend*

"*Hot Plastic* is a terrific read. It's smart, fast and sexy. It's also funny-sad in a way that really got me. Peter Craig has a wonderful eye for the young, for fallen innocence, for all the ways our world fails us. *Hot Plastic* has depth and intelligence. I highly recommend it."

—**T. Jefferson Parker**, author of *Cold Pursuit*

"As close to the day-to-day workings of modern con men as any sane person would want to get, *Hot Plastic* is a fascinating look at changing times on the grift."

—**Nicholas Pileggi**, author of *Wiseguy* and screenwriter of *GoodFellas*

"*Hot Plastic* is by turns funny, wry, painful, and nail-biting. Peter Craig's portrayal of life and love on the lam is penned with a savage elegance of language and insight that can stun you. This is a smart book by a real writer, and it'll con you out of a night's sleep before you know what hit you."

—**Daniel Hecht**, author of *Skull Session* and *City of Masks*

HOT PLASTIC

PETER CRAIG

HOT PLASTIC

HYPERION NEW YORK

Library of Congress Cataloging-in-Publication Data

Craig, Peter
    Hot plastic / Peter Craig.—1st ed.
        p. cm.
    ISBN 1-4013-0044-8
    1. Triangles (Interpersonal relations)—Fiction. 2. Swindlers and
swindling—Fiction. 3. Fathers and sons—Fiction.   I. Title.

PS3553.R229H68 2004
813'.54—dc21

                                        2003047887

Hyperion books are available for special promotions and premi-
ums. For details contact Michael Rentas, Manager, Inventory and
Premium Sales, Hyperion, 77 West 66th Street, 11th floor, New York,
New York 10023-6298, or call 212-456-0133.

FIRST EDITION

10 9 8 7 6 5 4 3 2 1

For Isabel and Sophie

ACKNOWLEDGMENTS

For their help with the details, both large and small, the author wishes to thank Caroline Jourdes, Natalie Kaire, Keith Kerns, David Martinez, and Amadou Ouedraogo.

Thanks to my wonderful first readers—Amy Scattergood, Scott Berg, Dan Weiss, David Sartorius, Dean Bushala, Judith Weber, and my family.

And, finally, thanks to Nat Sobel and Peternelle van Arsdale, for their hard work, good ideas, and impeccable instincts.

HOT PLASTIC

ESCAPE ROUTE, PLAN B

Because he couldn't take the punishment, riding in the front seat past sirens and searchlights, Kevin Swift rocked in and out of consciousness to the motion of traffic. He bled from his rib cage into a stolen coat. Time skipped blocks ahead. The last residue of sunlight glowed on a smudging vapor trail, a bright slash across the sky, and then it was gone behind helicopters and sharpened taillights. Another jolt ahead, shirt soaking and coat drenched, he gauged the missing time in sweat and shadows. The pain was relentless. No matter how he tried to wrestle free, the bullet was scorching against his bottom rib. He rested his head and kissed the glass. Rolling past ragged palm trees, squat motels, billboards between the frets of power lines, he wondered if blood loss could trigger a déjà vu—for either he had traced this route years ago, or he'd dreamed that he would die like this: in a commandeered sports car penned in slow traffic, with a useless gun, a phony badge, and his partner riding the clutch. While she tilted her head over the dashboard to find the helicopters, she told him to sit up straight as they passed another police blockade.

They were silent for each ring of the car phone.

"And by the way, I'm going to murder your father. I'm going to make it my life's purpose." Her hair was drenched with rancid water, her fingers covered with rust and grime. On her neck and forearms were the burn marks of sprayed gunpowder. Yet to Kevin she had always seemed most beautiful when placed before a backdrop of disaster. The garbage clinging to her seemed like the remaining viscera of some spectacular rebirth.

She whispered, "Don't give up on me, baby."

There was a dusty, sleepy quality of twilight that Kevin remembered from his childhood. Moving under a freeway overpass, through recoiling wind and into another neighborhood of stucco houses with caged windows, he recognized everything, as if his life had been a series of tightening revolutions around this single point.

"Look where we are," he said, and his voice sounded crushed and airless. "We were kids—"

"Shhh, honey. Try not to talk."

"And you still can't drive worth a shit."

"Don't criticize me. I've got enough pressure on me right now. I don't know if those helicopters are following us or not. It's a zoo up there. Are they news or police?"

"They're still circling the building."

"We're both going to keep our heads, and I'm going to get you to a hospital. Shit, I can't turn left here. Hold on a second. I know, I know— Jesus, people are such assholes in this town."

"I'm going to die because you drive like an old lady."

"You're not going to die," she said, with a tone half angry, half pleading. "Is he letting me in? Thank you." She gave a twinkling wave to the back window.

"This is the worst getaway in history."

She accelerated abruptly back into the flow of traffic, prompting horns from every direction. For a moment Kevin felt his heart throbbing in his side, then a sweep of pain rose so viciously up his spine that he began to retch against the closed window. She touched his shoulder, and said, "Oh, *Kevin*. Hang on. You're just sick from the shock. You're going to be fine."

"Elizabeth," he said, tasting blood on his teeth. "I don't want to die in traffic—just tell me how bad I am. And don't lie to me. For once in your life—"

"Okay," she said, reaching across and running her fingers along his face. "You're a train wreck, honey—you're bleeding all over the seat and you're as white as a ghost. But you're going to make it. I swear, on every dollar, as God is my witness, you and I are going to be sitting on an island somewhere under a fucking coconut tree."

Kevin turned his eyes back to the blur of passing shadows, and he thought he would rather curl up and sleep somewhere out there, in a stack of tires, an abandoned refrigerator, or the briar patch of a junkyard. He had learned everything he knew in those dark recesses, growing up like a weed through cracked pavement. "We never got away," he mumbled. "All that time, we were going in circles. Remember? We were right—not here, not here . . ." He made a gun's shape with his hand, poked his finger onto the glass, and pulled the trigger. *"Here."*

BOOK ONE  THE ACCESSORIES

1983–1984

ONE

An hour past sundown on a long summer drive, coming from the high desert in a Mercury Monarch, his father raced through a blind speed trap at the first decline toward a valley of blurred lights. The brakes burned; the roadside gravel sounded like popcorn under the tires. Quickly he shifted the mess of clothes in the backseat, and told Kevin to lie down and play possum until the cop was gone. "Those two bags, Kevin—have a nap on those. If you're getting sick, let's get some mileage out of it. We don't want this guy poking around in here."

Kevin climbed onto the bags and watched the siren flash through the back window. A few months shy of his fifteenth birthday, with something too wise in his narrow face and too alert in his wide gray eyes, he had outgrown this conceit of the helpless child. But when his father switched on the interior light, casting Kevin's reflection onto the glass and over the patrol car, he looked like a sick little boy—black curly hair sprawling and unkempt, cheeks flushed, nose reddened at the tip. Up until now Kevin had believed himself only to be intensely carsick. His appearance startled him and he lay down against the lumpy bags. When his father stretched back and pressed his knuckles

9

onto his forehead, they felt like coarse stones. "Hey, you do have a fever."

"I think I'm really going to throw up, Dad."

"Well, if that cop tries to search the car—puke on him. Play it up. Act like you're losing a kidney. Shut up, he's coming."

Kevin closed his eyes and listened to the crisp steps of boot heels approaching. "Evening, Officer. I know, I admit it—I was going too fast. To tell you the truth, I'm glad you stopped me." A flashlight shined through the open window, across his father's legs and onto a backpack overflowing with ripe laundry. "I got a sick kid in the car, and I got to be honest with you, I just panicked. He's hot as a firecracker, and I thought, holy smokes, we got to get this kid to a doctor before he starts hallucinating." The officer shined his light down through the glass to where Kevin lay marooned in shirts and socks. "How hot does he have to be to damage his brain? I'm just asking because I figure you guys get some kind of medical training."

Sternly the officer replied, "I think you have to be pretty sick for that."

"That's a relief. He's never like this, Officer. He's got my constitution. I mean, the kid can drink a gallon of Tijuana tap water and ride three hours on a bus. Not that he's ever *had* to. So, you know, once he started moaning about stomach pains, I just couldn't help stepping on the gas a little. You got kids, right?"

The officer checked his license and registration. As he returned to his patrol car for paperwork, Jerry stayed still, clutching the wheel and whispering, "Come on, come on, let's go . . ."

When the officer returned to give only a warning, "from one father to another," Jerry nodded his head in stilted agreement and said—as if reciting the motto for a secret society—"toughest job I ever had." Back on the highway he was superstitiously quiet for miles, until suddenly, speeding to merge with thickening city traffic, he began to cheer and thump on the empty passenger seat. "Beautiful work, kid. Fantastic. You're a natural—I ought to rent you out for telethons!"

Jerry kept yelling, so Kevin muffled his ears with a shirt that smelled like sweat and cigarettes. Feeling the car's lullaby drift, he fell asleep for a few dreamless beats, waking up with a jolt, his hair damp with sweat. He was now alone in the parking lot of a pink slab motel, somewhere near the airport and the nocturnes of idling jet engines. Diesel fumes hovered on damp air. Past the shadows of palmetto blades his father stood in a lobby window, talking to the receptionist, vigorously laughing at his own jokes, raising his chin to show a quivering throat.

Becoming suddenly more nauseous, Kevin scrambled outside just in time to throw up onto a sidewalk garden of white rocks and oleander shrubs. By the time his father returned, boots clopping, car keys rattling in his fist, Kevin was lying in an empty parking space. "Kev, you can't really be *this* sick, man. What is it, food poisoning? You don't hardly eat anything but pancakes." He knelt down onto the concrete and his aviator glasses flared briefly with passing headlights. "Look—help me out. If you're really falling apart on me, you got to speak up, man."

Kevin sat back against the car door and brushed the grit from his cheek. "I'm sorry I didn't throw up on the cop."

"I didn't want you to throw up on the cop, dummy. I just wanted you to distract him. Forget it. Now come on. We got a nice room—we're moving up in the world."

"Dad? What are we hiding in the car?"

"*We're* not hiding anything," he said sternly. "Whatever your crazy old man does, it's not your problem."

The room was a narrow stall of polyester curtains and beige wallpaper, carpet freshener and dust circulating through the air conditioner. Kevin complained that his joints hurt, and this new information seemed to alarm his father, who wondered if it was from sleeping in the car or some tropical disease. Even as Kevin lay down on the queen-sized bed, he was distressed by the way his father paced the room, ranting and cursing. In dangerous situations, Jerry usually became more self-assured. Kevin had once seen him cross the border in a stolen car, carrying five hundred film cartridges stuffed with rolled-up bills. In San Diego he had pimped a nonexistent prostitute to a group of drunken sailors, collecting their money and sending them to an abandoned room. He could smile through any lie, and hold court on cars, women, boxing, cockfights, cops, and dirty jokes with any combination of armed and angry men. But he was terrified of illness and betrayal, those surprise attacks from within the ranks, and all that night he alternated between grumbling and pleading at his son's bedside. "You've got to tell me, big guy, you got to tell me exactly how serious this is. Because if we got to hit the emergency room, it's going to take some planning. I can't just waltz in there with a puking kid—they ask questions, you know. All those doctors in their scrubs, they're just cops in blue pajamas."

The planes roared overhead as steadily as shore breaks. Kevin was awake for hours, a greasy sweat dampening his clothes and hair, while he listened to volleys of slamming doors along the hallway, toilets and hissing pipes. He finally slept a feverish hour; and then his father was standing over him in the glare through parted curtains, dressed for the day in a striped shirt with drooping collar flaps, clutching a paper bag. "I got you some primo medicine, big guy. Top of the line. And I want you to try to eat something." He held up an orange, peeled it with his thick, square fingertips, and tossed the rind onto the comforter. Kevin could smell pulp on his hands as he checked for fever.

"I want you to take some of this swill. It's going to taste like death—but—okay, so this shit is for the fever, and this one here is for the puking. This one is for the runs. How you doin' in that department?"

Kevin gave him a thumbs-up.

"Better just take all three." He started wandering around the room looking through drawers and opening cabinets. "*Damn it.* You need a spoon. You can't drink out of the bottle, that's just too uncivilized. Hold on—I got to go steal a spoon."

When he returned he was slapping the spoon on his thigh and mumbling to himself. The light had changed angles, deepening the dirty color of the walls. "You didn't eat your lucky orange."

He poured the pink ooze onto the spoon with such frowning concentration that Kevin laughed. "You look like a big monkey, Dad."

"I am a big monkey." Balancing the spoonful, he paused for a moment. "Hey, man? Can I ask you something?"

Kevin blinked a bead of sweat off his eyelashes, then grunted his permission.

"What kind of shit did your mother used to do?"

Kevin glanced past the unmade bed, to where, in a dusty path of sunlight, the smooth black handle of a revolver poked up through the tangled sleeves of his father's open suitcase. "The same exact thing, Dad."

"Okay. I was just asking. Point of reference. Now open up: here comes the fucking choo-choo."

TWO

That afternoon, as the shadow of the balcony railing slanted farther into the room, his father perched on a lounge chair outside and made phone calls. Every few minutes a plane rose, folding up its wheels, and Kevin found it amusing how his father tried to duck away from the sound with his finger in his ear.

"No, it's just that I got an unforeseen problem here. I got a sick kid on my hands. Let's meet where we said earlier and I'll figure it out—if we wait, we lose the window."

He lifted his glasses to scratch the bridge of his nose. While he talked to the next person in a more familiar voice, he wrote numbers onto the rubber flap of the lounge chair. He dialed again and spoke loudly over a descending jet. "Mr. Rubashov? My name is Jerry Swift— I'm a friend of Lenny's—Lenny Hutsinger? Can you hear me okay? Listen, I'm going to need one of your girls for something a little out of the ordinary, preferably somebody with some medical experience. No, no, *Jesus*—nothing weird like that. Here's the situation: I got some business I can't delay. I'm about to lose a year's worth of work here; but my kid has got typhoid or something. I just need somebody to sit with him, dial

911 if he chokes or turns blue. Somebody who's clean, okay—no drugs—somebody you can vouch for. That's right. Yes, sir, but you understand my predicament. I understand that, but those *baby-sitting services* are just narcs; I don't need DCFS crawling up my ass." With his hand against his forehead like a visor, he peered through the closed portion of the glass door into the room.

"No, sir—in fact she would be under strict orders *not* to do anything of that type. He's only fourteen."

Seeing Kevin awake, Jerry shook his head and slid the door shut all the way. Kevin watched the rest of the conversation without any sound except the murmuring air conditioner: his father crouched down, the phone buried under a tuft of wind-shaken, wheat-colored hair. Kevin held a slice of orange in his mouth. He was so sleepy in the stirring air that he closed his eyes and fell asleep chewing.

He woke to the sound of a straw slurping, the orange now a thin husk against his back teeth. By the far table, a girl was sunk into an armchair with a crossword puzzle propped against her bare legs. She maneuvered an ice chip in her mouth and twirled a pen around her fingers like a small baton. Kevin was disoriented by the dark windows and the changed rhythm of evening traffic. His fever had broken and the sheets were soaked. She had pulled back the comforters and placed towels around him, leaving a damp washcloth on the pillow beside his face. "So?" she said with her cheek bulging, spitting the ice back into the glass. "Did you see an irresistible white light?"

She didn't glance up from the puzzle. Wearing a short miniskirt and an oversized sweater with a collar wide enough to droop off one tanned shoulder, she looked like a teenage girl trying to trick her way into a nightclub. She had traces of kohl around her eyes, and glistening lipstick, but no matter how orchestrated her looks, she couldn't conceal a tomboyish quality to her face. Her cheeks and nose were scattered with freckles, the color of nutmeg, and her hair appeared bleached from lemon and saltwater and long summer afternoons, lightening into loose, feathery strands at the edges. "You were, like—legally dead all afternoon," she said. "Legally, medically. You know what I mean. *Clinically.* How do you spell 'Eurythmics'?"

"Where's my dad?"

"Don't worry. I have detailed instructions in case I have to take you to the hospital. Apparently I'm supposed to wheel you over in a shopping cart and leave a note stuck to your forehead. Your father is adorable, by the way. He was actually shaking. I didn't know there were still guys *that* lost—you know, domestically."

As he sat up to arrange the blankets, the blood drained from his ears and the room spun and settled like a stopping carousel. "How long have you been sitting there?"

"Years," she said. "Every few months I gave you a haircut and trimmed your nails."

He didn't want her to see him shirtless or in his silly pajama bottoms, so he draped a humid sheet entirely around himself and dragged his duffel bag past her to the bathroom. He went through his daily rituals. For almost a half hour he arranged the towels and toiletries into a symmetrical pattern around the sink, combed down his bushy hair, and repacked his duffel so that the shirts didn't touch the socks.

When he returned, the young woman had made the bed, and was now running her fingertip along the windowsills in a facetious search for dust. With fading reception, the television played a sitcom full of emphatic laughter, and Kevin dodged around the rabbit ears to pass her. In a phony British accent, she said, "Ah good, now that you're clean and presentable, I'm going to give you the rules." She raised her chin as she spoke. "I will not tolerate untidiness or mischief. Breakfast will be served at seven o'clock, no excuse for being tardy; I deplore laziness of any kind. And one more thing, you look very nice, a perfect gentle-man—but *do* please use the cologne a bit more sparingly."

"Who the hell are you supposed to be?"

Lapsing back into her hoarse, tomboyish voice, she said, "Shit. I thought it was obvious. I guess I need a flying umbrella." She sat down on the edge of the bed. "Hey—do they have room service in this hole?"

"Just a vending machine."

"You've got to hit your father up for a nicer place," she said. "What does he do anyway? Sell encyclopedias?"

"I don't think so."

She walked to the glass door and looked melodramatically at the darkness. "I daresay he's not a very good provider." Whatever character she was imitating, Kevin had never seen the movie; but he worried that if he admitted this, he would reveal something deprived about his childhood. In her normal voice she said, "You should find out what he does *exactly*. Maybe he sells coke to washed-up movie stars. And you know, Santa is very generous to kids who can rat out their parents."

"I'm not exactly a kid."

"Right, of course not. You're a grown man with footballs on his pajamas."

"I didn't buy those."

"No, no. I know. The tooth fairy brought them."

"You know what—don't even try to mess with me. You may think you're some kind of street girl, but I'm a green belt and I'll kick your ass."

"A green belt. Oh my goodness. Karate *and* pajamas. How thrilling."

"Just forget it."

"You should come over here and feel how my heart is pounding."

"You're crazy, aren't you? You're deranged. Are you on something right now?"

"Maybe I'm just in the early stages of your bubonic plague. Poor me.

Tomorrow I'll drop dead under a bridge somewhere. You'll be a murderer and never even know it." She dove onto the bed, rocking them both on cheap springs. "Actually I'm delirious from hunger. Do you think we can break up this little quarantine and go for a market run?"

So they crossed the street to the gas station, and each moment Kevin had a more difficult time deciding if she was a child or an adult. She bought beer and cigarettes from a man at the counter who rolled his eyes at her ID; then she shoplifted a dozen candy bars.

Back at the motel, they sat on the balcony with their legs draped through the railing, eating packets of powdered doughnuts. Sitting in a pleasant breeze, tinged with the flowery smell of her hair, he clutched the balusters and knocked against her shoulder. She laughed and said, "It's really touching that you're already so in love with me. I'm flattered. But before you get your hopes up, you should know I'm completely out of your league."

"Why? You don't think I could scrape together twenty bucks?"

"Oh my God. You are so dead. That is just so *wrong*."

She hit him in the shoulder with a lopsided fist, and Kevin jumped up, snickering, to flee from her across the room. As she chased him in narrow circles over the bed and around the carpet, she told him that she was going to strangle him and string him up by *his green belt*. He was an evil little man. The game quickly expanded into the hallway, and for the next hour they staged an elaborate barefoot chase around the motel, playing hide-and-seek in the alcoves of ice makers and vending machines, running up and down the stairwell with echoing squeals of laughter.

Up and down three floors and in a wide circle around windowless corridors, she chased him back into the room again, where he dashed onto the balcony. Quickly she locked the door. She stuck her tongue out at him and he pressed his crotch against the glass. "Oh, that's very attractive. You just cool off out there."

He put his lips onto the glass, at first kissing it tenderly; then he exhaled so that his cheeks inflated and his mouth spread wide.

"Wonderful," she said. "You know, I'm going to throw you off that balcony. Then I'll come in here and forge a suicide note."

With his breath he made a circle of fog on the glass, then drew a sad face into it.

" 'Dear world,' " she said. " 'I'm just too big a loser to go on any longer. I've been killed by unrequited love, and I leave my green belt to my criminal father.' "

When she unlocked the door, Kevin climbed over onto the outside of the balcony railing, glancing down at a three-story drop through palm fronds and into an empty section of the parking lot. She gasped and hovered in the doorway, as he crabbed sideways onto the neighboring balcony. He rolled over the railing and tried to open the sliding glass door. It was locked, so he continued to the next balcony, eventually climbing across the entire length of the third floor until he found an open passage through an occupied room. He tiptoed into the darkness, across the blue night light of the television, past a snoring old man and the lit outline of a closed bathroom door, to emerge in the bright hallway, where the girl ambushed him by leaping forward and grabbing his ear. She twisted it and dragged him ahead, whispering, "That was way *out of line*. Oh my God, you're psychotic."

Back in the room, with belts and sheets and the drawstring from a robe, she tied him to the bedpost while he tried not to laugh. "You're going to stay here until I can get an exorcist, *Damian*."

Throughout the ten o'clock news, she sulked on the bed, watching a report on a Korean airliner downed by the Soviets, until the game once again evolved and Kevin played the wounded prisoner of a brutal dominatrix.

"If you ask me politely," she said, "you may have another doughnut."

"Please, mistress, may I have a fucking doughnut?"

"Is that what you think is polite?"

She leaned down and smudged powdered sugar all over his face.

Just then, Jerry returned, nonchalantly dropping his bag and keys onto the cabinet. He cleaned his glasses with his shirttail, then pointed the frames at Kevin and said, "I'm not paying extra for that."

"He just got a little bit excited, sir. He's feeling a lot better."

"What the hell is that powder all over his face?"

"It's from a doughnut," said Kevin.

"You fucking kids are going to give me a heart attack. All right, all right—party's over. Let's untie the boy and you can get back to business." Kevin groaned and rose, easily extricating himself, and the girl dropped into the armchair hugging a throw pillow to her chest.

Massaging his temples, Jerry said, "So we're all fine, right? Nobody was injured; no hemorrhaging. Right? Fantastic. Thank what's-his-name for me—um—Mr. Ruba-somebody."

"Elia? Yeah, sure. I'll thank him." She gave him an awkward smile of tucked-in lips, which made a popping sound as she opened her mouth again. Kevin noticed a somber tension come suddenly over the room.

Without looking at the girl, Jerry fished a roll of cash from his pocket and wiggled off a thick rubber band. "So what are we talking about?"

"Listen, I'm not comfortable discussing business in front of your son."

"What does he care? He's seen money before."

"Could we handle the financial situation someplace else? Please?"

He gave a hiccup of air. "The *financial situation*. Everybody in this town talks like a pissed-off bookie."

"If we could go someplace more private."

"Well, maybe we should cram into the closet? That's private."

She grunted and rose, grabbing his elbow to lead him from the room. At first he seemed amused by her frustration, allowing her to escort him out to the hallway as if he were blindfolded and awaiting a surprise.

As soon as they were gone, Kevin unzipped his father's bag to find hundreds of credit cards held together in stacks with fat rubber bands. They were obvious fakes, with only names and account numbers embossed onto gray or white plastic.

"You've got to be *kidding*," said Jerry, just outside. "What do I look like—some kind of tourist?"

Kevin hunkered down and spied on them through the partly opened door, but the girl's voice was drowned by a stammering change in the air conditioner's cycle.

"I don't care if that's what you think your time is worth," said Jerry, "that's not the *service* you provided here. At least I hope it isn't."

She moved a few steps closer and her voice was audible in fragments: ". . . because I have to make a living, okay? We're not talking about anything else but my time, sir."

"You can't deliver a pizza and charge for filet mignon. You see what I'm saying?"

"No, sir. My time is my *time*. I don't see how there's any—"

"This is bad business, that's what this is. Flat-out unprofessional. And as far as I'm concerned, you don't deserve a dime now."

"Elia said this was all arranged. If you have a problem, you have to deal with him—"

"Oh, okay. I get it. Blackmail. *Great.*"

"I don't make the rules, Mr. Swift. You're putting me in a terrible position."

"You know what? Fine. Here. Go nuts."

Kevin eased the door open and saw the hallway strewn with leaves of cash. She stood with bare feet wide apart, her stiletto sandals wedged into a black velvet purse. His father waited, hands on his hips. "Whatever you think you're worth, kid. Jackpot."

From the disgusted look of her drooping eyelids, Kevin thought she would turn and walk away, crunching over the money; but instead she whispered something, stooped down, and snatched each bill as if she could hurt it. With the velvet purse dangling at her legs like a sling, she said, "This is just about the lamest jackpot I've ever seen." Finally she stuffed the harvest into her purse, gave him the finger, and crossed the hall in fitful strides.

THREE

Kevin told himself that the girl was like so many other vanishing faces: motel clerks, local kids riding old shopping carts, or hitchhikers with cardboard signs. They were features of a passing landscape, staying in his mind no longer than wind devils or drizzly afternoons. But something in her nature, beyond all the crisp details that stayed with him that night—her smile with the one indented tooth, like a sticking piano key, or the suntan-lotion smell that hovered in the pillowcase—something underlying the games and jokes had seemed filled with significance, like the whispered intensity of a secret pact. She had left so bitterly. He wasn't angry with his father: Jerry would always fight over money. But for the first time he wished he could apologize and explain his life. Kevin wasn't dragged along by some unfeeling monster; he wasn't a hostage—and he wasn't a child.

One bright morning when he was twelve years old, his father had arrived out of an approaching dust cloud along the dirt road. His mother had passed away that June, and by the end of the summer Kevin foresaw nothing but a lifetime of habitual mourning. Suddenly, fueled with milk shakes and French fries, Kevin and Jerry began to spend whole afternoons in batting cages, on ragged public golf courses, or riding go-carts around crooked stacks of tires, until Kevin believed that a new and easy life could be formed out of sunny days and spare change. Kevin's aunts spoke about his father with tense mouths, claiming there was more to redemption than a few skipped rocks. He had come off a three-year sentence for a puzzling list of activities (merchant fraud, check kiting, interstate trafficking of stolen goods), and they warned that everything he did had an ulterior motive. Years ago he had brainwashed Kevin's mother and she had only recovered in the nick of time. Enduring their criticism with a tilted smile, Jerry repaired the fences, rewired the chicken coop, built a backstop, fixed the crumbling chimney, telling Kevin stories up on the hot tar paper. "Back when I worked construction, couple of associates and I, we'd give a free inspection to some poor old bag, go up on the roof, knock down the chimney, then charge her an arm and a leg to fix it. Don't worry, Kev—they were rich and mean as badgers. Every last one of them. And I kept them from losing it on bingo and slot machines."

The three aunts and his grandparents would constantly discuss strategies for getting rid of Jerry, always returning to what Kevin's mother "would have wanted." Everyone orbited so tightly around her memory that Kevin believed she hadn't gone away, but had condensed into a black hole with strengthened gravity. Jerry would brusquely reply that she was dead and gone, and—more to the point—she wouldn't have *known* what she wanted; and they would cry and slam doors and discuss him between rooms for the rest of the night. Jerry remembered a vastly different woman, and Kevin knew his version far better than the revised, saintly one who had drawn a pilgrimage of doting relatives. "In her prime, Kevin—before the cancer and this whole conversion—in the old days when she didn't care where I got a car or a necklace, she was the kind of woman who caused traffic accidents whenever she dropped her purse."

By then Kevin mostly remembered the illness, and the way she had become preachy and demanding from her stale-smelling room, hating the food they brought her and expecting sudden and sincere tributes, as if proximity to death had earned her a kingdom of frightened servants. He was never comfortable beside her. He was ashamed by how he had refused to hold her as her body withered, and how he had resented her over those final months. She terrified Kevin with a long list of burdensome wishes—be honorable, decent, and happy, things she never would have told him during her healthy and volatile years. He hated the pitying looks his aunts gave him when he left the room, the way they mussed his hair and tackled him with unsolicited hugs; and he hated how the sickness had usurped all of his mother's original qualities. A few months after her death, no one spoke of anything but her Strength, Courage, and Faith, until Kevin felt that she had been worn down by pious generalities. He grew suspicious of the words, and craved instead his father and all the tangible grime and stink of a cursed life.

On the first anniversary of her death, Jerry had a disagreement with the aunts over the pruning of a tree, which somehow escalated, snowballing across the house through lit and dark rooms, gathering force. A little past midnight, his father came to his bedroom to say good-bye, and Kevin replied, "You better goddamn believe I'm coming with you." His childhood ended with the scraping ignition of a Dodge Dart. They filled the backseat with clothes, bedrolls, potato chips and soda, then pulled out along the dirt road, howling out the open windows. Jerry flicked his cigarette at the row of passing oak trees, leaned back in the seat, and said, "Keep smiling like that, kid—you're going to see the world."

It was never an easy life. Jerry moved between connections, from chop shops along the windy edges of the desert to cheap motels on the interstates. He tried to keep his work away from Kevin, leaving him in karate classes and game rooms, dropping him off for double features or with odd baby-sitters covered with blue-ink tattoos. Kevin quickly understood that no town was safe for more than a week or two. Jerry said that he was a barometer for tension, his fraying nerves manifesting in a passion for order: Kevin couldn't sleep in a new bed that wasn't arranged symmetrically; he would tie his shoes a hundred times until the laces lay in exact proportion to each other. Soon Kevin would eat only breakfast for each meal, and this eccentricity, which had initially amused his father, trapped them within a vast archipelago of twenty-four-hour family diners.

If there was anything he wished the girl could have seen, it was how much Jerry appreciated Kevin and his love of precision. He knew it meant that sometimes Kevin lost track of the larger picture, entire new cities with dingy horizons of phone wires and cypress trees. But he also understood his son's desire for mastery. Like an alien studying a new planet one tiny increment at a time, Kevin became obsessed with clocks, radar, fuzz busters, radio frequencies, police scanners, and revolvers. Jerry was careful not to get him "hooked on something new," because sleep and food were irrelevant to Kevin in the face of some new microscopic discovery. Mostly his father praised him, saying that someday he would be a scientist or inventor—or, at the very least, the greatest handyman the world had ever known.

Like any good partners, they each became indispensable to the other. Jerry relied on his son's patterns and organization, and often said that without him, he would get lost forever in the fast-food wrappers he threw into the backseat. But he could also tell whenever Kevin's meticulous nature was becoming too confined, when his son was trapped between pinions of a disassembled watch, with the irritable intensity of a boy who dreamed of controlling time itself; and those days, Jerry would spirit him away to the clutter of some nighttime carnival, or drive to a lake past dark, banks full of crickets and bonfire rocks, and they would swim or run or kneel on a beach in the tide, until the weight of so much anxiety was shaken loose and scattered, and the only thing between heartbreak and freedom was a thin tissue of air, torn open with fingernails, teeth, or a fist through the wind.

FOUR

Late afternoon in a restaurant near the marina, Kevin ate his ritual breakfast of pancakes and orange slices, while Jerry recovered from a tough hangover with a Bloody Mary and a withered celery stalk.

With his mouth full, Kevin said, "You're going to get killed and I'm going to wind up in some kind of boy's farm."

"They don't even have those places anymore, dummy. Reagan threw all those lunatics out in the streets with the air-traffic controllers."

"Everything fell apart at your meeting. Didn't it?"

"Tell me something. Have you ever gone without anything in your entire life?"

"Yeah. Lots of things."

"You might think that, but in most countries, kids would be thrilled to have what you do. Look around, man. We're sitting on the shore, in the sunshine. Seagulls flying around. You're having breakfast at three in the afternoon. That's paradise to some people."

"You're trying to move all those credit cards," said Kevin, sucking an orange. "It's ridiculous to pretend like I don't know anything. You're not a good enough liar to hide things from me."

"I'm the best liar in this city right now."

"I'll make you a bet. If I scam breakfast, I want in on it."

"You want *in on it*. Are you crazy? You think I'm going to involve my son with these animals? Forget it. As far as I'm concerned you don't know a damn thing. I don't want any accessories here. You're not a witness, you're not an accomplice—you're just a weird kid who needs a haircut."

"That makes me a kidnapping, Dad. And it sucks. You might as well put duct tape over my mouth."

"I'm going to put duct tape over your mouth—as soon as you get enough calories in there."

"If I get us a free breakfast, all on my own, then you have to tell me what's going on. I can still lie if I ever go in front of a judge. I'll say you brainwashed me."

"You'd sell your old man out like that?"

Kevin put the orange rind over his teeth and smiled.

"Fine," said Jerry. "I want to see this."

As Kevin paid for the meal, chattering away about the quality of service while the cashier hunted and pecked through register keys, he asked if he could have a ten to replace all of his crumpled singles. Cheerfully she gave him a bill while he kept counting and organizing the mess. Then he handed her back nine ones with the same ten reinserted into the bundle.

"Thank you, ma'am," he said, as he started to turn away. She noticed the apparent mistake. "Wait a sec, hon. You gave me nineteen here."

"Oh no. Did I really?" said Kevin. "I'm such an idiot. *Thank you.* How 'bout I just give you another one—make it easier."

The cashier smiled and handed him a twenty-dollar bill, and Kevin pushed through the doors, past his chuckling father, into the glare outside. Snorting as if trying to contain a sneeze, Jerry walked quickly to the

Mercury where he shooed away a seagull. Once they were inside the sweltering car on hot seats, he finally broke out laughing. "Did you see her lips moving while she was thinking about it? Man, I've never seen anybody get so confused. Fantastic, Kevin. Fantastic!"

"It's only ten dollars."

"It's the easiest ten dollars I ever saw. You've been watching everything, haven't you? You little shit. Roll down the window, for God's sake—I'm roasting alive in here."

All during that blistering afternoon Kevin waited in the car while his father ran errands, reluctantly explaining the ongoing con in the short drives between discount markets and peeling houses with bars over the windows. Apparently he needed to stock the shelves of a store that didn't actually sell anything, "to make it look real for any goddamn bank investigators." He ran into thrift shops and emerged with armfuls of awful pastel and lime-green clothes, leg warmers, and multicolored headbands, heaving them into the backseat. "You set up a fake business—it costs virtually nothing, and nobody ever checks the names. I'm just one guy on a team here and this isn't supposed to be my job."

At a ninety-nine-cent store he trundled out two shopping carts full of glass figurines, and threw them into the trunk with a shattering sound. "I was just supposed to supply the card numbers and get out of here."

"Those credit cards don't look like anything, Dad."

"They don't need to. That's white plastic. The accounts are the only things that are real. We've got plenty of merchants willing to put that bullshit through; they just take a little cut themselves. You can get *real* cards easily, it just takes longer and it's a pain in the ass."

They unloaded the car at a dilapidated mini-mall by the airport, where plywooded windows were covered with graffiti and the only extant business was a nail salon where two listless women stood in the doorway smoking cigarettes. Back in the car, the sun now fallen beneath the phone wires, Jerry continued, "See, we rent this little hole-in-the-wall store, make it look halfway legit, then in the first couple days we make huge deposits off these hot account numbers. Massive. Nobody's actually buying or selling anything, you understand—but we're charging five grand worth of ugly shirts to Mrs. Whoever in Wherever, Illinois. Understand? The banks, you know, all the different banks in the network, they wire the money into an account long before it even shows up on a statement; we wire it around into a bunch of other, smaller accounts; then, by the end of the week, we cash out and head off for a little vacation. It's a snap, but you need people with balls—not a bunch of crybabies."

"What happens to the woman in Illinois?"

"What woman in Illinois? Oh, *her*. She won't owe anything, kid. Just a headache and a few pennies a year in raised fees. Everybody pays a little bit, every month. It's like tithing. We're all part of the same big church and we're all paying our dues, you know. Welcome to the frontier."

Early that evening when they returned to the motel lobby, Kevin immediately noticed a woman's bare feet sticking out from behind an arrangement of shrubbery. Black and white clogs slipped off, her toenails were sprinkled with glitter that clung like silt around the heels. Kevin cradled a grocery bag in both arms, and after several paces he could see that it was the girl from last night, her reflection warped in the dimpled copper surface of the ficus pots. While his father was checking messages at the desk, Kevin slid past the branches and leaned against the mirror across from her. She wore white pants with a few smudges of dirt around the thighs; her hair was bound into a single doorknob knot like a tango dancer's; and in a crescent beneath her left eye, there was a thumb-sized bruise, yellow and violet. Her bottom lip was split. The rest of her face had suffered a counterstrike of makeup: a matching angry shade of purple over her eyes, and a paved layer of base.

She grimaced and commented on his sunburn, reaching forward to lift his sleeve off the sharp border of different pigments. Dropping back onto the bench, she lit a cigarette, exhaled, and watched the braided smoke rise through the leaves. Kevin said that he hadn't remembered to ask her name.

"Colette," she told him, with the softened note of a question in her voice.

Around the shrubbery Jerry approached carrying the rest of the groceries, and when he saw her, he made a sputtering noise. "Oh shit. It's the six-million-dollar girl. Get away from her, Kevin—we don't have the money."

"We're just talking," she said.

"Yeah, well, stop talking. Listen, miss, I don't know what's wrong with you, but don't try to get to me by manipulating my son. We're not going through this song and dance again."

"I need to talk to you. I'm getting out of here," she said. "Out of town. Okay? Probably out of the country. I'm being totally reasonable here. I just need the money you owe me; I need at least *half*—"

"I'm not listening to this."

She followed them toward the room and Kevin felt light-headed as she approached. "You can't treat me like this. If I wanted to make trouble, believe me, I could. You *know* the people I'm talking about."

"I don't know a damn thing."

She met Kevin's eyes while still speaking to his father. "I can call the police, you know. I can tell them what you've got in that room. I'm not somebody you can just push around. I had to cover what you didn't pay me last night."

Like a jaywalker on a highway, Jerry scanned the hall before he crossed to her, then he cocked his head to project a whisper more forcefully at her lowered face. "Don't threaten me with that kind of shit. Don't even fucking *try*—"

"I just," she said, with her voice beginning to tremble, "I owe a lot of money, all right. I did you a favor and I didn't even know you. I need to be making money every second to keep from drowning here and I can't do it, I can't take it. Don't you understand? I can't go anywhere else. Just please listen and don't look at me like that. If you knew me, you would be on my side. You would see how *scared* I am."

Jerry closed his eyes and whispered to himself. Somehow she had stumbled upon a magic word, confusing him and loosening his fists. He studied her face. Barely opening his lips, he said, "Yeah. So you're cornered. Everybody gets cornered sometimes. Doesn't make it my problem."

"Just what you owed me last night, it's enough to get me out of here. It would take so little for you to help me. Just the slightest bit of human decency."

"Well, right now there's probably some old lady with her ear to the door, so let's get out of the hall before she calls the cops on all of us."

She waited for him to unlock the door, throw down his bags, and find the light switch. As he hooked his boot around the weighted door, he glanced back at her, his teeth resting on his lips midway between a smile and a wince. He said, "You're right, okay: I'm the biggest son of a bitch in town. But we know that already. So come in—there's no more surprises."

She shrugged, then entered the room by ducking under his extended arm. Kevin had the electrified sense of a whole dangerous world in a siege outside the windows. Once his father closed the curtains, turned up the air conditioner, and threw his bag into the closet, a new plan seemed ready to unfold. Jerry spun a chair in a pirouette and mounted it backward.

"Look," he said. "I *do* know what it's like having this kind of thing hanging on you day and night. You're either somebody's pimp or somebody's whore in this world, and you sure as hell don't get a promotion from one to the other. I can't give you the money—now wait a second, wait until I finish—because I don't have it right this second. Ask Kevin—it's tied up in inventory. Now just *listen,* don't get all riled up again. I know you think I'm scum, but as soon as this shit comes through, I'm going to be rich. I'm not talking the kind of rich where you just worry about germs and commies, but enough to keep this kid full of pancakes for a long time. So my idea is this: lay low, hang out. Have a vacation for a couple days, you and Kevin. Go to the zoo. Whatever. Hell, the kid needs an education anyway—go see King Tut. And when I get through with this fiasco, I'll buy you a ticket wherever you want to go. Rio, Bali, Timbuktu. I don't give a shit. Throw a dart and see where it lands."

"Why would you suddenly do that for me?"

"Well—sometimes people have the same enemies."

"And that makes them friends?"

"No, friends are overrated. More like countrymen. You speak the same language."

She flashed a smile, and then, for some reason, blushed and glanced away at the floor. Jerry lowered his head to chase her eyes, and asked, "Is that a yes?"

"You better not be lying."

Because he said it was "the most gentlemanly thing to do" (which made Colette giggle for the first time), Jerry bought a separate room on the credit card that night. Kevin fell asleep in all his clothes, stretched diagonally across the comforter of the old room. He woke with a woman's pea coat draped over his shoulders. Humidity from the shower still dampened the upper halves of mirrors and windows. There were new bags in the room, a purple backpack and a leopard-skin valise, and Kevin assumed that he had slept through whatever dawn rescue mission had salvaged them from her previous life. When he tried the door to the other room, it was locked. Colette slipped out, balmy with damp hair and the smell of shampoo. As if Kevin had become younger overnight, she had a new patronizing tone, explaining that Jerry needed to work all day without distractions. Gripping his wrist, she whispered, "Come on, we're having a field trip. Don't make me get violent."

Jerry had loaned her the car keys for the day, and she was the worst driver Kevin had ever seen, stepping on the brake whenever she had an idea, hesitating to make a right turn into sparse boulevard traffic, and craning her neck to locate passing horns and shouts. When they finally made it safely to Venice Beach that morning, walking arm in arm past souvenir stands, street painters, and churro wagons, Kevin's light-hearted mood seemed to come mostly from relief that he had survived the trip. They sat at a café and watched tourists stroll past with balloons and visors, rosy cheeks and sunburned kneecaps.

For a long time, she talked about how handsome she found Jerry. After Kevin had stewed awhile, he made the mistake of disagreeing, prompting her to list his father's every attractive feature: a rugged hockey player's nose, big hands, and the relaxed way his neck and shoulders seemed to move when he walked. She liked his blue eyes on the rough canvas of his face; and most of all, she liked something in his voice, something like a comforting whisper in a storm, bold and con-spiratorial, which made her feel like any moment he might key her into all the world's greatest secrets. Kevin stopped listening and watched her face in the changing sunlight through ruffling sycamore trees along the beach. The bruise had deepened overnight, but without makeup, her eyes seemed more thoughtful, a startling green color like a deep stretch of ocean.

"Does he make any real money?" she asked.

"My dad? Sure, all the time. We're just laying low in that motel, you know. Usually we stay in the Grand, like—whatever. You know, a fancier place." He slurped his drink, and added, "With a pool."

"So according to him, this is supposed to be an educational day," she said, stealing a bite of his pancakes. "What do you want to learn? I'm just overflowing with knowledge here. Look at me. I can't keep it to myself any longer."

A man was walking past, fumbling through his wallet, a streamer of toilet paper dragging from his heel. "That poor slob," said Kevin. "I wonder how much cash you could make just off idiots like that."

"What do you say we go shopping, darling? That's the one area where I truly excel."

"I don't need to learn to *shop*, Colette. It's not exactly a science."

"It is if you're broke."

Her face was pink in the heat. She sipped her drink, crunching the last surviving chip of ice, and smiled at him with a closed mouth, lips stretched wide, a look so mischievous that it woke the little hairs on his arms and neck. "You don't have to do anything that makes you uncomfortable," she whispered.

Out on the beach in the noonday sun, using a handful of stolen Sweet'N Low packets and the car keys, she showed Kevin the basic techniques of shoplifting: pick up two identical items; throw one rapidly down the unbuttoned collar of his white oxford shirt so that it landed inside the sleeve, just under the armpit—or "in a fob pocket, if you're hopelessly traditional," she said; then conspicuously put the matching item back into its place. She was amused by the frustrated and determined way Kevin practiced this technique for over an hour on the scorching sand. She lay back on her wadded sweatshirt and purse, having stripped down to an orange bathing suit top. Kevin kept glancing at her, and each time she would open her eyes, facing him with a squint and her flat palm blocking the sun, while he quickly returned to his insistent practicing.

"You know what, Kevin? I've decided that you're a total maniac. Your father may *seem* crazy, but you're actually the real nutcase in the family. You've been standing there for an hour and a half throwing sugar packets into your sleeve."

"I'm a perfectionist."

"Perfectionism is for surgeons and architects. What you're learning is something people do to *avoid* that kind of effort."

"I just want to get it right, Colette. That's the way I am. If you show me something, I'm not going to do it half-assed."

"Well, then tuck your shirt in. That way, if it falls through, it gets hung up on the bottom. And then let's go boost some lighters, for God's sake. Show me what you got, little man."

They passed in and out of kiosks along the promenade, stealing chintzy rings, dolphin pendants, and glass bangles, watching each other in the convex security mirrors. Kevin could care less what he was stealing; but between each display rack, Colette bemoaned the worsening quality of beachfront crap, saying that if they worked this strip for an entire week they might accumulate the street value of a hamburger. Kevin was rapt with the task, studying only the size and weight of the items—agate earrings and Swatch watches—becoming so charged that his fingertips were tingling.

Prowling around T-shirt racks and under jangling wind chimes, Kevin overcame his sweaty palms and stampeding heartbeat by focusing on technique, cursing himself for each miscue, whether flubbing an easy shot into his billowing sleeve or gouging himself with a Japanese throwing star. Colette, on the other hand, was festive and improvisational and, like a daredevil, seemed to attract attention on purpose. Upon entering each store, she would start in the middle of a lurid speech about her sex life. "So anyway, he's a gunnery sergeant down in San Clemente," she said, somehow pitching silver bracelets into her sweatshirt hood as she loudly continued, ". . . and the guy had a kickstand practically. I mean, I'm a young woman—and *holy Moses*—I didn't think I had the equipment for that kind of ordnance, if you know what I mean."

At first Kevin thought that she was only showing off or trying to distract him. But he soon realized that there was a method to it. Though she drew a great deal of staring and suppressed giggles as she first came into a store, detailing a date's latex fetish or her own desire to dress up as Batwoman, eventually clerks and other shoppers looked away from her in embarrassment, covering their faces, shaking their heads, and she was ingenious about timing her thefts to the wincing reactions around her.

The banter wasn't always dirty. Apparently she read the cashier and whatever terrain of browsers, salespeople, and security personnel to decide which persona and narrative would provide the most cover. In a makeshift stall of African handbags and onyx talismans, she became a desperate and battered woman: "You can't call the police, because he'll kill me. He'll do it too. Look at my eye." She started to cry. As the staff whispered and circled at a distance, Colette broke into a coughing fit that became so hysterical she needed to hunch over and run from the store. Kevin assumed the game was over. But when he caught up to her on the bike path, she nudged him off stride and stuck out her tongue, showing him, on the tip, a tiny pair of earrings.

Amid scarves, Hacky Sacks, and incense sticks, she was an expecting mother loudly considering natural childbirth into a tub of Jell-O; and along a rack of jewelry and Vuarnet sunglasses, she was the snottiest princess on the beach, forcing a clerk to avert his eyes in fear: "Excuse me, Mr. Salesperson? A hundred dollars? You're not honestly trying to claim this is a real emerald chip, are you? Because I happen to have a cough drop in my mouth that tastes just like it."

Finally, in a store playing a hypnosis tape with the sound of the ocean (running slightly out of sync with the real ocean), while covering each finger with a different smoldering mood ring, she turned to Kevin and proclaimed: "I'm in love." She started returning the rings, every third one vanishing down her sweatshirt sleeve. "It's the first time in my pathetic life—that's for sure. Of course, I'm a little disappointed. I always expected that when it happened, it would solve all my problems. I'd live a good life afterward, never make any mistakes, never do anything stupid. Instead I just feel completely hopeless, like I'll have to go back to the grind in a few days and everything will be that much harder. Happiness just makes fun of people like us." She smiled at Kevin and added, "You're wondering—who's the lucky bastard?"

Just then, Kevin's shirt, which was tucked and weighted down with merchandise that had fallen to his beltline, was pulled loose by his sudden twisting motion toward her, so that two handfuls of worry beads drained onto the floor.

Colette grabbed his arm and said, "No, honey. They're not marbles." To the saleswoman she called, "Excuse us, he's made a mess again. We'll just go get a broom from the shop next door. I'm so sorry."

The saleswoman raised her voice behind them: "Excuse me? *Excuse me*," stepping out of the store and trailing them a few yards along the promenade. Colette clamped onto his arm, whispering, "Just walk, don't run, just walk," until the woman whistled with impressive volume and summoned two cops from beside an ice-cream stand.

Colette loosened her grip on his arm and said, "*Now* run."

They dodged through pedestrian traffic, balancing along a low brick wall, racing through a pickup basketball game and back into the crowds, narrowly avoiding roller skaters, rupturing through the joined hands of strolling couples, trampling over the flattened boxes of break-dancers and piercing through tambourine-jangling clusters of Hare Krishnas. He kept track of Colette only by the waving flag of her pony-tail, and once he caught up with her in an alley that smelled of Chinese food, he yanked the hood of her sweatshirt, dropping a trail of rings. She was laughing. "Pipe down," she said. "You're cracking under the pressure."

When they reached the car, she couldn't find the keys. She searched frantically through her purse full of trinkets while rhinestones fell from her sleeves and pockets, until Kevin grinned and dangled the keys in front of her eyes. She snatched them, but Kevin refused to let go until she tickled him under his extended arm.

She said, "If we're going to have any future as a criminal duo, you're going to need to grow up."

FIVE

Back at the motel, Jerry came to the door wrapped in a towel, bare shoulders steaming as he bored the tip of a washcloth into his ear. "Wait, wait," he said. "We need a drumroll. Both of you—close your eyes."

They stepped into the room with their hands over their eyes while Jerry hopped into his pants. "All right, no peeking. Whoever peeks is going to get a foot in the ass. All right, all right—open 'em."

In the effort to create a mood, he had tied ribbons around the room, but they drooped so lopsidedly that they instead seemed like strings on an amnesiac's fingers. Three presents sat on the bed. He had attempted to gift-wrap them with wads of old newspapers, comprised mostly of want ads and frowning underwear models. "I can't believe you got me a present," said Colette, and playfully slapped his shaved cheek. He handed her the smallest package, and she perched on the edge of the bed to unfasten the corners, spreading out the smudged paper as if she might frame it, then furrowing her eyebrows at the sight of a velvet box. "Oh, no."

"Hey, when things go well for me, they go well for everybody. That's just the kind of snake I am."

She eased open the box, then held up a gold chain with a sparkling droplet on the end, casting a wavering spot of refracted light onto her forehead. At first she frowned as if for an obvious fake; but then she made a stunned click with her tongue and the focus left her eyes, as if she were remembering something distant. An entire afternoon culling through storefront garbage had been overwhelmed by one tiny rock.

"It's real," said Jerry. "Go ahead and bite it."

She composed herself with a quick swipe of her fingers under her eyelashes. "You don't even *know* me."

"You don't seem very happy. If I thought you were going to be upset, I'd a' bought you a yo-yo or something. Hey, dingo—open yours."

"It's beautiful. Thank you."

"You see, we're all square. Open your presents, meatball! I started out this morning and I just knew everything was perfect. Ever have one of those days? Perfect! Ran out of gas right at the station—pulled up and bam—dead. Right at the pump. And I said, if that isn't a good omen . . ."

Kevin opened the first box, clawing through the wrapping to uncover a helmet detailed with a sparkly American flag.

"There you go. Put it on. Anyway, I did everything right today. Cleaned out the last account. End of story. Hey, look at Evel Knievel."

Kevin stood in the middle of the room with the heavy helmet over his head, muting the sound, making his neck feel thin. "What the hell is this for?"

"Open the other one, you moron."

He tore the newspaper and dug out a skateboard from the tattered shreds.

"That's the Cadillac of skateboards, kid. State of the art. Might as well have diamonds for wheels. I talked to every kid in the store and that is one cold-blooded board. I figure it'll get you out of the house more often."

Kevin was distracted by the thought that his father might be trying to get rid of him, to roll him away downhill toward a busy highway. No one was moving in the room.

"Why don't you go practice?" said Jerry.

"Right now?"

"Yeah, sure. We'll pack up in here. Colette will help me. Right, baby?"

Defeated and exiled, Kevin tried out the board on the long runway of the halls, speeding into the ash cans and ice machines. Because the wheels rolled too slowly on the spongy carpet, he carried it upstairs to the roof and burst out onto a flushed night sky, across an undulating terrain of tar paper around the bulkheads of elevator shafts and cooling towers, all penned in by a waist-high wall. A cool breeze smelling of rubber, soot, and palm dust swept off the low rooftops. Maybe he could get some benefit out of the stupid childhood toy. He imagined skating through the kiosks of that day, aisle to aisle, in this constant floating motion, or maybe department stores, suddenly deft enough to boost rings and real diamond necklaces while accelerating toward revolving doors.

Lost in the fantasy of weaving through display cases and escaping down escalators, Kevin began racing toward the stairs repeatedly, leaping off the board, kicking it upward into his hand and shambling downward. The moon rose higher; the traffic diminished below. He skated around the roof for another try, and when he rounded a bulkhead, he saw Colette against the faint western horizon.

"I've been looking all over for you," she said. Her lips sounded loose and she was sniffling in the warm wind. "Listen, I wanted to tell you how much fun I had. I got my money, so . . . Everything's fine. Everything will be okay. But I'm on my way again—off into the real world. I guess our love was never meant to be."

He pushed off harder and ignored her. Farther away on the tar paper, he could just hear the faint intonation of her voice, buried by the pestle of his wheels. He looped around her again, an elliptical orbit, and she called out, "Are you going to slow down enough to say good-bye?"

A jet ripped overhead and dissipated into a residue of thunder.

"I guess you're in your insane practice mode again. Just nod or something. Stamp your feet on the board twice."

"Watch this," he said, speeding toward the stairwell.

After barreling past the open fire door in a fluid motion, he waited too long and launched over the concrete steps. For a single stalling millisecond he saw the possibility of grabbing the board to negotiate the landing below; but the board twisted out from under him, and he hit the concrete in a tangled mess of splayed legs and dog-paddling arms. Colette rushed downstairs so quickly that a platform shoe shook loose and skipped toward him like the last rock in an avalanche. "You moron! You *freak*!" she shouted. "What are you *thinking*? Oh God, sweetie—you just murdered yourself. Don't panic. You're going to be okay. Don't move."

Beached beneath the fluorescent lights, where a gray moth batted and circled, he felt almost peaceful, until, warming up like an electric blanket, he began to notice the precise spots where he'd damaged himself: wrist, ribs, hipbone, back. His father's voice echoed from the landing below: "Kevin, you are a first-class bozo, you know that? It took you just over an hour to kill yourself with that thing. He's all right. That's why I got the helmet."

"Don't move him, Jerry! You didn't see it. He broke every bone in his body."

"Oh, stop. He didn't break anything—this kid's like a squirrel. He fell out of a tree once and he just ripped his pants a little."

His father grabbed him beneath the arms and hoisted him to his feet, and, despite the dizzy slice of pain from his ribs to his temples, Kevin was happy that his legs were intact.

"Let me carry that awful thing," said Colette. He slid his arm around her waist and, even with his wrist thumping at her side, he liked the feeling of butterfly breaths under her new T-shirt. His father took off his helmet and ruffled his hair, and they moved as one carousing, six-legged creature onto their floor, all the way to the door of the room. The phone was ringing. Kevin sat on the closed toilet lid while Colette soaked a washcloth for his cuts. She held his wrist on her palm. "You just get set on doing something, don't you? You forget everything else."

In the other room, Jerry said, "Who? *Who?* I'm asking you who called to complain. The kid just fell down the stairs—he's clumsy. Everything is under control up here. Oh, you got to be kidding." He hung up so violently that the phone rang like a service bell.

At the threshold he leaned inward with both hands on the door frame above. "We have to get out of here right this second."

"Jerry, his wrist is swollen."

"We have to go. *Now.* Somebody complained to the front desk, and that jackass just called the police on us."

"For what?"

"I don't *know,* Colette—they thought we were sacrificing a goat or something. Just let's get our shit to the car and don't look back. If you're going your own way, then *adios.* But I suggest you start running now."

Bags over shoulders, board tucked under his arm, Jerry stumbled down the hall, through a side door, ducking his head through swatting palm fronds. Colette followed and landed with her bags in a pile at her feet, hands on her hips. After the hard dash to the car, she was panting and flushed. She parted her lips, but remained quiet, with a look of childish confusion. Jerry smiled and ran his hand over the Mercury like a salesman in a showroom.

"It's not a white horse," he said. "But if you're interested, it's a ride out of town."

SIX

Besides his sprained wrist, which Kevin wrapped and rewrapped each night with a new collection of Ace bandages, the next few weeks became a catalog of bruises and abrasions: gouged elbows and scuffed knees, cheese-grater skin on the palms of his hands. He rolled into a cactus garden in Scottsdale, Arizona; bruised his tailbone trying to ride a low railing in Albuquerque. After a hard spill somewhere in the Texas panhandle, Colette studied his pupils with a flashlight, and swore that if he ever tried to leap off a retaining wall again, she would murder him with a shoe.

The board turned every rolling parking lot of horse trailers and Winnebagos into an amusement park, and initially Colette and Jerry had capitalized on his new hobby. Whenever they wanted time alone, the board would be sitting in the hallway, or tilted against the door like a *Do Not Disturb* sign with wheels; and Kevin would skate off cursing, punching vending machines and throwing himself headlong down an asphalt hill toward the parking blocks and newspaper stands in the distance. If he was bleeding badly enough, skewered on a holly bush or a cyclone fence, he would return to the room, knock on the door and claim that he needed stitches, eavesdropping on the whispered argument, until the door would open to reveal them both red-faced and hastily dressed, his father with a clenched jaw and Colette with her eyes unfocused, as if she were listening to a song in her head. "Sorry to bother you again," Kevin would say. "But I'm losing a lot of blood here and I started to get light-headed."

When Kevin was wrapped with gauze and surgical tape, Jerry would walk him around the motel, once fatuously claiming that he and Colette needed to take long naps because of their late-night planning sessions. Could Kevin please amuse himself in a less masochistic way? "I mean, do you *ever* land one of these tricks? It seems like all you do is fall down from different angles."

So Kevin would go to his adjoining room and practice throwing soap bars into his sleeves. A month into their eastward trip, he couldn't believe how his father and Colette had bonded, their initial maddening honeymoon segueing into an even more excruciating apprenticeship, during which, for long drives along I-40, over the Ozarks and into the Smokies, Jerry would lecture her about the fundamentals of the grift, from check kiting to white plastic to the old-fashioned pigeon drop and Jamaican switch. No matter how diligently Kevin memorized and practiced what he overheard during the long rides between motor courts and diners, where his father and Colette snuggled together in the booths and teased him about his fetishistic oranges and pancakes, Kevin still resented having been demoted to the lowliest bagman in this newly formed team. At night he would lie awake with the door partially ajar between rooms, watching their television flicker like distant heat lightning, and he would fantasize that someday he would devise his own con, some great ruse that would forever bear his name, immortalizing him like P. T. Barnum or Charles Ponzi, some heist so perfect that it would leave all the world's greatest hustlers in an impoverished trail of love and admiration.

SEVEN

One night in the first week of December, they went Dumpster diving
through a wealthy Maryland suburb of D.C., in a pickup that sounded
full of crickets at each bump in the road. They cruised through a neighborhood of giant houses and vast treeless yards. Colette wore a cowboy
hat slanted over her eyes; Kevin pulled the hood up on his black sweatshirt, like a monk's cowl. The night was unseasonably cold, and just
after one A.M. the air filled up with thin flurries for the season's first
snow, dusting the lawns and the long brick walkways, gathering under
the feet of jockey statues and the bark-covered clearings of dormant
rosebushes. The snow fell in spirals around the Doric columns of
porches and past weather vanes perched like crows against faintly
luminous clouds, but melted as soon as they touched the glazed
streets.

"Look at how these motherfuckers live," said Jerry. "You could make
a whole new continent out of their garbage."

"What are you waiting for, baby?"

"Just want some damn cover. Nobody's heard of a tree around here.

All right, this is good. I'll write the address. Now—Kevin, wake up. Not so loud this time."

Kevin and Colette slid off the seat and ran to a trash can at the base of the driveway. The air was spun full of flakes and Colette stood a few moments trying to catch them on her tongue. Kevin swept a puddle off the tarp over the back bed and unhooked the Bungee cords; he and Colette piled the garbage bags inside and he refastened the tarp over the lumps. Back in the front cab, with the defroster cooking a rancid smell, a radio commercial murmuring like a conversation in crossed telephone lines, Colette scrubbed her hands with napkins and spit some lingering taste off her lips.

"I think those people had a dead cat in there."

Back at the motel parking lot, in the diminishing snowfall, beside a highway of passing rigs and splashing tires, with his yellow dishwashing gloves and barbecue tongs, Kevin's job was to sort bills, carbons, and credit card applications from the trash. When Colette came out to check on him, jumping in place in only a robe and slippers, she laughed at the way he reconstructed each household into its own representative pile. While one house had a pile of microwave dinners—fish sticks and macaroni—along with trails of discarded double-A batteries, another was mostly empty cans of fruit cocktail and peaches, spent tubes of liniment, boxes from saltine crackers and Lorna Doone cookies, and moldering jars of pickle relish.

He explained his system to Colette: "The second house is some old lady losing her mind. She's got a bad back or something, and she probably doesn't spend much money on anything. There's definitely not a microwave in the house, no cable, and if there's a Beta-Max, the clock will be flashing midnight until the end of the world."

Colette laughed and blew into her cupped hands.

"But the other house has got kids, obviously. And they spend *a lot* of money on glow-in-the-dark neon crap; here's some ColecoVision cartridges—they even bought the Adam home computer and nobody bought that thing. And look at *this*: pieces of a Rubik's Cube. They keep buying them and somebody keeps taking them apart. They're impatient, whoever they are. But they believe in luck." He held up a piece of opened mail: a Publishers Clearing House envelope. "That's the first one of those I've seen open in ten houses."

"Kevin, do me a favor. Take a long, hot shower. And promise me you'll throw this stuff away when you're finished making dollhouses out of it. You're too cute to grow up into one of those people who hoards newspapers and cans."

Colette brewed coffee an hour before dawn, then sat on the linoleum of the motel's kitchenette to comb through the salvaged papers with Kevin. "Hon? We got a couple more preapproved applications. No Soc numbers, no maiden names. We got a lot of carbons, but the info is pretty spotty—we're going to have to send Kev door-to-door. Some of these people won't have listed phone numbers, but one house threw out an entire bank statement."

Jerry lay in his boxers on the bed, next to a nightstand covered with beer cans and a plastic motel cup full of bourbon. Staring at the ceiling, he rubbed his hands together rapidly like the forelegs of a housefly.

Kevin said, "That one was full of diapers."

"Oh, the one with all the bills? Ah, Jerry. They have a baby, honey. I don't want to sponge off somebody with a baby in the house."

"You always do this," he said. "The kid won't pay a dime."

"I hate that. There's so many other people we could find."

"The baby will be fine. In twenty years he'll be at Georgetown. Think of him as a little bundle of *credit.*"

Later that morning, Kevin woke to a radio alarm muffled through the wall beside his head. Colette was still working, wearing a Phillies jersey that hung to her bare knees, forging a petition of phony signatures, and rehearsing a telemarketer's greeting.

"Congratulations, Mr. Culpepper, this is *Janet,* from Diners Club International, and you've won—damn, what has he won?" On the cabinet beside the television, she had set out a clipboard and an orange sweat suit. She noticed that Kevin was awake and said, "I couldn't find a Little League uniform, so this will have to do. It'll be fine."

While Jerry drove Kevin back into the neighborhood, his hangover was so acute that he pressed a shower cap full of ice against his forehead. The day was sunny and the last lumps of snow had melted to white gravel. The houses now looked like fortresses of pilasters and windows. It was just past eight o'clock, and the last panicked stragglers were leaving the driveways for school. Two boys in woolen uniforms bounded down a sloped lawn to an awaiting car; three girls trotted past, wearing cardigans and kilts over leggings, carrying their books in plaid satchels. Kevin's mouth was parched. He was dizzy from the lack of sleep. The sweat suit now seemed ridiculous—a few chains short of a Grandmaster Flash groupie—and after trying to tame his curly hair with a comb and water, only the part remained, like a dent in the middle of his head. "Wouldn't Colette be better at this, Dad? I'm not good at the face-to-face stuff."

With the ice bag completely covering his left eye, his nose stuffed up, Jerry said, "Don't be a pain in the ass. You're a *youth at risk.* You're in some inner-city Keep Kids off Drugs program—whatever. They won't know what hit 'em."

Kevin struggled through the first pitches, talking to a maid through a peephole, an old woman in a monogrammed robe who gave him a phony smile before slamming the door, and one woman who spoke to him entirely through an intercom beside the doorbell. He explained that he had the day off from school to raise money for the flooded library or the collapsed roof of the gymnasium or a condemned science lab full of hazardous materials. Nothing worked, and he was certain that it was the orange jumpsuit. In the window of a glass door, he looked like a crash-test dummy. Waiting on front steps he became far more intrigued by the array of ornate doorknobs and locks, the zigzags of keyholes, with their subtly changing shapes from house to house, seeming more challenging and compelling than the people who emerged from behind them.

By midmorning Kevin found some success by pretending to have a mild stuttering problem. As long as he looked each mark in the face and smiled, he discovered that people were more polite when he seemed to have something wrong with him, such that by eleven o'clock he had developed a limp and a gnarled hand, along with a more effective story that he was collecting signatures to put a wheelchair ramp at his public school. Six women and three men signed and left their phone numbers, but the coveted Social Security numbers still seemed out of reach. Finally he landed upon the perfect combination of triumph and disadvantage, a young man with a dragging foot asking the pledge of one dollar per mile in the annual Laps-for-Literacy Jogathon; or a boy staring at the doorjamb to ask for a small donation to the Swim for Braille campaign. What Kevin lacked in social skills, he made up for in shamelessness. He was a participant in Bowling for Diabetes, Putt-Putt for Alcoholism, and a dance marathon to raise awareness of Hyperactivity Disorder.

But he was most proud of his response to one confused woman who asked why he needed her *Social Security number.* Raising his chin, he replied, "The school finance officer says it's necessary for tax purposes. You'll be sent a form in the mail, and your donation is tax deductible." He knew that if he had stumbled during his delivery, she would have caught him; but instead she smiled and complimented him, saying that any young man who could figure out the tax code was destined for great things.

Jerry was so pleased with the information that he gave Kevin a bonus of twenty dollars.

Outside a gas station, Kevin skated in lazy circles around Colette, in the phone booth. She opened the door and said, "They're going to think I'm in a roller rink, you idiot. Quit it for a second." He sat down on the board and swayed on the asphalt, watching the glare of late sunlight reflecting off the booth and gathering in the cloudlike edges of her hair.

"Good evening, may I speak to Mr. Culpepper, please? Well, congratulations, sir. My name is Janet, and I'm calling on behalf of Diners Club International to tell you that you've won the runner-up's prize in our annual membership giveaway sweepstakes." She flipped through her papers and rolled off an auctioneer's ramble of prizes: RCA XL-100 nineteen-inch color TV with remote, "runs cooler, lasts longer"; the all-new TRS-80 portable computer from Radio Shack; and a complete "luxury lanai" of wicker-rattan furniture. Her tone fluctuated between officious and pageant sweet. "Well, I could use some of your good luck, Mr. Culpepper. Anyway, sir, now to the boring part; this won't take long." Of course, she needed to confirm that he was the cardholder and that all information was current. She read his address, phone number, and wife's name; then asked *him* for his Social Security number, mother's maiden name, and place of birth. "Uh-huh. That's what I have right here in the files." After another lacquered congratulations, she promised it all within fifteen working days, then hung up the phone and winked at Kevin.

A temporary change-of-address form, forged for one resident out of a crowded household, would divert a stream of mail off the main flow and into a postbox purchased with a phony name. With the pre-approved applications or the information off carbons, they ordered virgin plastic or replacement cards, and they would arrive within weeks amid new offers. Jerry said this was the change of seasons in a con man's year, from Dumpsters and doorsteps to mail drops and stores. They slept in a different motel each night, and cruised new neighborhoods in rented trucks, back and forth through the industrial moats around Mid-Atlantic cities, where smokestacks fed gray skies and snowflakes fell like ash. They stopped each week at caged storage bins and postal warehouses where Kevin and his father unlocked their new cards from among the stacks of anonymous boxes. They started shopping, carefully at first, in towns where Jerry had connections to move stereo speakers, televisions, and silver.

Kevin was so fixated on the process that it surprised him whenever Colette would moan that they were terrible people, destined to a life in hell. So determined to improve his skills, Kevin usually forgot that he was actually *stealing* from anyone. Though deep down Jerry believed that anyone gullible enough to lose his money didn't deserve it in the first place, his mantra was that the marks would never suffer beyond a few cents of higher monthly rates and insurance; and this was enough to assure Kevin that thieves were embedded in the system like sin taxes and transaction fees. But every now and then, during a long drive on a listless afternoon or lounging in the motel room as snowplows scraped the pavement outside, Colette would confess her moral qualms about robbing anyone with children, tough lives, pets, elderly parents, or noble professions. Jerry said she needed to get over the idea of a perfect mark. It was rare to find a man both gullible and depraved.

Colette begged Kevin to grow up better than his father, which put Kevin in an awkward spot, imagining both a great heist to impress her and a life in the monastery to comfort her soul. As neither savior nor devil, Kevin understood the profound difficulties in stealing her affections. Late at night, when he would cease thinking about the logistics of new cons and stolen plastic, he would think of her, the way she could be thrilled and ashamed simultaneously, the way she was depressed by any glimpse of pure joy, as if disheartened by the size of her own appetite, until he believed that there was no puzzle as complex as a smart and unhappy woman.

On a cold, dry morning outside Columbus, Ohio, Colette surprised Kevin in bed with an orange and a stack of pancakes topped with burning candles. On the other queen-sized bed she had draped Italian suits, shiny dress shirts, and colorful ties, along with the miserable preppy clothes he was supposed to wear during scams.

"Fifteen was a bad age for me," she said. "I had a big pimple the entire year. I think I spent most of the time crying with a magazine over my face. But you—my little man—*you* have now got one lady-killing wardrobe here."

"How did you find out it was my birthday?"

"Your father wrote it on his hand last week. Don't get your hopes up, though, there's a good chance he's bathed since then. Anyway, you get yourself cleaned up. Don't take an hour. We're a brother and sister duo again today. And, Kevin, *please*, not so much cologne. It's going to lead the cops right to us."

That afternoon, they ran one of Jerry's favorite short cons for some spending cash. Down the aisles of a Christmas tree lot, they walked arm in arm under a crackling speaker of sleigh bells. As usual Colette was lost in her character, saying amongst the noble firs: ". . . and you know, he's even going to pay for Louise's hip replacement. And Becky's teeth. I swear, Jimbo, I think Santa Claus has got nothing on him."

Suddenly she stooped down and began looking around the stacks of bound trees, becoming confused and silent. "Did I drop my ring somewhere? I don't believe this." She got onto her hands and knees and crawled frantically under branches and along the fences of loose chicken wire, and when she stood up, her stockings were covered with straw and pine needles. The edges of her mouth quivered; her eyes dampened with tears.

Kevin abandoned the ruse for a moment to whisper, "Colette, are you okay?"

She flicked her eyes wide open and said through her teeth, "No, Jimbo—I'm not *okay*. I lost my *engagement* ring! Oh my God, this is the worst thing possible."

Stumbling dramatically as one of her heels broke, she ran toward the lot attendant, a thickset man wearing an orange parka vest like a deflated life preserver. Colette's hysteria terrified the man. She was crying mascara streaks and gasping with her mouth open so wide she looked to be choking. She'd lost the most incredible ring she would ever have in her life, at least eight thousand dollars, maybe more, and an heirloom. It had belonged to her fiancé's great-great-grandmother before the Crimean War (what wild ideas she threw into the mix), and he would never forgive her, never, not ever—maybe he would even call off the wedding. She had looked under every tree; her little brother had rooted around like a hound dog: "Get down on your belly and keep looking, Jimbo!" The attendant urged her not to panic. For the next half hour every customer and cashier searched around the needles and tree stands, while the attendant made an announcement—"Attention, Christmas shoppers, we have an emergency . . ."—until Colette commandeered the mike and promised a six-thousand-dollar reward, no questions asked, to anyone who found the ring. "Money is no object!"

She swooned into Kevin's arms. As he dragged her across the pine needles, he said to the attendant, "I'm going to get her home. It's okay. She's had a terrible shock."

He patted her cheek, a bit harder than necessary, and she climbed upright to recover herself, balancing on her toes and the one good heel.

With a sigh and an ingratiating pat, she said good-bye to the attendant, gave him a bogus phone number, and said she would return when the lot closed at midnight.

On the drive back, when a few tears thickened in her eyelashes again, she grimaced, cleared them with her knuckles, and told Kevin it was just the leftovers.

Then it was Jerry's turn, and Kevin had witnessed his side of the con in enough tree lots and pumpkin patches to imagine every step. Jerry would pretend to find the ring in a remote corner of the lot and would hold it up to the sunlight with one eye closed. "Looks like this sum'bitch is worth something." Careful to isolate the attendant, Jerry would ask if a reward had been offered; and he would move, talk, and mull his decisions slowly enough to let the mark's own scheme hatch. If the attendant was thick enough, he might even feed him the idea: "I bet this thing is worth three grand, at least." In fact, the attendant would claim, there *was* a reward: three hundred dollars, and he could have it right out of the register to save any further trouble.

"This might be worth more than three hundred, pal. My brother is an appraiser, and I think he'll say it's up there in the high four figures, maybe five—look how it catches the light." Jerry would leave with the ring; the attendant would grab him in the parking lot. With the restless smile of a novice swindler, he would admit that he hadn't been entirely honest. The reward was more (once Jerry had managed to work an attendant up to four thousand dollars for a fifteen-dollar cubic zirconia) and, of course, he could have the cash right out of the till.

While Jerry was out finishing the job in the tree lot, Colette took a long bath and Kevin sat on the bed picking the lock on her valise with a sheared piece of coat hanger. Each time he was successful, he briefly inhaled the perfume smell inside, then shut the flap to begin the process again. He was aware of every shift Colette made in the water. Her voice was flat in the tile-and-porcelain cove as she called out questions to him about his new clothes. Would he ever wear those nice suits? Didn't he think a con man should look good? After a long pause punctuated with mermaid splashes and the stampeding sound of water from the faucet, she asked, "Are you still alive in there, or did I short-circuit your brain?"

Jerry returned with a case of beer, a bottle of wine, and three submarine sandwiches. He threw Colette's share of cash onto the bathroom counter, and chuckled when she claimed that he'd mugged Santa Claus.

"Close the door all the way, baby. Kevin's right in the room here."

"Yeah, and he's not a Peeping Tom." A splash of rising knees, a scrape of draining water. She came out of the bathroom with a towel sheathed tight from her chest to the pallid tops of her thighs. "*This* is my cut? You're telling me you only made two grand?"

"He was tougher than he looked."

"Come on, Jerry. There's no way you'd walk out of there with less than three. Where's the rest of it?"

"Let's not do this again. You're tired. You get paranoid when you're tired."

"I can't believe you're going to nickel-and-dime me on this. I'm the one who does everything."

"Uh-huh. You throw a temper tantrum. How hard could *that* be for you?"

"I don't just stomp my feet out there—I go out of my mind. I froth at the mouth. Ask Kevin. Why do you think it's so easy for you when you go back? Because I'm a screaming lunatic and I make these people think I've lost the crown fucking jewels. And I've pulled this stunt now in every fruit stand and stupid fucking go-cart track in the country; so could I please have a little respect? You know what? Forget it. If you think that's what I deserve, fine. *You* lose the ring from now on. See how convincing you are."

"And you couldn't negotiate the back end worth a damn, Colette. You know that."

"I don't even hear you," she said, pulling water out of her hair. "You're not speaking English anymore as far as I'm concerned. You're speaking some pidgin asshole language I don't understand."

"Kevin? Am I nuts here?"

"Oh! Now Kevin is the mediator. Great father, Jerry. Great parenting decision. Oh, and I almost forgot: it's your son's birthday. But don't worry—I'm sure he'll have another one next year."

In the bathroom alcove she put on a new lilac nightgown, and as she returned to the mirror, she seemed distracted by how it gripped her around the hips.

Jerry leaned back against the counter. "We got a big week coming up with the new batch of cards. I'm not going to let this kind of suspicion get in the way right when everything is starting to happen for us. That's nice, by the way. Kind of shiny."

Swiveling in front of the mirror, she said in a softer tone, "Makes me feel like I'm married and having an affair."

"Uh-huh. And which one am I? The marriage or the affair?"

He waited, whispered something down the hollow between her shoulder blades. He stared at her waist, where the nightgown lay in ripples like water under a skipped stone, and began to trace them with his rough fingertips, head down and swaying slowly as Colette's eyes held Kevin's in the mirror.

"Hey, and happy birthday, Kevin," said his father. "No, I didn't forget. I just didn't have a chance to get away. Why don't I give you some money and you can run out on the skateboard and buy yourself something. Take your time. How's twenty?"

While with one hand Jerry pulled out his wallet and thumbed through bills, with the other he stroked around Colette's hipbone and the small of her back. His fingertips were big and square, and she bowed faintly to the motion of them like a skittish cat, staring ahead and brushing her hair. She must have perceived the tension in Kevin from clenched fists and flared nostrils, because her face grew steadily more distant, as if staring out a train window at a fleeting landscape, leaving Jerry alone to explore the strange new surface of the nightdress. "Give him fifty," she said. "I think his price just went up."

EIGHT

In early March bathing suits bloomed on the store racks and Easter decorations spread across every icy window. Whole families of mannequins faced the stark light in sunglasses and Bermuda shorts, mothers with picnic baskets and canary straw hats. Pressed zigzags of snow fell from the treads of galoshes to thaw in department store aisles.

To check the status of a card, they would buy candy bars or six-packs in a convenience store. Only once was a card declined as stolen, prompting Colette to retreat and leap back into the truck, idling behind a trash bin; they were southbound on a farm road before she'd freed the seat belt from the slammed door. When the cards cleared, the day would start with Colette's binges: brooches, topaz bracelets, diamond-studded barrettes. She'd give Jerry her fingers to kiss as she sank into a leather recliner. The promoted regional manager, his son, and pretty young wife, they celebrated up and down the escalators, lounging on bedroom displays and dollying out china cabinets. Colette would push out through the saloon doors of a dressing room to spin happily in a triptych of mirrors, while Kevin marveled at the giant stacks of televisions, a soap opera seen through the eyes of a wasp. Jerry needed power tools for fictional tree houses; Colette would stalk around every table and chair, mumbling to herself about its ideal place against the brocade curtains and over the Persian rug, trying to visualize a perfect harmony for their new chimerical home.

In a single week of manic shopping, they filled an entire moving van, a deluxe model with a door between bucket seats that linked the front cab to the storage in back. They packed to keep a passage open. When the last armfuls of clothes were thrown into the pile, they left town with Colette still taking stock in back, headed southbound on empty farm roads. Loaded up with caffeine tablets, Jerry drove straight through the afternoon and night, hollering his approval and disagreement at AM talk shows, as Colette rooted around in the stacks, an occasional fallen box rattling like aluminum stage thunder. Jerry laughed and said, "She's going to get buried alive back there."

When Jerry started singing along off-key to Johnny Cash songs, Kevin escaped through the cubbyhole door, back to Colette, past pillars of speakers, crates, and upended furniture. In a clearing amid the boxes and appliances, Colette had made a drawing room with a sofa, coffee table, chairs, and a wobbling antique lamp. The overhead light was the faint yellow of an industrial twilight, and the smell was like a burning tire. But even in the clutter, with the ground swaying beneath them, the close little arrangement of furniture looked homey and comfortable.

In her fake blue-blooded accent Colette said, "I'm terribly sorry about the state of things, but you know, since my husband went off to war we've been forced to retreat into the one room—to cut down on heating expenses."

Kevin crawled over the boxes and lay down on the sofa. All around him were Grand Teton cliffs of crates and lamp shades, suitcases fallen sideways, the cabriole legs of overturned chairs and snowdrifts of spilled packaging. On his opposite side, a linen chest supported an entire rack of cellophane-wrapped clothes. A table saw buffeted a ridge of ice coolers filled with jewelry and silverware, and a chandelier sat crookedly on top with its crystals dangling like icicles off the edge. In every crevice, she had stuffed a beanbag chair or a garment bag for support. When they hit a bump in the highway, snares rattled under a collapsed drum set, and a hidden cymbal rang faintly like the prelude to a magic trick.

For a while Colette continued spelunking over boxes in her tight jeans, hair ragged over her face, trying to stabilize one side of the mess. With a groan, she said, "I seem to have misplaced the tea kettle."

"I can't handle the English lady right now, Colette. Seriously."

She joined Kevin on the sofa, lifting his legs like a final piece of merchandise and placing them back down on her lap. "That's fine. You don't want to be associated with a fallen noblewoman. When you grow up, Kevin, promise me you'll have better taste than this. I remember thinking we were going to be jewel thieves lounging around on the Riviera. Instead we've got the world's largest collection of stolen power tools."

"Dad says a good chainsaw is worth as much as a stupid locket."

"And I'm sure he'll have my name engraved on it."

She lay down beside him. For an awkward moment, she nuzzled her shoulders against him, maneuvering until she cuddled up against his chest. They stared up at the yellow light, which flickered at each dip in the road, and he could feel each time the wheels lagged onto the lane dividers. She was rosy and humid from the work, and he inhaled the sweet fumes along her face and hair.

"So here's our plan," she said, louder now, as if they weren't so close. "When you and I get married, we'll have a moving wedding. Like on a train or a bus. No, not a bus, that's too white trash. I've had enough of these discount capers as it is. We'll rent out an entire train. So I'll be marching down the aisle—and I'm going to have a gown that drags through sixteen cars, so there'll have to be a lot of bridesmaids keeping the doors open, or I'll get tangled up and never escape. We'll be married by an engineer. Can they do that? Are they like ship captains? You'll have to get to work on that."

"When do you want to do this?"

"Oh, Kevin. Calm down. This is a long-term plan, sweetheart, not some whirlwind affair in the back of a truck. You're going to have to be patient with me if we're ever going to stand a chance." They had braided their legs together, and Kevin closed his eyes now and tried to visualize something to control his excitement. He pictured trash bins, security cameras, a slathering Doberman pinscher chained to a barbed-wire fence. He tried anything to save himself from the embarrassment, but her smell and the swaying motion in her ribs was stronger than any image he could conjure up; until he thought of a funeral, with rows of distant family in black, and he recalled the starchiness of his clothes and how he had stood stiffly with his aunts, afraid to scratch his legs beneath the woolen pants. Colette gripped his hand more tightly, and said, so eerily that he thought she had read his mind, "This is like a pharaoh's tomb. Do you believe in curses?"

"Stop that," he said. "I'm superstitious, sure—but there's nothing haunted about somebody else's credit."

"Well, I believe in the curse of Mr. Culpepper. Everything in here we'll pay back somehow, whether we like it or not. Might as well live it up now, I guess. But if I have to burn for something, I wish it wasn't this hideous couch."

A few hours later, while Colette was asleep in a recliner across from him, the truck turned off the highway. From the disoriented series of right turns, Jerry seemed to get lost in a grid of streets. They stopped and idled. A chain gate rattled open and someone hollered directions over the rumble of the engine. Outside there was the metal clank of stacked pipes, a frantic dog chasing the tailgate, facetious applause as the motor shut off. Jerry had a murmured reunion with someone by the front cab, while the dog's paws scrabbled against the side of the truck. "Get down from there, Sputnik. Where's your ball, girl? Go get your ball." When the back door raised open, Kevin could see blue sky behind coils of barbed wire and phone lines.

"I got a couple of stowaways in there," said Jerry. "Maybe I'll throw them into the deal."

"Shit, Swift—look at this. We talking about the truck too?"

"I need some coffee before I talk about anything."

When Kevin climbed out of the back, Jerry and his associate had already gone into a warehouse past shedding dandelions and a dismantled sink. The Rottweiler growled at him for a moment until Kevin put his hand out for her to sniff. She trotted away, distracted by some stench along the base of the weeded fence. Kevin found a secluded spot to pee, where severed screen doors rested against the high fence, their shaded backs pimpled with hornets' nests. When he returned to the truck, Colette was sitting on the tailgate untangling a length of hair in front of her faintly crossed eyes. The man was shouting in the warehouse, and it took Kevin a moment to discern that it was a joke and not outrage. Jerry walked back with him and introduced the man as Perch. He was considerably shorter than Kevin, but from the way he swatted him on the shoulder and called him "champ," he seemed to assume that Kevin was simply an overgrown child. Colette was also a forehead taller, and he rose onto the toes of his cowboy boots to greet her, smiling with his mouth shut, tongue slid behind his lips. When he stopped squinting, there were tiny, clean streaks radiating from the corners of his eyes. Jerry asked him how much he'd paid for a big place like this, but Perch kept staring at Colette, his neck tensed and shoulders raised. Distractedly he said, "Mmm-hmm. A pretty penny."

While they discussed business inside, Colette and Kevin took turns throwing a chewed softball to Sputnik. Colette whispered to Kevin that she needed to pee so badly she might explode. But when Perch returned alone to offer them coffee, she just shielded her eyes from the sunlight behind him and nodded politely to his long speech about quitting the game to raise attack dogs in the desert. "Mmm-hmm, but y'all got some crazy balls driving around like this. You come to the right place. We need an appraisal first, got to be proper about these things. Sure you don't want coffee?"

Colette shook her head. He put his hands up in the air and replied, "Okay, okay—your call, darlin'. Not going to hold you down and force it into you."

"Thank you."

"But you know what I think? I think you probably ain't old enough to drink coffee. Shit—you ain't any older than seventeen. You're just a baby, huh. A big, pretty baby with a mean look on your face."

Colette averted her eyes, and he seemed fascinated by the reaction, grinning at her profile, showing small, dingy teeth at the end of long gums.

"Where's my dad?" asked Kevin.

"He's inside, sport—don't worry about it. He ain't going nowhere. I just come out here to be a good host to you kids. It's going to be a little while before we're ready to unload this stuff, so, nothing I can get you? Some Cap'n Crunch? Maybe the prize is still inside! I can hook up one of these TVs and y'all can watch cartoons."

Perch put his hands out, showing scars on his palms. He had the faint foam of colorless stubble on his cheeks and a yellow texture to his eyeballs. Kevin said, "We're both fine. Thank you."

"Well, I'll get back inside then, talk things over with the Pied Piper." He laughed, a hard scrape, then walked back toward the warehouse with a clowning dance in his step.

"Colette? He has a bathroom. Everyone does. Even Satan has a bathroom."

"Yeah, right. One that locks from the outside."

Kevin groaned and told her that he would find it for her. He stepped through a dim doorway into the cool warehouse air, smelling of aerosol and bicycle grease. He noticed first how the light angled through the high transoms into spots on the floor, one of which shined perfectly onto the silver skeleton of a disassembled car. There were three stripped frames; but, on a row of foldout tables, it appeared as if there were parts from hundreds of others, whole boxes of brake shoes, flywheels, the cross sections of rotor chambers. Everything lay in the meticulously ordered piles of a collector: foreign and domestic tires, rows of bucket seats all ducking forward in a line, the plucked wings of windshield wipers. Along the far wall, past the cars, there was a region of other merchandise: washers and dryers, refrigerators, a stack of TVs in the same pyramidal arrangement of a department store.

Perch's laugh reverberated, and Kevin followed it through an alley of unfinished plywood walls to the stuffy office. The room was full of metal file cabinets and clamshell ashtrays; a dead geranium sat behind a barricade of green bottles. Perch had his face turned down and his mouth full of smoke. With a faint squeak of air, he said, "He's not a narc, is he?"

They both laughed, Jerry spraying loose potato chip fragments. He took the joint from Perch, touched the ash loose with his fingertip.

"Colette needs to use the bathroom."

"Oh yeah?" said Jerry. "And where do you fit into this little caper?"

Perch was laughing in shrill notes, but Jerry's face stayed hard, his whole body remaining still, just a thread of fragrant smoke coming through his fingertips.

"I'm finding it for her."

"So you two are *bathroom buddies* now? You're supposed to go out in the woods and take turns watching for bears."

At this, Perch was in such hysterics he put his head down and shook.

Jerry said, "Calm down, you idiot—you're going to bust a blood vessel."

Perch made a long, sighing release of air and said, "I missed this motherfucker. You got to come see me more often, you piece of shit. I'm going crazy down here."

"Listen to this. I need a second opinion here. This kid vanished all night in the back of the truck with her, and this morning, all of a sudden, he's in charge of her bladder."

Perch couldn't hold the laugh and he blurted it out through his lips. Jerry grinned reluctantly and said, "Get a hold of yourself, man. I'm trying to get a bead on this situation here—I don't need a fucking hyena as my counsel." He turned to Kevin and pointed with his smoking fingertips. "She's got you finding bathrooms for her now—what I'm wondering is, what else are you finding for her?"

Kevin took a hard breath through his teeth. He was gripping both sides of the doorjamb with his eyes down at the shedding carpet.

"Ah, he's a good boy, Jerry. Leave him alone."

"I'm not worried about *him*. Shit. What do you think I'm talking about here? Look at him—this guy is puberty on wheels, man. He doesn't have any control."

"Your will is not your own," said Perch. "It is a perilous journey, my boy."

"That woman—she's all about getting what she wants. Anyplace the road goes, you know what I mean?"

"She just has to take a piss, Dad. That's the only place the road is going."

"I'm talking straight to you right now—and you're not really hearing me, bud. She wants a bathroom—oh, sure. Now it's a bathroom. Pretty soon it's everything else. Then, suddenly, you're a slave. Standing outside a shoe store. Holding a purse."

Jerry frowned in an exaggerated and childlike way; then with his forehead raised into a stack of wrinkles, he took a hard drag and handed the roach back to Perch. As he thought, he seemed to chew the smoke in his mouth, until a wisp escaped as if from a blanketed campfire, and he added, his voice tinny and small, "I'm glad we finally had this little talk," and he laughed loose a cloud.

Eventually Kevin found the bathroom, a tiny, fetid alcove where yellow weeds from outside laced through loose boards and a bee ricocheted between a grimy window and a fractured mirror. Colette was still outside. She followed with her arms crossed and her shoulders hunched, and he stood guard because the door didn't lock. Sputnik roamed inside and trotted around, collar jingling, claws tapping on smooth concrete. When Colette came out, hair now tucked behind her ears, she inhaled deeply through her nose as if she had held her breath the entire time inside. "Let's hope there wasn't a hidden camera in there."

For the next hour they sat Indian legged in a clearing of cattail grass and made piles of little rocks on his skateboard. Colette told Kevin that she wanted to be treated like a lady for once in her life. She was her own woman, of course, and no, she wasn't going to expect some hero on a white horse. For God's sake, she would open her own doors, she would make her own money, pay for a meal now and then, it wasn't a question of petty things like that. It was a deeper sense of respect—for mystery and complexity—a kind of appreciation that perhaps couldn't be found around here, maybe not even in this whole stinking country. "See, I think it's about class, sweetie. You could soak that dwarf for six months in a spa and you wouldn't get the prison stink off him. And robbing every damn factory outlet doesn't add up to a Tiffany, you know. I think, basically, people take on the qualities of whatever they steal. If you're high end, then you've got some leeway; but if it's clearance sales at Pic-N-Save, then you're more or less competing with the cockroaches. I had to twist your father's arm to boost anything worth more than a few hundred dollars."

Three teenagers passed sideways through the narrowly opened gate. Perch poked his head out of the dim doorway, beyond a growing haze of gnats, and called to them in poor Spanish. The boys had stern faces and slicing eyes, and Kevin could tell they hated the little man from the way their bodies slouched at his commands. Listlessly, they unloaded everything onto the driveway; and then, in a haze of dust, they continued moving furniture along the path into the warehouse. Once they had moved the heavy appliances, they quickly grew impatient, and Kevin could decipher enough Spanish to hear them cursing La Perca as lazy and cheap and a *puto maricon*.

When Perch and Jerry emerged, their faces looked like they'd never touched sunlight, agonized squints and bright red cheeks. Perch had a gust of energy so uncontainable that he ignored all his assistants to play fetch with the dog in the high grass, each stride casting up more seeds and gnats.

"So?" said Colette. "What's the deal?"

Jerry stared ahead. The dog was hidden entirely in weeds, her movement only visible by her rustled wake. Perch stopped playing to pick the nettles from his arm.

"We're not through negotiating yet."

"You've been in there forever, Jerry! Should I pitch a tent?"

"If you got any sense at all, Colette, don't give me shit right now."

Perch tromped back, holding the pale side of his forearm upward.

The boys walked over and sat in a growing ledge of shade by the fence. The air, spun with dirt and pollen, had hit the hour when it seemed to have a dreamlike quality, quiet and luminously white, the sun coming slantwise through heat haze, the first afternoon shadows sprouting underfoot.

Colette whispered to Jerry, "Are those kids going to put back whatever he doesn't want—"

To interrupt her, Jerry raised his voice to Perch, "Well, let's get this over with so we can get on with the party."

Perch lowered his neck when he spoke. Jerry was a full head taller, but something about the little man's coiled movements, the stalking quality to his steps now, made him seem as aggressive as a mongoose hugging the ground. Perch said he could use the musical equipment, the washers and dryers, some jewelry—he had a person for that, and for cut ice—and he could take the electronics: stereos and speakers, Commodore 64s, ColecoVision, and the IBMs . . . "Now here's the bad news. I don't know how much I can do with the furniture, clocks, antiques, stuff like that. All this right here around the driveway. It's nice—don't get me wrong. But the man I know who deals with this kind of stuff, he's out of commission—"

Colette said, "Why didn't you say that before they took it out of the truck?"

"I like her, Jerry. She's quick. Must have kidnapped her right off the honor roll. No, this stuff is going to be hard for me to do much with. *But* some good news: I can probably strip down this truck and use a lot of it. I mean this is—what?—probably a six-cylinder engine in there."

"Jerry? If he takes the truck, he has to take everything."

"Shut up for a second, Colette."

"What? We're going to carry the rest of it out of here on our backs?"

"I understand it puts you in a bind," said Perch. "But really, if I bought the rest, I'd just be doing you a favor by taking it off your hands."

"That's an eight-thousand-dollar area rug," said Colette. "You're not taking it off our *hands*."

"Well, I don't do flying carpets, darlin'. So you can crawl back in your little genie bottle and let the boys work it out."

"This is ridiculous," she said, standing and brushing off her jeans. "We should've gone to a fucking pawnshop at this rate."

Jerry paced toward the warehouse and said, "Colette, come here. I want to talk to you for a second."

"I have a right to my say, Jerry. I worked harder than anybody for this."

"I want to *talk* to you. Come here."

"Don't order me around like a dog! If you want to talk to me, I'm right here."

"In private! Now. I'm starting to lose my temper."

"You don't want him to lose his temper," said Perch. "Trust me."

"Oh, great. Advice from his prison *bitch*."

Jerry seized her by the arm and, in one snake-quick motion, twisted it behind her back. He grabbed her under the shoulder with his free hand. As she grunted and stooped forward, Jerry muscled her ahead through the door. Just as Kevin sprang up from the grass, Perch snatched his wrist. "Let them have it out, kid. Everybody's excited. Let's calm down. Let 'em have a second. Ain't our business." He spoke like it was a far greater emergency than Kevin had first thought.

"Maybe it's none of *your* business, you stupid midget."

Perch clamped down on his wrist with his fat hand, each fingernail a hard yellow carapace over a bruise of grease. His tiny eyes opened wide, his jaw flexed, and he looked so ferocious that Kevin recognized within three racing heartbeats that he had misread the man, the place, and maybe the nature of his own life. A cloud passed in front of the sun. Kevin looked to the boys, who were all lounging indifferently with their hats or shirts over their faces. Perch leaned close to Kevin's ear and his breath was a burning field. "You little babies come in here and run around like it's the county fair—okay. Have a good time. But don't think I'm going to take one second of bullshit. I know your old man a lot better than you do. I've seen him do shit that would give you nightmares for the rest of your life. You want to insult me—now that we're man to man, go ahead. Insult me. But I'll show you the real world, kid. Do we understand each other?"

"May I please go get my skateboard?"

"Yes, you may. Because you asked nicely."

Kevin tried to skate off the queasy feeling in his stomach, but he hated how Perch stood there smirking at him; so he popped his board up to his hand and climbed into the front cab of the moving van. Ten minutes passed on the dashboard clock. He listened to Perch's boot heels in the dirt and the threshing sound of Sputnik in the grass. At first he was worried that Perch would follow him into the cab; then, after his heart had slowed and his stomach settled, he was more afraid that Perch might go into the warehouse. Kevin was fairly sure that his father wouldn't hurt Colette under normal circumstances, but this little man had brought out the worst in everyone, somehow turning everything he touched into a cheap commodity; and so Kevin waited by the window, temples throbbing, and planned to stop Perch if he approached the warehouse door. There were pipes by the wall inside; there were knives on the table.

He saw Colette stomp back outside. Because of a faint wind swinging her hair, he couldn't see her face right away, only her hands tucked into fists beneath her sweatshirt sleeves. She chewed her lip and ignored something Perch said to her. She saw Kevin in the mirror, and she joined him in the cab, climbing up behind the steering wheel as he moved to the shotgun seat. He was so relieved to see her unhurt and only more defiant that he wanted to grab her and kiss her, press his face against her freckled cheek. She was furious, gripping the wheel and shaking her head and starting a tirade about how she'd get back at Jerry, and Kevin was so overwhelmed by her fretful and beautiful profile that he could barely hear what she said, wanting to wrap her hair in his fists and smell it. She said, "If he wants to be an asshole and grandstand for that creep, he's going to regret it, I'm going to get him where it hurts. I'm being shoved out of this deal when I did everything. Can you please tell me what the hell I have to do for a tiny bit of respect here? These *boys'* networks—I swear to God. I'm like the Sally fucking Ride of con men."

Kevin took a shivering breath that lifted and sank his shoulders. She was perplexed by the gesture, and studied his face for a moment.

"Did you fall off your skateboard again?"

"No," he said. "But I would have killed him if he laid a hand on you."

She sat up straight in her chair and narrowed her eyes. "Who? The hobbit?" She wiped the sweat from her forehead with her sleeve. "Or your father?"

In the glaring mirror, they watched Perch argue with the teenagers, one side of his face glowing so that he looked like an overexposed photograph. "I would have cut his throat and left him bleeding in the dirt."

"Kevin, sweetheart. Let's calm down a little bit, okay? It's not a war, it's just a negotiation. I don't like it, I'm pissed off—but nobody needs to kill anyone for my sake."

"I need to tell you something."

"Don't tell me anything right now, okay? I'm still upset about this."

"I'm in love with you."

"Oh, Kevin. *Please*. I love you too, of course—you know I do, but I don't want to play this game while they're out there wrangling over a dinette set."

"You're miserable with him. Every day of your life. He's killing you and it doesn't make any sense."

"I'm not miserable. I'm frustrated. There's a big difference."

"We could leave. Together. You and I—we could strike out on our own, Colette. There's no reason why we couldn't. You've got all the personality and the style, and I'm an evil genius with the details. We could make a thousand times more money than this. We could go anywhere in the world—fucking Monte Carlo. You want to sit on the Riviera? You got it."

"Kevin, you're *fifteen* years old. What are you going to do? I don't want to drive this big truck out of here—do you? I don't even think I could back it up. Come on, be realistic. You haven't had your superstitious breakfast and you're delirious."

"What would I have to do for you to believe in me?"

"Stop this. Right this second. Your father is right over there and he can hear us."

"That creepy little dude is right, isn't he? You're like seventeen. If we were in school together, everything would be completely different between us. I could walk right up to you and ask you out."

"*No*, Kevin, don't try that—because if we were in school, I'd have a thirty-five-year-old criminal boyfriend, and you'd be a freshman whose lunch smelled. You would have less chance with me than the janitor. Forget it. And personally, I'm a little upset that you would choose right *now* to lay this whole tragic confession on me. I'm surrounded by testosterone."

Then his father came to the door and said the deal was made. Everyone could relax; the numbers were good. They'd borrow a car and buy some groceries. Champagne and caviar. Good cigars. As he retreated,

Colette yelled out the window that she wanted a decent room for once in her miserable life.

Jerry returned and said right into her face, teeth bared, "Yes, Your Majesty, whatever your greedy little heart desires."

That evening, when his father sent him out for groceries with four hundred dollars, telling him to grab everything expensive and impractical, Kevin had a plan to pocket at least three-eighty. Jerry was at the liquor store across an asphalt plaza; and Colette stayed back at the room, cutting her hair over the bathroom sink. Kevin first went to the general store beside the market and bought a needle and thread. Back in the market, he loaded two huge bags of dry dog food into the cart, and partially cut open the tops. With his hands hidden behind walls of toilet paper, he stuffed everything into the bags that looked like a luxury item—Camembert, andouille sausage, imported bubble bath—throwing handfuls of shedding dog food behind medicine and cereal boxes. He burrowed in travel magazines that showed exotic beaches, chalets, gondoliers navigating sun-glossed canals, and restaurant guides from Paris to Prague. For good measure he threw in a few women's magazines, with captions like *What He's Really Thinking* and *Seven Signs Your Man Is No Good*. He could find only lumpfish caviar, which, in a section amid salmon eggs and phosphorescent cheese, seemed to have been mistakenly categorized as bait; and in his quest for anything lavish, he was demoralized by aisles of pigs' feet floating in brackish water, massive bins of gumdrops, and whole expanses of Spam and canned pineapple that seemed more intended for a bomb shelter than a celebration. He nestled into the bag the only bottles of wine over ten dollars (Colette had once cautioned him about Blue Nun); he stabbed in Swiss chocolate bars, inexplicably overpriced salamis, a brood of little pink game hens; any crackers and cookies with the Union Jack on the box and all of the coffee from France. He resewed the bags while pretending to read a skateboard magazine, then checked out with two giant bags of dog food, a postcard, and six jumbo packs of toilet paper. The cashier smiled at him, didn't try to lift the bags, but simply called in a price check and rang them up. She asked him how many dogs he had.

"Two," he said. "But they're always hungry."

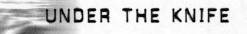

UNDER THE KNIFE

When Kevin woke under a spotlight, he could hear surgeons talking calmly through their masks about him. Around an open panel in blue sheets, they worked down into his chest, gloves and equipment covered with blood. He could see the respirator tube running outward and, in the periphery, hanging vinyl bags of blood and clear liquid. Everything was dreamlike in the bright lights, and though he could see the doctors rooting down into him, he felt detached from his body. It seemed stretched out across the room, as long as an afternoon shadow. He heard the whirling sounds of suction and irrigation as they were exhuming something from him. He closed his eyes and saw seagulls hovering over a landfill, felt rats burrowing through his clothes.

Rhythmically a blood-pressure cuff inflated and deflated on his arm, and when a nurse stooped down beside his heart monitor and announced his blood pressure, he perceived a current of exasperation and alarm moving through the room. He thought that he was controlling this readout with the images that floated through his mind, sewers and subway tunnels; but then, as if he had willed them into existence, he saw several cops walking outside the glass windows, sipping coffee, moving in a pantomime of a friendly argument. One of the surgeons was talking about infection, and the nurse replied, "He went swimming in *something*."

"Do we have any idea who brought this guy in?"

"Some girl," said another nurse behind the row of faces. "Hair all wet, clothes all dirty. Then she just took off before the police got here. See ya."

"Can we get the LAPD to stop gawking in the windows?"

The nurse said, "Aw, what did you do, you poor kid? Yeah, look at him. He's listening."

"His blood pressure is really erratic."

The surgeon stood up, glanced down at Kevin's eyes, his blue mask shielding his face like a bank robber's handkerchief. He studied the heart monitor and shook his head. "Look at his pulse. He's going to have to calm down now. Hey, down there? Don't start thinking you're going to get up and run. Okay?"

"Jesse James. I wonder what he did?"

"Some drug deal that fell apart," said the oldest surgeon with the gravelly voice.

"Five dollars says he's a murderer."

"Naw," said the nurse. "He's just another crazy kid, I think."

"A good boy who got himself shot. Probably dove into the sewers."

"Dr. Hollins doesn't like working on a John Doe."

"Let's have a little less chatter, please."

A few hours later Kevin lay in the tangle of tubes, breathing through a respirator, in a recovery room beside an empty bed. In the room there were two uniformed policemen, two men in blazers, a doctor, and a nurse. It was the loud nurse from earlier, her face familiar, as if from a dream, and she called the doctor when Kevin's eyes opened. He was the younger of the surgeons, and as he approached, he was laughing at something one of the detectives had said.

"Okay. We've got a lot of people anxious to talk to you, but we're going to get them out of here for a while. I don't think it's safe to take you off the respirator yet. But so far, you're responding well. You're in stable condition and the surgery went well. I'm going to explain your injuries to you. I want you to shake your head if there's anything you don't understand."

Kevin desperately wanted to know if he had been shot in his front or his back.

"You're one lucky kid—whatever your name is. The bullet fractured your fifth rib, went through both lobes of your right lung, and then lodged in the seventh rib. But the bullet didn't fragment, and you didn't have little pieces in there. By the time you were brought in here, the wounds had sealed themselves, so no air got into the chest cavity. Otherwise, you're a victim and not a suspect." He looked up at the officers and said, "Isn't that right? Officers, can we please clear out for just a minute?"

When he faced Kevin again, he added, "We had to remove the bottom portion of your right lung. But if there aren't any septic complications—any *infection*—you should be able to live a perfectly normal life."

"In prison," said one of the retreating cops.

As everyone left, the nurse came back into the room and gave him instructions about raising and lowering the bed. She showed him the paging button to use if his pain grew too severe. As she was talking, one of the cops returned, leaning over the bed and waving his badge over Kevin's eyes like the talisman of a witch doctor. He said, "Okay—he's got it. Kid, I'm Detective Daniels, Rampart Division, LAPD, and I got the unbelievably fucking exciting job of making sure you don't creep out of here like a snail. Lucky me, huh? You can't talk yet, I realize, but we're putting you into police custody anyway. So basically, here goes: you have the right to remain silent . . ."

BOOK TWO  THE APPRENTICES

1984

NINE

At the end of April the *Denver Post* printed a short article in the Metro section about a family of three running scams on furniture, electronics, and department stores from Maryland to Colorado. The leader was in his early forties, between six-foot and six-foot-two, with "light brown hair, blue eyes, and a muscular build." Colette read this aloud joyously in the motel room while Kevin claimed that his father hadn't done a push-up in ten years. "The woman is reportedly in her late teens to early twenties, described as 'attractive and talkative,' roughly five-foot-seven to five-foot-nine." She looked up from the paper and said, "Hear that? I'm a knockout."

While Jerry and Colette remained in that blurry region of general features, Kevin's description was so specific that it made him dizzy. "The third member is a young man in his mid to late teens, with dark features, his height approximately five-foot-ten, but difficult to determine accurately because of his curly black hair. He wears strong cologne. He has been seen carrying a skateboard. He sometimes wears designer suits, ripped at the knees and elbows. In larger stores witnesses state that he often plays with computers and other electronic devices. He appears to be most interested in technical gadgetry and may ask for help as he studies items in the store. Other witnesses describe him as being intense and inquisitive, with fewer social skills than the others."

Colette fell backward onto the bed and laughed hysterically up at the ceiling.

"Shut up," said Kevin. "You got me those clothes—it's your fault."

"I didn't tell you to skateboard in them."

That evening when Jerry read the paper, he nodded along solemnly, then rolled the newspaper up and pointed it at Kevin as if threatening a disobedient dog. There were going to be some serious changes. No more gallivanting through Radio Shacks in that stupid Armani suit. No more IBM computer games. No more conversations about binary code with the maintenance staff. Kevin was grounded until he learned to blend into the vast Midwestern landscape of politely bland people.

With his cheeks and earlobes growing hot, Kevin argued that he was a vital part of these cons; and he threatened that if they left him alone in the motel he would rob the front desk. His panic was not simply that he had been so accurately fingered in several malls across I-70, but that for close to a month now he had felt detached from the two of them, the most useless member of the team, banished in the evenings to his own room, the television always seeming to mock him with *The Love Boat* theme, nothing much to clear his mind beyond his repeated efforts to break into vending or cigarette machines. He wondered if Colette had mentioned that day on Perch's lot to his father.

He admitted that he was going through a stressful time, which Jerry might have intuited from his hobbies. Recently Kevin had learned to break into the jacks of fortress pay phones with a homemade tool somewhat like an Allen wrench, hooking up his own phone to bypass the system. On a hacker BBS he had learned to make his own blue box, and, using the toy whistle from a box of Cap'n Crunch, he could reproduce the 2600 hertz tone necessary to authorize a call. Each time he was successful, he dialed Jerry or Colette to boast about his ten-cent heist. He argued that leaving him out of the game would be a waste of his growing technical abilities, and might send him into a spiral of less healthy interests.

Jerry grabbed Kevin by the shoulders and steered him to the mirror. With a marker, he leaned over the cabinet and began tracing Kevin's features in the glass. When he was finished, the drawing was narrow, with hooded eyes and a faint dusting of shadow under a long nose. "See! You already look like a composite sketch."

About an hour later, while Kevin lay on his bed with a pillow over his face, Colette slipped through the adjoining door. It was the first time she had come to his room since that embarrassing day in the truck, and he sat up instantly. "I got you a present." From a stuffed paper bag, she poured onto the comforter a torque wrench and a sampling of padlocks and doorknobs. "Listen, Kev, he just got way overboard with all of that stuff."

"What's this?"

"I wanted to explain to you—he didn't mean to be so harsh. He wasn't saying that you were ugly or anything. You're handsome and you're not abnormal, and someday some girl, somewhere—"

"You don't have to apologize for my dad. I know him better than you do."

"It's just that you're sort of mysterious looking. Your father has a very trustworthy face, that's his gift. But you always seem more—how should I say it—well, you always look like you're plotting something."

"These are fucking awesome," said Kevin, holding up a pin-tumbler lock. "You even got these tube-shaped ones on the vending machines."

"Yeah, I went to a hardware store. What I'm trying to say is, when you're nervous, you look like a kid just learning to read; you move your lips. It doesn't mean that your ideas aren't wonderful, Kevin. In fact, your father is getting competitive with you about some of these plans. In a way, that whole speech was a compliment."

Kevin held up a row of long and flexible metallic strips, and asked, "What are these?"

"They're bristles off a street cleaner. You file them into different shapes and they make the best picks."

"How do you know that?"

"I once had a stalker who used them."

Kevin studied her face for a sign that she was joking, but she met his eyes and didn't budge.

"Are you serious?"

"You maniacs don't know anything about *me*. As far as you're concerned, I just materialized one day." She retreated a few steps and hugged her lean body against the doorjamb. "Just play with your new toys, Kev. They're a lot easier to figure out than I am."

TEN

Paranoid about the news article, Jerry claimed to know a disbarred lawyer who could give them foolproof new identities. "If the newspaper has that kind of info, the bloodhounds are right behind us."

But it wasn't until summer that Jerry hunted down his old associate Army Walsh, living with his longtime wife in a house on stilts, above a tidal flat of mossy rocks off Puget Sound. Kevin, Jerry, and Colette stayed with them over the Fourth of July weekend, all sharing one cluttered room. Bowls of smoothed bottle chips, translucent Japanese fishing weights, a ship's barometer and nautical clock, shell-studded picture frames, and candlesticks of carved driftwood, every decoration in the house seemed washed ashore. The wife moved in the jellyfish billows of a diaphanous purple dress; and Army, wearing only yellow gym shorts fraying at the waistband, his long beard dampened with beer suds, seemed not so much disbarred as shipwrecked.

The wife had known Jerry since the days when he ran a construction company as a cover operation, and Army—who barely spoke over the sound of the tide—had known him even eight years earlier, in high school, when the San Fernando Valley was filled with orange groves and

91

Jerry was a promising young car thief with a pompadour and sideburns. He was sent off to military school by his terrified and alcoholic mother (the widow of a tail gunner), then to a juvenile detention center in some godforsaken stretch of desert, where—"What happened again?"

"Yeah, yeah," said Jerry. "I escaped off a road crew and never looked back. Except when they caught me the next time. That's enough of memory lane—you're making me all fucking misty-eyed."

Three oily cats crawled around the porch and through the house. After Colette courted them with kissing sounds, she stroked the arching back of a tabby while ignoring the conversation. The woman raised her voice at Colette in the way some people blare at foreigners. The cat purred loudly; Colette didn't respond. Jerry waited for her, then finally said, "She's from Los Angeles too. Right, baby?"

Colette mumbled, "Just because you abducted me in L.A. doesn't mean that's where I'm from."

"Okay. We don't know where she's from, but we know it's not there."

"Well, good for you," said the woman. "One less person from California."

Colette whispered, either to the cat or Kevin, "I'm from Michigan—and a normal boyfriend would probably know that after almost a *year*."

"Kevin? Would you like to play a game, honey?" asked the woman. "We have Chinese checkers."

"Oh, don't get him started on something," said Jerry. "He'll never be able to stop. The kid's got a screw loose. Just watch him tie his shoes— he's the reason they invented Velcro."

Colette cleared her throat and said, "Don't be an asshole, Jerry. You know you'd fall apart without him."

"See this! This is my crew here," said Jerry. "This is every day of my life with these two."

Jerry and Army talked briefly about business, while the woman cut up bits of cheese and placed them onto Wheat Thins. Jerry bragged that his friend, after serving sixteen months on fraud charges, had become a wizard with new identities, so determined to stay hidden that he had invented a mob of aliases to protect himself. "You're looking at about fifteen people here." One of his fake identities was a notary public; he had contacts within the DMV and Social Security offices. They walked around the porch, mumbling their plans, until Jerry finally returned and announced that the three of them would assume the identities of "deceased children."

Colette's mouth curled down in horror. "I'm not going to be a dead kid, Jerry!"

He refused to argue with her. They had been on the road a long time, and if she thought the Secret Service, the FBI, and the credit card bureaus weren't closing in, she was being naive. "Let him do his work, Colette. He'll give us three people without histories."

"Blank slates," Army said with a damp lisp.

Later that night, they sat around a bonfire on the rocky shore watching Seattle's fireworks splash up from behind dark hills and radio towers, the delayed, disembodied thunder reaching them long after the fleeting sparks. Colette retreated to sit by herself on a broken slab of concrete near the top of the beach. Kevin found her, sweatshirt tucked over her bare legs, her chin on her knees.

"I am so tired of your father's hippie underground railroad."

Kevin said, "I bet I could forge a birth certificate. Doesn't seem *that* impressive."

As the tide rose and now sizzled at the edges of the bonfire, Jerry and his old friends reclined in the smoke eddies and laughed up toward the stars.

"I've never understood why people like smoking that stuff. I just get hungry and think everybody hates me."

"Why didn't you ever tell us you were from Michigan? We were just south of there—we could have stopped, we could've said hello to somebody."

"And I'm sure that would have been a magical time."

From the raucous sound of their distant voices, Kevin could tell that his father and the couple had started recounting memories again, this time with more bluster. The ambient light was faint enough to see plummeting bats around them. Colette grunted at a moving shadow.

Quietly, Kevin asked if she'd been near his age when she ran away from home. Instead of answering him, she started making a circle of pebbles beside her. Farther down the beach, past slanted trees with exposed roots, three sparklers shed into the damp rocks. "Close. I think I was sixteen. So you've still got a little time."

Somewhere a cherry bomb screeched and spat. He asked why she left home, and at first she chuckled as if she'd never confess such a thing; but something about the tone around the fire, or the way Jerry's age became suddenly more visible by proximity to his weathered friends, made her seem lonesome. No matter how irritated she pretended to be with Kevin, he had a sense that she shouldn't be left to herself. After a long silence, she promised to tell him everything, her whole life story if that's what he wanted, as long as he swore not to pass anything on to his father.

Jerry stood up to go swimming, stripping to his boxer shorts in front of the smoldering fire while the others laughed that he was insane. His body was silhouetted against the flickering light, wide shoulders and broad chest, as he walked gingerly on sharp rocks. "I don't care about any cold water, you crybabies! Colette! Let's go swimming, baby. Let's show these pussy little forest people what we're made out of." She sat still as he repeated her name, until he finally gave up with an exaggerated wave of his arm and crossed the rocky beach to the dock. As he dove into the water with a hard splash, followed by a shocked howl that echoed around the trees, Colette leaned all the way forward as if to tell Kevin a ghost story.

As a little girl she shared "a rat-hole apartment" in Saginaw, Michigan, with a mother, "who looked just like Ann-Margret," despite her tendency to slam crystal meth and indulge a parade of jittery and abusive men. A straight-A student who skipped several grades—"I could read at like *four*"—Colette rode her tasseled bicycle home one day to find all of their belongings outside in the snow. For some reason, she characterized this eviction as if it were a dashing assistant deputy coming to rescue a talented child, though she did betray some shading of genuine horror when she mentioned how a social worker undressed a Barbie doll and asked if she had been touched on the plastic hinge. From the motel that night, her mother had gone out to turn a trick and get high, never returning, and at seven or eight years old, Colette had apparently lived in the room on her own for a week until the neighbors called the police.

From there she went into the sprawling system, where she solved the problems of every chaotic foster home, redecorating the squalid rooms and transforming violent orphans into lovesick admirers. In the next four years, she lived in seven different houses, "putting up with your occasional, you know, really bad apple." Finally, when she was eleven, she landed in a foster home run by a devout Lutheran named Cassie Doerfling. Cassie made her living off foster kids and sometimes had more than fifteen or twenty in the house. "It was a scam, I guess, but she was basically an okay person—*strict*." She made everyone in the house pray before bed and meals, attend church and Sunday school, study the New Testament and memorize verse; but the work seemed a small price for a woman who cooked meals and never raised her voice or fists. In the house, Colette became very attached to the younger kids, writing plays for them to perform, devising games, and sewing costumes. For a long time she described all of the toys and fairy wings she made for these girls, but mentioned only in passing the Armenian twin brothers who eventually set fire to the house.

"Then in junior high, you know, other girls can be pretty cruel—and I just didn't have anything. I wasn't going to be that kid in the home-made shirt, you know, who smells like mothballs. So at thirteen or fourteen, I was shoplifting everything I wore. By the time I was in high school, I dressed like a model. You should have seen me. If I stuck around, I would have been voted Most Likely to Wind Up in Paris."

At fifteen, the end of her sophomore year (which should have been her senior year if she had really skipped grades), she had an art teacher who fell instantly in love with her. Here Kevin noticed for the first time how she spoke toward the hills and sky whenever she was exaggerating, and how she played with something on the ground beside her whenever she passed closer to the truth. As she ducked down and sorted through the pebbles, she explained that she had been caught stealing art supplies, and that the teacher had threatened to have her expelled, continually bringing it up as a mild threat during their affair, which was consummated in his Buick.

"Maybe he was a little bit of a sleazebag," she said, "but he went crazy over me. He would call me and talk all night about how he was leaving his wife. I didn't believe him or anything—but, I guess I just wanted to hear that kind of thing." She was drawing with a stick in the damp sand around her. "One day his wife found some letters we'd written to each other, and he basically panicked. He said he wanted to take me out of town—he didn't want to lose me. I don't think he wanted to go to jail either. I was sort of depressed, because I didn't love him; but I guess all I'd ever been waiting for was a *ride*.

"I called Cassie from a pay phone in Ohio, and when she picked up, I was too ashamed to say anything. She knew it was me, and she repeated my name a couple times, told me to stay safe, said Jesus was with me, and I just hung up. I don't feel guilty about anything but that, because *really*, she was my mother. She raised me. Everything solid and stable in my life had come from her, and then I just left her like she was a stranger. Like somebody that rode next to me on a bus."

She played with a thread from her cut-off jeans, coiling it around her ring finger.

The art teacher drove her all the way to the Pacific Ocean, chattering about his dreams while she watched the landscape change from galloping crop rows to scrub brush and canyons. "First thing I thought when we got to L.A.—I was amazed at how ugly palm trees really are. Big dusty brooms full of rats. We wound up at this motel on the west side. Basically he got really weird on me—a little violent—and I just started crying, kind of freaked out about the whole situation. We had a huge screaming fight and needed to change motels before the cops came. I guess we made up, temporarily. But when he was asleep, I took all his money and credit cards. I stepped right out into the night. Bought some clothes, some luggage. I had a great time, actually, all dressed up and shopping, salesladies hopping to my side when they saw I had some sugar daddy's cards. I knew he couldn't call the cops to report them stolen. But he canceled them, one by one, and then the celebration sort of faded away, and I scraped by however I could. It got worse every month. Ugly shit, you don't even want to know."

She turned and, for the first time, seemed to acknowledge Kevin sitting beside her. Her hands were buried under her loose sleeves, but she rubbed a sweatshirt cuff along the side of his hair.

"About a year later, there *you* were—asleep with a fever in a motel bed, traveling with that big crazy sea monster over there. It's fate, I guess."

The couple was now shouting at Jerry about jellyfish as he backstroked around the dock. He blew a plume of water over his face and yelled, "Who are you people? The fucking Coast Guard? Let them take their best shot."

Kevin asked, "Why don't you want him to know anything?"

"What do you think we're doing here, Kev? We're going to trade in our whole histories. Like a set of hot speakers. He doesn't want to know me any better than this, honey. Maybe that's what I like about him."

ELEVEN

Mostly by posing as a genealogist, Army had accumulated certified copies of birth certificates for practically an entire graveyard. While Colette found the process the most nauseating depth she had ever reached, Kevin couldn't deny himself a morbid fascination in absorbing the identities of stillbirths or tragedies on rainy highways. Why should there be any disrespect? If there were organ donors, why not document donors? If anything, it gave him a feeling of determination, to live a thrilling and adventurous life as a tribute. In his most macabre fantasies at night, he imagined there would be some otherworldly communication with this graveyard sponsor, a whisper in his head or an occasional breeze that pointed him in the right direction like the tablet on a Ouija board. He hoped that his new name would come from a boy who had gone out gloriously—in a fiery plane crash or on a sinking ship, or, as he told Colette one night while they sat on the porch, torn apart by wolves. She hit him on the shoulder.

Once the plan moved forward, however, Kevin was livid that his father refused to make him sixteen. While Colette clearly leapfrogged several years, maybe half a decade, to become the twenty-two-year-old

Esther Barrick (d. 1962, complications from pneumonia), Kevin was forced to regress a full four months in Douglas "Dougie" Herman, because Jerry claimed it was the only father-son duo he could find in Army's ghoulish files. Kevin was further disheartened that the two had died when a fishing boat capsized, the sort of hapless vacationer's death that made him imagine his guiding spirit in tall rubber boots and a floppy hat. "Were they at least eaten by sharks?" Kevin asked.

"I don't *know*, Kevin. It doesn't matter."

Jerry, Colette, and Kevin began a long, nervous process of Social Security forms, DMV lines, and passport offices where prominent signs threatened six-year prison terms for fraudulent applications. During a driving test, Colette ran over a long stretch of pylons and jeopardized the entire scam. She was more irritable than Kevin had ever seen her, and in every new ID picture she was partially hidden under a cascade of messy hair.

For many years Kevin had instinctively believed that morality was the symptom of a dark and mysterious disease, a kind of tremor in the soul; but while Colette's conscience made no sense to him whatsoever, he was unable to sleep at the thought of her suffering. His efforts to comfort her seemed only to make the situation worse. One night, while she was sleeping on the couch to avoid Jerry, Kevin went to her and hovered beside her. She was awake, staring at him through threaded eyelashes. He told her that she shouldn't worry about Cassie's God, because to Him, an identity was little more than a bar code. "You see, it's just hidden numbers within the stripes, which are there to help the computer isolate the actual code. It wouldn't be hard to get some stickers and, with magnetic ink, just print a whole bunch of new bar codes. We could go put them on beluga caviar, and it could show up as gumdrops. But it wouldn't actually *be* gumdrops."

"Kevin, go back to bed."

"What I'm saying is that if you're worried about your eternal soul and that kind of stuff—it's still the same. You've just got like a new sticker on the outside."

"Wonderful. I'm now a box of gumdrops. I feel so much better."

The next morning, while they waited in their car during the ferry ride, stalled in a wavering tunnel, Colette said she wanted to find the cemetery and leave flowers for her new alias. Jerry snapped, "You're being fucking ridiculous, you know that. I'm getting really sick of these *moral cramps*, Colette—"

"Oh my God. Okay, Jerry—if I don't agree with you, it must be because I'm having my period. That's great. Whenever a guy says that, it means he's completely baffled by anything more complicated than a lawn mower."

"Listen, baby. I need you to calm down and think a little more realistically. All right? You have a very screwed-up sense about the world sometimes."

"Of course I do. I died of pneumonia in the sixties."

"It's paperwork. If you're going to put some kind of significance into paperwork, honey, then you should get on the next ferry to hell right now. It's not voodoo, it's not a volcano sacrifice: it's *red tape*! Ask Kevin."

"Kevin doesn't think it's red tape. To him it's fucking necromancy. I'm not going to ask him, he's more twisted than you are."

"We steal identities every day," said Jerry. "Why should it be different because the person is dead? Why is it okay to steal a credit card number, but not a name? You're going to have to get this shit straight, Colette, or you don't belong out here. *Now,* I don't want to argue anymore on this tugboat, because I got nothing but coffee in me and I'm going to puke if I keep talking."

She was quiet for a few rolls and dips beneath them. Finally she said, "It's just terrible to have to do something like this."

"Then go work for the Peace Corps. Dig latrines. You don't get to pick and choose. You don't get to ride somebody's Visa card for five grand and then be Mother fucking Teresa about this."

"Why are you always so angry at me, Jerry? I don't even get to say my opinion?"

"I'm angry because I hate phony righteousness. Right now it's all on me, and that's fine. If we get picked up tomorrow— Colette, you'll say you were kidnapped, and Kevin will pretend to be some idiot savant who doesn't know anything but computers. But time will go by, and you'll have to make some choices. You're not thieves right now, you're a couple of shoplifting babies. And you're toying with all these little ideas about yourselves—'Oh, I only rob from *bad* people,' or 'I only take what I deserve,' 'I'm too good to do *this,* but not that.' Give me a break. If you want to live outside the rules, kids, then there's *one* moral: protect yourself and your crew. That's what I'm doing. So don't rely on me, expect me to save your asses, cart you around, and then act like you're *better* than me because I'm willing to use anything I can. So far you've only seen the good times. When it gets bad, and believe me, things can get motherfucking awful—then you'll change your tune, baby. I don't care what you believe in, I don't care what the name on your little phony license or that little phony passport says—you'll find out *exactly* who you are. Both of you. Goddamn it, I'm seasick!"

TWELVE

In Seattle, with the last dwindling set of cards, they rented a hitch and trailer, and filled it with fur coats, toolboxes, and, at Kevin's request, a collection of newly unveiled Macintosh computers. The trailer rattled behind the bumper of their orange Chevy Nova, which smelled sweet from leaking antifreeze. In Deer Lodge, Montana, worried that prolonged exposure to fumes might cause brain damage to his already slaphappy crew, Jerry traded the car with a fence who claimed to need only the bell housing of its transmission.

"In my day, when you stole a car, you used the *whole* car," said Jerry. "Like the Indians did with a buffalo."

By then moving cash had become far more work than moving themselves. Money orders needed to be accumulated at less than three hundred dollars apiece to avoid a record with the authorities; humble bank accounts had to be constantly circulated from one to the next, a simmering pot constantly stirred. In late July, Jerry opted for an easier way to wash the money, closing out many of the accounts to buy thick booklets of traveler's checks in his new fake name, which he could cash at any lobby or convenience store without attracting much attention. At first Kevin thought his father's sudden proclivity for tourist sites (the soak in the Mammoth Hot Springs where Colette was a lone pink bikini in a herd of black one-pieces, or the souvenir rampage through Custer's last stand) might be nothing more than a ploy to cash bulky checks discreetly. But as Jerry became more cavalier about hotel prices, snubbing the usual motor courts in favor of hotel compounds with squelching arcade castles under portcullis doors, indoor pools of cavernous echoes and chlorinated air, thumping cowboy bars and all-you-can-eat buffets and air conditioners as powerful as jets, Kevin began to assume that these traveler's checks had unleashed the giddy momentum of amusement-park spending.

With a feeling as if he were avenging the death of his alias, Kevin (a.k.a. Doug Herman) underwent a surge of new abilities like nothing he had ever experienced before. He learned to make picks with bicycle spokes and brick straps, forming the snake, the rake, and the half diamond. Closing his eyes to reconstruct the internal shape in his head, feeling the pick bounce in the keyway according to the resistance of each pin, once he learned to visualize the dark and detailed terrain, he could feel the sheer line, keeping the pressure right, applying torque and turning the plug; and when he had opened his first Ace-type tubular lock into a vending machine, dropping the back panel and loading his shirt with pretzels, gum, and wadded dollar bills, he was so proud of himself he needed to bury his face in a pillow to muffle his hollering revelry. He couldn't contain his enthusiasm, so he refined it. Breaking through two panels into a pay phone with a homemade key, or scrubbing the padlock into a hotel storage room, he closed his eyes and imagined Colette as a damsel-in-distress, chained to a tree with a progressively more elaborate series of disk-tumbler and pin-tumbler locks. Delirious upon each new success, he filled his pockets with jackpots of spilling quarters. Town to town, his duffel sagged under the weight of coins. At two A.M. in Sterling, Colorado, he broke into the Miss Pacman of the Ramada Inn game room, fishing out a few hundred coins and, using information off a technical manual he had stolen in Denver, resetting the high scores to confess:

```
I__     100000
TOO     _99999
K__     _99998
UR_     _99997
MON     _99996
EY_     _00000
```

When Jerry noticed, he only commented that Kevin's scams weren't very lucrative, that they netted at best a few added pounds of loose change and a trunk full of licorice. But Kevin could tell from the rolling eyes and crossed arms that Jerry mostly disapproved of the lone-wolf quality to his style, the way that he would slink out of his room past midnight to reprogram solitary pay phones along the highway, or how he thrived in the strange new frontier created by compact discs, learning to reseal shrink-wrap with an iron, so that he could buy his favorites then return them for a full refund.

Maybe it was the focus on technology that most rankled Jerry—the "phreaking"—which appeared to a veteran con man like a form of poor sportsmanship. This new breed of grifter seemed to him like a mechanical rat living in the loose wiring and the broken-up aftermath of Ma Bell. Why rob a machine instead of a gullible clerk? If that was the goal, why not take a sledgehammer to a slot machine? After all of his rants about no morals beyond protecting his crew, Kevin began to see that his old man *did* have a clear ethos. He found any robbery to be unseemly if it didn't involve a phony smile and a handshake.

"I'm just worried you'll electrocute yourself or something," he said. "Salespeople have less volts running through 'em."

Kevin took the challenge and tried to show his father that he wasn't entirely without "people skills." After all, it was a season of teenagers. In every hotel there were dozens of awkward and shouting youths. Kevin stalked the pool and tried to read this landscape of wild, cannonballing adolescents. Chewing, spitting, interrupting their bragging monologues to punch a younger sister, some of them didn't seem like real people to Kevin, but flickering carnival games of frustration and impulse. Their intimacies were startling and unpredictable. A girl from Minnesota, with a railroad of steel in her mouth, wanted to show him her appendix scar; a thirteen-year-old boy bestowed on Kevin a single M&M, like a pearl, then confessed that his mother was upstairs "porking" her new boyfriend. Most disturbing were the shrill safety-monitor types who took it upon themselves to uphold the Commandments of the Pool, some of whom were so bossy and officious that Kevin began to fear the shallow end as a hatchery for future police officers.

Among the fifteen-year-olds, some had their own foolish ambitions to commit crimes—kicking like SWAT teams on the Plexiglas windows of soda machines, storming the hallways in paramilitary gangs to tamper with fire alarms. As if he had confronted a tribe of early humans, Kevin couldn't help but find their ventures hopelessly unsophisticated. But he was impressed by how easily these young men could be convinced to steal from their own parents, especially if they believed a baggie of oregano was "Humboldt County" or "Acapulco Gold" (the more the name sounded like a soap opera, the higher the price). He skateboarded in the parking lot with shabby young boys who boasted about unlikely sexual conquests, fat bowls of Maui Wowie, lines of pure cocaine, or tickets to see Iron Maiden in concert; so Kevin would sell them ground-up NoDoz or forged tickets to Ratt in Grand Island, or, once, a mashed-up ball of melted Tootsie Rolls and paprika pawned off as a Thai stick.

Colette despised anything to do with drugs, and when she learned of the scams she demanded that Jerry punish his son. Kevin argued that he wasn't a drug-dealer, but an *anti*-drug-dealer. If he didn't exist, these ragged and rebellious teens would have a far better chance of finding *real* drugs. His father agreed, but he also acknowledged Colette's point that the phony drugs might serve as "gateway spices." To contain what he saw as a growing "sibling-type rivalry" between the two junior members of his crew, he imposed a mandatory one-week break from the grift.

Even while scrubbing locks, practicing forgery, and devising new cons, the hiatus was excruciating for all of them. Jerry needed to unwind with an evening of casual lying, claiming to be a Hollywood producer, a tennis pro, or a diplomat, sometimes all three. Colette liked to model new swimwear publicly, usually making an appearance at the prime poolside hour (right after the news). She'd adjust her bathing suit over the hollows of her flexing hip joints, strut down the diving board like a fashion runway, dive prettily into the water, then linger beneath the surface long enough to let compliments and whistles start from the men in the hot tub, who looked like pink missionaries in a boiling cauldron.

Somehow the week of leisure gave more venom to the arguments between Jerry and Colette. Kevin would only deal with them one at a time now, for it was too much effort to read the shifting terrain between them. Argument and silence, sarcasm and hard breath. A shout, a scuffle, a breakdown. The reconciliation: kiss, nuzzle, and locked door. Kevin could never tell what caused a crisis, if it was Colette breaking the cease-fire to buy a watch with a credit card she hadn't tested, or Jerry flirting with a waitress at the Pancake Palace. They were clearly happier when there was a common enemy, and Kevin found himself enjoying the evening when they allied to peek around opposing edges of a curtain at a police car outside. But afterward, while Jerry's adrenaline quickly faded (he lay down shirtless with a beer on his stomach), Colette stayed charged all night, and couldn't sleep without dancing, drinking, browsing store windows.

One night at the end of the moratorium, she decided to go out on the town by herself, in jeans so tight they seemed bolted onto her by the brass rivets on the hips. Jerry said she was sure to win a blue ribbon tonight, ready for the big hoedown—St. Cloud, Minnesota, city of burned-out lights—where a toothless goalie was just waiting to buy her a margarita. "You know, Colette, there's no prize for attracting the most losers."

"Tell me about it."

Most of that night Kevin heard his father wander the suite, sirens on the TV, the damp syllables of opening beer cans, the ascending and finally stammering note of a peeing cascade. Kevin came out of his adjoining room and asked his father how he could let her go out like that. "Did you see how she was dressed?"

"Give me a break, Kev. I can't control that woman any more than I can control you. I'm too old. You kids are killing me here! I need an old woman, man—somebody as *tired* as I am."

Colette returned midway through the Carson show, mumbled, and dropped her handbag. Stepping in front of Kevin's open door, she lobbed her stiletto sandals up to her hands with two chorus-line kicks. Sounding vindicated by the reasonable hour, Jerry said, "Didn't stay for the double feature, I guess."

"Can we please stop fighting for once?"

"You're the one who's fighting, Colette. I'm just watching TV. But you should have seen Kevin—he was pacing all over the place. He was worried you found somebody else to mooch off."

"Great, I'm surrounded. You know what's wrong with you, Jerry? You're cheap, you're lazy, and you don't respect anybody or anything but yourself."

"What makes you think I respect myself?" asked Jerry.

Kevin could see her gesturing at him with the heel of her shoe. "I just went for a walk, but I realized something. My scams have *made* us. Everything in this room, I paid for. That lamp—mine. That shitty fucking painting—what the hell is that?—mine, I paid for it."

"It actually belongs to the hotel."

"This suite, that couch, the fucking car downstairs. Me, I paid for it. Not Kevin and his bathtub full of quarters. Not you and your stupid fucking network of prison buddies or your card catalog of dead babies— *me*. You just sit there with a beer and point. Like a fucking caveman. You tell me what to do, and I *do* it. Day after goddamn miserable day. And you know what?"

"You want some credit."

"Yes! I want some credit! I want you to say something—like *Thank you* would be a start, or *Good job, Colette*, or *Nice going, Esther*, or Barbie or Toots or whatever fucking name I have this week. Tell me something nice, Jerry. For once in your lying cheating life, give me something I can use."

"Come over here, Colette. I want to explain something."

Kevin tried to sleep with a pillow tight over his face, and he nearly suffocated himself. When he tiptoed over to close the door, they were talking in a subdued tone on the narrow couch. Colette's bare legs were curled up on the pillows, her head riding on the camelback motion of his chest. But her eyes were open, and she looked more adrift than comforted. In a tired baritone, Jerry was talking about prison. It was a horror story—about the echoing screams of young kids and eyeballs cut open with smuggled razor blades, beginning as the usual speech about the hell he'd seen. But somehow it became a lonesome country-western love song, about how every long night of his life he had dreamed of a woman like her—quick-witted and beautiful and tenacious. It was more than Kevin expected from the man. He told her that if he could buy her safe passage out of this life, hers and Kevin's, he would; but it was hard with a teenage son always pressing to know more and a tiring and insatiable young girlfriend who wanted to devour the world. Think of the pressure on him. "You need to know that we're together like this partly because of you. You keep us up and running. I know it and Kevin knows it. I'm not a good person, Colette—I never claimed to be, I don't *want* to be, and you can't expect me to be. But look me in the eye and accept me as a snake, and I'll tell you whatever you're waiting to hear: I need you, I want you, I hurt for you, down in the dust, honey, down in the dust of my bones."

She interrupted him with kisses that sounded like determined sips at a scalding drink.

THIRTEEN

Late September, they stayed in a penthouse suite in Minneapolis, which overlooked a river and the torches of autumn trees. Downtown was arranged so that they could pass between buildings through enclosed skywalk bridges, like transparent tubes for hamsters, an entire city of sinuous walks under glass, from the fresh carpet to the food-court tiles, where along the paths there were bazaars of business clothes, luggage, and travel clocks. Kevin would scout out the best corner shops so that Colette could return in character, dressed in her tweed skirt, chiffon blouse, rolled hair framing a steely expression. As a peace offering, Jerry now let her open accounts on her own. She posed as a succession of eager young ladies pitted against condescending bankers: a timid farm girl with a new job in advertising, a cosmetology student from Winnipeg, the heiress to a chain of frozen-yogurt stands.

One account she set up jointly, for herself, as Esther Barrick, and her stepbrother, Douglas Herman. While sitting in the plush chair across the desk from the banker, Kevin became bored and distracted, wondering if there was some way to access the computers and divert electronic-funds transfers; and Colette, to his great displeasure, decided to pretend that he was autistic. "He doesn't really hear us right now," she said to the banker. "But I like to think he does in his own way. Honey? The account is in your name also, with me—Esther."

"You'll be the custodian of the account, ma'am. He won't be able to access it until he's eighteen."

Irritated, Kevin stared at her devilish eyes.

"Honey? Eighteen. That's just a little over two years. One, two. I don't think he understands. He's a whiz with binary code, but if you get beyond that, he just starts shrieking."

Kevin was still pouting at dinner that night, as Colette and Jerry broke into fits of red-faced laugher. They dined at a French restaurant, celebrating the birthday on Jerry's fake ID; and they had so firmly united to ridicule him that Kevin believed the fighting was over. There was a white tablecloth, a basket of fresh bread, four bottles of wine, Kevin's cola in a burgundy glass, but no pancakes anywhere on the menu.

Jerry proposed the first toast—"To the Credit Card Fraud Act. No one is ever liable for more than fifty dollars."

Kevin toasted the microchip; Jerry drank to the USA; Colette abstained. "Oh, go to Russia then," said Jerry. "Fucking boycotter. To the best country on earth and their gazillion gold medals and the little rumproast gymnast who won it all. Here's to check floats and preapproved credit, virgin plastic and the promotional toasters for every new account—Colette, you could make a stack of toast all the way to the moon."

"Oh, Jerry—boy, are you loaded."

After dinner, they strolled down a cobbled walk toward the parking garage, savoring a new chill in the air. Colette was wearing a cloche hat pulled low over her forehead, and Jerry became rowdy at the idea of her twirling in a circle and throwing it into the air. There was a hint of belligerence in his tone that sped Kevin's strides and slowed Colette's. Up ahead, beside a bench, Kevin waited, and he was amazed that this request had already escalated into an argument. Colette refused to be his "Mary" fantasy; and Jerry, talking in slurred jokes that verged on shouting, guiding her along with his wobbly shipmate's walk, claimed his fantasy wasn't *that* Mary anyway, but the black-and-white, apron-clad Mary.

"I *know*," said Colette. "She isn't in my repertoire."

"*Repertoire.* Repertoire! Listen to you, for God's sake. Come on. Throw your fucking hat in the air. Why won't you ever do a single thing I ask? It'll make me happy. Please. Pretty please with sugar and a big cherry on top."

"Jerry, I don't want to. It's a good hat."

"She's worried about the hat! Oh Jesus, you are a princess."

"Probably everybody that comes here throws their stupid hat in the air. It's not funny, Jerry. It's like going to Paris and wearing a beret with the Eiffel Tower on it."

"Everything is a goddamned negotiation with you."

"Now I wish Kevin's alias was sixteen," she said. "Jerry, don't you ever find it troubling that your son can hot-wire a car, but he can't drive it?"

"Throw the hat! I bet I could go out and find any woman in this city, and she'd be happy to throw her hat in the air for me. All night. We would just stand here and she would do it over and over. She'd throw anything I wanted."

"Good for you, Jerry. Then maybe she'll throw herself off a bridge."

In the car Jerry's driving had the same syntax of drunken speech: abrupt stops, fitful accelerations, and gratuitous lane changes. Kevin jumped out at the hotel and waited by the bellhop stand. The car twitched, full of sealed wind. After an accidental honk, Colette stepped onto the pavement and smothered the second half of Jerry's insult by slamming the door. "Do whatever you want!" she shouted, as if to the car itself, which hiccuped forward, fumed its engine, and squealed into a left turn past dark office buildings.

As Colette entered the hotel through the revolving door, Kevin slipped into the chamber alongside her and trapped them in place by spreading out his feet.

"Kevin, not *now*. I'm not in a good mood."

"Listen to me, Colette. This is over. I'm watching the two of you and it's breaking my heart. I've got a thousand dollars saved. We could leave right now, you and I, and we could turn it into ten thousand."

Their collective breath was steaming the glass of the narrow compartment, and already there was a small crowd forming on both sides of the door. Colette wiped a strand of hair from her face and said, "Congratulations. That must be twice your weight in quarters." He released the door and they raced out in different slaloming paths across the congested marble lobby.

He caught up with her by the gold-plated elevator doors, their wobbly reflections in the surface, and grabbed the arm of her pea coat. "Don't ignore me, Colette."

"A thousand dollars and ten thousand more," she said with a sad quiver in her voice. "With all your studying, you have to know that a girl like me would need another zero on both of those numbers. Please don't grab me. I *hate* being grabbed."

The elevator doors opened and split their reflections down the middle, and on the inside they scooted to opposite sides to make room for a bellboy with a loaded cart of luggage. Staring up at the panel, they waited in silence for three floors.

Kevin said, "I'll rob a bank if I have to."

"It isn't just about the money, Kevin. *Please.*"

He whispered, "I love you so much my teeth are numb."

"See a dentist."

"I'm dying, Colette."

"Or a doctor."

"I could rip off every room in this hotel to cover us."

"Maybe a shrink."

"I'll just beat up this dude here and steal his uniform."

The bellboy looked from side to side.

Colette sighed facetiously and said, "Oh, I'd do anything for a man in uniform."

"All he ever does is cut you down, Colette."

"And all you do is bother me."

"That's not true. If I'm bothering you, then why are you still here?"

"Because I'm not ready to pry open the escape hatch and leap down the elevator shaft. See—we're *here.*" The car settled and the doors swung open, and as she strode out she turned to the bellhop and said, moving her head to meet his eyes past the closing accordion doors, "By the way, sir, it was all a joke."

Kevin trailed her down the hall while she tried to speed up and lose him. Suddenly she kicked off her shoes and ran full speed away from him around the bend. He knew that in all his life he would never again find a woman who ran with such beautiful abandon, with those lean, strong legs and her unraveling hair. He caught her on the stairwell landing and held her tight against the railing. "I'll hit the fire alarm," she said.

"No, you won't." He waited to catch his breath, then explained, "There's a little white squirt of paint that comes out and it makes it easy—"

"Oh, shut up!" she said and started to cry. To his astonishment, she leaned forward into him and put her face against his shoulder. She sputtered in his arms, sniffled, and said, "Why do you have to take everything *apart*?"

"You'll leave with me then. Tonight."

She shook her head against him, either to say no or wipe her eyes.

"I can't stand to think of him ever touching you again—"

"He *doesn't* touch me anymore, Kevin. That's the problem. He just yells at me."

"We'll pack our bags. We've got the money in our joint account too."

"That's nothing. That wouldn't last half an hour. No, Kevin. Just hold me for a second. *Please.*"

He held her and smelled the salt of her tears, the smoke and lilac scent of her hair, and he felt the slowing pace of her breath and heartbeat beneath her dress. Then she pulled back and looked at him with a pink and softened face, raw newborn eyelids and a dampened mouth, and through leftover tears she faced him and said, "I need you right now. From the bottom of my heart, Kevin, I *do* need you. But if you have any sense at all, stop pressing me like this. I want you to come back to the room with me, and just be a human being. That's it. Don't say a word about stolen cards or master keys or anything like that. Just come back to the room and *wait.*"

"All right," he said quietly. "Wait for what?"

"I don't know, Kevin. For tomorrow, for your father to come back, for something in this fucking world to make sense. Just wait. And for once in your demented life, don't ask so many questions. For *me,* if you love me, if you really honestly love me—then you have to shut up and do what I say."

For the next two hours, they sat in her dark room and watched television, Colette prone on the bed, Kevin upright against the headboard. The news, the talk shows with sizzling applause, a late-night show of music videos, it all came and went like headlights in the rain.

"Should I be worried?" she asked. "About your father, I mean?"

"I'm not."

The networks signed off with the national anthem and they moved to separate rooms, Kevin reclining on the couch, Colette pacing in her dark bedroom. He could tell that he had slept only by the crick in his neck and the changed taste in his mouth. Soon the gauze of the curtains seemed to glow faintly, and garbage trucks rattled outside.

"Kevin, honey. Wake up. It's past five."

"He probably went to breakfast."

"Right. Okay. You're the resident expert on that. I'm sorry. Go back to sleep."

At the first hot light in the curtain ruffle, they took turns showering; ordered breakfast and ate the toast, the oranges, the buttermilk pancakes, but left the two domes of eggs standing on their minarets. They both wore terry-cloth robes. Colette whispered to herself over a crossword puzzle. To Kevin it felt like they were a somber married couple. Neither spoke. Silverware clanked and the thickening traffic honked outside like arrows of passing geese.

"It's eleven," she said. "Did you ever know him to be gone this long?"

"Maybe he was too drunk and got another room, closer to the bars."

"If he did something to himself, I'm going to just kill him. I mean, torturing *me* is one thing, I'm getting used to that, but if he's really hurt or in trouble, how the hell are we supposed to know? Okay—calm down. If he was arrested, he would call us."

"No, he wouldn't."

"*Yes*, Kevin. He would too. Don't be ridiculous."

"If he got arrested he'd make sure we weren't implicated in anything."

"Don't talk like that. It's still early, we don't know anything yet."

The trembling quality of her voice made Kevin realize that his father truly might be in trouble, either smashed into a brick wall or arrested at dawn with a hooker and a bottle of Thunderbird. It simply hadn't occurred to him before that his father could ever be in danger of *anything*. Jerry was the height of casual human ingenuity. He was a natural phenomenon, like sunlight or wind, and the notion that the man was somehow vulnerable seemed to change the texture of everything around them. The traffic moved haphazardly in the streets below; everyone on the hotel staff suspected them; the FBI was camped out in the office building across the street; and their lives could end, just like this, not with a flash, not in a glorious burst of fire, but with a confusing and surreal morning. Jerry could vanish like Colette's mother—and they wouldn't know for years what had happened. It could have been a pinch in a strip club, or a hobo who whacked him over the head with a plank.

They hit the phones. While Kevin tried motels, motor lodges, and the YMCA, using every alias he knew (even an old one from his dad's construction days), Colette was across the suite talking to nightclub managers. By three o'clock the rooms were littered with torn pages of slashed numbers, but not a single lead. Colette came into his room and said, "Now I'm officially freaked out."

"He's going to be all right."

By evening Colette had called the area hospitals, waiting on hold, painting her toenails. "Should I call the morgue?"

"Quit it with that. I'm going to make a list of police divisions."

"He better be in the hospital. With a big concussion. Or liver poisoning. That's how I feel right now." She raised her chin, and spoke with a tight mouth. "His appendix better have ruptured at dawn, and he better be on his deathbed eating Jell-O through a straw, because if he's not—"

"Stop it. We'll find him."

"I'm going to kill him with a salad fork."

At seven o'clock, when the sky was dark, Colette sat quietly by the window with her bare feet pressed against the glass. Kevin stayed under a single light in the bedroom amid torn papers, calling motels in the suburbs, working until he glimpsed the somber look on her face reflected in the glass.

"Listen," he called out. "I'm going to take my board and go look for him. I can cover half the city, I swear to God."

"When does your offer expire, Kevin?"

"What offer?"

She made a frustrated kissing sound and replied, "We can leave tonight. Anywhere I want to go."

"Colette, listen—it lasts forever. But let's make sure he's okay first. I just can't stop thinking he got arrested or fell in a manhole or something. That doesn't change anything."

"You don't have to explain, Kevin. I don't think we're in any state to fly off to Cancun anyway. Maybe someday. We'll go look at the departure screen and treat it like a buffet. Pick whatever looks good."

Kevin clutched his skateboard over his chest and exhaled. "I'll try the drunk tanks—"

"You're going to do what you have to do. We're mercenaries, Kevin, and let's just not pretend otherwise. Just for future reference, don't use words like *love* anymore. It's a very sensitive word and it wears out quickly. Romeo barely says it, but John Hinckley filled up a whole journal with it. To put it in your terms, it's a currency that's pretty easily devalued."

"Colette, I'm just going to go look for him. That's all. He could be bleeding to death in an alley, and even if he's a jerk to you—he's still my father."

"Pretty soon you're saying it whenever you hang up the phone or whenever you leave. It turns into an apology. Then it's an excuse. Some assholes want it to be a bulletproof vest: don't hate me, I love you. But mostly it just means—*more*. More, more—give me something more. A couple years from now, when you're on your own completely, if you really fall in love, if it really comes to that—and I pity you if it ever does—you have to look right down into the black of her eyes, right down into the emptiness in there, and feel everything, absolutely everything she *needs*, and you have to be willing to drown in it, Kevin. You'd have to want to be crushed, buried alive. Because that's what real love feels like—choking. They used to bury women in their wedding dresses, you know. I thought it was because all those husbands were too cheap to spring for another gown, but now it makes sense: love is your first foot in the grave. That's why the second most abused word is *forever*."

Kevin sat down on the arm of the couch, still hugging his skateboard. Outside there was a flurry of sirens and ambulances, followed by rustling pigeons off a nearby ledge.

She said, "I'm not going to lie to you, Kevin. In some perfect hypothetical world, if you were older and your father wasn't in the picture and I was less screwed up, then maybe you and I would be some kind of fairy tale. But I've been sitting here telling you exactly who I am, and you haven't put down the skateboard. Maybe you can't sleep, maybe your teeth are numb, maybe your head's in the clouds. But you need your father more than you need me. Go find him."

FOURTEEN

At ten-thirty that night Jerry returned to the room: sunburned, in a giant pair of pants, with his hands up for surrender. He thought his story was a riot, and seemed mildly puzzled when Colette refused to look at him from the bed. Late last night he had driven out to a lake with a case of beer and drunk it while he sat on the hood, overlooking the water. He had passed out in the backseat until the upholstery heated with sunlight, then rose around noon to find a secluded spot to "do some business" in the trees. Not twenty minutes later the car had been towed, with his bag and wallet, his pants and shoes, twenty-two discarded beer cans and a roach in the ashtray.

Penniless, in his boxer shorts and T-shirt, with only his wits and some useless car keys, he took to the challenge like a hustler's chess problem. For hours he traipsed through the woods in his underwear— "like some Bigfoot documentary"—until he found the clothesline of a campsite, where he stole pants and a damp pair of canvas sneakers. He walked miles back into downtown, avoiding the highway patrol, until he was too hungry to continue. He stopped at a diner, where he ate practically everything on the menu. When the check came, he claimed to have left his wallet in the car. He gave the keys to the hostess as a show of good faith, and set off again to find the hotel. "Luckily you had the room key, Colette. Otherwise the cops would have been here by now. We'll need another car though—fast."

"You went out to the lake alone. Just to what—go fly-fishing?"

She finally faced him across the dim room, but without her eyes focused, like he was only some sound in the dark.

"Oh Jesus, baby. You don't fly-fish in a *lake*. And no, I had a lot on my mind." Jerry put his arm around Kevin and shouted, "He thinks it's funny! At least somebody around here has got a sense of humor."

Colette's eyelids were swollen. Kevin couldn't imagine how his father failed to see the wreckage of papers, broken lamps, and clothes in the room, like a storm had blown through a shattered window. When Kevin left the room, he expected shouting to start, but they were silent all night.

The following morning, over breakfast, Jerry seemed to have accepted that Colette was angry, but his normal run of apologies and promises did nothing more than stiffen her in the chair. Beyond the fact that the car had been towed and the clock was ticking on Minneapolis, he didn't seem to remember details of his own story. Colette asked him if his hickey had come from a squirrel, and he replied that he had bumped into a tree branch.

"I think her husband came home," she said quietly. "And you had to throw on whatever clothes you could find, because yours were scattered around. And then you ran outside and *voilà*: the car's been towed. That's the one true part."

"I don't think you want to call me a liar, Colette."

"You're a professional liar."

"Yeah, but this is different. I only lie when there's money involved."

She stared down, licked her lips, and said: "Then we'll have to find out how much I'm *worth*."

That afternoon she kept to herself in the hotel's lounge, reading at a far table and refusing drinks from men at the bar. Passing her on the way back to the room, Kevin asked if she was okay. She responded with a curt, "Of course," giving him the same vacant look that she had shown his father.

That afternoon, beside the theaters in a mall, Kevin stole her a gold pin from a jewelry store. He felt a gust of nostalgia as he looked at two identical items, flipped one perfectly into the inside fold of his sleeve, and placed the other back in its spot. But when he looked at the pin later, it was a tacky scarab, fit only to melt down and fill a tooth. He knew Colette would consider a tasteless gift to be worse than a deval-ued *I love you*—for he now believed that the dividing line between suit-ors and stalkers could often be determined by an appraisal. So he tied it into his shoelaces like a cocooning insect.

When Colette found him that evening, she glanced at it and said nothing. Squinting, with only business in her voice, she said, "I'm going to need your help with a scam. Your father isn't doing anything but fronting some cash, that's it. You don't have to think, and you don't have to be on anybody's side. I don't need your heart or your soul—I just need a decent pair of hands."

FIFTEEN

For her first solo assignment, Colette was determined to find the per-fect mark. In Madison, Wisconsin, she left the new hotel disguised as a student wearing a backpack, a knit cap, and a douse of patchouli oil. She quickly filled a legal pad with observations about various candidates: a classics professor, a claims adjuster, and a presumed surgeon who later turned out to be a distinguished-looking hospital janitor.

Jerry passed the entire first day in a grim bar, hidden from daylight, scraping wet labels off his beer bottles. He hated this university hamlet with its bike paths of joggers and baby carriages, a lake full of pedal boats. "All these little rosy-cheeked punks make me want to blow up a juice stand."

He complained across the bar that his woman was going to kill him with visions of grandeur. To Kevin, he added, "She's never going to be satisfied with a wallet, let's put it that way. She's going to want some poor bastard's whole life. Whoever she picks for this little con of hers, she might as well *marry* him."

He stared vacantly at a football game on the shelf above the bar.

"Look—I know what you're thinking, Kevin, so don't say it. She's a very smart girl. And it's hard to be too intelligent when you're a woman. They get spoon-fed even more bullshit than we do. It drives any girl nuts who's smart enough to notice it, and that's why all intelligent women are insane—write that down if you have to. They live in little shoe-box prisons of perfumed horseshit."

He swigged the last dregs from his bottle, then nodded his chin at the bartender. "But she's got to stop fucking around and just admit some things. She's a greedy bitch. *Personally*, it's a pain in the ass; but professionally, it's high praise. She just doesn't direct her energy. All this setup now: she's got to find Mr. Right, and everything has to be as perfect as her wedding. This is a job. Look at our bartender—you think he goes home and writes in his diary about that bottle of scotch? No. And neither should we. We pick one asshole off a pedal boat, ride him for a few Gs, and get out of town."

"Then why let her do it?"

"Look, I'm going to tell you something and it doesn't leave this bar. Okay? I've had a lot of partners, a lot of—business associates—and in some ways Colette's the best I ever worked with. She'll turn a store clerk inside out; she'll get people so hyped up they'll listen to anything she says. You've got this crazy ability with details, little technical things—but that woman can read the landscape like nobody I've ever seen. Ask her a few questions after she leaves a giant store. She can describe the look on everyone's faces from women's wear all the way to sporting goods. She can look at twenty clerks and pick the one who'll run a hot card. She's got that sense of people. But, see, it also scares her. Like being too stoned in a crowd or something, and she needs somebody to walk her through it. Anybody who sees too much stops being able to move. You wind up being one of those video-store clerks with a 160 IQ, or this bartender over there—he was a fucking summa cum laude."

As the bartender looked over at this, frowning, Jerry toasted his empty beer and said, "Yeah, one more, Einstein."

Two weekends before Halloween, Colette asked Kevin for a favor. She wanted him to turn his technical expertise to the ancient and underappreciated craft of pickpocketing, which would be a helpful shortcut in a scam she described as "a ballet colliding with an opera." True to his usual form, Kevin practiced the new skill intensely. He hung coats and pants over chairs, bumped them, and lifted out wallets. She replaced his dummy wardrobe with a baggy blue suit. As she hung this suit from doors and shower stalls, it began to have its own haunting personality, startling Kevin when he woke up to find it dangling from the curtain rack, or mocking him from a standing lamp, its pockets always refilled, its wallet hidden among the lumpy decoys of breath mints and folded-up papers. During each practice run the suit waited for him across the hotel room like an unwavering enemy in a duel.

By the third night, Kevin needed work on a moving target. Colette played the mark, sauntering across the room. Kevin would bump her, dip his extended fingers into the pocket with a scissoring motion. After an hour, she said, "Stop feeling me up, Kevin. And you have to be quicker than that. More fluid."

It was an exciting and agonizing dance routine, rehearsed into the giddy hours of the night. But Colette was in no mood for joking, not when he playfully frisked her, especially not when he bypassed a coat to wedge his fingers into the back of her tight designer jeans. "If you can't stay focused for this—tell me. I have a hundred contingency plans here."

"I can, I can. I *promise*. No problem whatsoever—no more messing around."

While she was asleep, Kevin grew so curious about this perfect mark that he climbed out of bed to snoop through her notes. With turbulent penmanship she had sketched so many details about the man's daily patterns, indulgences and weaknesses, tastes and merits, that Kevin felt a pang of jealousy.

> Meets lover for lunch,
> Does all the talking—
> Hides wedding ring
> Inside alligator wallet.

Some observations read to Kevin like little cramped haiku:

> Red Mercedes-Benz
> Backseat: books, flowers, papers
> Never carries cash

The following night Colette returned, threw down her bag and hat, then leaped up and danced on the bedsprings. They were in business. She pronounced her mark the worst and richest man in Wisconsin.

When Kevin began to piece together some of her plans through the growing pile of notes, receipts, carbons, and mail, he was astounded by the way she seemed to work her con in reverse. She had operated on the theory that the most expensive jewelry store in town would attract a significant percentage of philandering husbands. He asked her about this while they were practicing one morning, and she nonchalantly replied, "Diamonds are pure guilt or lust—to any man except Liberace."

The mark was a university professor and, apparently, a noted author. Like an eager freshman, Colette was thrilled by each new discovery, purchasing his novels and reading them in her bed with a scrunched, horrified face, happy to proclaim that he was a talented but pompous writer who had completely objectified his female characters.

Over the next thirty-six hours she used the man's bloated ego to dig up more information than on all their Dumpster dives combined. Posing as a journalist, a student from freshman lit who had a nagging question (and obviously a schoolgirl's crush), and, at last, a woman from the payroll office who had lost the files on him, she could easily have written the man's biography. She developed for him a deep and almost erotic hatred.

He was having an affair with a graduate student, it seemed, and Colette had known this since the first day he'd browsed through the jeweler's like a circling hawk. Intending to bilk the man out of some ungodly sum, she referred to his wife and young lover as if they were her teammates; and sometimes, eerily, she would begin speaking to his wife while reading through the course work or plotting out schemes.

"You know, Darcy, this literature racket is a joke," she said. "Every woman in these books is a suicidal idiot: Madame Bovary, Anna Karenina. It's like this guy is teaching a class on easy marks."

She woke Kevin before dawn on the morning of "phase one," and reviewed with him a calendar that predicted the mark's activities in fifteen-minute intervals. She had a map of the university, annotated with flourishes of her handwriting, and she explained to Kevin that today was the day. Posing as her mark's mistress, she had called around town to change a reservation, and—like a hacker eventually stumbling onto a password—she had found the exact restaurant where they were set to meet for lunch.

Just as she had predicted, the mark emerged from Helen White Hall at a few minutes after ten, bought coffee at a nearby stand, and began heading across the crowded quadrangle. The man was in his mid-fifties, gray, with shaggy eyebrows and a stocky build that seemed to give his walk an added crotchety seriousness.

Dressed in a tie-dyed shirt and a knit Rastafarian hat, Kevin pushed off and began trailing the mark on his skateboard. Colette's notes were accurate down to the exact path he walked and the crosswalks he used. He headed through the shops along State Street to buy his mistress a gift, and as she had hoped from his days of covert browsing, he ducked into Good's Jewelers. Just as she'd said, he came back out through the revolving brass doors hiding a bag in his overcoat pocket.

Kevin could perceive only enough of this scam to admire her eye for detail: he even recognized the overcoat. The mark stood on the corner sipping his coffee, trained to ignore the droves of students around him, his tie a crimson pennant in the brisk wind. Kevin pushed off and began scuttling downhill toward him. He swerved among pedestrians, zeroing in on the mark, the light just changing from green to yellow, the students with their backpacks and books stepping off the curb. Kevin's fingertips tingled, the board clattered under his feet, and his vision reduced into a predator's narrow focus until everything became blurry around the edges of his target.

With a thud Kevin skated right into the man, intentionally knocking the coffee onto his shirt. Scrambling and muttering apologies in the parody of a stoner's voice, Kevin patted all around the man's coat and pockets. In the midst of this orchestrated tangle, Kevin was most surprised by the intimacy of the act: the man smelled like cigars and bleach; his body was soft under the girdle of a tight blue shirt. After a few explosive heartbeats, he was back on the board, skating away, and the mark still sat on the ground, disoriented among a pack of other students in similar psychedelic shirts. The bottom of the mark's coat pocket had left a trace of lint under Kevin's fingernail; and the wallet was warm and scaly and felt vaguely alive. He crumpled the jewelry store bag in his fist, and said to a passing group of girls: "I'm a magician. I'm a grandmaster, a black belt—Bruce Lee. Oh, I'm a bad man."

From around the bend Colette was approaching in sunglasses, a scarf tied over her head and a rolled-up newspaper tucked under her arm. The quality of her strut, the angle of her raised chin, the tilted smile—all filled Kevin with such a gust of joy and affection that he broke into laughter. He skated to her and slipped the wallet and crumpled bag into the fold of the newspaper. Around the next corner, he sat and caught his breath on a bus-stop bench. Everyone stared at him. "I'm an all-star," he boasted to the other people around the bus stop. "Don't worry, I'm not crazy, ma'am. I just aced all my finals. I'm summa cum laude."

That evening, pretending to be the wife, Colette called every credit card company to go over suspicious charges on the cards. She made a list of places the professor had bought gifts, claiming anyone arrogant enough to have an affair on a Visa card deserved worse than the "evil poetry she was about to unleash upon him."

Though Kevin was not entirely sure what she planned next, he explained the con as best he could to his father, sitting beside him in the bar where Jerry had long since gained the status of a grumpy regular. "She's already got enough information to take the guy for a lot—she can do his signature, she's got all his info. But for some reason she's waiting on something else. Weirdest thing, Dad—I go to all this trouble to steal the guy's wallet and some fancy necklace, and she drops it off at the lost and found of the restaurant where he had lunch. She had it a couple hours at the most. Then she calls his office, pretending to be a waitress, leaves a message with his secretary. Says someone found it. She didn't steal a thing but a couple of receipts, and the mark never even reported the cards missing."

"Face it, Kevin. It's a disaster. I'm losing hundreds every day just on her back-to-school wardrobe."

Just that night Colette bought new clothes, and when Kevin saw them hanging around the room, each dress and coat in the thin membrane of its wrapper, he worried that she was planning to elope with the mark. She bought a gold wedding band that closely resembled his ring, so snug that she had to slide it on with Vaseline.

"Why does it need to be that tight?" asked Kevin.

"Because I'm *with child*."

She asked Jerry to play one simple role: check out of the hotel on that afternoon, load the car, and meet them at six-thirty, when they would leave town immediately. "Probably with every cop in the city on our tail," he said.

Kevin's job was to follow her from store to store throughout Madison and create diversions. But the task was complicated, and she briefed him on the various tendencies and psychological profiles of salespeople all over the town.

Before dawn Colette was already getting dressed. She had duct-taped folded shirts over her belly and now unrolled panty hose that she squeezed over the bulge. Once assembled in her lavender maternity dress, she appeared to be somewhere in the second trimester, and for a while she practiced a gooselike walk with an arched back. With makeup she emphasized the plum coloring of the circles under her eyes, thinned out her normally heavy lower lip with pale contours, and ground in the powder of an anemic complexion.

It was a blustery morning, wind tugging the trees, chapping Kevin's nose, when they set out in their bundled coats and scarves, Colette looking ten years older from the makeup and her changed movements. The stores were just opening.

Quickly Kevin began to understand the first layers of her scheme. In a couple of hours with the "lost" wallet, she had created six department store accounts off his Visa while pretending to be his young girlfriend. She had already run up massive charges. Now, after taking a few days to learn the schedules of clerks, careful to make sure she faced a different staff, she returned as *his wife*. She complained that she had found receipts but never seen any of these elaborate gifts—mink stoles and diamond earrings—"What on earth is going on here?" If any salesman was unsure of her tragic position and her loutish husband, she would break into tears. To any man she would become both lost and flirtatious, playing on any protective impulse and begging him to "bend the rules."

"Let's close that account, please. I don't need any more humiliation. And I'll need you to change the billing address for those charges. You see, my husband is going to be moving out soon. I won't tolerate this. Here's where he'll be. It's our house in the Berkshires—maybe this *bill* can greet him there."

The sympathetic salesmen diverted enormous credit card bills to a random address in Massachusetts buying Colette added weeks while she further played her tortured status to add other items onto the accounts. At a Robinsons-May, Colette had scouted a righteous and bitter young saleswoman, who willingly colluded to charge another thousand dollars to the professor's Mastercard, using only the number, the expiration date, and his wife's tremulous signature.

The final stop was the infamous jewelry store, where Colette described a staff that had "only one kindred spirit." Kevin entered first, past the ringing bell, chased by a few tumbling maple leaves that settled on the floor. From Colette's notes, he knew that Barbara was the day manager, and Carl was the most officious salesperson; and he knew it would please Colette if he could divert them both, open a perfect lane to the sympathetic and highly suggestible Sheila, who was rearranging a display of velvet boxes. Kevin yelled to Carl that he wanted to buy a present for "his sophisticated lady friend." When Kevin began pawing at mobiles of bracelets and pendants, Carl rushed over and asked what he had in mind.

"She's a jewel, dude—top-notch. The smartest, most beautiful, heartbreaking ass-kicking babe you ever met in your life. She'd go through you like a slice of cheesecake. There'd be nothing left but the sweater vest."

"Well, she sounds like she may be out of your budget. May I suggest the university bookstore. They sell *geodes*."

"Hilarious. I want to talk to the manager. I'm coming in here ready to throw down some serious coin, and you're talking fucking geology. I don't have time for that. My dad's top brass in Silicon Valley and I'm coming in here with serious *plastic*, my man. I got a credit line that goes deeper than hell and I'll fucking use it just to shut your ass up."

Barbara emerged from the back to try to calm the strange aggressive customer, while Sheila watched fearfully from across the store. Just then a bell on the door rang and Colette stepped up to Sheila. She said a quiet greeting. Carl noticed her, so Kevin twirled a display of hoop earrings, dropping a few. Carl was blushing with anger and complained to Barbara that he had said nothing whatsoever to provoke the young man, who had without warning become violently rude.

Meanwhile, Colette had begun her routine. She put the stolen receipt on the counter, and then placed her wedding ring on top of it. She said, "I was wondering if you might help me. You see, I found out that my husband has purchased some merchandise here."

Kevin had to fight to keep his eyes away from Colette, for there was a magnificent thread of suppressed hysteria in her behavior, reined in by a pathetic attempt at dignity. Jerry's standard rule was to do everything with brash confidence, to muscle the mark into position; but here Colette played such a sad figure, straining to be noble, that she immediately bypassed any suspicion. Sheila was a younger woman than Kevin had expected, perhaps in her early thirties, with an expressive face that seemed like a canvas for dread. She had a perfunctory manner that was quickly befuddled, and she appeared to empathize with any show of suffering. "It's not my birthday, and it's not our anniversary," said Colette, with an ironic lightness in her voice, "so I can only assume it's a gift to help get me through my *pregnancy*."

Kevin couldn't hear Colette's next move because he had broken into his own monologue: "I walk in here and this dude assumes I'm broke, like some thug off the street—that's, like, a form of discrimination right there. I could be a fucking prince for all you know."

"You don't need to use that kind of language."

The phone rang and Carl answered. Colette and Sheila moved to the farthest corner, where Sheila was now studying the receipt to keep her eyes averted. Colette said, "The problem is, I haven't been seeing any *jewelry*. If you catch my drift—I think our only hope would be a set of rings. For the sake of—" And she glanced down at her belly. "And of course, look at my ring. It's nothing. It's from the days when we were kids. I haven't seen a piece of jewelry in ten years."

Onto the glass display case, Colette unfolded a photocopy of the mark's driver's license, as well as his credit card information.

"Because I don't particularly agree with my husband's taste, among other things, I think we should go ahead and open up an account. Here's all of his information. Believe me, he'll prefer we do it this way, rather than get into a serious debate about all of the secretive little things he's been purchasing over the past few weeks."

"Okay, ma'am—are you authorized to—let's see here—"

Collette looked down at her bulging stomach and said, "Believe me—*I'm authorized*. If he can afford a two-thousand-dollar necklace, he can afford to save his marriage." She pressed her finger onto the glass and continued, "I want those two rings. We can have them sized later. Don't be alarmed, Sheila. I'm having the man's child. The least I can do is go out with a fight."

Sheila was so confused by this dialectic that she read the information again. Colette looked away long enough for her eyes to dampen; then she leaned forward to rivet them on Sheila's face.

Meanwhile, Kevin chose a pair of drop earrings with gold-plated ankhs and the eyes of Re, and he littered the display case with crumpled bills, which Carl helped smooth and count while still on the phone.

Sheila said she needed to talk to her supervisor first, and Colette grabbed her by the forearm, entreated, "This isn't about policy—this is about two women who understand each other. Do you honestly think a man cheating on his pregnant wife is going to have the audacity to complain to your *supervisor?* This is one of those moments, Sheila, when policy and humanity don't see eye to eye." She quickly cleared the water from her eyes, sniffled hard, and stood up straight again.

Sheila's nostrils flared and she looked at Colette with bulging eyes, altering from sympathy to a startled admiration. Colette waited, then smiled. "I want these two rings engraved with this message. I realize it's a rush, but I'd like to pick them up this evening, before six o'clock." She slid a piece of paper across the counter.

Sheila's pale face had boiled into ruddy cheeks. She whispered that she hated her job anyway, and Colette responded, "You might be changing your life someday too." With the tone of speaking to a genuine confidante, she confessed, "I really do love him. He taught me everything I know. I used to think I couldn't live without him. But—if the respect isn't there, you have to demand it any way you can. Don't you?"

Sheila began punching numbers into the credit verification machine, looking up finally to say, "You've sure got guts."

Colette reached across and affectionately touched her shoulder. "It's just about my only redeeming quality."

All day, before the rings were ready, she shopped for her two boys, buying Kevin a ratchet set, a police scanner, a new suit, and a Farrington machine, used to emboss credit cards; and for Jerry, a monochromatic outfit of blazer and slacks, which he seemed to regard as the skinned hide of a dream lover.

"At least I have something to wear at my funeral."

They packed everything into the car except Colette's favorite leopard-skin valise, which she ordered Kevin to lug along to the store, claiming that she might need something for the endgame. Kevin gave her a suspicious look under his drooped eyelids and disheveled hair. She asked if he objected to being her porter.

"Am I going to carry it to the border?"

"I haven't measured the distance exactly. Do you charge by the mile or the foot?"

It was a frigid evening. The windows frosted and obscured the orange-and-black Halloween decorations, cardboard witches and handkerchief ghosts. Kevin trundled the valise along behind her, tempted to pour everything out into the street. He had a pathological distaste for being a bagman. He imagined her chasing down spilled underwear and blouses as they scatted like blown leaves; but when the image faded, he was alarmed to have felt a sudden and almost prophetic bitterness toward her clothes.

He waited outside while Colette moved in the portraiture of lit windows, past an arrangement of severed mannequin hands, fingers beset with the gaudiest cuts of stone, and two clasping black hands with matching oval-cut diamonds, like a wedding of shadows. A new salesperson checked the receipt, then retrieved a bag, which she handed to Colette with an unknowing smile. The cold wind had paused; the air hovered and thickened, until distantly spaced snowflakes drifted down. When Colette left the store, the flurries strengthened enough to speckle her sleeves and net in her hair.

She ran across the street on a faint tissue of snow, leaving footprints from her ballerina shoes. Kevin followed her into a parking garage, where they stood under the cement canopy and watched, through steaming breath, as the landscape disappeared under silver and gray. "I'm in my element again," she said, and there was a nervous tremor in her voice. A fluorescent light flickered over puddles, and, a level above, someone tried to start a flooded car. She reached into the bag, opened the cardboard package, and parted the velvet box like a clamshell. "I wonder if you already know what I'm going to say."

"Don't do this to me," whispered Kevin. "Not after all this."

"Repeat after me: 'I, Kevin—'"

"I said *don't*. Don't mess with my head. Don't make me into some kind of a joke."

"I'm not, honey. There's no easy way to do this. 'I, Kevin, do hereby proclaim, that I will never forget you, or any alias you may choose, as long as we both shall live.'"

"I'm not going to say some little speech you wrote."

"I want to give this to you. Okay? It's to say thank you and that I—"

"If you think I'm putting that fucking thing on my finger—after all this—"

"Don't be so pigheaded, for God's sake." Snowflakes were thawing in her eyelashes, and when she grabbed his hand, her skin felt like a cold rag. "I'm trying to do this in a civilized way, and you're not helping."

"If you *leave* now, Colette, right when things are rolling again, then you're fucked in the head."

"Oh, don't sound so much like your father. Can't somebody ever have feelings for me without using foul language? Now, come on. I'm going to miss you too, so we should end on a decent, classy note for once in our lives. We don't get to do this again, so let's not drag it through a puddle."

"Just wear one on each hand then. Collect them for every finger."

"Okay, so you're angry at me. Fine. But try to see beyond that, please. Haven't I at least been a good friend to you?"

He was so stung that he moved away from her to the edge of the lot and faced the streetlights around the naked trees. "I can't believe you made me carry your bag all night."

"You know I have to go; you've known it longer than I have. We had a great run, didn't we? Come on, Kevin. Am I just supposed to be miserable because you want me to stay? Look, I'll always appreciate your father for what he taught me, but there's a lot more in the world than digging through a minister's garbage and plundering a Kmart. All I want is for you to put this ring on and tell me you'll remember me."

"I'll remember you, Colette! I don't need a four-thousand-dollar string around my finger."

"God, you are so impossible." She grabbed his fist and tried to pry his fingers apart, clenching her jaw. "Open your hand." As he let her pull open the fingers, he lost track of everything else but the look of her face, eyes downturned under damp lashes, the smooth curve of her forehead. She was sliding the ring onto his index finger and it was freezing cold. "It's too loose. I didn't realize your fingers were this slender."

"What if I just found you again someday—"

"God, you have incredible hands, Kevin. I might have noticed if they weren't *all over me*."

"What if I found you again in a few years? Would you want to know me again?"

"A few years is another lifetime. Wear it on your thumb then. Like a married hitchhiker."

"You should at least say good-bye to him. He isn't a monster, you know."

She lifted his fingers, kissed him on the knuckles. "Of course he is.

So am I. And so are *you*. We're three little trolls, and it's better we find our own bridges. Watch after him, okay? He isn't taking very good care of himself."

She hoisted up her valise with a groan and walked, listing against the weight of it, down the path of streetlamps and under the churning wind, where she moved in shambling steps under each heave, dropping the valise for a rest, and raising it again from a gouge in the shallow snow. He watched the halting journey all the way down the block. She looked back from the corner, waved to him, turned east, and disappeared behind a store. In the tinny light between a van and a pickup, Kevin tilted the ring to read the inscription:

A SECRET BETWEEN US: ELIZABETH

For a second he thought it was a mistake, that she had used the name of the professor's real wife. Then it occurred to him that Colette had been an alias all along; and with a sudden pulse down his bones he understood that she had just introduced herself, at the very same moment she'd said good-bye.

SIXTEEN

Walking downhill, Kevin could see the lake wrapped with ribbons of clouds, thick trees emerging through mist. He watched his feet. The snow was just deep enough to make a chewing sound under each step. He found the meeting place, and waited under an awning while the yellow siren of a snowplow approached. Once it had passed, with its scrape and two-tone heartbeat, headlights came on from a parked car across the street, shining through a silk web of ice. Kevin opened the door with his sleeve, brushed off the bucket seat, and sat beside his father, who lit a cigarette and stared up at the parchment of snow on the windshield. His window was cracked and he blew a slim thread of smoke past a ridge of clinging ice. He didn't speak for a long time, handling the cigarette like it might convince him of something, until finally he asked, "Did she pull off the job at least?"

"Yeah, she got them. But she's not coming."

"She had a lot to prove."

"Let's just go. I'm sick to my stomach."

Jerry tilted the cigarette up and tapped ash into the snow. "She say anything?"

"Bunch of stuff I was supposed to tell you. I don't remember any of it. You're sure smoking a lot more, Dad."

"She took her share, man. And then some."

"A ring, a little spending cash. Big deal."

"She left me a nice letter, thanking me for how much she'd learned, and a whole load of shit. Touching, huh? Except, guess what? The whole note was in *my* handwriting."

"What are you talking about, Dad?"

"She's been practicing for six months—'oh, just using it to get better.' Meanwhile, she can do any signature like a fucking rubber stamp. So, most of the traveler's checks are gone, no big surprise there. Most of the cards—okay, I can deal with that. But she bled about three-quarters of the bank accounts into some hole I can't find. I don't even know where the money went. Sure, she nailed her professor, but she got us too."

"You're kidding me?"

"I'll be surprised if we got a nickel left by dawn. She tore us up, dingo. She burned the fucking house down."

"Naw, she'll leave us something."

He started the car and let it rumble for a while. The defroster began to heat two grease-paper stains on the windshield. "If I ever see that little whore again I'm going to snap her fucking neck."

"She'll leave us *something*, Dad. She was just showing off. I *know* her."

"I know her too! So she distracts us with some drawn-out con, and generously leaves us with ten percent of the accounts. What is that? A commission? I'm supposed to be happy with that? I worked like a goddamn ditchdigger for that money."

"She did all the work."

"Oh, fucking hell. I don't even believe you're going to sit here and say that. She just did what I told her."

"Obviously not."

"Kevin—cut this shit out." He held up his palms at the steering wheel, making a halting motion. After he took a slow breath and nodded with his lips tucked, running the windshield wipers under a froth of washer fluid, he pulled onto the street, his only visibility through slush and calving ice. "We're just going to drive."

On the salted highway they moved in a spindrift from under trucks and buses. Jerry scrambled through radio stations until he landed on a high school football game, apparently leaving it there because the road thickened with snow and he needed to clutch both hands to the wheel. The car was filled with whistles, cheering, a rickety war drum, the announcer calling off yard lines. When Kevin flicked off the radio, his father said, "Fucking pretty girls, man. *Pretty* girls. Cheerleaders!"

"She took what she thought she deserved."

"Uh-huh. That I know."

"I don't hate her for it."

"Well, you're growing up and you're entitled to your own pussy-whipped opinions."

"I think if you ever gave her any credit for anything—"

"Check and make sure she didn't run off with one of your balls too."

"You just shit on her all the time—it's your fault as much as anybody's. So don't go calling her a whore all the time. You're the whore. You're the one who just sat around and made her do everything."

"First of all, you obviously don't understand the term very well. Of course a *whore* does all the work, that's what a whore is. But—whatever—I don't want to have a fucking semantic argument. Second of all, you should've read some economics when you were roaming around pretending to be a student. The people with the big ideas *are* the people who make the money. Not the cocksuckers who do the legwork."

"Right. Big ideas, like going through the garbage."

"Let me clue you in on something, because I got a little more insight into this than you. She was a piece of work, she had a lot of brains and spirit, but *believe* me, she wasn't worth half of what she took."

"You can't even admit you got played."

"I admit she's a backstabbing cunt. The only way I'm keeping my eyes on the road right now is by picturing her dragging from the bumper."

"I really wish you would just shut up for once, Dad."

"Oh, I get it. All of a sudden you're a tough guy and I'm some punk that everybody can dump on. You don't know me if you think you can talk to me like that. I tell you what, tough guy, I'm going to pull this car over. We're going to find ourselves a nice, quiet spot to have this conversation like men."

He left the highway, past the bright beacons of gas stations and all-night diners, into a snowy town of crossing power lines, sprawling junctions of wires now piled with frost, past the border of dim streetlights to where the road was unplowed. They passed a school where the chain-link fence was a clotted strainer of ice. Jerry fishtailed around turns. He skidded into a supermarket parking lot, bouncing a tire over the curb, where he spun doughnuts around the streetlamps, grinning at the centrifugal force in the car. Holding the bandoleer of his seat belt, Kevin put his head back against the seat and closed his eyes.

With a last forward slide, Jerry stopped the car and stepped outside, leaving the door swung open. The sound of rigs sizzled on the wet highway. When Kevin stepped outside, the air was still, a layer of cold settled down heavily upon the ground, rich with the acrid smell of chimneys. They were alone except for shopping carts of caught snow, and the campfire flickers of televisions in distant windows.

His father took off his jacket and draped it over the hood of the car, then began rolling up his sleeves. He stuck his glasses into the crust of snow still on the roof, lenses outward like a lone spectator.

"Now that you think you're such a tough motherfucker, let's see something."

Kevin lolled his head back and groaned. "Oh Jesus, Dad! Come on."

He walked right up to Kevin, tilting his face in front of his nose as Kevin stiffened back against the car. His father's eyes had blackened and the skin on his face looked as if it had stretched tighter over his bones and teeth.

"You want to talk to me like I'm some kind of bitch, then you got to show me something. Come on, you little pussy—show me something. Show me you got something better than crying."

"I don't want to do this—it's ridiculous."

"And it's not ridiculous for you to sit there and pick me apart like some spoiled fucking princess? Hell, you're going to be sixteen years old in a few weeks. We got to start planning for that debutante shit. You're going to need a gown and a fucking tiara."

Kevin jammed his hands into Jerry's shoulders, trying to push him away, but his father's weight barely shifted. He smiled so broadly that the streetlight caught in his teeth. "What are you doing, trying to give me a backrub? Tell me that's not the hardest you can push, because that shit ain't even going to get the tension out of my neck. What do you want, huh? You want to give me a kiss instead?"

Kevin reeled back and slugged him as hard as he could in the chin. Jerry stood up straight, holding his hand over his mouth and nodding, like he was sampling a swig of wine; then he shook his head, and with a sudden, blurred look in his eyes, shouted, "You just made it into the Girl Scouts with that one!" He threw a jab into Kevin's shoulder that sent a shiver to his legs and head, his whole body caving around the spot. Kevin had no idea people hit each other that hard. Bent sideways, he started to walk away from the car, and Jerry stalked along his side. "Tickles, doesn't it? What do you have to say now, huh? Want to try the other shoulder? Even it out a little bit?"

"I'm going to fucking kill you in your sleep with a steak knife," said Kevin.

"Just the sort of chickenshit I thought. Where you going, you running away?"

Kevin turned and charged him, grabbing him around the waist and driving forward until Jerry hit the car with a thud.

"That's it! Good boy. Use the legs. All those wheelies, you got good strong legs—that's where the power is. You can hook your legs behind mine to get me onto the ground—not now, I'm *expecting* it."

While he was still talking, Kevin threw his fist straight up, landing an uppercut under his jaw that made a sickening clack on his father's teeth. As if his mouth were full, Jerry said, "Ah, fuck, I bit my tongue." Seeming more frustrated than angry now, he grabbed Kevin's shoulder blades like handlebars, steered him sideways, then threw him down. Kevin lay on the ground and watched Jerry rub his cheek. "Get the fuck up, Kevin! You don't *ever* lie down in a fight. Get up! Your ribs would all be broken by now. You're fighting like this is some after-school special."

Kevin rose and drove at him again, locking around his waist, and Jerry said, "Okay, drive with your legs. Good—you got a grown man's legs. You got to hold on tighter than that or I'm going to pry your arms off and tear you in half. And what if I did this?" He poked right into his kidney, which flared so painfully that Kevin tasted a mouthful of bile. "See! You got to tie my hands up if you're going to stand a chance! Don't lunge into me like that and leave my hands free—that could've been a shank in your side. You're thinking there's rules to this, kid—and there's no rules. Protect your neck and your nuts and show the other guy he's got to kill you to win. Don't plan your moves either—you fall into a pattern. You got to be unpredictable."

Kevin stepped back and saw his father crouching down for another charge. This time Kevin led with the crown of his skull, knocking right into Jerry's chin with such a click that he worried he'd smashed his teeth. He slid his arm up behind the shoulder blades to pillory his father's hands. Jerry said from a smudged mouth, "Better! Good head butt!"

They stopped. They stayed in a tangle of arms, with Kevin bent down and his face at his father's sternum, and they became still enough that Kevin smelled tobacco and sweat. Jerry was waiting, hovering in this strange, straitjacket hug against the body of the car, a calm pace to his breathing. The lull came so suddenly that Kevin was disarmed, and despite all his efforts, he was crying against his father's shirt. He expected Jerry to peel away and throw him into the snow again if he heard it, but instead his father stayed locked in the hold, listened, and let Kevin cry for a long time. Finally he pulled his arm loose and draped it around his back. He said, "No, no, you're not such a punk."

Kevin took a few slick breaths, heard his father's heartbeat, barely raised. When his father unthreaded his other hand, they stayed tilted against each other.

"I understand, kid. It's all out in the open," he said. "We'll leave this behind us." He breathed a dip in his chest. "I'll tell you something though—with a woman like that, a woman like her—I *know*. Some things hurt and you can't do anything about it. The best thing is to get up, fight like hell, and don't look back. You might lie down bleeding on the concrete someday, or lose a few years of your life to some bullshit charge you don't even remember, but you're just numb for that. Nothing ever hurts much worse than this."

Kevin stepped back and stared ahead at him, their breath evaporating in clouds. Jerry smiled at him and wiggled his top tooth, a tint of blood over his teeth and gums.

"Promise me something, Kevin: this will be the last time we say a word about her. Swear on it. Because I loved her too, kid. She broke the bank, but I loved her too."

THE WEDNESDAY
INTERROGATION

By evening, Kevin was breathing on his own in short swallows of air. In the post-op recovery room, the blinds were opened onto wide skies, a few helicopters circling in the dark. In the corridor beyond his open door, Kevin heard the changing of shifts with passing good-byes, laughter, conversations trailing in different directions. Detective Daniels was telling a story to a group of laughing nurses and interns; but Kevin could hear them teasing him as he began to complain about his assignment.

After a silent interlude, Kevin heard Daniels greeting some of the newly arrived staff, sighing to each about his boredom.

"You mean he hasn't tried to escape yet, Chief?" asked a passing voice.

"Don't you start in on me now."

Kevin found what he thought was the TV remote, but it began raising the bed. Daniels heard the mechanical sound, and hustled into the room. "There we go. Frankenstein. He's alive."

"Barely," said Kevin in a soft, hoarse voice.

"Time to answer some questions."

Daniels made phone calls, and less than a half hour later, two plainclothes detectives joined them in the room, Hartwell and Gonzales. Hartwell was a heavy, pinkish man with prematurely thinning hair, and Gonzales had a large mustache that drooped over his lips and seemed saturated with coffee droplets. Kevin said he wouldn't make a statement without a lawyer, and they proceeded to pull chairs around his bed anyway.

Gonzales held up a picture of one of Kevin's father's associates, Lenny Hutsinger, who had been brought into the team at the last minute, and who irritated Kevin with his sloppiness. In the mug shot he looked drunk, facing ahead with his long, greasy hair and sideburns. "I don't know his name," said Kevin. "He's an idiot, though. I hope he gets twenty years for whatever he did."

The next picture was of the collusive girl from the hotel staff. It was hard to recognize her right away without the uniform, and because her eyes were swollen and her face looked blotchy. Kevin said, "I have no idea who that is."

"She described *you* perfectly. She said there was a kid there in his late teens or early twenties probably, with black hair and a great big scar on his cheek. Does that sound familiar?"

"I'm sure there's lots of people in that hotel with scars on their cheeks."

Gonzales showed the picture of one of the buyers, the kid with the long, sleek goatee. "This kid got shot in the leg and he's over at County USC right now. Probably talking about *you*."

"Well, either you guys shot him or his own friends shot him—because I have no idea who he is."

"Last picture." He showed a young man on a slab at the morgue, the wheezing kid, the one who had lost his mind that afternoon. Kevin tried not to react at all. "This kid didn't make it."

While Kevin evaded questions, Daniels moved to the side of the bed and began taking his prints, rolling his thumb and then fingertips across the ink blotter. There was a sporting quality to the interview, since they were trying not to reveal whatever they already had. Kevin knew his fingerprints would unravel a great deal of information, so he gave his list of aliases up until he'd fled his arraignment one day, years ago, in Minneapolis. Accidentally, they gave him a piece of information in return. Hartwell asked, "You have any idea the location of the girl?"

"Which girl?"

"The one who left you here."

Gonzales put his head down and took a deep, aggravated breath.

"No, I don't know where she is," said Kevin, smiling despite himself.

"Don't fuck with me, kid. We got a witness saying that two people car-jacked him in the alley outside his restaurant—a man and a woman, both soaking wet, both smelling like shit. The guy was bleeding all over the place. I'm going to assume that was your blood too when we found his car, so I think it's obvious we got you on at least grand theft auto even if you can't remember a goddamn thing. Now—why don't you at least tell us who shot you?"

"Did I get shot in the back?"

"I don't know. What was going on up in that hotel room? A drug deal?"

"No, no drugs," said Kevin. "There was a deal, but it was—complicated. I would just call it a big family disagreement."

BOOK THREE  THE RAP SHEET

1985–1986

SEVENTEEN

Midnight at a truck stop where an electronic billboard flashed the going rate for diesel, sirloin, and a shower, they celebrated Kevin's sixteenth birthday with a meringue pie and a chorus of waitresses. Christmas passed in a hotel lounge in Rawlins, Wyoming, as they exchanged gifts of cash and watched baton twirlers on a mounted TV. In a casino, dodging blowout party favors, Kevin picked eight pockets on New Year's Eve, 1985, while Jerry remained at the bar rallying investors for his phony patent (a fireproof building material made from recycled ice coolers). By the end of February they were still running short cons between the Rockies and the Sierras, crossing the high desert of snowy yucca and tumbleweed, past the mountain storm floods sitting like pooled mirages. They headed toward distant casinos that contorted on the horizon, elongated in haze, like ships flying unknown colors.

The scams were as effective without Colette, but the daily routine never recovered. Kevin had forgotten how prone his father was to mishaps, like running out of gas on the salt flats, where Kevin had to walk all day along the roadside, expecting any moment to hear the cinematic screech of a vulture; or how often they arrived past dark in towns overloaded with conventions, loan officers or beef wholesalers, not a vacant bed until dawn. This basic disorganization of their lives worsened Kevin's superstitions, and Jerry found it absurd and torturous that his son needed fresh oranges in the middle of distant windswept deserts, or how, if deprived entirely of his rituals, he would sit for hours in the front seat picking and re-picking the same padlock as if in a trance. It only worsened the problem when Jerry tried to get his son to go "cold turkey." Kevin's suitcases now needed to be composed as if each article was a vital organ in a living creature; and his "symmetry fetish" intensified until he could lose a half hour adjusting the height of his socks. So Jerry never again questioned the sanctity of a lunatic's breakfast, and whether in freezing campgrounds or hunting lodges or over an oil drum beside the forgotten monolith of a drive-in movie screen, his father would grease a pan and pour out globs of flapjack batter with a cigarette in his mouth.

While Kevin appreciated his father's efforts, he was often frustrated by Jerry's inability to distinguish his eccentricities from his real interests. For instance, throughout the spring Kevin had plumbed through flea markets and pawnshops to find a magnetic reader and encoder, finally discovering the stripped-down subassembly of a credit card swiper in a science surplus warehouse outside Boise. In each motel room, under the fluorescent bathroom lights until dawn, Kevin hovered over this gadget as if it were the Holy Grail. Jerry thought it represented a final breakdown, an obsession with the smashed remains of a toy. At the public library in Salt Lake City, Kevin studied the manufacturer in the *North American Technical Directory*, along with books on magnetic flux reversals and programming languages, and he experimented to discover the use of five wires coming off the assembly; soon he could connect the swiper to the joystick port of an IBM PC Jr., writing a simple Turbo Pascal program to read the card. Jerry was not impressed with the weeks of binary gibberish Kevin sucked out of the backs of credit cards, even when Kevin tried to explain his enthusiasm for deciphering a fantastic new language. "There are three magnetic tiers in that stripe back there," he said as they drove toward Reno with a trailer rattling behind them. "Tracks one and two are all of the information about the cardholder and the account, and everything else."

"So what, Kevin? Why do you need to go into all that to use somebody's card?"

"That's what I'm trying to tell you, Dad. You can reprogram that. You just need a magnetic encoder. The card can have anything you want on the front—your name, my name, anybody's name. And you could redo the magnetic stripe to send the charge to another account. What I'm saying is, you can use one alias to put charges on a thousand different cards, come home every night and reroute the bill in another direction. It's better than white plastic, Dad—you don't even need a clerk. All you need are the numbers."

Jerry nodded at the road ahead of him, looking faintly seasick at the thought of yet another new frontier. As if Kevin were becoming a mad scientist whose obsessions his father needed to escape, Jerry began once again to buy adjoining rooms and aggressively seek companionship at night. With an abandon Kevin hadn't seen since the early days, he threw himself into flirting with any dirndled waffle-house hostess or sarcastic short-order waitress with a pencil stub behind her ear. Kevin rarely paid attention to Jerry's spiels or the women who joined them in diner booths with the sudden squeak of bare hamstrings across Naugahyde; but it did bother him that the fiasco with Colette had caused such a nosedive in the average IQ of his dates. Dozens of women commented that Kevin was "smart and fascinating" (meaning "serious and strange"), mostly because a palpable look of dread came over him whenever he heard an inane giggle at one of his father's corny jokes.

Once it became clear that Kevin could ruin any potential date (by, say, lecturing a casino cocktail waitress about the randomization process of slot machines), Jerry had to resort to bribery. They established a "courtship fee" in which Jerry paid Kevin twenty dollars to act like a normal sullen adolescent. For months this price didn't vary, until one night in Reno at the end of spring, when Kevin returned from the computer lab of the university, his father ushered him quickly into the hallway to offer him a hundred dollars. The toilet flushed behind them. Kevin was curious to see any woman who could raise the rate so abruptly, but Jerry guided him all the way to the elevator. "Where's your skateboard? Go reprogram Miss Pacman or something. Just let your old man have a little of his own fun once in a while."

Twenty dollars had seemed a reasonable amount, enough to be useful while still preserving the tone of a joke; whereas a hundred felt off balance, like a buyout. From his new room Kevin called them, and when the woman answered, he pretended to be a confused room-service waiter. She had a voice so babyish it sounded falsetto, and she broke into laughter at Jerry's mumbles in the room: "Sto-ha-ha-hop it, baby— it's *ro-hoo-hoo-hoom* service."

Kevin hung up the phone and stayed on the edge of his bed for a while, staring at the floor. He had no idea why he felt so defeated. He splashed water on his face, then skated along Virginia Street, weaving through pedestrian traffic and picking several wallets off easy targets (men in pleated slacks with their arms draped heavily around their girlfriends). He hid for a while in a gas station bathroom, culling the cash out from among the receipts and cards. As souvenirs he kept the weathered pictures of babies and basset hounds, a grinning couple, a woman in a dim kitchenette toasting with a Styrofoam cup. After counting just over six hundred dollars from the night, he expected some greater sense of accomplishment; but he felt only sluggish, as if he had gorged himself on tasteless food. He missed Colette and hated her for leaving.

The following morning Jerry didn't answer his phone. After Kevin beat on the door for ten minutes, he finally appeared, climbing into his jeans. The room was saturated with a musty, bear-den smell. He had removed the mirror from the wall, leaving only hooks and wires, and the tables were covered with glasses of auburn liquid. A pair of red satin panties inflated weakly over the air-conditioning vent. The woman was buried under pillows and blankets with just the bend of an elbow visible. Jerry explained in a gravelly voice that they hadn't gotten much sleep, and he would give Kevin another twenty for the game room if he'd come back in a few hours. The twenty kept rolling up at the edges like an old scroll. Jerry sniffed it, tried to smooth it flat on a wall, and finally handed it to Kevin. "Just put this straight into the change machine. And we should all meet for lunch. We have a lot of important things to talk about."

Lunch plans changed into dinner plans, and at six-fifteen they met in the coffee shop that still served breakfast, where they drank tomato juice and listened to the distant clatter of slot machines. Jerry looked as gray as a vampire, while the woman was more yellowish, like an old newspaper. Kevin didn't look directly at her, but with sly glances he tried to figure out why she'd raised the stakes so heavily: she *was* an attractive woman, closer to Jerry's age, although he hated to think that any good-looking contemporary could spoil a functional payment plan. Years ago, she might have been *very* pretty, with her dimpled cheeks and wide mouth; but now there was a frizzing in her rusty hair and worried lines around bloodshot eyes. She looked like a long history of Saturday nights. Her voice was high and sweet, so deliriously cute that Kevin thought it sounded like a helium-induced party trick. Maybe Jerry liked her dedication to silliness. She never spoke in full sentences, but made animal and car noises and sweeping gestures. She rendered the feeling of sleeping all day by whisking her flat palm over her head with a whoosh; she indicated her mental state by twirling her finger around her ear and saying, "Cuckoo." It would have been easy enough to assume she was insane; but it appeared more as if she had taken a vow never to be serious, replacing language with some placatory cheerfulness.

Jerry said, "Now Douglas, I just want you to relax for a second, I don't want anybody to panic here. I want us all to be friends. Last night was a wild night."

"Whoo-wee," she said.

"But Melody here is obviously one spectacular lady. I don't want a whole lot of trouble about this, *Douglas,* because I'm the dad here. I can make my own decisions. I still can't believe this little lady doubled down on thirteen and won—but I guess that's what happens when it's your night—and believe me, *Doug,* it was her night. She was coming up big. This is Lady Luck, right here. We finally met her. We came down here at three A.M. and played some more, and then—what was it, about dawn, baby?"

She made a rooster sound.

"The point is, *Dougie,* when you know, you know. Sometimes you got to just roll the dice. Go for it in life. So we went ahead and got crazy."

"I have no idea what you people are talking about."

"We got hitched. You're looking at the new Mrs. Daniel Herman."

"She married your phony name?"

"It's not a phony name—cut it out. He's kidding. He'll try to do things like that—you got to be on him like a hawk." He finished his drink with a last swig and slammed it down. "So how about a congratulations? I'm going to have another Bloody Mary. It's my honeymoon, for God's sake. Look at him, he's speechless. What's the matter, kid? You've never heard of a whirlwind romance?"

Kevin put his hand across the table to shake hers, soaking his cuff in her tomato juice. She tried to wipe his wrist with a napkin, and she was shaking. Her hands looked spotted and old, as if they'd had a more difficult life than the rest of her. She excused herself and scurried off to get towels from the bathroom. Kevin watched her move in mincing footsteps, then he glanced back at his smirking father.

"Dad—if you're going to start running sweetheart cons, why couldn't you find somebody with money?"

"So you just assume I'm not serious about this?"

"I thought those chapels weren't allowed to marry drunks."

"No, you can't get a *tattoo* if you're drunk. Everything else is—you know—pay as you play."

"This is the lamest scam in history."

"Hey, look—we've been on the road a long time, kid. Maybe a little change of pace would be good. She's here promoting some little business, and she's got a condo back in L.A. Why not? We'll settle down, have some home-cooked meals. Do the whole picket-fence thing. I'm not saying I'm going to stop working—but she doesn't need to know a damn thing. And I tell you what, I think it would be pretty sweet to come home for once and have some fucking *stability* in our lives. Besides, she's a lot of fun, Kev. So why don't you just calm down and try to let your old man be happy. Okay, shut up now, she's coming back."

Kevin sat quietly, thinking for the first time that Colette really had run off with everything, not just money or both of their unwieldy hearts, she'd stolen all the plans. They were off the map, out of gas, and stuck with a hitchhiker.

EIGHTEEN

Summer in the San Fernando Valley came like a hot pause in the weather, skies the color of a dirty window. Kevin and Jerry moved into Melody's basement-floor condo in Reseda, where every afternoon, feet and knees would appear at the top of the entry steps, descend through slats of venetian blinds, and finally become whole people between ferns and wind chimes. Melody had enough friends to fill a bleacher. They swooped around the place with wedding gifts and bottles of wine. They all loved Jerry, who invented personalized lies for each of them: he had motorcycled across Africa, worked on the McGovern campaign, smuggled guns, lived in an ashram. He was a real find, a leathery wise man found in the desert, hosed off, put in decent clothes, and eased back into society. Melody seemed to have achieved great status among her girlfriends, as if she had domesticated a gorilla, somehow taught him to use a toilet and wash dishes. Kevin found it irritating to listen to her brag about Jerry on the phone as if he were an abandoned chair being reupholstered. She described his past life by humming space-age horror music, and her feelings for him as, "Uh! Oh my God. Fireworks."

Jerry seemed to have lost the will to get out of bed. He slept until two in the afternoon, watched cartoons while he ate cereal and drank beer, took a few "business" phone calls in the evening, then went out to do errands for an hour in just his shorts and sandals. In the evenings Jerry sometimes sat alone on the couch tuning an acoustic guitar that he never got around to playing. When Melody came home, she was always filled with tree-house enthusiasm, and they would retreat into the bedroom for hours, emerging sometimes through plumes of smoke, fidgeting, sniffling, talking in rapid voices, chewing on their lips and fingernails, stifling laughter that turned quickly into coughs.

Melody owned a small company that manufactured party favors, and her ultimate dream was to expand nationwide, improving on all the little deficiencies and clichés she saw in the industry. The rooms were already crowded with knickknacks and Kevin sometimes felt like he and his father had become part of the collection. Gag cards, festoons of withering balloons in the kitchenette, little toy mice in miscellaneous uniforms. Jerry seemed to hate the piñatas even more than Kevin did, for they often lay decapitated in the closets and cupboards.

But there was one very good thing about the apartment complex. Because of aggressive algae, the pool was drained in late July, becoming a skateboarding paradise. Kevin spent most of his time perfecting a backside ollie off the deep end wall. By August he could almost land a three-sixty kickflip, surviving brutal falls that brought cheers and respect from the other skateboard rats who'd found the empty watering hole. Despite his strange olive-colored suit pants and his mop of black hair, they respected Kevin's insane disregard for his own safety. For the first time in his life, he began skating in a pack. Word spread quickly that the new kid could pick locks off gates, opening a world of construction sites, dried viaducts, and the asphalt dales of elementary schools. Under highway overpasses they perched on the steep slopes and smoked buds off dented soda cans, and at night they hovered outside convenience stores while Kevin robbed pay phones and parking meters. They packed into Pintos and sagging El Caminos, cruising in circles and hollering at pedestrians; and Kevin learned to drive amid bursting smoke-filled laughter. In quiet moments the longing for his old life still seized him like an undertow, but he felt protected by the new clamor of his friends with their bottle rockets, skinned elbows, and bloodshot eyes; and he was certain that he had found his natural habitat in this broken sprawl of shopping plazas and concrete slabs.

Often Melody would confront him late at night when he returned home, looking proud of her resolve, as if conquering a bad habit. She blocked doorways, clutching the drawstring of her pink terry-cloth robe. He would look at her chapped nostrils, her perpetually stuffed nose on a delicate face, and wonder how a woman so obviously jacked to the ceiling on something could criticize him for avoiding the condo. In a voice meant for puppies and small children, she told him that sixteen wasn't an *adult*, and boys shouldn't stay out so late. She urged Jerry to start a curfew, and she began a system of reward points and demerits. But her system was applied hysterically. Once she docked him a million points for coming home late, and eventually every infraction provoked such an inflated response that the points seemed like the currency of a collapsed nation. Soon he came home only on rare occasions, to drop off laundry and stare into the refrigerator.

That fall his father enrolled Kevin in Taft High School as Douglas Herman, an average student from Bremerton, Washington, whose files had been destroyed in a fire. Jerry complained that this procedure was the toughest scam of his life, because the administrators hounded him for more records and new documents: immunization proof, exam scores, and transcripts. "These people are worse than the FBI," said Jerry. "They need to know if you've ever pissed in the shower." He needed to soothe Melody's doubts, first over the vanished records, next over Kevin's dreadful grades. Jerry needed to intercept calls from the school and testify in front of curious and concerned teachers. He was a first-rate apologist, holding the faculty at bay for an entire month. Finally on a Thursday evening in October, he needed to meet with "an ungodly quartet" of schoolmarms, consisting of the vice principal, guidance counselor, and Kevin's two most officious teachers.

Kevin waited in the car, then skated for a while in the parking lot. Coming from far across the quad, his father's loose, drifting walk had been replaced by the concerted flat-footed strides of a man trying his hardest not to run. When Kevin saw his eyes—that thousand-yard stare—he rushed into the car and strapped on his seat belt. Jerry slid into the seat beside him and gripped the wheel.

"Douglas?"

"Don't call me that."

"You're not doing a very good job here."

The sky was the color of concrete, rapidly darkening, and they both stared ahead at a stucco planter of ivy and weeds.

"Dad? Nobody has fucking consulted me about *anything* here. Okay? So I don't know what angle I'm supposed to be playing with this whole school thing. I'll tell you the cons I've been running, they're nothing big. I broke into the storage room and I stole the teachers' guides. Who cares? So there's a few grade books missing. So what? What's a vending machine here and there? Besides, I tried to order some stuff on some teachers' credit cards and they were all maxed out completely. These people are losers, Dad. There's no money in this entire place."

"I don't know if they've got you on any of that. They're just going on and on about your *interests*. Jesus, Kevin, you don't ask these people about ATM networks. What do you think this place is—prison? You made fake bar codes for a science project? And what's all this shit about algorithms? Your fucking math teacher probably can't even do that shit. What are they?"

"Oh yeah. Algorithms. That's the launch code, Dad. The magic decoder ring. If I could just get to that and forget all this other crap, I could make my own credit card numbers out of thin air. Perfect—ready to use. It's just a simple formula. Well, not simple—but you know. If I could get that down, we could get the fuck out of this situation."

"Kevin. You can't even pull off being a high school moron because you got to take the school apart. Just bring your teacher an apple, shut up, and draw naked chicks in your notebook."

"Just don't say we're sticking around here, Dad. Right? You've got her accounts? You've got something going with Melody's business?"

"Kevin, I'm not ever going to be a completely normal dad. But listen."

"Don't tell me we're *really* living here. If there's no scam, Dad, what is the point?"

Jerry lowered his voice and said, "I'm making money, Kevin—I've got investments. But Melody is onboard with us. She's a good little businesswoman and in the long run—"

Kevin dropped his head against the dashboard and said, "Oh, fuck. Just shoot me, Dad."

The automatic sprinklers came on and splattered briefly across the windshield. Jerry waited for them to chatter all the way across the ivy before he responded. "Listen, Kev, I'm going to level with you here, because this is another one of those times when you might be missing the big picture. There's only one reason to go to high school. Get yourself *laid*. Okay? That's the only reason any man ever showed up for this crap in his entire life, and I dare any rocket scientist to prove me wrong."

Kevin nodded down at his feet, exhaling, and admitted, "Yeah, but the girls think I'm a little weird, Dad." The water drummed across the glass.

"You *are* weird. But that's okay. Find yourself a weird girl. They're everywhere, man, those cross-eyed chicks with big feet. But they're animals, man, tigers. They're the undiscovered country. Fucking terra incognita. If I could go back in time, I'd have some kind of goddamn harem of those girls. Think *low self-esteem.* Besides, they're smart and resourceful and someday they're going to look good enough to humiliate all the pregnant cheerleaders. They'll get their teeth fixed and strut back into the reunion, a bunch of little Napoleons with big hair and shoulder pads. Just close your eyes and imagine what they're *going* to look like—investments, baby. Stock options. And I guarantee you when you get some Betty's shirt off in the dark, you won't be asking about the prescription on her glasses."

Jerry started the car and ran the wipers, snagging a leaf of ivy. In a moment of quiet admiration, Kevin replied, "Okay. I'll make you proud."

NINETEEN

During midterms, Jerry's model girl was supplanted by Kevin's real and unavoidable attraction to a completely different type of young misfit. Shortly before the first exam, someone set a roll of toilet paper on fire in the girls' bathroom, evacuating the entire school and delaying the test. Each class was required to stay together on the football field, and, by the far hash mark, in the loose gathering of colonial history, he saw a sophomore girl arriving late with a skateboard, combat fatigues, thin-braided strands of blue hair, and a look so guilty and mischievous that Kevin was simultaneously drawn to her and lonely for Colette.

Her name was Denise, and she enjoyed throwing rocks through plate-glass windows, spray-painting the foundations of unfinished minimalls, hiding drugs in her vast collection of stuffed animals, head-banger music, whittling homemade bongs, and decrying the hypocrisy of her parents, a contractor and a child psychologist. She spit constantly, blew giant pink bubbles, slept at her desk, and usually ate alone. She was vulgar, antisocial, and Kevin was hooked. They skated late together around the drained pool or the abandoned elementary school. Kevin would take absurd risks to impress her, and later they would sit together on the ground, boards in their laps, and compare gouged elbows and knees. Past one o'clock one night in November, she draped her legs over his while they sat by the tetherball pole, shielded from the boulevard by the handball backstop. She shared a badly rolled joint with him and talked about her family, her "materialistic" mother and her father the philandering pig.

"Yeah, my dad is philandering and materialistic too," said Kevin, taking a drag. "But he's up front about it, so . . ."

"That's all the difference, right there," she said. "Like, be what you are. Don't be all, like, fucking—you know, high and mighty and shit . . ."

Kevin had no idea why, but she reminded him of Colette, without any of the qualities that made him feel like beating his head against a wall. Maybe she was a younger, more straightforward version of her, somehow stripped of the easy ability with words, a bit rougher around the edges, dressing in the same clothes every day and usually stoned. They had nothing in common physically, and Kevin was sometimes annoyed by Denise's slouched and moping posture, the way she walked alongside him kicking broken glass and rocks. But there was something in the quiet moments like this, under the autumn stars and streetlights, that brought Colette back, like a ghost.

"You know, you remind me of somebody I used to have this giant psychotic crush on," said Kevin.

"*Bonus.*"

He sat there for a long time on the asphalt, lost in thought, staring at her face, determined to kiss her as soon as she looked up. She never did, and finally he asked, "Would you run away and call the cops if I tried to kiss you?"

"God, you freak. Not *even.*" She stubbed out her cigarette. They leaned together, into a union of smoky breath and the sweet residue of Life Savers, and he felt the smooth underside of her lip, and when he sat up, the cold wind felt crisp on his tingling skin. The world seemed a dark and unpredictable landscape.

That winter break, as he turned seventeen in secret, he began the nightly routine of climbing to her cramped bedroom full of Anthrax and Megadeath posters. They would lounge on her bed together, sharing a bowl. He would explore her body while she lay naked and pale and motionless, quivering slightly whenever he tickled her by accident. She was so quiet that he sometimes forgot she was there. But, undeterred, he knew he had found a hobby to rival any magnetic strip encoder or algorithm. Unabashedly he studied everything he could find on sexual techniques and the female anatomy, running back to her lit window each night with his head full of new ideas, always to find her stoned and willing, her body stretching out flat as if for an experimenting scientist.

One night around Christmas it occurred to Kevin that she was becoming progressively more reserved, as if waiting to be tied to the bed. He asked, "Are we getting better or worse here, Denise?"

"Doug, I have to tell you something. It's, like—important. I've been putting it off—"

"Because you know yourself better than I do—I mean, no matter how much research a guy does, no matter how much prep time, some- times you got to talk the plane into the runway, you know—"

"I really think we should, like, see other people. I like you, but I just—"

"You mean a threesome?"

"No, I mean, like, you know, breaking up. I totally want to stay friends, but you're just, like, so—like *focused*—and I'm, like, not ready for that."

Initially, Kevin took this disappointment rather well, with a mild sense of failure, rationalized as a beginner's overeagerness, and maybe a twinge of pain in his chest, a rock in his throat. This was only natural.

When he joined his friends skating under the freeway overpass later that night, they were all high, cackling with hoarse laughs, breath steaming in the cooler air, and he endured their ribbing, refusing to join them in any negative commentary about Denise. When asked if she had "another dude up there already," he threw a beer bottle, which smashed on the concrete over their heads. Everyone stood and spread out across the slope, each apologizing to him and trying to calm him.

"Anybody who talks any shit like that is going to get a piece of glass right through the eye socket and into his fucking brain. Understand? I'll break into your houses when you're sleeping, I swear to God, and I'll piss on every fucking thing you own."

He was impressed by how emphatically they apologized, conceding an entire six-pack as a peace offering.

Second semester, Denise had a conspicuous new boyfriend. She went through an astounding transformation. By February she dressed in a jean jumpsuit, wore her hair in a crimped mop, and abandoned her skateboard in favor of a white leather purse. The boyfriend, Kip Larson, was the son of a real estate developer. Flush with easy money, Kip apparently sold cocaine "for the adventure." Wherever Denise went, his hamhock arm draped heavily over her shoulders. In mid-January, she wrote Kevin a letter in which she thanked him for giving her "the confidence to be herself and date other people," and blamed their sudden breakup on the fact that "in three whole weeks," he had never once said that he loved her. Though his eyes throbbed, his lungs burned, and he couldn't sleep at night from rage and humiliation, he was determined to behave rationally.

He forged magazine subscription orders so that Kip's parents were inundated by S&M fetish magazines in their son's name; he hacked into the school computer via the lab at CSUN and flunked Kip in every class but wood shop. He filled their pool with instant Jell-O, and when the family was gone for spring break, he impersonated the father, left a credit card number, and had a locksmith change all the doors. Out of his trash, he found information for Kip's very own American Express account, and—in a quiet moment of unsung victory—encoded it onto the magnetic strip of Daniel Herman's MasterCard, charged a thousand dollars' worth of massage oils and dildos at a sex shop, then dropped it down a storm grate. He called the school psychiatrist, pretending to be Kip in the throes of a bad acid trip; and when school began that Monday, he snorted with suppressed laughter upon hearing that Kip was in the office with a social worker, "undergoing evaluation."

During a lull in the battle, on a rare night when he was home at the condo, Denise called and Melody brought the cordless phone to Kevin in his room. "It's for *yooooou,* Doug." She mouthed the words, "It's a girl!"

He put the phone to his ear and mumbled a greeting.

"Doug? You have to stop this shit you're doing to Kip. If you don't, we're going to call the police. I don't know what you call it exactly, but I know it's some kind of a crime."

Melody was lingering in his doorway, watching and nodding expectantly. She whispered, "Is she asking you out?"

Kevin grimaced and waved her out of the room, but she wouldn't leave.

"Listen. If we could just discuss this matter at a more convenient place—I could meet you somewhere."

"Just stop. And Kip's dad is in real estate and he knows mobsters, okay? So you're totally dead if you keep this up."

"Okay, Saturday night then. Right, right. Bye-bye."

Melody gave him a wink and quietly shut the door.

The following afternoon, Kip and several friends in muscle shirts met Kevin in the parking lot, walked him across the school into a shaded spot behind the physical plant, and worked him over. Though his ribs hurt and someone had stepped on his neck, Kevin wasn't impressed by their performance. They went about the beating with the dutiful nature of PE calisthenics, finishing with a flourish of stomping Converse sneakers while he curled up in the gravel like a pill bug. Doubled over, he skated across the neighborhood to Denise's house, and, finding no one home, crawled through the pet door and hid in her room.

He waited for hours as the windows went dark. Showers hissed in the walls, the phone rang, the garage door rumbled in the floor. He heard dinner downstairs with clanking silverware, growing louder until an argument erupted. Muffled in the walls and carpet, he could hear Denise screaming at her parents, screeching and crying. Someone broke a dish, and then came a tremor of racing footsteps up the stairs. The contractor shouted and the child shrink admonished him. Denise stepped into her dark room, turned on the lights, and reared back against her closet door when she saw Kevin on a pile of stuffed animals.

"It's a bad time for this—I'm sorry."

"Oh my God, you are *such* a psycho."

"I'm really not. I'm just single-minded. This letter you wrote me, I have a few questions about it."

He unfolded the letter from his pocket while she moved all the way into the corner. Her posture relaxed when she saw his swollen face. "What happened to you anyway?"

"Your boyfriend and his goons. They had to resort to violence. I'm actually flattered. It's a sign of weakness. Means I'm getting into their heads."

She sat on the edge of her bed and clasped her hands together. "God, you're like honestly all fucking Batman and shit over me, huh?"

"Exactly," said Kevin. "*And* Spider-Man. I want to make you an offer, Denise. Will you hear me out on it?"

She looked up with a worried face and nodded.

"I'm having some problems at home too. With my stepmother. She's like a schizophrenic bunny or something, and I can't take it. I want you to come away with me. Get the hell out of the valley, and head someplace better for people like us. The fucking Riviera maybe."

"Where's that?"

"My point is, I've got skills, Denise. I got ten Gs saved up. You and I together could turn that into a hundred inside of a month. Wherever you want to go. Throw a dart at a map." He looked around her walls at the assorted headbanger and satanic posters, and continued, "You don't have a map, but you get what I mean."

"Like Vegas?"

"Well, it's not very ambitious. But *okay*: Vegas."

"You really have ten grand?"

"Denise, I'm a magician, I'm an alchemist, pure science; I can get money out of a *stone*."

She nodded for a long time, until she seemed stuck in the motion, as if dancing subtly to one of the bands on the wall. Finally she replied, "Okay. Bring the money on Sunday night, and we'll hit Vegas. No, wait. *Monday* night. Monday is better."

Kevin packed for the rest of his life. Headphones, passport, cash. His father appeared to have withdrawn all the money from the local accounts, because when Kevin searched the apartment he found shoeboxes and drawers filled with hundred-dollar bills. Boxer shorts, a favorite shirt, the lucky diamond wedding ring on a chain necklace. He was preparing for a border check and a deserted island. His skateboard of disintegrating sugar maple and his two torn pairs of jeans. Favorite CDs (Iggy, Black Flag), favorite books (*The Killer Inside Me* and *Endless Love*), two boxes of Bisquick, a bag of oranges, and finally, for the first leg of the trip, he picked the lock on a cabinet and stole Jerry's .38 revolver.

He hadn't seen Denise in the time between their agreement and the designated night, but he assumed she was ready. At a little past two in the morning, he waited at the spot for an hour; then he moved to the hedges beneath her dormer window. He waited another hour, then climbed the drainage pipe along the side of the house to perch on the roof beside the windowpanes. The room was dark, empty and sealed. The posters were intact, but the mattress was bare. There was no more clutter on the shelves. It was a Spartan museum exhibit of her life.

He climbed back down, leaping the last few feet into the hedges; and he waited until dawn, while the house developed as a silhouette against gradients of lighter gray, details of windows and shingles clarifying slowly, hatching awake. Lights migrated from room to room. Then the garage door slid up to reveal her father, fishing for car keys in his pocket, a sweet roll held in his teeth. The morning was grim and drizzly and Kevin stood at the garage's mouth, beyond a curtain of dripping water, his curly hair dampened flat onto his forehead. "Excuse me, sir?" He raised his voice over the drumroll of thickening droplets. "I don't want to bother you, but I'm a good friend of Denise—and I was wondering if she went somewhere."

He nodded with the roll still in his mouth, placed coffee on the roof of the car, took a bite, then in the midst of chewing seemed to become angry, finally pointing at Kevin with the dental imprint on the roll. "She doesn't need any more friends like you, pal."

"Can you tell me where she went, please?"

"Drug rehab. And when she's out, she's going to a different school. So move on, kid—or I'll call the police."

As Kevin skated home on the damp pavement, he was shivering, so enraged that he could no longer visualize Denise. Instead he pictured Colette burdened with shopping bags, his father stranded in front of Melody's TV. When he saw the condominium complex rising like a drab prison complex, he hated the place worse than any tragedy in his life. He passed through the door and the hair on his neck rose.

Right away Melody was there with a rehearsed speech, wagging her finger in his face. He snatched it and twisted it backward, until Melody yelped; and then, responding to some gathering velocity, he grabbed her by the throat and jammed the gun up against her mouth. Her eyes bulged, her lips turned white. She tried to speak but only a lisp of air came loose. When he let go, she staggered back, robe flown open, tattoo of a compass beside the thin stripe of pubic hair, old bruises on her gardenia skin. She bundled herself up and quailed in the corner of the living room. Everything was disconnected; Kevin couldn't relate himself to the splash of events in the room. His father was standing naked in the dark doorway, and Kevin winced and looked away.

He heard Melody sniffling, a ticking on his father's teeth. "First of all," Jerry said calmly, "killing somebody is a bigger commitment than marriage, you know, and I don't think you're ready. Second of all, you should pull the hammer back if you really want to scare somebody."

"Are you crazy?" shouted Melody.

"He's dusted up on something, just wait for him to come down. Put the gun away, dummy. You're all right."

"I want the rest of the money in the house and I'm getting the fuck out of here."

"He's a bully. He's never been anything but a bully. He's going to kill us both."

"I'll give you some money," Jerry said. "But I wish you wouldn't go like this, Kevin. It just doesn't sit right. Besides, guns are for people with no imagination. You're better than that. Put it down, Kevin."

"What is happening here, Daniel? Why are you calling him *Kevin*?"

Kevin was suffocating on the air between them, so he turned and left with the gun at his hip, refusing to look back even as he heard a scramble and a wail from Melody. He was too angry and disoriented to plan his next move. His board was overturned in ground cover, and as he grabbed it, he heard doors slamming in the complex. After he had skated for close to an hour in the empty pool, he saw police cars racing past the back gate, pulling around to the parking lot without sirens.

He climbed the fence, crossed the street, and from the other side of the boulevard, watched as more vans and squad cars gathered. They parked haphazardly, slanting into one another, doors opening rapidly and deploying SWAT teams that ran to the stucco pillars around the stairs.

For a moment, Kevin was astounded that some hysterical phone call from Melody could provoke this level of tactical response. He walked toward the police cars with theorems of probation in his head: first offense, assault with a deadly weapon, mitigating factors. When he saw the piñatas piled around the unwinding yellow police tape, one of them placed upright on the hood of a squad car, he recognized his miscalculation. There were nine cars, far too many for a mere domestic dispute. He tried to figure out the relationship between the events. Had a neighbor called the cops? Had there already been a stakeout around the complex?

Suddenly an officer led Melody up the stairs with her hands cuffed behind her. She was crying uncontrollably with the pitch of anger and disbelief, and when he tried to guide her into the car, she shouted that he was hurting her arm. With a sick feeling in his stomach, Kevin realized that this moment had always been coming, like a card in a deck, and it was a divine joke that he had roused Melody and his father from bed on their fated day. Or maybe the shouting in the apartment had precipitated the raid. As a cop began to smash a piñata with a night-stick, Kevin knew everything as if recalling it from a nightmare: he knew the money around the apartment was from scams that had persisted too long and become careless; he knew his father and Melody had been conspiring together; and he was not surprised when out of a papier mâché horse spilled forged deeds, fake IDs, and leaves of hundred-dollar bills.

The star attraction under tiers of spectators, faces hanging out windows and families clustered on flights of stairs, Jerry rose out of the basement apartment in a circle of officers. Unlike Melody, his face was placid. Wearing a wrinkled white dress shirt and a tight pair of yellow shorts, he looked as if he'd been arrested out of the hamper. The sun and sky moved in flickers off his glasses, and his hair was blowing loose around his face.

Two shorter policemen reached up and placed their hands on his head to guide him down into the car, but he stood upright, and it was awkward to see two uniformed men straining to touch his crown of unruly hair. Then Jerry looked right at Kevin, smiled, and nodded slowly, a gesture that could have meant anything, and his lips opened into a crude circle around his gapped teeth, tightening and shrinking slowly like he was blowing out a candle, mouthing a lone syllable: *Go.*

TWENTY

In the spring of 1986, Jerry awaited trial in the Los Angeles County jail on over fifty-five charges of forgery, fraud, and money laundering all stemming from a single year in Melody's apartment. The scam that had ultimately led to his arrest was one that might have worked in the old days, when he remained constantly on the move; but over the past six months Melody, with her cramped condominium and her inexhaustible supply of cocaine, seemed to have given him a sense of invincibility. He had begun forging quitclaim deeds. Day after day Jerry had been driving out into the relentless sun of the valley, searching for weeded lots and crumbling buildings, anything that appeared to have been abandoned by its owner. After looking up the deed in city hall, he would study the owner's signature, practice it for a few days, then forge the property over to himself for a negligible price. There was no line of defense against this con other than a bleary-eyed clerk in the records office, who would stamp it through, plug the new details into a computer, and return to the doldrums of paperwork around him. Jerry would wait for the title, then borrow money against the new property. The problem was, several DEA officers were already watching the steady flow of cocaine going in and out of Melody's condominium complex (the top floors apparently worse than the basement); and they became suspicious about Jerry as well. By the time he was arrested, he owned eleven earthquake-damaged houses, a condemned gas station, six abandoned lots, and a cluster of concrete slabs for a lost trailer park. Kevin knew that he had probably skateboarded through some of his father's land.

On April Fool's Day, while Jerry was still awaiting trial in the county jail, new charges accumulating each week, Kevin said good-bye to Douglas Herman in a quiet ceremony along a short industrial twist of the Columbia River through Portland. Washington and California state IDs, a learner's permit never matured to a driver's license, a passport never touched with a stamp—he could never have guessed the failure and loss he experienced as he watched the papers scatter in the currents, drift downstream, and vanish into the murky water.

He became Quentin Casellas, a suicide from West Seattle, whose untimely end seemed to haunt him far more than his carefree former alias. Kevin shaved the black locks from his head and was surprised by the long, slender quality of his face, the width and openness of his eyes. He dressed in combat boots and torn T-shirts and jean jackets covered with anarchy symbols, and in Portland, he found hundreds of young ragged teens around a lingering punk scene, kids who congregated with skateboards and cigarettes in the drizzle, under bridges and around the doors of clamorous shows, sweatshirts tied around their waists, girl-friends with dirty hair, angry pimples, and sad blue eyes.

He had followed his father's guidelines. He visited Army Walsh and his doting, sympathetic wife on Vashon Island in Seattle; he accumulated documents from the easiest first (the state ID) to the riskiest (the passport). But with paperwork fit for a high-class fugitive, he sank penitently into a landscape of Greyhound terminals and runaways. He fell in love with panhandlers. By summer, he had moved the length of the

West Coast, San Diego to Seattle, eight times, leaving a city whenever the police seemed to recognize him. With an apostate sadness, Kevin didn't run any of his old scams. He lived in exile among the other travelers, shivering until welcomed into the sleeping bag of a ripe and drunk and luxuriously warm girl under the concrete pillars of the Willamette Bridge; scavenging crates of free just-expired groceries along the slick cobblestones of Pike Street; sleeping and sharing cigarettes in flophouses full of dirty backpacks and spilling laundry and a lone kitchenette with a boiling cauldron of instant noodles. They slept outside, barricaded within backpacks, in chains of interlocked legs in Golden Gate Park, guarded by a single scrawny dog in a bandanna who growled at every squirrel. They hovered in lines outside clubs and listened to the rhythmic collapsing sound of drums inside, negotiating their way in to fight in mosh pits and pop amyl nitrite in the bathroom. There were rarely any good drugs; more often a kid would deaden his face with airplane glue, hover over the fumes of gasoline until he puked and his eyes grayed. Kevin never touched the stuff, and he had a reputation for being abnormally clean—at least, among the abnormally filthy.

In late June, Kevin called the L.A. County jail to learn that his father had been transferred to the Lompoc Penitentiary. He was rattled by the thought that his father might have gone through the trial and been sentenced already while Kevin was in some time warp of hopping trains, fistfights, and sex in sleeping bags. On a southbound bus he tilted against the window and slept through passing stripes of light and shade. He woke to see ruffled veils of blown rain, loamy pastures of mud and green, where fat droplets spotted the window. There was a sublime desolation, so vast and beautiful at times that it could refashion loneliness into a feeling of sudden liberation. Over the Cascades, through the forests and a passing storm; through the vineyards at night, where the shifting brush strokes of sky faded into pyrite stars, his life reduced to nothing more than weather and traffic and conversations with people he'd never see again.

It took him a week in Lompoc to devise a suitable cover for visiting his father, for he worried that a seventeen-year-old son might become either a key witness or a ward of the state. Instead he was Quentin Casellas, a young journalism student at Fresno State. When Jerry stepped into the visiting room in an orange jumpsuit, sporting a new handlebar mustache of blond and gray, something in his abstracted eyes made it clear that he was prepared to meet a stranger.

TWENTY-ONE

"It was a disaster, man. I'm glad you weren't around to witness it. I
fired two lawyers and I thought about defending myself." Across a layer
of thick Plexiglas, streaked with the same grease rainbows that covered
his glasses, Jerry talked into a phone with crackling reception. "Every
one of them was whistling the same tune, and then the third lawyer
gave me the exact same advice as the other two, and *I took it*. Copped a
plea. Might've faced a nickel otherwise. I'm glad you got a haircut, Kev,
but other than that, you don't look so good."

There was a faint bruised coloring on the loose skin under his
father's eyes. The forked tails of two new tattoos emerged from under
rolled-up sleeves, the same faint blue as the veins on the pale underside
of his arm.

"And how's Melody dealing with the strain?"

"Hey, don't do that. Sure, she gave a statement against me to get
herself off with just probation. I don't blame her. At least she sends me
naked Polaroids."

"I don't want to hear about that, Dad." As the guard paced behind

Jerry, Kevin changed his tone, saying, "No, sir, it's more of an article on the kind of environment that produces a man like yourself."

Once the guard was out of earshot, Jerry chuckled and said, "What the fuck was *that*? You pulling some kind of con like that up north?"

"Actually, I've had kind of a bad period, Dad. I just—I guess I'm trying to stay clean, you know?"

"That's okay. You mean like a regular job?"

"Well, no. I mean—some panhandling, and just—traveling—" He couldn't face his father's disappointed eyes as he spoke. "You know, just moving around. Maybe a little shoplifting, I guess. Misdemeanors mostly."

"What the hell is the matter with you, Kevin? I'm the one in jail. If you were talking about getting a job as some kind of computer genius, you know, then that's different."

"I'm not going to get a job as a *computer genius,* Dad, just because I can tamper with shit."

The handlebar mustache seemed designed to frame a new, drooping shape to his mouth. There was a stranded and lethargic quality to Jerry that seemed like the culmination of a year on Melody's couch, and it reminded Kevin of the way the biggest and most ferocious animals in the zoo stare out of the shadows with something eerily close to human desperation.

Jerry said, "Kevin? I fucked up. *You* didn't. You don't have to go live like some kind of castaway. Look, Kevin—you're going to be eighteen in what? March?"

"That was the old alias, Dad. My real birthday is in December."

"My point is, I was on my own at eighteen. I went and joined the army, but that counts."

"You were in the army?"

"Yeah, yeah. There wasn't a war or anything—I just farted around in Germany playing cards. Hustling. What I'm trying to say is, you got to grow up here. The army gave me a real sense of, you know, discipline. Shit like that. You got to get tough. I don't want to hear about my son *panhandling*—that shit's for junkies. Besides, there's a lot of good con men in the army. It's just like prison, but they give you a gun."

He looked down at his hands: they were like separate embattled creatures, cuts and scabs on his knuckles, shop grease like sediment down in the lines of his palms. Two fingers looked broken, swollen and curled, as if refusing to unlock from a fist.

Kevin had chewed the cuticle around his thumbnail down to the blood, which he tasted as he looked up to meet his father's gaze.

"I don't want to join the army, Dad."

"Then at least toughen up. I'm going to be pissed off if I got to hear about you begging money on a street corner. You were raised better than that. You got first-class skills, kid. You can do shit that nobody knows how to do—except maybe a few gypsies. And the Nigerians—they're *always* ahead of us. This isn't *you*, Kev, bumming cigarettes under an overpass."

Jerry shook his head and closed his eyes, reloading, and then he leaned closer to the glass, which pulled him away from the mouthpiece and made him more difficult to hear. "Kevin? The world is yours: don't be a pussy. *Now*, with that out of the way, I need a favor."

With ten minutes left to talk, Jerry shifted tone completely. He was serving time for lending institution fraud, wire fraud, mail fraud, document forgery, and other offenses. "But there's a few accounts and safe deposit boxes still out there. If the feds start finding accounts and old mailboxes out on the East Coast and in the Midwest, man, I'm looking at a long drop in here. Most of that was under a different name, and I'm sure they're still piecing that together. Money sits in limbo too long and the paper trail just gets hotter."

Kevin asked, "Which accounts are we talking about?"

"Everything we did, all across the whole Midwest, out to the coast— you remember. With you-know-who. Whatever *she* didn't get to."

"Right. *Her*."

"The person whose name we don't ever say out loud."

"Got it."

"Because we don't want to invoke her fucking evil bitch spirit—"

"I *remember*, Dad. Jesus."

"So for your article, right, I was basically born rotten . . ."

Kevin was confused by the shift in tone, until the guard crossed behind his father, glancing down. Jerry waited, then continued, "Now, quick—listen up. Those accounts are still open, Kevin. Like little wounds. The FBI starts piecing those together, I'm looking at a whole new ball game. I mean, we ran up a fortune out there. I don't know if you were old enough to realize the kind of volume we were turning over."

"What do you want me to do?"

"Close them down. Stop the bleeding. You do that for me, you can keep half of whatever's left."

"Half?"

"Don't try to negotiate, you little street monkey. I'm still your father. I got a lot of information put together, and I'm finishing it up now. Get a mail drop and I'll send it to you. Everything from those days. Will you just be a pal and help out your old man? However bad you think it is in here, it's about a hundred times worse."

He smiled and for the first time Kevin noticed the missing tooth beside the canine.

"Don't fight too much in there, Dad."

"Me? I'm an elder statesman. I'm a mentor. Take sixty percent."

"I'll do it, and I'll keep whatever I find."

They glowered at each other through the smudged barrier.

"You must really think you got me over a barrel," said Jerry.

TWENTY-TWO

The image of his father's crooked fingers stayed in Kevin's mind, and seemed with their bent paralysis to point him onward. In Grand Junction, Colorado, the mail drops contained nothing more than credit card offers, sweepstakes offers, and flyers about missing children; in Wall, South Dakota (home of a large pharmacy that served an excellent twenty-four-hour breakfast), Kevin found a pile of coupon booklets and an unused two-year-old MasterCard, with a few months left before its expiration. Staying in roadside dives that advertised color TV and air-conditioning, Kevin spent his long, lonely hours working over a reassembled card swiper, stealing the three-tiered magnetic codes of every extant card, and rewriting them on the magstripes of hotel key cards. Night after night he would scan numbers and plumb the mysterious depths for four-digit PIN numbers, each card a new puzzle, and when he succeeded, he would take cash from ATM machines, which were beginning to process credit advances as shared networks spread across the country. In Kearney, Nebraska, along a stretch of sagging wires and fast-food chains, he unlocked a long-forgotten postbox to find six different sets of promotional checks from Visa, all of which he forged and cashed in nearby liquor stores.

He lived in such a perpetual state of concentration that time seemed to fall past him, the sun wheeling overhead through hot skies and cirrus clouds, miles of landscape passing during a nap on a Greyhound bus, day and night becoming irrelevant, sleep seizing him when his focus lapsed. He fell so headlong into the process, invigorated by the idea of redoing all the old cons in his own way, that he scarcely noticed how his superstitions and rituals were growing wild and extreme and overpowering. He no longer trusted motel beds, but lay in his sleeping bag on the floor beside them, with his own air mattress that took a meditative hour to inflate. In his backpack lay a precise internal layout of clothes, incriminating cards, cash and equipment, oranges, a portable cooking stove (upon which he made breakfast in bathrooms amid all the accoutrements of a chemistry lab), and pictures—hundreds of stolen wallet pictures—that he would place across the untouched bedspread to study each night, staring down at the souvenirs from each pickpocketing, a crowd of tiny smiling faces. He would hover over them, feel the weight of so many people and so much stolen credit; and he would say, depending on his spirits, as if to a cheering crowd of benefactors or an angry jury, "Thank you, thank you, thank you, thank you," to every unsuspecting face.

Some curse was released from those mailboxes; at each stop he was reacquainted with the frustration from his days on the road, with his father and "her." In the rare moments that he stopped working, he felt the old pining, that breed of intense loneliness that recalls smells and expressions from missing people. But he was always angry with *her* for his loneliness. Several times, his longing became so intense that he mimicked his father. He threw himself at a truck stop waitress who, surprisingly, seemed to like anyone with "nice eyes" and both of their front teeth. He went to a strip club and made himself a spectacle, sliding five crisp hundred-dollar bills into the G-string of a gyrating farm girl. He lingered in a department store, touring the bedroom and dinette displays like a childhood home, then offering to pay for the armfuls of clothing held by a chatting pair of young women and a beleaguered but attractive mother of two. "And that lady with the screaming kids over there," he said to the cashier. "I want to pick up the tab for her too." The shoppers themselves were baffled, and looked as if the gesture might be a prelude to some parking lot abduction; but the cashier, who obviously had enough downtime to imagine fairy-tale princes among the aisles, was charmed by the game.

In Madison, he felt betrayed by every familiar store and street corner. He closed a small checking account with a slapdash letter of information from Esther Barrick and a mediocre forgery of her signature. He didn't even care about the remaining few thousand dollars. He had it sent as a cashier's check to another mail drop; and after cashing it at a shady hardware store in Milwaukee, he pitched every dollar into the cups and boxes of panhandlers.

"You're an angel," said a stooped old woman.

"Don't say *that*," Kevin called, walking away backward. "It's just Reaganomics, ma'am."

In Minneapolis, he returned to the joint account that Colette had created for Douglas Herman, Esther Barrick as custodian. He found a cheap motel and hunkered down for a long ordeal of paperwork in a city where every alley and store window felt like a traumatic memory.

On the phone, Jerry sounded as if his mouth were swollen. His words mashed together and he whistled faintly while he talked. Kevin asked him about the sound, and he shouted, "Whatever. I broke a tooth on a meatball."

"Is there a dentist you could see?"

"Hey—it's hell to get quality phone time in here, so don't waste it talking about this shit."

"I'm just having some minor problems. I'm coming across all the accounts that *she* started. Tons, in fact. I need Douglas's papers back. Is there anything Melody kept?"

There was a long pause on the other end of the line, filled with echoes. "You got to use that high school. They'll have everything."

"You-know-who left a bigger trail than I expected out here, Dad. By the way, how is Melody?"

"Sends her love."

In the background there was a man screaming at the top of his lungs.

"Taking care of yourself?"

"Shit yeah. Got a conjugal visit last week. Mel wore a negligee under a trench coat."

"I don't want to hear that."

"And she did everything I told her," he said, whispering. "Boofed in a dozen joints like a goddamn mule. That's first class, man."

"Dad, I'm kind of nauseous."

"My advice to you, if you ever get pinched, have some weed where nobody can find it. It's gold in here, man."

It took Kevin three weeks to replace Douglas Herman's key documents, by pretending to enroll in a community college, prompting his high school to send mimeographed copies of every old ID and record. After a long stay in a St. Paul dive, he was relieved to think that this scavenger hunt would finally end. Here was the last hurdle, the final pittance of stranded cash, but the night before the final withdrawal he had a sinking, desolate feeling, as if he feared losing something for good.

That morning, he thought the teller was wearing Colette's perfume.

He watched the twitches on her face while she typed and read the screen. She filed the copies of his new Social Security card, Hennepin County driver's license (a ten-day ordeal), and a counterfeit birth certificate copy, notarized by a ghost, the signature with the bogus medallion stamp. She found the account and swiveled the computer monitor toward him on a hinge, so that Kevin could see rows of green digits. At first, he was so startled that they looked only like a chaotic chain of hieroglyphs. He tried to maintain his composure. He reread the names: Douglas Herman and Esther Barrick. The account balance:

67,155.96

"Would you like to make a withdrawal, Mr. Herman?"

As if he were staring at a magnificent portrait, he felt a swell of pride and affection for Colette. "No," he said, surprised by the laughing sound in his voice. "I'd like a summary of all the account's activity, please. As far back as you can go."

TWENTY-THREE

The pattern of deposits showed that Colette gravitated toward old-money towns and resorts in the East. For a few weeks in Newport, Rhode Island, the deposits were a steady one thousand twenty dollars a week under the alias of Sheila Bath (which had a biblical ring when inverted on documents). In East Hampton, she made two wire transfers a week at nine hundred fifty-two dollars, from a trinity of names: Mary Beale, Molly Defoe, and Violet Beauregard. She was a hydra of aliases. Each time one was severed, two would immediately spring into its place; and by the second page of this printout, it appeared to him that she created names exclusively to feed this account. He researched each name, for he believed they might have a message embedded in them. Augusta Gordon, for instance, turned out to be Lord Byron's half sister, with whom he had fallen madly in love; and Evelyn Rafter, once he had whispered it to himself a thousand times, seemed to him a twisted, fairy-tale pun. Whoever and wherever the benefactress, the deposits and wire transfers remained for almost six months in a specific pattern between $1,020 and $952. She floated around Boston for a few months, vacationed for two weeks in southern Maine, only to return for a determined stint in Manhattan, with over twenty names and fifty ATM locations, before suddenly fleeing north and making an abrupt numerical shift: a deposit of $1,067 through a mall in Plattsburgh, New York.

The names behind the wire transfers had distracted him; there was a more specific meaning in her choice of numbers. That winter she moved in zigzags through Quebec and Ontario, through a chain of high-priced hotels with their own ATMs in Toronto, her movements looking like a primer course for a young fugitive, until eventually she snaked back across the border between Windsor and Detroit, and the account went into a brief hibernation. Had she made amends with her foster care mother? Or had she been arrested?

One night, while he had been mulling over the numbers, an idea came to Kevin with such force that he cursed himself for not having seen the possibility right away. That awful day in Madison, Colette had given him a police scanner as a parting gift. He realized that each deposit was a police radio code. 952: Please report on conditions. 10-20: location? 10-67: person calling for help. They came like digital smoke signals. When the account had awakened a month later, she was back in the eastern corridor, becoming more elaborate with her messages, until a two-week period in Baltimore read like an encrypted diary: 10-11 (visitors present, exercise caution); 10-45 (what is the condition of the patient?); 5150 (emotionally troubled); 910 (can handle this detail alone). Had this been a partnership that went awry? Was she running sweetheart cons?

He hoped she was still on the other end to find a returning message; but when he deciphered the final series of deposits, he became depressed. Over a week in Manhattan, she relayed: 484, 484, 484, a day-long space—like a dash of punctuation—and 487. Then she disappeared. For the last seven months there had been only the vegetal growth of interest. The sequence probably meant that she had been charged with three counts of credit card fraud (say, theft, forgery, and illegal use). The list's emphatic ending, grand theft, Kevin thus took as the heaviest charge, the one for which she was likely to serve the most time. Had she gone upstate, taken the hit? Or had she jumped a bond and now considered the account too dangerous to use? He was trying to read a splash from the way ripples struck the shore.

He imagined the frustration Colette must have felt transmitting for so long without a response, and his mind filled with morbid images: Colette in an orange jumpsuit and shackles; Colette as a frazzled, amnesiac hitchhiker first seen in the Florida panhandle, later found in a mangrove swamp between tentacle roots, nail polish still bright on soiled toes. He took his board out, rode in the cool nighttime air with his eyes closed, and meditated on the best possibilities for her: she was in Florence, touring the museums, or shopping in Rome, robbing that better class of people. There would be no denotation of lira small enough to match a police code. With all the cash and positive witchcraft he could summon for the moment, he skated to an ATM outside their favorite hotel in downtown Minneapolis—and deposited two unwieldy clumps into the account: $104 (message received), and $108 (in service).

Then he walked inside and purchased a room, the final transaction in the short resurrection of Douglas Herman.

Dismally lonely that night, he wandered through the escalators and bridges, and eventually into a wide upscale clothing store in a cove off the skywalk. While flirting, he anonymously bought an entire wardrobe for a shopping woman and made the attractive saleswoman promise not to reveal him. He watched the women joke about a secret admirer, then, as the saleswoman closed up shop, he lingered and asked her out for a drink.

In a hotel lounge that he remembered well, they shared a bottle of wine and talked about their careers. They moved upstairs, crossing the marble floor, kissing and giggling in the elevator behind gold-plated doors, and ravaging each other in a sweep of tangled covers, booze, and room service. Suddenly Kevin, delirious with a disconnected feeling of love and loss, told her the truth about his life. "My name is actually Kevin Swift." She lay naked beside him with wide eyes. He said he was a thief and a con man, hoping to someday rival the great work of his father. He said he had been in love in this hotel like never before in his life, and probably never again. He had never been in jail, but he had committed well over a half-million dollars in fraud, and he had been involved in a few million more. Was he a rich man? No. They spent it faster than they stole it. They burned it off like kindling in an oil drum, like coal down in a train's fire hole. Quietly the woman rose, dressed in the faint light, bra, skirt, blouse, and shoes. She thanked him for an interesting night and left the room. Kevin had a hunch she would call the police, but for some fatalistic reason, he rolled over into the sweet-smelling dent in the pillows and fell asleep.

When he awakened there were two guns on him, and three more officers digging through luggage scattered around on the floor. Kevin lay naked on top of the sheets. The radio alarm was playing a classical station, escalating from a forlorn violin solo to a clatter of cymbals. "Don't move," said a cop. "Stay right there, buddy."

"Can somebody throw me my boxers?"

Flashlight beams were moving across the carpet, until finally someone turned on the lights.

"Hold your horses, kid. We're still tracking 'em down."

TWENTY-FOUR

After the arraignment, Kevin was transferred from the courthouse into the Hennepin County jail to await trial. Passing through reception, he listed and stored his possessions (jeans, chain necklace with diamond wedding ring, four hundred and fifteen wallet pictures); he took his mandatory shower in a tile chamber echoing with the animated conversation of two guards; he filled out paperwork; and when he carried his folded blankets and pillows down the walk, keeping his feet inside the yellow line, he felt time slowing to a narcotic drip.

After a night of intermittent sleep under permanent fluorescent lights, taking turns on watch detail with two young drug dealers and a jittery car thief, Kevin was granted his phone call. He considered calling a bail bondsman in Minneapolis, but he could think of nothing legal to offer as collateral. Melody was his last resort. When he reached her, she was on her way out to work and he heard loud television commercials in the background. Kevin explained that he was in jail and she made a bleating siren noise into the phone.

"Really, Doug," she said. "I always expected this call, sooner or later. Just not this much later."

"Don't get preachy on me, Melody—you were in on every vacant lot."

She made a buzz like an angry wasp. "Wrong answer. Your *father* was doing that to fund the company. If you were around for anything, Doug—"

"You knew everything, you liar."

"Yes. Ding. You're correct. That doesn't mean I'm a criminal."

"Yes, it does. You were convicted of a crime."

"What do you want, Douglas? You want to apologize to me for all the headaches you caused?"

"Look, we don't need to pretend that we like each other. But we're family, and I need help. I need you to talk to some bail bondsmen around town here, in Minneapolis, see if you can scrape together enough to get me out of here. My bail is a lot higher than I expected, and they're going to need collateral."

She made a whistling sound to simulate a cartoon character falling off a cliff, but the splat never came. "I don't have any collateral, Doug."

"You have your business."

The television shrieked in the background.

"Melody? Are you there?"

"I'm here."

"Melody—I'm going to take this like a man. I'm no risk to you."

"Doug? Or Kyle or Keith or whatever your actual name is—can I just explain a teeny-weeny, itty-bitty little thing to you? My business is my life. And let me tell you why—"

"Can you just think about it?"

"I will think about it. But the problem is, Doug—I'm better now. Your father is better now. We've learned our lessons—"

"You put an ounce of marijuana up your ass!"

"Did Jerry tell you that? Oh my Lord. I can't believe he said that.

Whooo-weee, what a day, what a day. I'm going to be late—I have community service Tuesday mornings."

"Melody, *please*. I'm just a petty thief. I'm a pickpocket. I'm a gentleman. I can't fight worth a damn, and I'll never last in here."

"I'll think about it, Doug. Okay? I have to go—honk-honk, that's my carpool."

He boiled and brooded, hating Melody and her catalog of jittery cartoon sounds. One night at the end of the week, a group of wolves, stirred by some undercurrent of restlessness, circled around the bunks looking to start a war, wanting to test the newcomers. Kevin fought badly and hard, earning some Pyrrhic respect by continuing to shout and kick and defend himself, by refusing to "punk up," taking his beating and never surrendering even when the kicks and jack-hammering fists began to seem life threatening. The next day he moved like an old man, his joints aching, his face soggy, his left eye swollen shut. Ribs tender, jaw misaligned. When he heard his name on the overhead speaker, his first instinct was to be furious with Melody for waiting so long.

When he passed through the last swinging doors and out into the slanted autumn light, his face patched with crisscrossing surgical tape, he needed to wait a moment on the steps to let a gust of illness pass. He sat on the balustrade to recover himself. The wind was cold. His skin was wet and clammy and he was shivering inside his clothes. He looked out at the terrain of passing traffic, sidewalks, bare trees full of brawling finches, a plane cutting the sky overhead, the gutters and the weeded lots filled with trash; and he wished he could curl up in an abandoned lot and sleep for a year. Where was the bail bondsman Melody had sent? Was there anyone carrying a message from her? Stopping in the middle of the steps with the flow of pedestrians around him, his white shirt flapping in the wind, he looked everywhere and didn't see a soul. He waited and massaged a cramp in his neck, and it was by mere accident that his eyes rested on a woman across the street.

In the broken spaces between moving cars, she stood motionless, one high-heeled shoe crossed over the other as the wind sculpted a black dress over the outline of her hip. To hold down a wide-brimmed hat, she had placed a single fingertip on top of her head in a pose like a wind-up ballerina. When she took off her hat and gripped it in both hands, he recognized the girlish swaying in her shoulders. He moved down the last steps to the curb, where he faced her as if across a wide river. She looked down at her fluttering dress and traced her own contours with the swooping hand of a magician's assistant, as if to say, *amazing, but true*. It was Colette.

She nodded at him, then hailed a cab with the hat. Just as he stepped onto the street, a gasoline truck pulled between them, showing him his own warped reflection. When the truck pulled away, she was gone, and he wondered if everything had been a mirage formed out of sleeplessness and paranoia. But the cab approached from the opposite direction and stopped in the middle of traffic. The door swung open and she slid back to give him room. He lowered himself onto the seat, springs scraping and popping, and she saluted the driver with two fingers.

From her shorter and sharper haircut, a splash of blonde, to her makeup (the faint layer of base that covered her freckles and eyeliner that circled cold green eyes), from her fluttering black dress to her upright posture, she seemed like a different person. While she was more beautiful than he remembered, her scent filling the car more lavishly, she seemed icier, with an expression of warlike intensity.

"Do you need something for your face?" she asked quietly.

"I'll live."

They rode for a while in silence, glancing at each other, and she gave him a look that he didn't remember or recognize—her tongue moving behind her lips, her ropy muscles flexing along the jawline. With strained calm, she said, "Aren't you going to ask how I found you?"

"Don't expect me to kneel down and kiss your feet, Colette. You scorched us. You have no idea what you did to us. My dad went crazy after that—forging deeds to old dirt lots and moping around all day. You *killed* us."

Her reaction was baffling to him, for she looked over and nodded along, as if forced to humor a lunatic, then she calmly lit a cigarette in the breeze through the open windows. "Let me ask you a question. I'm sure you're angry, but just try to listen to this."

Kevin crossed his arms and rotated to face her in the backseat, determined not to fall victim to any flurry of sweet talk. She took a long, meditative puff, the smoke gathering and spilling from her mouth, and then she asked, "At what point did you fall off your skateboard and damage your brain completely?"

So shaken by her unexpected tactic, Kevin was silent, while she looked forward over the driver's partition, chin high in the air.

"What are you talking about?" asked Kevin.

"Are you now the dumbest person that's ever lived? You must be. You're going across every state closing down my old accounts. You even forged my aliases to close down a few of them. Do you think I didn't *know* which safe deposit boxes were being watched by the feds? Do you think I was just forgetting money here and there? I've worked my *ass* off to stay in front of this shit and you just gave the feds a fucking dot to dot of everything we've ever done."

Kevin's swollen lips and cheeks began throbbing. He said, "I didn't realize—"

"Let me tell you my situation, please. Our old friend the professor, the perfect mark, he hired a private investigating service; and so did the jeweler, and so did Visa and Carte Blanche, and everybody else. They put together a hell of a rap sheet on that little alias, Esther Barrick: she's wanted in every fly-over state, and I'm not talking about fraud and forgery. I'm talking about a long rap sheet of larceny charges. This is one of those times, Kevin, when you got buried in a little game, a little technical procedure, and didn't pay any attention to the big picture. You just took a bunch of dead ends and turned them into a blazing hot trail of pixie dust right to my perfect *ass*."

Shaking, Kevin pointed to the cabdriver.

She said, "No, don't worry about Luther. Luther is getting a cut of my last dollar. Aren't you, sweetie?"

Luther waved from the front seat.

"You're lucky to God I have connections giving me the story here, Kevin—so we can put a stop to this. You checked into our old hotel using the same fucking name! And that's not the worst of it. You tried to put two ATM deposits into a *frozen account*. From the same hotel where you were staying! I would think that someone who grew up on the fucking *grift* would have a little more wits about him than that."

"I got nervous thinking about you—about all of this. You're right, I lost my head."

"A while back, in New York, I pled no contest to fraud and theft charges, with Colette as my name—and they never made this connection. I did ninety days, Kevin, and it was like a whole separate lifetime. If I go back down for any of this showboating two years ago, I'm looking at six, maybe ten. I'm looking at a prison matron I call *Mommy* until I'm thirty. Now let me ask you one thing: in your opinion, why is there a new warrant out for me, one that's got the lovely Esther Barrick listed as a key alias? That's right—because you put it together for them. In back-to-back fucking days you cashed out accounts from both names, and you did it all over the country like that. Thank you very much, Kevin. I'm sorry about hurting your father's ego—but you just finished *me* off."

Kevin was trembling, unable to sort out his rush of different emotions. He turned and steadied himself against his open window, closing his eyes into the gusts of wind, until he had a clear thought and turned back to her. "Then why are you here? Why would you hire somebody to cover my bail, and take all these chances? If the trail is so hot now, why didn't you just leave?"

She crossed her legs in the other direction, rearranging the folds of her dress like a tablecloth.

"Because two years ago you were trying to impress me and I was trying to impress your father, and we didn't think about how hard these people would follow up on *big* boosts—not chainsaws or video games—but the big shiny stuff. And because, when I was down for three months, I realized that I'm not going to have too many friends in this life. I might as well go help the one I used to have, even if he is some kind of blithering idiot savant."

Kevin shook his head, dizzy, feeling his heartbeat in the swelling under his eyes. His mouth was so parched he needed to lick his lips and teeth. He said, "I don't know what you're saying to me."

"Let me put it to you this way, *darling*. I'm all out of options. I cashed my last working account and the rest have just been frozen. There's an APB out for me and anyone else with a clever name who looks like me, and I'm not going to prison again. All I've got is one clean passport, a tub of hair dye, a taxi driver here who's willing to talk to bail bondsmen and keep his mouth shut, and—maybe—an old friend who doesn't want to face six years because of the scams he did with *me*. Minneapolis might not be clean, but I bet we can fly from Duluth to Winnipeg, connect anywhere else from there. Do you have a passport? It can't be Douglas Herman."

The cab merged onto the interstate and they sat in a crosscurrent through open windows, rigid amid fluttering clothes and flapping hair.

"I have a perfect one, brand new."

"Then I think we should try to outrun this mess—somewhere, somehow." She rolled up her window and took out a compact, tracing a pencil along the edges of her lips. "After all this time, Kevin, you're finally going to get what you asked for. We'll run away together." Her mouth looked angry under the strokes of the pencil tip, and then she slammed the compact shut. "But something tells me it won't be a dream vacation."

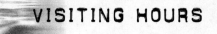

VISITING HOURS

Daniels so hated his assignment of guarding a hospital room that he would unburden himself to any sympathetic ear. By Friday, the staff was tired of him, preferring his counterpart, a grim LAPD detective who read financial magazines and never spoke. Kevin was the only person left who would endure his tirades, and soon a kind of stranded friendship formed between the wounded suspect and the fidgety young cop. They watched the mounted television together, groaning at sports bloopers, commenting on women or arguing about politics (the criminal was in favor of gun control, the officer opposed).

Daniels became a great source of information about the outside world. He solved the riddle of the bullet, relaying news that the entry wound was in Kevin's back, which seemed to have dishonorable implications for both of them.

"Does it mean somebody fucked you over?" asked Daniels.

"No," said Kevin. "It means I finally got *caught*."

Probably against orders, Daniels admitted that police had no idea of the whereabouts of the other two suspects in his "posse," and it was Daniels who brought him the exciting news that his fingerprints had turned up a list of warrants across America and even overseas. They were two active men forced into inactivity, and Daniels seemed to admire Kevin after realizing that he was more than a casual thug.

"But your crew, man—they sure left you for dead, didn't they? Personally I'd be pretty POed if somebody did that to me."

"They'll be here."

"Oh, yeah, right. Like you're going to bust out of here, huh. Good luck."

"There's just you and some hospital security."

"But you can't even get up to piss, man. Give me a break."

They played a few hands of gin (he was a miserable card player, who moved his lips while he considered his moves), until a nurse came in to announce the arrival of Kevin's mother. Daniels said that she had already given a statement to the police. Kevin found all of this baffling, and said that if it was his mother, he was somewhere in the afterlife. "Stepmother," said Daniels. "Whatever."

Melody came into the room on platform shoes, taking tiny shuffling footsteps. She carried a picnic basket with novelty balloons tied to it, each in the shape of some medical device: a syringe, a bottle of aspirin, and a thermometer. Kevin asked if her theme was the Jersey shore, and she responded only with a humming sound. She hugged him, catching a balloon between them, and immediately she began pitching her new line of fortune cookies to Daniels.

She offered the entire picnic basket to him while describing them as "cooperative cookies," or "riddle cookies" (she hadn't yet landed on a name). Kevin had been around this cop long enough to know that he would tear through them like a grizzly. He was drawn to sugar, and would leave his post only when some passing orderly announced that there was birthday cake on another floor. Right away he began stuffing fragments into his mouth, explaining with his mouth full that he hadn't eaten all day. It took him a while to notice, however, that his fortunes didn't make any sense.

Melody squealed at his discovery and told him the concept. Individually they were meaningless. But each scrap of paper was part of a larger, more elaborate fortune. "I mean, who eats one fortune cookie? So this way, you have the space to say something meaningful—not like 'You will face a tough decision someday.' You get to treat it like a puzzle. You'll love this message, by the way. It's one of the best."

Daniels took the puzzle and began laying out snippets of the fortune on the empty bed. When Melody finally turned to Kevin, her lip was quivering. "Oh, Douglas. They searched my house, they searched my kitchen. They confiscated all of your father's office equipment. They took everything but the junk in the garage. You lied to me. Whenever you're around, something terrible happens to your father."

"I think it's a reciprocal thing."

She handed him a single cookie and whispered loudly, "Don't *eat* it."

"What?"

She made a throat-cutting gesture, then nodded rapidly and pointed at the cookie, beginning to walk backward out of the room. "It was nice meeting you, Officer."

With his mouth full he wished her luck with her company, then turned back to his disordered fortune.

Kevin smelled his fortune cookie—it was embalmed with sugar and some other form of shellac. The slip of paper read "8:15," which he initially thought was some biblical reference. But on the opposite side he saw his father's handwriting, shrunken and cramped: "Cop immobilized. Security clear. Be ready."

BOOK FOUR  THE LAM

1986–1987

TWENTY-FIVE

Colette sold the arrangement like this: they were professionals now; they respected each other's accumulated skills; anything they did to support themselves on the road needed to be safe and discreet; and there was no way that any romantic entanglement could work. The speech came in staggers through airports and dark flights, and sounded so rehearsed to Kevin that he nearly laughed. Time had given him perspective, a sense of Colette's unendurable emotional baggage; and secretly, he swore never to trust or forgive her. After two years, she was more composed, more competent, and perhaps more clever and attractive. But he was no longer helpless beside her. If anything, he felt lingering embarrassment from those days, as if having awakened with a hangover and only a vague memory of some shameful act. For some reason, Colette simply needed to set limits on their "working relationship," a clumsy preemptive strike that assumed complete love and devotion despite his slanted mouth and chuckle of disbelief.

"I think I can handle it," he said.

From the moment they touched down on foreign soil, passed nervously through customs with authentic passports, and moved outside into the clutter of taxicabs, crowds, and ancient ruins, Kevin knew he could ignore any condescension from his new partner. No matter the risks, no matter the constant worry about Interpol notices, he had found an irresistible new playground. The Acropolis. The Parthenon. They were the birthplaces of common thieves, and he saw in the thousands of passing tourists, a predator's destiny. No matter where they traveled, Kevin reaped wallets from the predictable herds of Americans, following them like a wolf alongside migrating caribou. Beginning in Greece, crossing to Italy, and moving along a northerly trail, he was amazed by how it appeared that the same browsers from shopping malls now turned up outside the Medici Chapel, or jostled for cheap religious icons around the church of San Lorenzo. Young couples in matching anoraks stormed through chapels in hiking boots; the old couples, with T-shirts tucked into the waistbands of zipper-covered shorts, snapped pictures of spires with their pockets spilling. Because he looked Italian (to anyone *but* an Italian), he fashioned himself a convincing ID badge for a fictional tourist council and sold bogus citywide passes to all the museums. He discovered another athletic talent in his pursuit of the fanny pack (which seemed to have proliferated across the globe). Scissors tucked into his sleeve like a pincer claw, with a quick bump and a *scusi* he would snip them loose from their owners. It was even easier in a crowd jostling its way through a turnstile. Back to Colette, he carried the bounty of packs like a spear fisherman, piling the cash into the center of ruffled bedcovers among traveler's checks, passports, mints, pocketknives, sunglasses, birth control pills, asthma inhalers, and miniature phrase books.

"*Sono incinta ed ho l'asma.*"

"I know you think it's easy to run away after this kind of hooliganism, but there's probably a line forming outside the American Express office right now. We should get going before they sic Karl Malden on us."

They disagreed about the safest ways to scrape together a living. While Kevin argued it was best to accumulate small thefts amid crowds of gawking tourists, Colette believed that the sweetheart con was her only meal ticket. A week later, as they passed through Cannes, Colette began dining with a minor French director, having fabricated her own racy autobiography (a Mississippi childhood, a censored adult film, and a breakthrough role in a low-budget feature). The gull was probably in his mid-fifties, but looked far older, with a giant shock of unkempt white hair and small bewildered eyes on a weatherworn face. Strolling arm in arm with Colette, he seemed deliriously charmed by his young prize and her twangy accent, while Kevin waited nervously for the payoff. As he stood outside restaurant windows and watched, Colette lay her chin on clasped hands in a posture of enthralled listening. Her earrings like shards of a fallen chandelier, gown glimmering for a palace reception, Kevin was heartbroken by the beautiful and deceitful sight of her. After all the groundwork, all the dinners and gifts, the ruse was a simple credit card heist that milked the old man's accounts for a few extra francs, blurring the line between crime and simple gold digging. When Kevin criticized her for wasting a good mark to buy evening gowns and shoes, she replied, "Would you rather I bought nothing but oranges and waffle mix?" Swiveling to view herself in dressing-room mirrors, she wouldn't stop talking about the mark's incredible palate for wine, or his ability to quote poets and philosophers. He was everything she coveted on earth—so why take him for anything more than the tasteful gifts he was already willing to buy her?

"Oh Jesus," said Kevin. "Please tell me you're kidding. You want to run off with some senile frog who thinks you were an underage Mississippi porn star. Good idea."

"Well, I was—sort of."

"You're Elizabeth Olsen from Saginaw, Michigan."

"Why do you always have to bring *her* up? I'm sorry I ever confided in you, Kevin. If I ever have two happy nights in a row, you remind me that I'm secretly a cow."

Colette stayed too long with the man, became too enamored of his stories, and only when she discovered that the director was married did she leave town with Kevin. She boarded the train, and, once inside the swaying ligature between cars, she confessed: "You're right, okay. I'm getting too attached to the marks. I know that—couldn't help it. He was just so supportive of my work."

On a listless morning, they moved westward past seaside villages, crossing a narrow spit of raised sand between the ocean and the glassy marshes, all the way to Bordeaux, where Colette succumbed to a lingering head cold. Kevin suspended his work to take care of her, bringing oranges, aspirin, and secondhand books. In the evenings, while she sniffled on a mound of pillows, he read to her from *The Arabian Nights,* and she was so inspired by Scheherazade that she made him read until his voice broke, sinking down onto her side, eyes as open and attentive as a child's. She believed that several chapters proved conclusively that women were superior swindlers. Scheherazade was really the first great hustler. "That was just a sweetheart con," she said. "If they taught women things like this in college, instead of reading about all those hysterical housewives throwing themselves in front of trains, well, then we'd really be somewhere. She played that con every night. That's the kind of patience *we* need over here, Kevin. One day at a time."

The theory bothered Kevin not because of any reverse chauvinism, but because she had now developed the sweetheart con as a career. Even worse, their agreement to steal discreetly meant that she now seemed more interested in flattery than money; and the compliments that had most delighted Colette infuriated Kevin like a wallet full of prepaid tour vouchers. She was the "prettiest gal" some Texas oilman had ever seen. That wasn't a tribute, Kevin said, it was a pageant score. *Pretty* wasn't the adjective for Colette. She probably wasn't an adjective at all, but a verb, a zigzagging line traversing an old movie map, a rise of the chin and a crooked march in uncomfortable shoes.

When she had finally recovered from her illness, Kevin stole eleven wallets, risking a beating from the local thieves; and after pooling his take with their last francs, he bought pearls for the twenty-fourth birthday of her new primary alias. During a last dinner in Bordeaux, once she realized that the gift was safe, that he had legally purchased them, she blushed all the way past her neck and into the cleft of her dress. She thanked him, and perhaps for the first time they stared at each other like two resourceful adults. She lowered her head to clasp the necklace, then glanced up at him with a fearful expression.

He knew then that if he touched her, she would rear back as if stung. Maybe she would disappear into smoke, he thought, leaving a pile of rings, bracelets, and clothes on the chair, with the pearls nested in the middle.

TWENTY-SIX

After a loop through Spain and two frenetic weeks in Barcelona, working the crowds amid flame spitters and street vendors, they headed for the border with France. The train had moved fretfully all afternoon, until finally, far from the last village bells and lights, as evening changed every window to a mirror, it gathered speed for a final descent through the mountains. Passing between cars, an American tourist struggled ahead with his bags. Assuming he would disembark in minutes, Kevin bumped him, picked his pocket, and continued back to his compartment.

There amid the unpacked bazaar of hanging clothes, Colette was sketching an old Spanish woman across from her. Kevin sorted through the plunder. He found a postcard from Valencia folded into the wallet and began writing a note to his father on it. Suddenly the train stalled on the cliffs with a hiss of air. After a few minutes, clanks and hollers came from underneath the wheelbase. Colette saw some nervous flush on his face and said, "Don't worry. They've got a crack team down there fixing it with a rock."

For an hour they were stalled in the cliffs, Colette loyally shading every wrinkle in the old woman's face, and Kevin straining over how much to tell his father in the cramped space of the postcard. Without looking away from her drawing, Colette said, "Dear Dad, I hope you're making a lot of new friends in there . . ."

Kevin stopped and looked up at her, his ears and cheeks burning. "Don't. I mean it. You're not allowed to say a word about him."

"My God, Kevin—such animosity. I bet *he's* even gotten over it by now."

"As far as you're concerned I don't have a father."

"I'm not entirely sure you did. You know, you should say *something*—just so he doesn't think you're all alone."

"I'll tell him I'm with a porn star from Mississippi."

She blanched and tightened her lips. "She wasn't a *porn* star—she had a desperate phase in her life. I forgive her, why can't you?"

Colette held up the portrait for the woman to regard and, despite a remarkable likeness, the woman shrugged. The train resumed, speeding to a lullaby motion as it traversed coastal mountains, alternating between stretches of moon-trailed sea and the recoil through tunnels. Suddenly, in the midst of a downhill turn, Kevin glanced at the corridor and saw the American stumbling ahead with an attendant, who appeared listless, worn out by the indignant tourist. They were stopping at each compartment to ask about the lost wallet. In a scramble Kevin gathered his backpack and began stuffing Colette's things into the valise.

"Are you having another attack?"

"We got to get out of here. Now."

He led Colette to the caboose while she watched him with bewildered eyes. Kevin counted the turns of the track, snapping his fingers and patting his jeans, relieved only when he saw a hook of lights along a distant shoreline.

"Kevin? Don't tell me you were stupid enough to roll somebody *on* the train."

"I thought it was pulling into the station! I got homesick. I had a weak moment, okay. Here—we're slowing down."

"Kevin—you're very good at this. But how the hell are we going to make it over here if you keep pickpocketing the most aggressive tourists in the world?"

They hadn't heard of the little village where they stepped off, Cerbere, but the hour was so late and the station so deserted that they couldn't find a redcap. As they wandered through, two customs officers waved them past without looking up from a card game. Outside, Kevin trailed Colette in the dark carrying her heavy valise and his backpack, while she moved erratically, stopping every few yards to survey the sparse windows and lights furrowed into stone cliffs. A dog barked from somewhere above. "I don't even know if we're across the border. Does that sound like a French or a Spanish dog?"

Around the shore where each light smudged onto the water beneath, the train slid away under a trail of violet smoke. They ascended a steep hill to a plateau where the road narrowed and a homey restaurant sat perched on a high ledge. Everything was closed and locked, but in a lit window there was a man sweeping the floor around a snug arrangement of pink tables. Colette traipsed through a small garden to tap on the window. The man searched the windows as if a bird had flown into the glass. When he located the drumroll of Colette's fingernails, he drooped his shoulders in exasperation. He pointed at the sign on the door. "*Désolé mais on viente juste de fermer.*"

"Oh, thank God," said Colette. "We're in France." The man came to the door and Colette broke into a negotiation in broken French, finally cajoling him into selling them leftover bread and some wine. She was pleased with herself, and she skipped far ahead of Kevin back downhill, the wine bottles clanking in the bag, and a single stale baguette carried like a rifle. Kevin said that they would never find a room this late; he was going to circle around the dark shoreline on the opposite side of the bay to look for a secluded beach. She didn't want to sleep outside, but he heard her following him from the jingling of the bottles. A few hundred yards past the ambient glow of streetlights, his eyes adjusted to the blackness and the sky was a vast canopy of stars, the ghostly trace of the Milky Way along a sharp outline of cliffs. The lights of the harbor now looked like a beached constellation. They scaled boulders and slid down a chute of loose driftwood toward the listless slop of tide over pebbles. He pretended not to hear Colette's complaining, until she called for help, whereupon he backtracked to find her clinging to a damp, slanted rock. He reached his hand out, and she said, "Not me, Tarzan. The wine."

Trundling the luggage and groceries, they crawled over the last wet footing to a clearing of gray, pocked sand, penned on three sides by black cliffs. Colette laid T-shirts and jeans into a quilt on the damp sand; and Kevin struggled to make a perfect circle of stones for a campfire. He splintered some old boards stranded at the top of the beach, and used maps, hotel bills, and stolen passports as kindling. "Good thing we carry around so much evidence," he said. While Colette uncorked each bottle of wine with his pocketknife, Kevin carefully lit and fanned the fire, the map igniting through the center like an image from a war film.

"Now I really feel like a fugitive," she said, handing him a bottle.

"Fugitives don't drink fucking Beaujolais."

"You're officially not allowed to criticize anything I do from now on."

"Every dime we live off comes from me, Colette. I don't see any of your new shoes or underwear paying for our train tickets. I paid for *this* dinner as far as I'm concerned."

"Oh—and stale bread makes you the king. Man hunt wallet. Man get food!"

For a while they lay on their backs, eating crust in silence. His skin warmed with fire and wine, Kevin rose and stomped a few paces to the water's edge, where the wet sand shined like opaque glass. He started undressing. He threw his shirt into the air behind him, and when he stepped out of his jeans Colette covered her eyes and asked if he was having an episode.

"I can't listen to you anymore. I'm going swimming."

She peeked at him as he was pulling down his boxer shorts, and she squealed and buried her face under her arms. "I'm totally unprepared to see you naked right now!"

He stepped down the slope into frigid water, his skin rippling to his neck and his muscles stiffening. Colette gave a facetious hoot from above that echoed in the cove. With a determined gasp of air, he dove forward and immersed himself in stinging water, leaping upward and shouting before finally sinking back down again to endure the chill.

"You big baby," she called.

Kevin goaded her to join him, daring her with chicken noises. Rising in the flickering light, she pulled off a sweatshirt, guarded by her own long, fidgeting shadow on the uneven rocks behind her. She paced ahead to twist out of her shirt. With mermaid wiggles, she slid her skirt down her legs, seesawed ivory panties down off her hips. Her collarbone suddenly distinct in a strike of moonlight, she leaned forward to unhook the bra, then covered her breasts with her forearm, trudging awkwardly into the water with shackled footsteps. Her ribs butterflied for a scared breath and she fell forward, straining her head upward and away from the splash, breaking into a startled dog-paddle as she came toward him with tenacious puffs of water.

"Oh, my God, that's cold." Her pale face bobbed ahead in darkness, teeth chattering. "You're such a bastard. I hope a big fish comes and bites you on the pecker."

They swam far out into the darkness, seeing only the smudged lights of the village along the opposite shore. He offered a piggyback ride back, and when she accepted, he felt how her skin had retained more warmth than his, sliding slantwise across him, breasts on his crawling shoulder blades. Once they reached the shallows, Kevin dropped to his knees. She rushed back to the dwindling fire, and climbed into a pair of his clean boxer shorts, pulled on a sweatshirt, and cinched the hood so tightly that only a small porthole circle of her face remained exposed. She threw Kevin his jeans, covering her eyes again.

They drank another bottle of wine and warmed themselves from the inside out; and soon, with the stars now fogged over and streaks of mist gathering on the surface of the water, they were overcome by giddy laughter. "Oh God," she said. "Where's Frommer anyway? Where is that five-dollar-a-day wimp?"

They lay down with their heads on bunched clothes, facing each other, and her voice trailed off. Under the faint glow of the fire and fog, Kevin could see the spellbound look on her face, sleep having seized her like an undertow. He closed his eyes and heard a rustle of wind. He dozed and woke to the lull in the fire, the beach filled with haunted mist. Colette had burrowed into him, her elbows shielded her chest and her body clenched into a ball, her nose pushed beside his neck. So Kevin slid downward to position his cold face in the path of her warm exhales.

He closed his eyes and woke again to nibbling kisses. Now the clouds were distinct around fissures of opening sky. The air was a cold assault around their fortified groove of beach. He tipped his nose into the shared breath between them, and they kissed in tiny sips, lingering in the humid air between mouths; and during these few unreal moments he wondered if she was awake or asleep. He paused and her eyelashes threaded open. She peered at him with slightly crossed eyes, and when he ventured another kiss, her first instinct was to give a pleased and affectionate hum. But then some other part of her consciousness woke and she bolted upright as if she'd heard a siren. "What did we just do?"

"It's almost morning."

"Did we do something? Oh *no*. Please, don't say we did something, because that would be a huge mistake . . ."

"You were just kissing me a little. Relax."

"Oh Jesus, I'm going to kill myself."

With a dejected voice, he replied, "It's a good thing I'm so self-assured."

She dropped onto her back, hair fallen in tangled corkscrews of sand and salt. "Listen," she said. "I'm sorry if that was abrupt. I love you, Kevin—you know that. I've known you longer than anybody in my whole life. It's just that this sort of thing can't happen between us. It's understandable: we were cold, and if a person is cold enough they'll kiss a Saint Bernard."

"Just keep talking. Maybe you won't *have* to kill yourself."

"Well, maybe I'm the Saint Bernard. Did you ever think of that? God, that wine must have been turned. I'm trying to say we can't lose our—professionalism."

Kevin looked around at the scattered clumps of blowing laundry, the opened suitcases littered with kicked sand, the discarded bread bag and the empty wine bottles piled among the blackened campfire rocks, and he replied, "Yeah, that's key."

"We have to promise to forget this incident, to not let it change anything. Put up your hand and repeat after me: I, Kevin Swift, do hereby swear—"

"I'm not saying anything under oath. Quit it with that." Kevin began piling the bottles into the grocery bag, shoveling sand onto the ashes, growing angrier as he picked up trash, until he burst out: "You *love* this, Colette. You were all over me, and now you're just thrilled to sit there and condescend like this. I think you kissed me just so you could act like I made a move on you."

"That's right, Kevin. I planned this whole thing. I bribed the engineer to stall the train, and I called ahead to make sure there wouldn't be any rooms or food, and I tricked you onto the beach and got you drunk, all so I could challenge your manhood—while I have sand up my ass."

"Jesus. Challenging my manhood? Fucking Scheherazade over here—I forgot. Give me a break, Colette, you wouldn't even know what to do with my manhood." He continued over her peals of laughter. "You're so used to crazy old men with prostates bigger than their wallets, you'd flip out. You'd run for the border. You'd run crying back to the bayou—you *porn star*."

She stopped laughing abruptly and stomped away across the beach, her black hood inflating in the wind as she climbed onto a rock in the distance. Kevin kicked more sand onto the campfire, noticing little fossilized papers that hadn't burned; then he began folding the clothes and packing their bags meticulously, talking to himself as he organized his backpack in the ceremonial layout. He hoisted up her dress and swatted the sand off it, and when she looked at him, he draped it to his side and waved it like a matador's muleta. He called, "I love how your tantrums always come whenever there's work to do."

Once he had packed everything and buried the fire, he walked to her and was bewildered to see her face streaked with tears. "Oh, Colette. Come on. Big deal."

"It *is* a big deal. You have no respect for me. And I was stupid to think that you would understand me, because you're exactly like he was, in every possible way—except you take an hour to pack a suitcase."

"What do you want from me, Colette? You came back for me, and no matter what you say now, you *wanted* me to come with you. Why? If you hate me so much, if you're so disgusted by the thought, why not leave me to rot in prison?"

"God, you're so stupid."

"What did you expect from me? Huh? You wanted me to be your little mascot again, didn't you? You wanted me to chase you around and make big sad moon eyes at you whenever you felt bad, whenever you were really lonely. You didn't want a partner, Colette—you wanted your fucking *teddy bear*."

"I hate you so much right now. You don't know anything about me, Kevin. Nothing."

"I know everything you say is bullshit. I keep thinking there's some kind of theorem, some formula. I'd feed into it all the crap you say, and it'd go through the formula, and come out as what you really mean—which for every single thing would be 'Help me, I'm a miserable drama queen and I need more attention.' "

She looked away and wiped her eyes with her knuckles. "I was so right." Her face pinched up as she gritted her teeth and squeaked, "You were my only friend left in the world, and now everything is ruined."

"And after what we've done together, do you seriously think it's because you kissed me?"

"Yes," she said calmly. "The rest of it is business. That's the dividing line right there. And I have a curse on me. If I ever have any feelings for a man, he turns into a sociopath."

"I'm already a sociopath. Come on—let's go clean this shit up and get back to work. I'm tired of being broke. We need to scam some French toast."

She took long, ponderous breaths, staring at the village gables and ship masts in a break of mist. "I'm an unhappy person," she said.

"No shit. There's lots of unhappy people and they still manage to clean up their campsites and not leave evidence lying around. Let's get to a city and get hooked into something. My dad was right, you're only as good as your connections—and this fucking *Let's Go* grift is a pain in the ass. We'll get some solid new aliases and do some real work again."

She waited, and after a long time he climbed up onto the rock beside her. To his surprise she leaned her head against his shoulder, a gesture that seemed more than a cease-fire: it was a sign of exhausted trust. He kissed her hair, still rich with campfire smoke. She said, "Don't be mad at me—please. I just don't think we know how to control things once they start. Every wallet turns into a fiasco out here, and every kiss turns into a sweetheart con. Somebody always has to lose."

Staring ahead at streaks of light emerging onto the water, Kevin said, "You keep talking about ruining something. Why worry about that? We've been ruined for a long time. I'm good in the ruins; it's my hometown. You ruined us like nothing you can imagine, and here I am. I ruined you and you came back for me. Now you're just getting too worked up about everybody's fucking *savoir-faire* over here. You're thinking this is some ladder to sophistication. But where you see culture, I just see a different kind of trash. The tourists, trinkets, the same cheap crap spreading over the globe—the world is ruining itself faster than we could ever hope to keep up. Everybody ruins whatever they *need*, whatever they put their grubby hands on, year after year, until it's so ruined that it's a new fucking thing altogether. All we can do is ride it downhill. So please, for me, don't think about some ceremonial friendship you have to protect like an endangered species. That's the last straw. I'm a weed, a cockroach—you can't kill me with a rock. And you can't scare me about ruining us. In fact, I hope you'll ruin me again someday, some way that makes it all new again. Gives way for a few tougher weeds to sprout up in the scorched fucking earth. But right now—forget it, we're too broke. We follow the course. I'm learning and I'm not going to miss the big picture anymore. You either want to work with me or you don't. I don't trust you and you don't trust me. But I respect you from here all the way back to that dumpy little motel in Inglewood, where you ruined me the second I laid eyes on you."

He stared right into the blacks of her pupils, and he saw that she was curious and amused by this speech.

"Colette? You're a good thief. Now stand up, forget all the crying and the kissing and the sand in your ass, and let's go make some money again."

TWENTY-SEVEN

That winter Kevin and Colette rented separate rooms in Paris.

North of the Porte St.-Denis, amid the clutter of West African markets, Kevin rented a room in a boardinghouse where every curtain smelled thick with hashish. He covered the walls with wallet pictures. In a cabinet beside his camping stove, he kept fifty boxes of pancake mix, and the room was always a stale mixture of kerosene and citrus rinds. At night, he snapped awake to the sound of arguments and two-tone sirens, and again in the morning to the clatter of raised store cages and unloading trucks.

The local authorities weren't accustomed to pickpockets who escaped down cobblestone streets on skateboards, pulling rail slides off medieval fountains or running over the hoods and tops of cars stranded in traffic to escape down Métro tunnels. Soon every gendarme and pickpocket in town had heard of the young American who was feeding off tourists like a glutton, able to whisk off fanny packs with a deft pair of scissors or slice a camera strap without stepping off his board. Through the labyrinthine streets of the rue Mouffetard, insinuated into stone, he navigated past howling crowds and kiosks, dumping the evidence into trash cans, which he would reclaim in the first light of dawn as the green-uniformed sanitation crews worked the streets on motorcycles with tanks of soapy water. He could leave a single hotel lobby with a dozen wallets; by evening he could fill a bathtub with traveler's checks. With a hot calling-card number and a shoulder-surfed PIN, he would call Colette to brag, "I'm a god here. I've got wallets from sixteen states and Manitoba." She would tolerate his bluster, so long as he brought her an occasional peace offering of cards. He was reveling in a city with so many burrowing escape routes, so many hapless half-drunk tourists; he was an outlaw at the peak of his skills. But Kevin was far too conspicuous, and he learned quickly that the police weren't his only concern.

In January, after he was beaten up in a Métro tunnel by a gang of African pickpockets, he learned where to pay the requisite protection money in each arrondissement: Algerians who controlled his neighborhood, a Brazilian transvestite who oversaw the nights in the Bois de Boulogne, and the Eastern Europeans who pimped and ran strip clubs from the rue St.-Denis to the bars near Stalingrad Square.

One morning near the carousel in the Montmartre, the cops grabbed Kevin just as he had tossed three wallets into a trash can. A German tourist had been robbed, and apparently Kevin matched the physical description, though he doubted he had hit any Germans that week. The police led him into the back of a cramped hatchback, where he was nudged in beside a young Frenchman. Dressed in a camel-hair coat, a satiny red shirt, and slacks with pinstripes, sitting nonchalantly with his legs crossed in the cramped backseat, flicking ash from his cigarette out a tiny opening in the back window flap, he looked to be the victim of some polite mugging. He was the other suspect, and Kevin wondered in what possible world they could both fit the same description. His fellow thief was tall and had a pale, almost bloodless complexion, with thin lips, prematurely thinning hair the color of dust, and, on his long, distinguished face, glasses consisting of two tiny round lenses.

Kevin never admitted to speaking any French in these situations; but the suspect spoke English well enough to translate all of Kevin's feigned outrage. The act amused him. When the police conferred with the German, the young Frenchman whispered, "I translated everything wrong. I said you were guilty. They will send you back to America and give you the gas chamber."

When the German tourist didn't finger either of them, they were released with a warning. Kevin and the other suspect left together, chuckling, then had a drink in a bar around the corner. His name was Pierrick, and within an hour he seemed less a person than a fuming atmosphere of smoke and opinions. His bottom lip always perched outward into an expression of irritated surprise; and his voice had a suffocated quality, as if his words traveled downward in his throat.

Kevin never would have expected them to become friends; but after their initial meeting, Pierrick found him each day, dragged him to cafés, and expounded theories of American savagery in which Kevin was both listener and proof. He would berate Kevin for an hour for his ridiculous high-top Converse sneakers or the skateboard; yet he took great offense if Kevin avoided him. Two days passed without a conversation, and on the third, he found Kevin on the steps of the rue Lepic, and petulantly said, "So you're avoiding me again. I should have given you to the police when I had the chance."

Pierrick was thrilled by the prospect of having his own personal American buffoon to ridicule, to berate over international policies that Kevin didn't know (from expansionist fast-food franchises to tariffs on moldy cheese). He loved ranting about artists Kevin didn't know and writers Kevin hadn't read; and when he asked if there was any education at all in America, Kevin happily replied, "Just burgers and handguns, dude." Pierrick was delighted. Here was a perfect specimen, without shame. A cannibal. A young man who felt no remorse at eating with his fingers or chugging his wine. In fact, Kevin even played up his boorishness, as if to exert some confused sense of nationalism.

"I keep wondering if I should explain a faux pas—or if I should let you live in your perfect blissful stupidity. I think any attempt to teach you would just corrupt you in the end. I think the jungle is all we have."

Financially, meeting Pierrick was a great windfall. He knew nearly every street hood from Aubervilliers to Bastille; and he bought as many passports, traveler's checks, and ATM cards as Kevin could harvest, without even haggling, preferring instead to marvel at how Kevin could rake such profits out of the passing hordes, while seeming to understand so little of what was important. "You are Michael Zhordon," he said to him.

"Who?"

"You play a sport and you're fantastic. If you *think,* you fall apart. That I love. So don't think. I'll order something you can eat with your fingers."

Kevin endured the criticism, used Pierrick's connections to move stolen cards and cameras, and was content for a while with the pattern of his days. But the more money Kevin made, the more he supplemented a radically different lifestyle on the Left Bank. Mademoiselle Augusta "Gussie" Gordon (a.k.a. Colette, Esther, Elizabeth, etc.), despite a few intricate cons of her own, developed such an exorbitant routine that she needed constant loans. Paris, for her, seemed a lavish form of denial. Her apartment near the Jardin des Plantes was well over twelve thousand francs a month, all for a garret with a sloped ceiling and an obstructed view of the Seine through the steel bridges around the Gare d'Austerlitz. When Kevin toured the flat, he needed to duck his head, and he was distracted by the rising volume of traffic and teeming children who wandered below in field trips outside the natural history museum.

They would stroll slowly, arm in arm under the bare trees, feeling a tremor in their ankles as the Métro passed beneath the ground. She would offer to buy him lunch at a favorite brasserie, then ask to borrow money when the bill came. She dragged him through her haunts, the open-air markets along tight streets, where she would linger over a bracelet and he would buy it for her, claiming he was branching out with his stolen phone cards and long-distance PINs. "Don't take any extra risks for my sake," she said.

She knew a thousand people, all of them believing some nonsense about her being a rich American studying art: stylish girls in burgundy coats on their way to music classes; handsome men who pulled over on mopeds to offer rides. With expensive lessons, her French had improved dramatically; and she seemed, like so many of the "good" Americans, to live in constant gratitude to the Parisians who tolerated her. He would tag along with her during her weekly pilgrimage to the Musée d'Orsay where she liked to sit and sketch, or through the park in a break of sunlight; she loved to be watched. He even attended expatriate poetry readings with her at cluttered bookstores, where she was friendly with the other Americans, all seeming intoxicated with their faux exile. After she began writing her own poetry in the empty spaces around her drawings, Kevin brought Pierrick along to one of her own readings. Kevin was charmed only by the look of thankfulness in her eyes each time she glanced up at the small audience. She had found a style so lovely, so fitted to her seductive shape, the designer skirts and blouses, the anachronistically coiled hair, that men surrounded her afterward to bombard her with compliments, and Kevin left the store feeling panicked and lonely, with Pierrick walking beside him and mulling over his cigarette: "Horrible! Every poem she read was worse than the last. It was some kind of fantastic torture in there. Oh, but there was that something, just something about her that said: *America*. I looked at her and I thought—that woman is the Statue of Liberty."

"Oh, fuck, Pierrick. Don't start with her now."

"I have to meet her."

"Just shut up about it, all right? I'm warning you."

"What? She's with you? No, no—I don't think so. She wants to improve herself—you can see it on her face, every word she says. She wants to climb as high as she can. *You*—you live in the sewer. You could never have a woman like her. Women like her have to *give up* on themselves completely before they'll go with a man like you. They have to be married for twenty years and weigh a hundred kilos. They need disasters. Catastrophe. They have to have a choice between suicide—or you. That's your only hope, really, that she'll have a fabulous breakdown. If you're really determined, I can get her some heroin. With a junkie, you might stand a chance."

"You know, I have a boiling point."

"You want my advice? Get her on the needle."

"I don't want your advice."

TWENTY-EIGHT

In late February the police detained Kevin again. It was a cold day with dirty flecks of snow dappling the windshield, and he listened to questions in French while answering in English. Kevin was astounded to realize that the police knew about the Interpol green notices and the charges facing him in America. They knew Gussie on the Left Bank, his contacts on the Right, and they were curious about the Eastern Europeans in the nineteenth to whom Kevin paid protection money and sold phone cards. They seemed to have neglected to arrest him only out of some jaded big-city indifference to outside pressures, a sort of tacit insult to the American authorities. After Kevin played dumb for hours, they finally let him go with a threat: stop stealing on *their* beat or they would spread a rumor that he was an informant, then wait for him to float ashore in a canal. Kevin left the squad car admiring the gendarmes, feeling that he had just witnessed a great display of street pragmatism, an ethos not much different from a veteran crook's.

He went to Colette that afternoon to ask her to leave the city with him. He had guidebooks for trendy expatriate hubs like Amsterdam and Katmandu.

"I'm not leaving, Kevin. Extradition is probably twice as easy from those places. You said yourself, no one can convince the French to do *anything*."

He urged her to change apartments at least. It was likely they knew about her ongoing con, in which she had fabricated an American realty company and arranged house exchanges, taking fees from businessmen as they left the country. Working from a migrating office with only a broken computer and a stalwart plant, she duped three people into paying sublet deposits for fictional apartments in New York and Los Angeles.

"It's the same routine, Colette: dye your hair, pick another pretentious name, change flats. I've been buying protection from some people up in the nineteenth, and I can get decent new passports through them. I figure if we don't do any more work, we've got a few weeks. But this is serious, Colette. We've gotten too comfortable here."

The following day, Colette gave him a strip of passport pictures along with an opened letter addressed to him that she'd retrieved from the mail drop outside the city. It was from USP Lompoc, and throughout the Métro ride Kevin was furious that she would read his mail.

He read the letter on the train.

Dear (YOUR ALIAS Here):

Thanks for the postcard. I figure you've written me an average of one word for every month I've been in here. I cherish them all. This month I'm going to dedicate myself to savoring your creative grammar, which has a nice Daniel Boone quality to it. By the way, the postcard itself really brightens up the place . . . ah, Valencia! I'm a big hit around the yard with such fancy shit coming to me. Several people have already offered me punks and cigarettes for the thing, but I've turned them all down. How could I part with your groundbreaking spelling? You also say you're traveling with "an American woman, but plutonically [sic]." I'm not sure if that means she's a nuclear element or Mickey Mouse's dog, but she sounds like a keeper. Perhaps she could write the next letter for you, so that I can feel less guilt about your miserable public education (no wonder I had so many goddamn parent-teacher conferences).

> Sincerely (notice how it's spelled with two e's),
> Your indestructible father

The letter stayed in his mind all the next day, and, despite the mocking tone, Kevin imagined his father watching over him as he went about his errands. He believed that if Jerry could see him moving among the powerful and dangerous, that he would approve of his son's ease and competence. The best chance of buying foolproof documents would be to talk with the Czech off the rue du Crimée, Jirka, to whom Kevin already paid a weekly cut of his earnings. Never go alone to ask for a big favor, Jerry had once told him. But, at the last minute, Pierrick backed out, claiming he had a peptic ulcer and would be unable to handle the diplomatic drinking of Eastern Europeans. He promised to trail Kevin and periodically check the windows for trouble.

Late afternoon, the skies already dim and heavy with approaching snow, Kevin knocked on the chained restaurant door. A goon in a stiff sport coat frisked him and led him inside, dorsal muscles so lumpy that his arms hung outward as if toting pails of water. Chairs lay upside down on the tables under a stopped ceiling fan. Jirka stepped out from the bathroom in a shirt with a tic-tac-toe design printed across it, Adidas sweatpants, and loafers without socks. Kevin handed him an envelope full of cash while he was still drying his hands, and, after tossing aside wet paper towels, he counted through the money.

"Very good, Jack." For some reason, Jirka had always called him Jack, and Kevin was too nervous to correct him, both because of the man's formidable demeanor and because it was possible that Kevin had once used the name. "The rate goes up next month."

"Why?"

"*Spring*—big time for tourists. There will be money on the street, my friend. Ask the taxi drivers. Everyone pays more in the spring."

"I already pay more than anyone, sir—"

"Because you are new here, my boy. And you are American. You are the only American stealing in Paris right now. You should be proud. You are like the writer Henry James. You steal only from *other* Americans."

"I don't know him."

"Of course not. Americans don't even know their own writers. In Czechoslovakia, we watch all the cowboy movies; we read your best writers, drink your best whiskey, we know everything about your bank robbers and gangsters. Then we meet Americans and they don't know anything but what happened yesterday. I wonder what you do all the time over there."

"I'm probably not the best ambassador."

"Oh, very sly. You *do* know your Henry James."

"Okay, if you say so. Listen—I need help with something, sir. I have a small problem."

He was a head shorter and he put his moist hand on Kevin's shoulder. "Of course, of course. We have a drink first, my boy. The American thief!" He hummed the theme song from some movie, which Kevin recognized only from ice-cream trucks. "Let me guess. You need a loan? You get some bitch in trouble?"

"Nothing like that, sir."

"Okay, then we have a toast to nobody in trouble!"

Jirka shouted in loud Czech at the bodyguard, who poured three ample glasses of whiskey. They toasted while the bodyguard drank with the gasping sounds of a thirsty child. Kevin was irritated by the smile on Jirka's face. Cautiously he explained that he needed passports, first-rate documents. The best money could buy. Jirka reddened with swallowed laughter and replied, "Yes, it is no problem to do this. There is a woman who works for me, ten minutes from here. But you must understand: her family is very close to me. To my heart."

"You know how discreet I am."

"You American boys, you always say something. Anything for pussy."

"I know better, sir. I don't know anything about whiskey or American writers or any of that, but I know what's important. This is an emergency, and I need two passports. One for myself, one for my lady friend." He slid the picture of Colette onto the table. "And there's no reason she needs to know anything about where they're coming from."

Jirka peered for a long time at the photographs, nodding his head as if reading a letter full of expected news. Then he glanced at Kevin with his hard, sallow eyes, and said, "Who is she? A girl you fuck?"

"No, no. Just—it's a long story. A friend."

"A *friend*," he said with a sneer. He waited a long time, staring furiously at the picture, then he lightened all at once and replied, "Okay! Whatever you say, my boy! You're a good worker and I take your word."

He stood with a groan, paced to the bar where he picked out a bottle of wine. He yelled at his bodyguard to unlock the chains, and gestured for Kevin to follow him. Quickly the three men set out into a dirty snowfall, flakes melting as they touched the ground. The two Czechs jaywalked without looking, so that a few drivers leaned on their horns. In the wintry darkness, children were running in stone playgrounds of grinding, rusty carousels. Across the street, Kevin saw Pierrick, who stood watching as they entered a tall drab building.

The elevator was broken, so they climbed the stairs past a swirling sound of televisions. But the bodyguard became so out of breath after two flights that he lit a cigarette and gestured for them to continue without him. Jirka was still berating him as they reached the ninth level and pushed through a fire door into a hallway of painted cinder blocks, where Jirka knocked on a door and shouted, *"Immigration!"*

A very old man greeted them, hoary eyebrows shagged over his eyes; he smiled painfully and hugged Jirka with a series of little pats on his back. Immediately a stewed, vegetable odor filtered into the hall. Kevin stepped inside, heard the mewling of an infant, felt the blast of a radiator. Through a sheet hung over the kitchen doorway, an old woman pushed out, strong torso over the pleated drape of a wide skirt. The old couple and Jirka vanished behind the sheet and Kevin listened to a mix of greetings in French and what seemed to be Russian. The curtain brushed back for a moment to show a fleeting postcard of squalor: hanging pots on a line overhead, a dark, snow-streaked window, light the color of weak broth. Kevin studied the clutter of the front room: porcelain ballerinas, a music box with a revolving Star of David.

The young woman who emerged next from behind the curtain was so improbably clean and well dressed that it seemed as if she had stepped out from a wholly different setting. She wore a black sweater with a loose weave, cinched around the waist by a silver belt, and airy slacks that billowed as she walked. Kevin thought it must be the incongruity that made her seem so lovely. The sleepy quality of her face, matched with the contrast between her black coiling hair, pale skin, and dark eyes, made her appear so beautiful that Kevin felt unprepared to negotiate.

When she asked if he spoke French, he told her: *"Pas suffisament bien pour parler affaires."*

Her English accented with damp consonants, she said, "You are American then."

"Yeah, but I don't have to have an American passport."

"Americans can't have anything less."

Jirka introduced the young woman as Irina Pashutinskaya, and when Kevin shook her hand, he felt crusts of Super Glue dried over her fingertips. They poured the wine, toasted, and talked business. Kevin explained that he had access to stolen passports, but he was out of his element here and didn't have equipment to do the plastic laminate and dry seal. Irina responded that her work wasn't the cheap tampering done by most of these people-trafficking rings; on the contrary, she used the same magnetic ink as the consulate to re-codify the inside covers; she legitimized each page with real entry and exit stamps. She had helped physicists, engineers, and artists into North America and western Europe. "People who come to me are not *fugitives*," she said. "They are intellectuals. But I cannot talk business as much as normal, because my baby is sick—his stomach. Excuse me for one moment."

Kevin sat stunned: all his life he had fantasized about working so easily with magnetic ink and printers. Jirka and Irina were arguing about the baby. They also seemed to assume that his French wasn't good enough to understand their comments about him. Irina first said that Kevin was handsome, launching Jirka into a crude tirade. She calmed him by saying that Kevin (Jack) didn't seem to have any money;

Jirka assured her that he earned well. But over the course of the conversation he referred to him as the *"crétin d'amerloc"* (American dumb-ass), and expounded some theory that all Americans believed their farts were too precious for their asses. Irina scarcely reacted, but when Jirka ordered her not to sit so close to Kevin, pointing at his crotch and saying, *"C'est un dégueulasse de pervers!"* she yelled at him in Russian, and abruptly lowered her price a thousand francs per passport. Jirka shouted in Czech, while in calm, arbitrator's English, Irina replied, "Instead of worrying about me, why don't you go to the pharmacy for the baby?" He lunged forward as if he might slap her, while she stretched out her neck to offer a smooth cheek as a target, her martyr's expression disarming him, sending a surge of violence rebounding inward around cringing shoulders. He whisked his coat off the rack, plunged his arms through sleeves, and slammed the front door hard enough behind him to shake the pictures crooked.

"He worries," said Irina.

They waited in silence in the hot room.

"So you're from Russia?"

"No, no, no—we are *Ukrainian*. And you see, my family is Jewish, and when you are Jewish in Soviet Union, you have Jewish passport. You cannot have same travel privileges. This is why I have so much experience and I charge a higher price. To be Jewish in Ukraine, very dangerous. You have to be *smart*. He is angry now because he thinks my price is too good. So he says I must like you. But he says this—dirtier."

"Yeah, I caught some of it. Listen, I want to talk to you about something beyond this deal." His eyeballs tingling with excitement, Kevin explained that he had a cache of stolen documents. "I never have enough room to keep the stuff, it's coming in so fast." He wondered if they could work out an arrangement by which he could fence passports directly through her, not his current middleman—"because he's kind of a snob and I'm tired of him dumping on me all the time."

Her eyes widened throughout his speech, but Kevin wasn't certain if it was for the offer, the passion of his delivery, or his difficult slang. "Fine, yes," she said. "I can use them maybe."

Blatantly Kevin suggested an exchange over dinner, at a restaurant near the Bastille Opéra—dark, private, free of cops. The faint rhythm of uncertainty in her English made him exaggerate his gestures, until she began to watch his swooping hands rather than his face. She agreed to the restaurant, and there followed an uncomfortable pause, broken when she asked pointedly about Colette's pictures: what were the specifics of her order?

"Oh, don't worry about *her*. I mean, her documents don't have to match mine, if that's what you mean. Make her from anywhere. Make her an Albanian refugee."

She smiled, showing small wine-colored teeth, then covered her mouth.

After another silence, Kevin pantomimed rocking a baby in his arms and asked, "And the father?"

She smiled in a tight pucker, gestured to the kitchen, and said, "The baby's father is not my husband. He is *married*, but not to me. Complicated."

The radiator in the room seemed to have intensified, and she was sweating around the temples. With a rush of excitement, Kevin reiterated the time and restaurant, gave her an awkward Parisian kiss—more head butt than farewell—and left the apartment, passing the bodyguard who stood fiddling with a cigarette lighter. On the stairwell, he met Jirka plodding back upward, red from exertion and cold, carrying a white paper sack. Jirka blocked the path and lay his palm against Kevin's sternum, using the gesture both as a threat and a chance to rest his tired weight. "So? Everything is happy?"

"Ecstatic," said Kevin.

Jirka continued up the stairs, then turned at the landing to make a throat-cutting gesture, calling back, "Now you keep your big American mouth shut, or I cut out your tongue and nail it to this door."

TWENTY-NINE

He saw Irina four times in the next week, bringing to each rendezvous a thicker bundle of stolen passports wrapped in shopping bags. They would meet for lunch, then stroll the city. Lunch merged with dinner, dinner matured to drinks, until Kevin believed he was engaged in the first traditional courtship of his life. They would talk idly about fantasies as they walked along the Seine. "I always dreamed about someday tapping into an automated clearinghouse," said Kevin. "In the States, they're these regional computer centers, they store millions of electronic transactions every month, all of it on magnetic tape. Everything for electronic deposit. I used to get a knot in my stomach dreaming of those places."

Dryly she replied, sliding her arm through his, "I always prefer to break into credit card bureaus. Do you know Chaos? And Inner Circle? They hack into credit bureau computers every week."

"Sure, sure, but they're mostly hacking into the TRWs just to check the limits on cards that are already hot. I know all about that, and I actually had offers when I was in the Northwest. Mostly that's older credit card thieves offering kids a little gum money for some research. But you can use those time-sharing services now—like Compuserve—and order stuff with just account numbers, never even showing your face. It's not as developed yet as it will be. Mark my words."

In a break of sunlight through the first cherry blossoms, she told stories about the European ATF1 car phone in the early eighties and how with simple hardware and an FM receiver, it could make free calls to anywhere in the world. She recommended Jan Jacobs's seminal work, *Kraken en Computers*, which mentioned, not by name, several of her contacts in the Netherlands, who were responsible in their impulsive youths for rerouting all the phone lines between Holland and Denmark. They strolled past street painters and talked whimsically about art fraud. Perched together on bridges, shoulders touching, they watched the barges move up and down the Seine, and she told him about the mythical French con man who had once gathered investors for diverting the Ourcq River in order to speculate on water.

Sitting outside at a café in slanted winter sunlight and breeze fragrant with approaching spring, he told her he admired anyone who could work so deftly with magnetic ink. She blushed. She waited silently and patiently in her chair, espresso steaming, chin beneath the raised collar of her coat.

"I don't want to brag or anything," Kevin said, lowering his face. "But I once encoded a MasterCard account onto a strip of VCR tape."

"Yes, I've done it with audiotape."

They sighed together and sipped their espressos.

By the third date, they made self-conscious efforts to discuss their families, though it was clear neither was comfortable during these moments. Kevin admitted his father was doing time for fraud, and she said that her mother and father would disown her if they knew of her activities. Her parents had grown up in Odessa, sophisticated people, but they had been relocated to the country in the seventies. Her brother had been killed in the early eighties. She would only say that he had made "deliveries" for a living. "You remind me of him. But of course you are nothing alike."

Motored on caffeine, adrenaline, and sunlight, Kevin slapped the table and said, "It's like we had the same childhood. I was *constantly* relocated."

She watched him with sleepy eyelids, sipping, and finally responding with a wry smile, "But you are terrible. Such distractions. A week already and I do no work on your passports."

At first Pierrick was irritated by the lost business, but he became so curious about the mysterious document forger that he actually trailed them in order to spy on dates. Often Kevin noticed his little car parked outside cafés. He made no effort to hide his snooping, and instead criticized Kevin's itineraries, claiming no woman would ever sleep with a man who frequented such tacky places. They were behaving as ugly tourists from opposite sides of the Iron Curtain. Kevin explained that Irina shared his aesthetic of junkyards and plastic, and his fondness for her only grew with the realization that she was indifferent to all the social minutiae of Paris.

Still Kevin had no clear idea what she thought of him, until one afternoon as it grew dark, Irina was suddenly, irrationally afraid to return home alone. This anxiety was the first vivid emotion Kevin had seen from her, so he seized upon it as a show of intimacy. Together they rode the curling oxbow of the pink line, never taking their eyes off each other; and on the walk along the Canal St.-Martin, he reached out and held her hand, feeling her surrender hers to him as delicately as an heirloom. He kissed her once outside, once again in the stairwell, and she deflected his impulsiveness with patient, close-mouthed volleys. He whispered that he wanted her so badly he was dying. She had a furrowed, concerned look on her face, as if he were becoming unmanageable, whispering his devotion between kisses, until she relented with a stoical tone, "Yes, okay. But do not talk so much about dying, please."

She guided him upstairs, then across the living room, and in ten silent strides he was inside a strange hot bedroom between a gurgling radiator and an empty crib. He sat on the unmade bed and listened to the mumble of a conversation. The baby fussed. The grandmother raised her voice. Irina finally returned to the room dandling the infant against her shoulder, blouse still unbuttoned from a breast-feeding. Shushing either the baby or Kevin, she did a rocking dance and sang songs in Ukrainian with a susurrus of kisses and whispers, before finally laying the infant into his crib. When the room was silent, she stood upright and said, "Okay, quick now and not too noisy."

She had the matter-of-fact demeanor that Kevin expected, undressing herself and nestling into the bed beside him, complimenting his adroitness with bra straps. She talked to him throughout their encounter in a whispering tone, as if they were collectively breaking into a vault. "Not quite right," she said, "a little lighter touch—yes, yes, better. More like that." Her body was a rolling pale terrain in the moonlight, moving purposefully, and when he sank down under the covers, she said, as if responding to a business meeting, "We could try that." Once they had finished together, technically proficient, as synchronized as an ice-skating team, Kevin was satisfied, but oddly distant; and he wondered why he felt like he had made a terrible mistake. She was everything he wanted. She was a genius. True, the sex was mercilessly calculating, but Kevin mistrusted the sort of bluster and abandonment of romance novels.

With their own swelter of humidity over the radiator's warmth, a trace of breeze slipping through the open window, Kevin soon faded into an uneasy sleep. When he woke a few hours later, Irina was sitting on a chair across the room nursing the baby. The room was filled with gasping sounds, and Irina looked lovely and ruffled, dark hair spilled down over white shoulders, naked in the chair.

"What's the baby's name?" asked Kevin in a drowsy voice.

"Jirka," she said.

Every trace of sleepiness was gone immediately, and Kevin leaped out of bed and hunted down his clothes on the floor, whispering, "Oh no, no, no. Okay—Irina—I really *like* you, but—"

"I can have my own life, Jack. He is married, he has a big family—and I don't want to sit here and be a slave. I am a grown woman. I am independent of him. I am not one of his whores."

"Holy shit. Irina, listen, I don't want this to end either, okay. I'm really happy—*theoretically*. But then we need to go deep, deep, deep underground with this stuff—I mean, if we're really going to stand a chance here, we need to take precautions. Seriously. Disguises, hotel rooms, fake IDs. I mean there's just no other way."

The baby had fallen asleep and Irina stroked his forehead. "Yes, okay. But as you see, I can deal only with one child at a time."

THIRTY

Kevin had only briefly introduced Pierrick and Colette, so he was sur-
prised that during the weeks of his preoccupation with Irina the two
had become friends and gossiping partners. Pierrick attended all of her
readings and eventually assumed the role of her steady matinee date.
Though Kevin was troubled by the familiarity that had developed
between them, he was relieved to witness her allowing Pierrick to correct her French pronunciation, something she wouldn't have tolerated
from a legitimate suitor. What bothered Kevin most was how centrally
his affair with Irina figured into every conversation. They had created an
entire cinematic fiction of his romance, filled with inside jokes; and now
Colette demanded that they meet Irina officially, with all due pomp and
circumstance.

Three nights later, Irina met them for dinner on the Left Bank, stepping out of the cab so made up that Kevin believed she might be in dis-
guise. Colette was warm and friendly, kissing Irina's cheeks and telling
her she must be a saint to put up with Kevin. Irina responded dryly that
Colette looked just like her passport photograph.

"Oh, let's please not talk about work, honey. Someone might be wearing a wire." Then Colette whispered into Kevin's ear: "She's *adorable.*"

Throughout dinner Irina's posture was as stiff as her hair, and Kevin slumped down around his soup bowl like a prisoner. Colette would occasionally disrupt the flow to ask questions about the Ukraine, hobbies, and future plans, while Irina answered in stern monosyllables. Kevin had expected Colette at her loudest to dominate Irina's retiring manner, and initially she did. But soon it seemed, inexplicably, that Colette was in the more strained position. She tried to engage Irina in a hunkering private conference of whispers, but when Irina wouldn't lean away from the table to meet her, Colette waved it off, launching into a series of self-effacing jokes. Soon the isolated flurries of conversation between the two women seemed like a bitter tennis match, in which the improvisational player becomes flustered by the robotic consistency of her opponent. Colette spiraled off into a long soliloquy about how all she ever wanted was "some kind of *life.*" Her face was flushed in blotches, her lips heavy with wine. She threw her hands around comically, but with a tremulous threat of hysteria.

Kevin paid the bill, and outside they walked in silence, until Colette saw an alley cat and stooped down to beckon it with wiggling fingers. She pursued it under a parked car, dampening her coat and dress to offer her hand. Brushing herself off as they continued onward, she seemed devastated by the rejection from the cat, and, twice as drunk as Kevin had thought earlier, she talked in a sighing tone about how dreadfully unfair the French were, spoiling their awful little dogs and treating their cats like viruses. As they were about to say good-bye, she broke into a fit of sneezing, first suppressing each into a cranial hiccup, and then finally bursting outward with full force. Kevin and Irina waited for a pause to wish her a good night, but each time they tried, she halted them while holding her palm like a partition over her nose and mouth.

Finally she regained her normal respiration, and she grabbed Irina by the shoulders, speaking with woozy melodrama, and said, "He's my good friend, and I'm glad he met someone . . . so . . . like the way you are. I mean that."

"Yes, all right," said Irina. "It was a pleasure to make your acquaintance."

"*Exactly*," said Colette. "To a new era! And don't ever forget—" She closed her eyes for a moment as if falling asleep, clutching Irina's shoulders now to maintain her own balance. "If you hurt him—don't do it. Because he's, like—important. To me, that is—not to those people over there. But to *me*. So—that's what I have to say. I'm a dangerous bitch, honey, when I want to be."

"I believe you, yes. You seem like it."

Pierrick smoked with a sepulchral disappointment on his face. After all the promising weeks under his tutelage, Colette had regressed into a living, breathing faux pas. He took her arm and nodded to Kevin that he would make sure she got home safely. Pierrick led her away, his strides tugged off course by her staggering.

Finally alone on the Métro, Irina said, "She wants you for herself, I think."

"No, no, no—she just drank too much. I've actually never seen her that drunk. So don't judge her based on that."

"She does nothing but embarrass herself. I don't judge, I pity her."

"There's no reason to *pity* her. She was trying to be friendly to you, and she got frustrated. You were a little icy."

Irina shrugged and looked away.

He tried to temper his comment by adding, "It's all right. I didn't expect you two to get along anyway."

"There is no problem. She is like every American woman. She talks, blah blah blah, and she says nothing. We don't have to think about her anymore now. She is stupid and I don't have time."

"She's *not* stupid. In fact, she's excellent at her work. She's just not very organized. There's a big difference. I don't want to have an argument, Irina. She wanted to be your friend tonight, and you were so superior. You were just determined to snub her all night long."

When they reached their exit, he saw from the accelerated pace of her stride that she was offended. As they walked to the apartment, he tried to apologize by placing his arm over her shoulder, but she twitched away. Though her face looked angry and unforgiving, she still asked, "Are you coming upstairs?"

"You know I can't. I'll work it out, I'll figure out an arrangement, but I just don't feel comfortable—"

"Fine," she said. "Go sleep with your stupid friend."

"Stop that. We don't have anything between the two of us. I'll come by tomorrow, during the day. We'll talk over the plans." He leaned down and kissed her on her cold cheek, and she walked away under spaced yellow lights.

When he was back in his grim room, undressing for bed, there came a tentative knock on the door. It was his Algerian landlord in his undershirt, hair mussed and eyes bloodshot. Kevin hadn't been there in three days and he expected this was some confusion over his weekly rent. The Algerian spoke slowly, making sure that Kevin understood: the police had been here earlier. They had looked through his room and asked questions. With a series of reassuring shoulder pats and handshakes, Kevin promised him that everything was fine, he had nothing to hide, except a collage of wallet photos, which they had evidently confiscated.

With the landlord pacified, Kevin stayed away from the room all night, returning only to shower at the first clatter of trucks. Standing at the counter of a bar downstairs, he drank one espresso to open his eyes, then he raced to Irina's, hoping the night had quelled her anger enough for him to describe his near miss. Head down, he took the stairs two and three at a stride; he burst into the hall, and noticed only at the last moment that her apartment door was wide open.

Police were everywhere. The old couple sat on the couch, shouting orders as if to movers, while the cops emptied cabinets and sorted through files. Irina sat on the floor, hands cuffed around her baby. She glanced at Kevin and gave him a look of pure contempt. Then she straightened her shoulders and pointed at him, saying to the police that a "buyer" was right outside.

Kevin stumbled backward, clambered downstairs, and hit the street running. For the next few hours, he stopped at every phone booth, repeatedly trying Pierrick's and Colette's answering machines. He couldn't return to his room. Irina was a linchpin; the police would trace lines outward from her, tacking document fraud on each thief and racketeer up the ladder. She would have two incomplete passports for Colette and himself, so he needed to warn her. By late afternoon, he still couldn't find Pierrick or Colette, and he cursed his incompetence and his pathetic connections. He was resting his forehead against the inside of another phone booth when he was startled upright by a jeweled ring tapping on the glass.

Outside stood Jirka's bodyguard, with two other men beside him, both in blazers and stiff blue jeans. One of the men opened the door. "You," said the bodyguard, reaching inside. Kevin thought of biting his hand. "Come," said the bodyguard, with a tortured accent. "Come heyre. Beekh traughvle."

There was a sinister courtesy about the bodyguards. As they walked, the youngest fanned three cigarettes in his mouth, lit each, then, with an expression of having drawn the shortest straw, handed one to Kevin.

They humored him by using crosswalks and waiting for the lights to change. They turned down an alley and entered the restaurant through the clanking prep kitchen with its simmering smells of chicken stock and garlic; and they guided him up the stairs. From the stilted friendliness of the men, three bad actors on their way to a surprise party, Kevin expected a gun to click against his temple at any moment.

He sat on the couch and waited. Jirka stood in the bathroom, his thinning hair slicked down with water, his shirt buttoned partway, a towel over one shoulder. He focused on the mirror while lathering his face. The only light in the front room was from a shadeless lamp sitting on the floor, which cast top-heavy shadows against the chipped wall. The windows were blotted with steam. Humming a muddled rendition of an old country song, and eyeing Kevin sideways as if he meant to be clever, Jirka began shaving himself with a straight razor, over his cheeks with a sculptor's care. When he had finished, he buried his face in the towel and grunted, then paced over to Kevin with dabs of cream still on his ears. He said something to the three men, then made a crumpled smile at Kevin, nodding with an expression that evolved into a strange, fatherly look of disappointment. "My boy," he said. "We have some tragedy here. Terrible news."

"Mr. Lubek, I just want you to know that I'm as upset about this as you are."

He pressed a finger to his lips. "Shhhhhh. Shut your fucking mouth now. I want to know. Who fucks up here? Who talks to the police?"

Kevin's throat felt clogged.

"Let me explain something to you. And listen very good. *Irina*—she does work for people only if I approve them. Maybe forty or fifty clients. Some very important people. She is always careful—she is a *serious* person."

"That's what I really like about her—"

"Please, don't talk. Only understand. Five years now, she works—no trouble. Nothing. I *love* her, I protect the family. She is my secret." He breathed so hard that his center of gravity seemed to move between his shoulders and waist. "Now *you*. You come, and—how long I don't even count. And police. Police, police. Everywhere. Now, I wait right here—and you tell me *why*."

"Mr. Lubek, I swear to you, I have no idea what happened."

Jirka sat on the arm of the couch, stared at the windows with a lamenting face. Kevin could feel how the other men moved around him in predatory circles. He tried to perform for them, showing a relaxed respect and mutual concern, but he betrayed the facade with gulping breaths, like a caught fish on the deck of a ship. Kevin said, "*I* want to know what happened. I'm as angry as you are."

"You think I am angry?" Jirka stood again and wandered around the room, and then turned and gave Kevin a look of exaggerated pity. "Angry like a little child? Right? I kick and scream, boo-hoo. I lose my favorite toys. Yes?"

"No, not like that. I didn't mean like that."

"I want to explain to you. I am angry when the cooks fuck up downstairs. I am angry when my children don't go to school. This is very different. When I am twenty-four years old, in Pizen—close to *your* age, I think—I have to kill a man who steals from my boss. I cut off his fingers, and I let him bleed—because I want him to know what he has done, to learn something—and then I cut his throat. I am not angry when I do this, I know this is part of the contract."

With his voice quivering, Kevin said, "I'm sorry if I was careless, but I don't see how anything is my fault."

Jirka sat and brusquely put his arm around him, rocking Kevin back and forth until the amiable pose changed into a firm clamp at the side of his neck. "You don't see because you are still a boy—grabbing things.

You don't even know the rules. When you steal from tourists, you *borrow* from us. It's okay—you can cry if you are afraid. You need to learn some things, and I can teach you."

With a rill of saltwater coming from his nose, Kevin said, "I didn't do anything."

"Listen to me, my boy. I work for people, and sometime—tomorrow, next week, I don't know—they will come to talk to me. Because they have problems now. These are people you don't want to meet. They don't care about your pretty girlfriend, and how you are angry, and it was all—accident. Yes, I know about you and Irina. But that is nothing compared to this. Maybe they will kill me. Because this is my responsibility. You are my responsibility, and my *mistake.* Do you understand?"

"I could try to find out what really happened."

"It doesn't matter what really happens. You are thick in your head, my boy." He flicked Kevin on the tip of his nose. "Are you so surprised? You think life is so valuable? It's nothing. I take it whenever I want. It is just another thing you carry with your wallet and keys. You live like a thief—anyone can take it from you. You Americans don't know anything. You think you steal what is already yours. You make this deal with me a very long time ago, my boy. Don't you see? Every time you put your hand in someone's pocket, that is just a little handshake with *me.* But I'm tired of talking now."

Two men grabbed Kevin under the arms and hoisted him over the back of the couch. At first Kevin cooperated, but when he saw Jirka click open the straight razor, he swam frantically against their weight, sprawling his legs around the doorjamb to hold himself outside the bathroom. They threw him onto the floor, where he scrambled away like a mouse, until they caught him again, someone pinning him down with a kneecap in his back. They carried him this time like pallbearers, a man to each writhing leg, fat hands cinching his wrists together. In a flurry of clawing they threw him into the bathtub, where his head struck the faucet and his tailbone bruised against the porcelain. He lost his wind for a few moments and strained to breathe. When Kevin finally sat up, Jirka was perched on a waste bin beside the tub. He grasped Kevin's cheeks in his palms, squeezing and steering his head around loosely. "So sloppy," he said. "You are such a little boy, you cannot even shave right. Your father should be ashamed."

They sprayed and piled a froth of shaving cream onto him, into his hair and eyes, over his nose and mouth until he was drowning in menthol. He felt the first pass of the razor up his cheek. "What does she see in him?" asked Jirka. One of the men laughed in low hiccups. "Let me ask you something." The razor moved up the curve of his neck with the sound of a striking match. "You think of no one but yourself." There was the flashing burn of small cuts, and Jirka said, "Oh, stop moving. You don't want me to have another accident." He pinched Kevin's nose tight in his fingers. "Lift up. Like a rat." He raked the blade over his top lip and Kevin felt another cut. "So many people are hurt." Within a few seconds, Kevin felt a searing burn as they doused cologne over him. Someone turned on the faucet, scalding hot, and they shoved his head down into it as he flounced from side to side to protect his face and eyes. One of the men cursed that he had burned his hand, while Kevin climbed up, scalp throbbing with heat. Jirka stood at the washbasin, rinsing the razor. "You are as pretty as she is now!"

He took a long time replacing the blade, then tested the new one against his fingertip. "Okay—stick out your tongue. Like *this*."

Kevin clamped his mouth shut, and one of the men stomped him on the head, so hard that he felt momentarily dazed. "Open, open, open. I am tired of your crying and your big fucking mouth."

Kevin wept in a paroxysm, reddened and sick, and he barely had the air left in him to say, *"Please."* The bodyguard grabbed him around the throat with both hands and squeezed until Kevin thought his neck would snap, and as his mouth gaped open, Jirka tilted the razor and held it sideways against the inside purse of his cheek. The bodyguard released him. Kevin jolted for air, trying to recover his breath without moving his lips, feeling the cold blade nudged against the hot skin.

"Yes, good. Very still. If you move, I think you lose your tongue." Jirka's eyes were yellow around the edges, flat, and Kevin thought he looked dead, skin graying and a wisp of decayed breath through his teeth. Then he smiled, and said in a tone that sounded almost loving, "I wish you would be a man and stop crying. Show some courage, some—what is the word?" Kevin closed his eyes and waited with the steel rubbing faintly on his teeth, while Jirka hunted through his vocabulary: pride, faith, respect—he couldn't remember. "God will know. His English is better than mine."

With a sudden yank, Kevin's face was tugged upward and dropped with the sound of a fishhook pulled loose. He fell against the side of the tub and saw a scattered spray of blood along the porcelain. He tasted thick, sweet iron; but he was unsure where it came from. He didn't recognize his own blood. He sank lower and, with one eye open, he watched as Jirka shook the syrupy blade, washed his hands, unbuttoned and changed his shirt. Then Kevin saw the redness mixing with the lingering water around the drain, thinning like wine must. The pain was far away. Whatever had happened, Kevin hoped that this might be an insignificant slash on the corner of his mouth. He felt his tongue—still intact. As the blood netted in his eyelashes, he had faith, even as the pain began to clarify into a sloppy strand across his cheek. When he touched his mouth, a surge passed through his eye socket, jaw, the hammer of his ear; he felt his heartbeat in the gash along his mouth, and he saw blood as thick as resin in the creases of his palm.

The men wrapped towels around Kevin's face and lifted him from the tub, their gentle caution seeming to be inspired by a fear of touching his blood. They carried him downstairs as he stumbled between them. He heard the kitchen, the cymbal crashes of pans, the knocking on cutting boards. The smells seeped through the towel. Someone called, a door swung open, the air outside was cold and the wind sounded like fleeing steps through trash. Blood dampened his collar as they guided him through a network of alleys until he could hear the trickle of water through metal grates, a barge splashing ahead, carousel music in the distance. One of the men yelled for someone to clear out of the area, and from the sound of voices over water, and the feeling of bottled wind, he knew he was right at the branching dead end off the Canal St.-Martin, across from Stalingrad Square. He felt a gun press against the bunched towels.

The man holding Kevin was stiff and upright, pressed too close, so that Kevin saw his chance: bending in a snakelike twist, he coiled his legs back around the man's feet; then he threw their collective weight backward, tripping them both. They fell together, and Kevin felt the suddenness of the dip as a move he knew from his childhood karate classes and play-fighting with his father. While the man panicked at his loss of balance, throwing out his arms and losing hold, Kevin was patient, and in the split second of falling, he untangled himself to roll gracefully off the pavement. In a few racing heartbeats, he leaped to his feet and ran, the towel unwinding behind him. Each stride burned the cut in his face. As the two men chased him, Kevin bypassed Stalingrad Square and kept running. He was already dead, it seemed, so unreal were all the lights and windows. Farther south, he lost his strength again and needed to hold tightly onto the rail to descend the Métro steps.

He came to the turnstile and found a ticket in his pocket like the inheritance from a previous life. He heard the men coming through the tile labyrinth behind him, so he climbed onto the tracks and ran into the Métro tunnel, through the darkness full of rats and electrical conduits. The train was approaching and he ducked into an alcove between girders, where he crouched down and watched the lit windows rush past like a flip book of bright faces, each a small wallet photograph, until with diminishing clanks the train was gone.

He didn't know if he had passed out; another train startled him, crossing near his extended legs, a bright, shrieking alley of coats and fluttering newspapers, which left behind a whispering, hollow recoil, draining into silence. Then he heard voices. Echoing. They were coming. Someone was howling, amused by the echo. Laughter. No, they were younger voices: *children.* He saw their thin figures coming through the fretwork of tracks and wires. How long had he been down here bleeding? He saw them leap the rungs, avoid the voltage along the central conduit, he saw the swinging movements of their arms, the spray paint cans, the backpacks, a saunter in their shoulders: they were African kids. Graffiti taggers. One found him and frantically waved for the others. *"Regarde!"* They stooped around him, whispering. Kevin muttered, *"Ne m'amenez pas à l'hôpital.* Go to—*Place Monge."* They picked him up and walked him down the tracks and raised him onto the platform. With a dreamlike efficiency, they were on a train; Kevin was across from a woman in a brown business suit who asked startled questions he couldn't understand. Kevin was shivering and one of the boys laid his coat over his shoulders. *"Place Monge? Quelqu'un pourra vous aider là-bas?"*

Kevin nodded his head, then mumbled, "Just no hospitals. *Je suis recherché."*

Soon they were out in the darkness again, under a smudged pattern of windows and streetlights, shadows and voices moving past; and as the boys helped him onward, he heard passing reactions to him, as if he were cutting a wake right down the path of onlookers. He told them, right, left, *gauche, droite*—seeming to make decisions indiscriminately; until suddenly he recognized a street market and knew all of the buildings, and he said to the kids, "*Ici, ici, très bien.*" They carried him up steps to the intercom, where he had a sudden moment of doubt: was this the old apartment or the new one? As if it were no more than a lucky number, he pushed a button to the flat, leaving a bright spot of blood, and within seconds heard Colette's voice through the speaker. The tallest boy said, "*S'il vous plaît, s'il vous plaît! Il y a un monsieur américain ici qui vous demande et il est blessé avec un grande coupure au visage.*"

She responded in rapid French, which Kevin didn't understand. Then in English she said: "Kevin? Is that you? Come through that door in front of you. I'll be on the stairs."

They pushed forward, everything accelerating through rooms and doorways to a spiral staircase where Colette rushed down on bare feet. She was fluttering in clean white organdy and a skirt, and she grabbed him around the waist, gasping as all of them ascended the corkscrew of stairs, repeating, "Oh shit, oh shit," until they were through her open door and into the soft lights of the front room, where he heard a jazz trumpet, smelled dinner, saw plants and books and cozy shadows. She led him to the bathroom where a fluorescent tube flickered overhead. He watched her turn and touch one of the boys' faces, and thank him profusely, "*Merci, merci, mille fois!*" and the boys scattered throughout her living room at some offer of food and drinks. There was another man, British, who wandered into the doorway with a wineglass close to his sweater vest, who looked pale and bewildered, and said, "Good lord, Augusta, this man needs a hospital."

"Richard, if you want to be helpful, go get a pad and pencil from the kitchen and let's write down everything we need."

"Who *are* these people? There are three black children ransacking your cupboards."

"Now!"

She crouched over Kevin, and he saw that her sleeves and the front of her blouse were already drenched with his blood. Her face, pale and scared, had streaks of red across the chin and cheek. "We can do two things. I can take you to the hospital, and then we—handle the police when they come. That may be our only choice. Okay? Or I can try to close this myself."

"You," said Kevin.

"Don't just say that! Just because I was a seamstress for a bunch of foster kids, that doesn't make me a surgeon. You don't see yourself. Okay—calm down. I can *try*." Her face scrunched up into a panic, until she relaxed herself again with determined puffs. "I've done a stitch before when I was in jail. It's called the vertical mattress, and it'll just close it. That's all. But this is a complicated spot, sweetie, and even if I can clean it and do this, I'm going to leave a scar like you can't believe. Do those kids know how long this cut has been open? Richard—there you are, shit. Get one of those kids in here. I need to ask him something. Wait, write this down first. Go to the pharmacy right down the street, and get—*write it down!*—spray-on Lidocaine. Have one of the boys help you, your French is a wreck. Get catgut sutures, antibiotic ointment, and saline. I don't know the needles, so just get all of them, and—tape! Closure tape. Tons of gauze—and some sanitary napkins, we need something to soak this blood up. God, what am I forgetting? I'm a fucking mess. Did you write it all down?"

"You're mad, you realize that."

"Let's step up in a crisis here, Richard! Move. And don't answer any strange questions or I'm calling your wife!" She petted the damp hair from Kevin's eyes, shushed him, and said, "I'm shaking a lot. I don't know if I can do this."

He grabbed her hand. Bloody fingers dovetailed.

"I'm going to get you a little whiskey, sweetie."

He faded out and back. Beside an arrangement of end tables and reading lamps, he lay on his back and saw the ceiling's intersecting rings of shadow and light. He felt a bee-sting pierce and a flutter through his skin; the thread slithered into his cheek with a rustling sound straight under his ears. Under her half-moon reading glasses, she was sobbing as she wound each stitch, so that it appeared to Kevin as if she were absorbing the spilled pain off his skin. Slowly, she grew more focused, and finally showed the same frowning concentration she gave to her drawings. The tugs were sturdy now. Her pupils widened and he saw little coin-shaped images of himself. Her hair was unraveled and stuck together at the tips with his blood. She paused, momentarily distracted by his watching eyes. He mumbled, "I love you."

"Shhhh, stay still." She picked up his hand and kissed the skin between his fingers, then in her airy, play-acting voice, said, "And please don't say anything that you'll regret in the morning. I might just follow through and sew your whole mouth shut."

THIRTY-ONE

In the greasy mirror of the truck stop bathroom, Kevin peeked under the flayed edge of the surgical tape to see a dried crimson groove, cinched together in an upward curl of stitches like a baseball seam. She had done a tremendous job for a novice. Along the buckled pink riverbanks of skin, he saw no sign of infection, despite a hangover in his bones. He didn't remember much after having found Colette last night, but as he now walked back outside into a wind scented with gasoline, he noticed a change in her behavior. From the car she trotted toward him, hair in streamers, blouse like a wind sock. She lay her fingers on his face and neck. No fever, no swelling. It was a miracle, she told him. "We'll get some antibiotics when we get there, just to be safe."

As Kevin groaned and struggled into the car, a few fat raindrops fell against his arm. Pierrick pumped the gas, cigarette pushed into the wind, trailing ash and sparks.

By afternoon they'd made it to an abandoned cottage, beside a small farm plot of lumpy, fallow mud, where crows swarmed between the eaves and a crooked fence. Around back, behind the cottage, in tall grass bowed down under the weight of a recent drizzle, Colette and

Pierrick pried off the boards over the windows, all the while Pierrick swearing that the owners—his aunt and uncle—lived in Paris and wouldn't return until summer. After they had broken in and helped Kevin through the door, Pierrick reminisced about his youthful imprisonment here, and the years in which this was a functioning fifteen acres of sweet-smelling alfalfa crops, chickens, and fat farm cats.

In the single streak of light, a belt of orbiting dust, Kevin lay on the couch under a blanket that smelled of mothballs. Colette and Pierrick continued working loose the boards until every corner was visible: stone floors and rafters spun with cobwebs. Pigeons cooed in a nest high above, and below, bird droppings spotted the armchairs and the dining room table. Weeds had grown up and died along the kitchen wainscoting, so Colette gathered them for kindling in the stove, blowing on damp logs until at last the mildew and mothball smell was overcome by a perfume of wood smoke. Kevin lay on his aching tailbone, shut his eyes, and listened to them claim the space. From a dark alcove, Colette cheered at the discovery of two unopened bottles of port.

Returning from a bedroom, Pierrick announced that his aunt still paid some of the bills. "The phone works," he said. "I don't believe it."

"Don' u'a' phone," said Kevin. "I'n nonna shranga you wi' d' cord."

"You lost too much blood, I think. You are delirious."

"His mouth hurts, don't make him talk. He means there might be taps on all the phones back in the city, so everybody has to show a little discretion."

"Some real outlaws. One in the kitchen, one on the couch. I am surrounded."

Kevin sipped his port and dozed as he listened to their conversation at a wooden table, drifting in and out of anxious sleep. Every few minutes or hours they would rouse his attention with some adamant comment in French or English, and he would strain his neck to see them sil-houetted beside the flutes of burning kerosene.

At the first bright slash of sunlight through the east-facing win-dows, he woke with his shirt soaking wet. The room smelled of thick coffee and cinders. Colette and Pierrick had gone and left the door tap-ping open in a breeze. A rooster led a chorus of faraway dogs. Kevin wandered the house huddled in the blanket, bare feet on cold stone, then outside into light the color of dust and straw, the ground and fences netted with raindrops drying in the grassy heat, the landscape a bunched quilt of green and yellow squares, some fields of bare earth, hemmed with blotted bushes, and a sunken stream that twisted through the terrain like an indented scar. Crows perched in every tree, calling and suddenly flying upward in tornadoes of black. Such terrible disrepair: there were leaves from before the last snowfall now in a sticky, decomposed film over the pathway; and farther back, a decrepit chicken coop was filled with bristling dandelions, the wire chewed open, look-ing like a monument to some last stand between birds and foxes.

The first day rushed along with the calm diligence of Colette's chores. She gathered wildflowers for a wine bottle vase; cooked a zuc-chini frittata, which burned on the bottom but remained edible at its higher elevations; she hung up and cudgeled the dust from a faded Turkish rug; and she washed their shirts and underwear in a sink of cop-pery water, hanging them on the restrung laundry lines. Pierrick said that she had transformed overnight into a housewife; she replied that she had always done all the housework as a child, it was a form of prayer. Trailing smoke, Pierrick followed her all afternoon, refilling her glass.

"And if you're the housewife, who will the husband be?" asked Pierrick.

"Someone who doesn't ask a lot of questions," she said.

Kevin watched her legs move under the light dress. As she twisted to find her glass of wine, he was drawn to the curve of her waist and her dancelike movements. He hadn't allowed himself to feel this way in a long time, and now that he did, anxiety attended each trace of longing. She blew a strand of hair from her face with a pouting lower lip, and Kevin recognized the gesture so vividly from her younger days that it made him nervous.

The light faded and they heard baying dogs on a distant farm, so riled that Colette worried they smelled her unfamiliar cooking. To drown the noise, Pierrick found a monophonic radio in a drawer, and he left it on a crackling talk show filled with cascades of applause and static. Colette and Kevin passed a few hours playing hands of rummy. She reacted to every rustle and wince he made on the couch, checking his bandages, her fingers smelling of caramelized onions. Now that he couldn't talk, she seemed desperate to understand whatever he might say. The mere act of reading his eyes meant they stared at each other and waited, taking deep breaths, and wondering. Kevin thought that she was falling in love with her own crude signature on his face.

After the card game, they walked outside to see a broken shard of the moon. Kevin paced on the gravel, his knees still throbbing, wrapped in his blanket, while Colette stretched against the hood of the car. She was clowning for him. She made facetious pliés, a tipsy pirouette, hair swung loose, and then circled him with *pas de course*. She grabbed him around the waist and they moved into a tentative waltz together, hands interlaced and upright. But he winced at a stab of pain in his side, and she quickly helped him upright.

"Oh, I'm sorry—honey. You must have some broken ribs."

The house was a flickering lantern against purple sky, a filament of smoke trickling up from the chimney. They noticed Pierrick moving through the bedroom with a lantern, searching for something in his bag. He began to dial the phone. Kevin loped into the house, grabbed the phone, and hung it up. Pierrick's hands fluttering in exasperation, he shouted, "I was only calling a close friend!"

Kevin tried to say that he didn't trust Pierrick's friends, and Colette needed to translate a portion of his garbled sentence. It was amazing to Kevin how much she could suddenly intuit his thoughts.

"*You* are my friends," said Pierrick. "So you don't trust yourselves then."

"He's right, Pierrick. We just need another day or two so Kevin can get his strength back—but if you start calling everywhere, we'll have Interpol down here within an hour."

Kevin rushed to a pad and began scrawling his response in dull pencil. Colette took the note and said, "Oh, sweetie, your handwriting is as bad as your voice."

For the next hour Pierrick mumbled to himself and pretended to use the phone, placing mock calls through an imaginary operator, to presidents, kings, and commissars, until he was appeased in the kitchen by a new tidbit of conversation about his childhood. Kevin couldn't stop thinking that something was wrong with Pierrick's behavior, something *too* cavalier for a lifelong thief. He was a gossip, certainly—but he wasn't foolish enough to spread rumors around the remaining thieves and mobsters in the city. So Kevin slipped into Pierrick's room and rifled through his things. While Pierrick and Colette spoke in French in the kitchen, Kevin picked the lock on his suitcase, and filched a heavy day planner filled with scraps of paper.

With the lantern, Kevin walked out the back door, heading to behind the chicken coop where he sat in the wet grass and shined the light over the book. Page upon page of ordinary, alphabetized names—for a while it appeared to be nothing more than an ambitious social document. But soon he came across some alarming notes.

He saw Irina's initials and address in a corner; he saw the name of Jirka's restaurant in a long list of other businesses. A whole series of numbers followed, on first impression looking like a cryptogram; but Kevin thought they might be the numbers of accounts and safety deposit boxes. Had he followed Irina from her apartment each day? The details multiplied. There were lists of banks and money changers, names underlined, *sparbuchen* accounts and a series of dates. On another page he had sketched a tree of connections, Irina's initials in the center sprouting off other names that Kevin didn't recognize: Algerians, French, Russians, and a spattering of question marks throughout. It was a flow-chart of money-laundering schemes and document trails. An ache ran through Kevin's bones. He walked back through the house, returned the book to its place, and fell into the couch. Colette told him he was ghastly pale.

He scrawled with a pencil: "You + me—talk. Important!"

She looked at him with lowered, serious eyes, and said, "You'll be able to talk a little better every day. Wait until you heal a bit more. Then tell me everything you've ever wanted to say."

Kevin stayed awake all night. The moon fell low enough to shine under the eaves and project a cross of shadows from the window sash onto the far wall. For an hour Kevin was so tense he might have attacked Pierrick if he had seen him wander to the bathroom, but he paced to clear his mind.

Early that morning, just as the sun was coming over the lumpy horizon and roosters were crowing on a nearby farm, Kevin and Colette went for a walk along the road. His knees still ached, his lungs still burned, but she was patient and waited for him to catch his breath. She checked the gauze: he was bleeding a little, but it was clean. Kevin touched her face and thumbed the fledgling hair along her temple as she looked up at him with yielding uncertainty. They had made it a mile or so from the house along a road beside stone walls and budding trees. They stepped onto the damp grass as a black car gusted past them, and then they rested on a pile of bricks beside a field of corrugated dirt.

"Kevin, I can't do this anymore," she said. "I just looked at you that night, and maybe it was how afraid I was, or maybe I was just imagin-ing—" When she paused, he grabbed her hand and put his fingers to her lips. She seemed to like this overblown gesture, though he needed it now simply to communicate.

Feeling the movement in his stitches, he said, "Purrick. 'S'an'in-whormant.'"

"Wait, slow down," she said. "I can sort of understand you. Does it hurt to open your mouth all the way?"

He nodded, then closed his eyes and concentrated, ignoring the pulling feel in his cheek. "He's a rat." His *r* sounded throaty and remark-ably French without full movement of his lips. "He ratted 'em out." He pointed back to the direction of the house, where a cloud of lit dust still swirled from the passing car.

He made a series of clear gestures to explain: he unlocked a deposit box, he signed a check in the air, he dialed a phone, and made the sound of a siren, and for a sinking moment he thought that he was communicating like Melody.

"Okay, let's just be calm," she said. "Did you see something, or is this just a hunch?"

Kevin pantomimed scribbling into a book.

"You saw his notes? Oh God. And you don't have any doubts?"

Kevin shook his head. The crows were moving in new patterns in the distance, flocking up toward a path of trees along the creek.

"Oh my God, Pierrick. You son of a bitch—you fucking *collaborator*. I don't believe this. Okay, okay—calm down. Let's piece this together. Why would he do it? Maybe he was trying to get out of doing some time, I guess—maybe he's been doing it for years. I never saw him actually steal anything, so maybe the cops support him. God, I'm never going to trust another human being again. Okay, okay—but the point is, he took us here, and I have to believe he's at least *trying* to protect us. Is that completely unreasonable? Maybe he gave the police a lead—but it's possible he didn't intend for us to be directly involved. Otherwise he would have had us a long time ago."

Kevin clenched his face and pointed to the damp gauze.

"Well, that's true. So he used you. You led him through like the white rabbit. A tourist in his town."

Kevin nuzzled his finger into his forehead and made an imaginary gun.

"Does that mean somebody is going to kill us? Or we're going to kill him? I'm not trying to be contrary, sweetie—I'm just trying to make sure I'm picking up the right nuances. I was never any good at charades."

Kevin lowered his eyes and glowered at her; he pointed to his chest, then at her, and made a saluting wave toward the house and Pierrick. With a somber tone she said toward the house, "What is it about me that makes everybody run to the police? All right. It's you and me, Kevin. We don't ever let our guards down again. And you're right—we go back, we get our things, we don't say a word. Steal his keys or you hot-wire the car. We'll get out of here and we'll never look back. We've still got the old documents—maybe they'll get us through some tiny little checkpoint in the Pyrenees. Do you really still trust me, Kevin, after all we've been through?"

He shook his head, but opened the top buttons of his shirt and pulled out a chain. Dangling from the end of it was the engraved ring. Her eyes dampened, but she quickly blinked them clean and replied, "Of course you still *have* it. You're a pack rat."

They took almost a half hour mounting the dirt road and descending through the farmland back toward the cottage, all the while Colette's arm around Kevin, who was wincing with each step. She went over the plan a hundred times in a frenetic whisper: "We don't say anything, we just leave. Should we disconnect the phones? Right, of course, we should disconnect the phones."

When they reached the cottage, Kevin paced slowly toward the house. Maybe it was only the sudden jolt of endorphins from the pain, but everything around him now seemed already to have the texture of a memory. When he noticed fresh tire tracks in the mud beside the gravel driveway, he knew. All around barn swallows filled the air now, a huge disseminating splash off a roof in the distance. The air was sopping with loamy earth, a tractor growled behind a smooth hill; he was noticing details with an electric clarity.

When he walked inside the cottage, past the door partially open and rocking with the wind, he smelled fetid sweetness, metallic and carnal, and his stomach and chest revolted. He covered his nose and mouth with his shirt. Flies sat on the floor and along the ridges of chairs, some of them stalled under heavy air. The rooms had the shocked clarity of a crime scene. An open door, an end table struck slantwise, a mud print from a dress shoe on the rug.

Pierrick lay on his side in the bedroom. Eyes open, mouth parted as if skewered on a thought, Pierrick looked almost ready to stand and greet him: it was amazing how intact the front of his face remained, even as the wall behind him had been sprayed with fragments, and the mattress was saturated like a cotton ball with blood, which dripped steadily onto the floor in a coagulant puddle. A lone fly crawled through the damp tendrils of his hair, skimming across a cheek to settle in the septum above his purple lips. It seemed a poor counterfeit of him. The skin was too gray, the bristly hairs on his face, growing like stubborn weeds, shaggier than ever in his life.

The hinges creaked as Colette stepped into the house. Kevin rushed back to stop her, putting his hands up and trying to lead her back outside. He was surprised that she recognized the smell of blood so immediately. When she reached the frame of the door, she covered her mouth and squeaked, her skin turning livid, her breath in pounded gasps, until she walked out of the house shaking her head and repeating, "No, no, *no*," as if it all were an argument she refused to accept.

Kevin took stock. The rooms were murals of their fingerprints. One footstep of softened mud was the only possible image to exonerate them, and it was blurring slowly in humid air. How long before the body was discovered? How long before some farmer deciphered the frantic quality of all those distant, barking dogs? There was no possible way he could clean all the flaked traces of Colette and himself from the room, so he assumed they would be suspects as well as targets, and that the best alternative was to move fast and keep moving, now and forever. He thought of his father, and knew that he was right: there wasn't any halfway in this life.

Colette sat in the center of the weeded and muddy field beside a softened groove of old plowing. She had thrown up, everything tinged violet by last night's wine, and as Kevin approached she hurried to cover it with mud. She tucked her hair behind her ears, streaking dirt onto her cheeks and ears.

She asked, "Are these the same people?"

Kevin nodded.

"You're awfully nonchalant, aren't you?"

He stood and offered her his hand. She looked back at the house, sighed, and brooded deeper into the ground, muddying her clothes. She tried to speak with an ethereal calm, but it came across as her imitation of aristocracy. "Part of me thinks he should be entitled to some kind of funeral—even if he is a rat. We're not savages. He was a very ceremonial person. I know he lied to us about practically everything, but I'd like to think he still enjoyed our *company*." She covered her face, and when she emerged again from behind cupped palms, the coloring had returned to her cheeks.

"Don't do that, Kevin. Don't just look at me like I'm crazy—I'm serious. We're the only people left to pay our respects. I'm not the kind of person to just walk away from that. He deserves something more than being left in a filthy room."

She grew suddenly angry at some cold practicality in his eyes. She stomped back to the house, and when he caught her, she was approaching the phone like the ledge of a cliff. He ripped it from her hands and tore the cord from the wall. Colette turned up her chin and spoke to him down the length of her nose, seeming to have gone insane behind a character of superior gentility. "I am not going to subject myself to some sordid plot here. If you're planning to dump the body in a creek, then count me out. I am a decent person and I intend to do things properly."

He was so angered by her false behavior that he seized her by the arm and began pulling her toward the door. Even in the midst of a scramble, Colette clawing at his arm and fist, shouting and straining to pull loose, Kevin noticed something grateful in her movements: she had taken to the fight with the quickness and drama of having expected it, perhaps even *wanted* it; and, as he manacled her wrists, while she kicked at him until he grabbed her around the waist and threw her into a bundle over his shoulder, legs writhing and hands scratching at him, he felt how much stronger she was than she was letting on, the wild power in her flanks and thighs. If she truly wanted to resist him, especially in his injured state, she could easily have done so; but there was a slightly yielding quality to her movements, as when a dancer allows herself to be lifted, and as Kevin trudged with her toward the car and she called him a thug, he nearly laughed at his sudden surge of love for her. He believed that he was freeing her from the burden of guilt, somehow, in the heart of this tangle, stuffing her into the car as she slashed fingernails and spread her legs outward onto opposite sides of the door (what an incredible ordeal trying to force a strong Midwestern woman into a Fiat), and he understood for the first time that, unlike him, unlike his father, Colette lived every day with the confused dream of somehow becoming an honest woman.

As he drove away, she recovered quickly to say, "We should leave an anonymous call, at least. Okay—from a train station. I just hate the idea of leaving him there."

Kevin glanced at her, seeing her wide, terrified eyes, then he touched her shoulder and shook it with camaraderie. She smiled bashfully, looked back out the passenger window, and replied, "How badly did I hurt you with that little tantrum?"

He put both hands over his heart, throwing his head back melodramatically, while she reached across to steady the wheel.

THIRTY-TWO

That afternoon, Colette made an anonymous call to the police from a provincial station, reciting the address in French with a phony German accent, then slipping back onto the train just as it began moving again.

Struck with sudden colds, they slept three lost days in Lourdes, near the border, over a courtyard of street minstrels. A nearby church tolled its bells, blending with the first insistent thumps of a disco in the hotel's lobby, a metronome in the floorboards that continued until dawn. They ate crackers, cheese, and antacids; they drank cheap picnic wine and a carton of orange juice. Colette seemed almost to welcome her wretched state, wandering in loose pajamas, blowing her nose like a bagpipe, moaning in bed amid the crumpled piles of tissue. She broke into tears while brushing her teeth, and when Kevin held her, the crying gave way to a fit of sneezing against his bare chest, apologizing with each emergent gasp of air.

On the third day, Kevin wrote a postcard to his father and asked her to fix his spelling.

I wanted you to know that everything has fallen apart for me out here. The Old Country isn't any picnic either. But I'm still alive, still on the move. I'm traveling with a woman you remember well. I know your blood will boil to hear it, but she's my last real friend, and probably the only thing I love in this world—except for maybe your sorry ass.

Stay tough, your son

Colette's eyes flickered around the card as she proofread it, and when she looked up, she was flushed in her cheeks. From under his collar he reeled up the chain and swung the engraved ring like a pendulum.

Her bottom lip lay caught between her teeth. "We were such kids."

He unclasped the ring and started to slip it onto her finger. Her hands shook as he did, and she began to cry with a face that looked tortured and angry. He stared into the expanding holes in her eyes, and said, in the first tense words of his returning voice, "You know everything I want, and I know everything you need, Colette. So what if we're dangling our feet in the grave? We've been through hell together—and it's nothing. Nothing we can't handle."

That night they catnapped a few restless hours clutched together in their clothes. The room smelled of coal smoke. She woke around midnight and for a long time they lay on their backs facing the water-warped map of the ceiling. She was breathing unnaturally, with shivers that curled her back and lifted her shoulders. They moved closer in slow advances, until finally they were tracing their hands over each other, in a way that seemed to Kevin like two blind people trying to decipher each other. He had imagined this moment with her so often, and although there were qualities that he had guessed correctly, he found himself most stirred by the details he had dreamed wrong. The bouts of childlike playfulness he had expected, the giggles with foreheads touching and hot blasts of air, the way she made a fuss over fishing off his socks and flinging them away; but he was more surprised by the moments of cathedral quiet, how slowly and steadily they kissed, teasing and goading, fleeing and returning; and he was amazed that she was so bashful, covering her breasts as he undressed her, forearm across like a sash until she could hide herself against him in a warm press.

There were shifts between playful and determined, chasing and quiet reunions, slowing and speeding, until a serious current overcame them, and their bodies grew tense, and they seemed to make each other hungrier. With her legs wrapped over him, feeling trapped in a closed circuit of voltage, he was wincing, unable to wait but waiting, as they rolled again and she perched upon him and leaned forward to bury him in a curtain of fallen hair. He peeked sideways to see in the mirror the beautiful tensing machinery of her back, then once again watched the quivering of closed eyes. He was startled by the way she appeared to be communing with loss and sadness, until gradually it seemed to him a breed of wisdom, a sudden sorrowful clarity at the center of anything real, which overwhelms as it passes. The body is too tender to endure it long enough. Pleasure becomes heavier than pain. The skin turns electric, protecting and imprisoning, and everything falls an increment farther away from the touch; until all that's left is a room, like a shell, quiet, where two people are sealed under a hot sheet, in a mystified pact: she sniffles, while everything for him is one layer down, underwater, past where light can reach, and once she has stopped, and he watches the faint oncoming dawn in the windows, believing her coiled body against him is consolation for the end of the world outside, he asks why she's upset; and she replies, "I just suddenly had this sinking feeling—that I wanted to go home."

THIRTY-THREE

In a windswept village deep in the mountains of northern Spain, Kevin found the local priest sleeping in a small office off the stone church of San Pedro El Viejo. It was a sweltering July afternoon, and Kevin already had sweat stains expanding across his tuxedo shirt. Like the church with its dusty stone floors and its altar of wavering candle flames, the priest seemed to be an unassuming little man. He was taken aback by Kevin's excitement and faltering Spanish. *Tengo que casarnos, mi mujer y yo*— he needed to be married in time for the six o'clock train.

The bride-to-be was already causing a sensation around the tiny village, hiring local girls and seamstresses to help put the finishing touches on an ambitious dress, which she had sewn herself during the last eight weeks of difficult and continuous travel, hiding it and laboring over it in youth hostels and cheap *hospedajes*. In cluttered marketplaces of saffron, dried peppers, and North African jewelry, she shopped for Spanish lace, pearls, and silver—never boosting even a single sequin, because she had sworn that the wedding would be the first entirely legal day of her life. The thought of this elaborate mystery dress put a knot in Kevin's stomach, but he was determined that she have her moment in this picturesque village, far from access roads and Interpol green notices.

The priest tried to find his glasses. It was summertime, the season of tourists hiking the nearby pilgrimage trail of Santiago with backpacks and sunburned knees, and he seemed accustomed to their photo ops and intrusive requests. He was undoubtedly wary of his church being used as a novelty site for a bizarre Eurailer, especially one with a gigantic incriminating scar on his cheek.

Clearing his throat, he asked if Kevin or his fiancée were Catholic.

Speaking in a hybrid of the two languages, Kevin explained that his girlfriend had been baptized Catholic in Michigan, then raised in a Lutheran foster home, and that he was a devout, practicing agnostic.

Kevin didn't catch every word of his response, but the priest appeared to ask *why* they wanted a church service if those were their beliefs.

Kevin thought about this for a long time, sweating in the hot and cluttered office. When he looked up at the priest to answer, he started crying for the first time since he'd been a boy. In English, he confessed everything. He was a pickpocket, a con man, a hacker, a phreaker, a liar, and a thug. Never in his life had he felt anything like guilt or shame, only pride in his work, a desire to improve and diversify; but he had been scared one night, nearly killed, and he had seen the death of a friend and traitor, the effect of which was to make him feel the tug of violence in acts that he had once considered sport. He could no longer pick a pocket or cut loose a fanny pack without feeling that he had nearly murdered someone; and he found it progressively harder to lie to the faces of open and well-meaning people—not because he admired or understood them, but because they seemed somehow vulnerable, fragile, easy targets for the *real* wolves out there: because he sympathized with them now—God only knew why. Maybe he had been frightened enough to feel pity for the frightened; or maybe he had been chased long enough to no longer think as a predator; or maybe, more likely, he believed for the first time that he *had* something in his own life worth protecting: "She's crazy and impossible and I'm losing my mind—but I know if I lost her somehow, there's nothing in the world that would be worth more than a trinket."

The priest nodded along at the waves of Kevin's speech, with a nervous expression. When Kevin finished, he knew that the man hadn't understood a single word. But for some reason, he took Kevin's hand in his, patted him on the fingers, and agreed to perform the ceremony.

At a quarter past four, the pews were filled with the local villagers, children giggling and play-fighting, a great buzz of expectation about the fugitive American wedding in their town. The church doors burst open in a wash of sunlight, and out of the clouds of spiraling dust, Elizabeth "Colette" Olsen walked down the aisle carrying a bouquet of orange blossoms, in a sprawling dress of ivory silk and inlaid pearls, with a fifteen-foot-long veil that ten laughing young girls carried behind her. The vows were read in Spanish, and they answered, "I will," until in a gust of spontaneous festivities, they were cheered out of town, amid the throwing of rice and improvised confetti, escorted all the way to the empty station, where on the platform the bride closed her eyes and threw her bouquet, which soared backward into the air, and landed on top of the ticket vendor's booth.

When the train arrived they settled into their compartment, Colette looking buried in a cloud of white lace, Kevin now drenched with cologne and sweat. They lowered the window and waved. Colette blew kisses to the children who ran after the train. Then, as they gathered speed past the ringing bells of the intersection, the last flags of drying laundry, out into the scrubby landscape of ranches and hills, she collapsed into her seat by the window and made a tired and pleased humming sound.

Kevin said, "We'll be legends in that town."

Her face was slack with relief as she stared out the window, sunlight and shadows passing over her like a shifting spotlight. Her eyelids looked drowsy and Kevin hardly recognized the peaceful expression.

"When do we have to make San Sebastian?" she asked dreamily.

"Tomorrow at nine," he said. "We'll have a few hours to spare. But we're traveling under the names of . . ." He searched in his bag for the passports, worrying suddenly that he'd lost them in the rush.

"How did you get that priest to agree? That must be the biggest trick you've ever pulled off in your life. And our real names too."

He felt the passports down among his clothes and exhaled deeply. "It's a miracle."

Three hours later, she had fallen asleep with her head in his lap. The sun vanished and the moon passed with them through a chain of interlaced lakes. He stroked her hair, stooped over and guarded her like a treasure. Through a village, the train nearly grazed house fronts, squares of light falling away slowly enough to see the blinks of home interiors, snapshots of a hundred lives, the flashing of tables and chairs, vases and windowpanes, old women pulling curtains shut, gardens and doormats, brick pathways; then past bells and waiting farm trucks, sidewalk trees slowing, until with an earful of depressed air another train punctured the space beside them, and everything became a wild montage of windows, a flicker of silhouettes. Colette jolted wide awake and blinked up at him as if he were a floating ghost.

"What is it?" she asked. "We're in trouble."

"No, no," he said. "Not yet."

THE THURSDAY
NIGHT SHIFT

Whatever Melody had coated her fortune cookies with—Seconal, tria-zolam—Daniels began acting drunk by around seven-thirty that night, slurring his words during a bitter harangue about how much his father hated him. At a little after eight o'clock, he climbed onto the neighboring bed, yelled at the television, and nodded off to sleep. Whoever had masterminded this escape, they had picked a potent chemical, for while Daniels snored, roseate patches developed on his cheeks.

Less than ten minutes passed before an orderly came into his room, head down, carrying a bedpan. After three strides he knew it was Colette. Out of the bedpan she unfolded a jumpsuit that had been tightly packed, and she laid it out across Kevin's legs. It looked to be the uniform for a medical-supplies courier.

"The shifts are changing right now," she whispered, as she began disconnecting the IVs from his wrist, pulling back the sheets. "Listen close, honey, because we're behind schedule. Get in this uniform. Out in the hall—turn right, go about twenty steps and pick up the clipboard and the yellow ice cooler marked 'Live Organs.' You're delivering a heart for a transplant. You're going to have about thirty seconds to get downstairs, down to the lobby. Go to the front security desk, and say there must have been a mistake. That's it."

"I don't understand."

"*Trust* me."

"Why should I?"

"Because I'm here."

"Colette, I don't even know if I can walk."

"You can do it. I found your father, by the way. I've never seen him so genuinely *beside himself*—so I spared his miserable life. You go where the security guard tells you and we'll be there."

As she was leaving and he was climbing painstakingly off his bed, he called to her, "Colette? It's not really somebody's heart in that package, is it?"

"No, sweetie. It's nobody's real heart." Then she slapped her hands melodramatically across her chest and, through fake tears, said, "Except *mine*."

BOOK FIVE **THE FINAL SCORE**

1988

THIRTY-FOUR

At the border with Canada and the port of White Horse, Montana, in a cramped Toyota Cressida with the windshield wipers swinging at a downpour of cold rain, Kevin and Colette gathered their documents and whispered their plans. A horse trailer idled ahead of them, taillights flaring. "We'll be fine," said Kevin. "He's not even going to come out of the booth. Look. There's probably a meth lab in that trailer."

When they pulled ahead, the customs agent looked at their Wyoming licenses—easier to counterfeit because they still lacked holograms—and came out of his booth in a green poncho, shining a flashlight over their staged display of backpacks, camping gear, and crumpled-up maps. Colette placed her hands against the dashboard, as if preparing for a collision, and Kevin reached forward and touched her fingers. She relaxed, held his hand; they began a conversation, first as a mere diversion, about a real moment when Kevin was terrified by a hissing raccoon in a rustic motor lodge bathroom. Like every performance now in front of cops, customs officials, or suspicious onlookers, it became an exercise in positive energy. She rested her head against him and they proclaimed their happiness; and Kevin only lamented that they never quite felt the same purity, the same staunchly unwavering optimism when they were safely alone.

The customs agent waved them through, and they were in good spirits, passing under the black clouds, searching through the gravelly radio stations. "We're home. We should get a bottle of champagne," said Colette. "If they have one in this neck of the woods."

They found a desolate roadside motel between a billboard covered with snowmobiles and a neon sign that advertised HBO, partially obscured by pine needles. They were still high from their successful border crossing, and they made love on top of the motel comforters, lounging for a while afterward in the darkness, listening to truck tires slice past in the rain. When Colette took a shower, Kevin went out to find groceries—and possibly champagne—feeling that inevitable downshift in mood as their real situation became unavoidable. She would be genuinely upset that he couldn't find any goddamn champagne, and he would be demoralized by the state of his career. They were down to a few hundred dollars.

Certainly, there was a practical reason why they had done so little work during their long meander across Canada: their goal was to re-enter the States, and this required as little noise as possible. They had wanted to hide, and they learned to scurry from town to town as unnoticeably as mice. But their long hiatus was also the result of Colette's fairy-tale idea of marriage, what Kevin considered her own specific form of lunacy. She believed that matrimony itself was purifying, and that any descent back into criminal activity would jeopardize all other aspects of their life together. Kevin found it difficult to go "cold turkey," but it was as if one binding contract made it impossible for Colette to think illegally. She would pout and cry and harangue Kevin if he so much as devised a simple lottery scam.

She could startle him with the depth and intensity of her gratitude if he preserved this illusion; so his entire life became dedicated to the idea of "going clean," as if it were something far more magical than the ditch-digging or lumber-stacking jobs he was likely to find. Of course, the problem was that a talented con woman had a certain standard of living. There were only so many weekly-rate motel rooms she could tolerate before they needed the Hilton in Vancouver. Where was the money supposed to come from? Colette didn't seem to care. In her mind, she was an honest woman now, and her husband was obligated to devise a working scheme, both legal and lucrative; and when he criticized this, she responded with her own catalog of perfectly reasonable problems—her inability to find a job in retail because they were always on the move, his obsessive and imprisoning jealousy of her whenever she went out to pound the pavement—until Kevin believed that marriage was that rare scam in which both sides considered themselves the easy mark.

In a mini-mart a few hundred yards down the slick highway, Kevin needed to hollow out a bag of dog food to buy groceries. When the bleary-eyed clerk rang up the bag, Kevin asked him about the AVS machine for swiping credit cards, claiming that he was starting his own company. The man had no idea beyond the basics, but Kevin was only trying to steal the shop's merchant ID numbers, which he found on the underside of the machine, a different sequence for each credit card.

Kevin had been working underground, away from Colette, quietly, on a project that he believed might eventually lead to one huge payoff. In computer rooms and universities, he had at last uncovered the algorithms of several issuing banks and credit cards, meaning that he could create "well-formed" account numbers that would show up as valid to any authorization system. Leaving with his dog food bag, he called an 800 number from a pay phone and, using the shop's merchant ID, verified a few of his fictional numbers. They would work, but the process was cumbersome: ordering goods via the phone or by mail, setting up single mail drops or delivering to motel rooms, fencing the merchandise and beginning again—it would never make a man rich. As Kevin stood there in the phone booth with the raindrops splashing all around him, he dropped his head against the glass.

Two years ago he had believed, like a religion, that if he ever made a credit card generator, he could sell it for a million dollars. A week ago, on a hacker BBS he'd seen hundreds of them for sale. Credit card numbers were bought and sold as cheaply as a dollar. With the improvement of modems, he saw no way that credit cards could even be in use much into the '90s. He understood his father's exhaustion; he understood the fortitude and inviolate hopefulness needed from a working con man who must adapt, year by year, to technology and new waves of younger and more resourceful thieves. The hustler's life span is shorter than a mosquito's. Train robbers controlled the landscape only until there were manganese vaults, then safecrackers inherited the cities. His father had grown up in an era of check forgers, advancing into white plastic, when magstripes and holograms on cards suddenly gave rise to identity theft. AT&T crumbled and the phreaker rose in the aftermath; the modem appeared and the hacker emerged; but in the end, no matter how many scavengers fought and rooted out their predecessors, nothing truly changed. The grift was a blue-collar endeavor, day by day. There was never enough money to retire, hardly enough to catch your breath, maybe, in the best times, just barely enough to dream.

Kevin was so lost in thought that he was only startled to the present because a Mack truck shined its headlights in his face as it went splashing past him. He noticed that the phone was an Echotel from the early '80s. Overwhelmed with such nostalgia that a lump formed in his throat, he broke into the front panel and used an old blue-boxing trick to make a long-distance call. "I'm looking for prisoner number 10376-106, please."

Jerry had made parole nine months earlier, and his most recent halfway house now had him listed at an address in Duarte, California. Kevin was thrilled that his father had received no additional time. He took down the number, then—worrying about a passing car—reassembled the phone and returned to the room.

Colette lay on the bed in satin panties and a camisole, watching a movie filled with hysterical screaming. When Kevin began taking apart the phone, she said, "I don't want to come all this way and get arrested by phone cops the second we get into the country."

"Right," said Kevin. "You'd rather pay fifty dollars for a call. Okay."

He stretched the cord as far as it would go, then sat in the hall with the door partially open. The corridor was long and gloomy and there didn't seem to be anyone else in the motel. The phone rang and then his father answered, his voice coming through crackles and the murmured conversation of a crossed line.

"You little bastard, I've been looking everywhere for you. How the fuck are you? Did they catch you finally?"

"No, I'm in a little dive in Montana. You got my letter, right?"

"Oh, Jesus. Sure. Are you two still together?"

"Yeah, we're still together. What is that supposed to mean?"

"Hey, don't jump all over me. Gut reaction. I was surprised, that's all. I figured it must have been—well, anyway, congratulations. What do you know? Two married men. We ought to get together and have some kind of . . . barbecue or something."

Kevin smelled a sharp chemical, and when he looked through the crease in the door, he saw that Colette, still on the bed, had begun painting her toenails. He lowered his voice and asked, "Are you still working, Dad?"

"Hold on a second." After a few moments of rustling, opening doors, and different textures of ambient noise, Jerry said, "Sorry. I got to be careful around the little missus nowadays. We can talk now."

"I'm going flat broke up here, Dad."

"Well, I can't believe you *married* her, dummy. She must have tied your dick up like a fucking boat knot. Of course, you're broke—"

"Don't do this, okay? I don't need you to judge me—she's a different person now."

"I always suspected something. I think she planted some kind of homing device in your ass."

"If you're not going to talk to me, I'm going to hang up. This is costing about ten dollars a minute. I just wanted to find you and ask if you're doing any work."

"Why aren't you making any money? She's the most talented bitch in the country."

Kevin breathed out through his teeth, then spoke slowly, "She's tired. She wants out. I don't blame her, Dad—she's been working hard since she was sixteen, and she's worn out. We're all like thoroughbreds, and you don't have that many years on the track. I know that now. You win a few races, and then it's the glue factory."

"Unless you get put out to stud."

"She wants a regular life, whatever the fuck that is. I want to know if there's some trick to it."

"So you called *me*?"

"I figured you must have some idea. You must have thought about how to call it quits."

Jerry started laughing on the other end. "Let me tell you something, Kev. You want out of the game—you got two simple choices. First choice. You drop everything right where you are, you walk up to some foreman, say, 'Please, sir, can I pound some nails for you,' and you ride off in the back of his truck. He'll pay you absolutely nothing, and you'll look at him and think he's lower and dirtier than the worst mugger. You'll live on a can of corn chowder and six beers a day, and if you're lucky, you'll find something decent on TV before you fall asleep. You'll scrap and save and someday you'll find a better job. If you're lucky, the feds won't ever catch up to you. The statute of limitations will run out, and you'll be your own man. You'll have a nice little exhausting life and a woman who's pissed because she can't have anything nice, and maybe—if she's tougher than I think she is—she'll stick around and put on weight and have a couple of screaming kids. You'll love them and you'll do your best, and you'll feel like crying every night at how much they have to go without—and then one day, when they've grown up and decided they hate you, and your wife won't talk to you anymore, and you're on some kind of disability because some day laborer dropped a fucking bathtub on your foot—you'll die. Probably something to do with the liver."

"What's the other choice?"

"I don't want to diminish it, kid. Because if there's a heaven, I sure hope it's for those fucking people. The better man goes that way. Those are the fucking heroes, the goddamn philanthropists. Those people have got my undying admiration, and luckily they don't have credit cards—"

"Dad? Shut up. What's the other choice?"

"Buy your way out. Grand style. Get your ass down here and go to work for me. I can use you. I got something huge and it's watertight. You'll make a *killing* and never look back."

THIRTY-FIVE

A featureless sky, miles of unbroken fences and rolling sheep ranches, high valleys skirted with snow-capped mountains, they headed south through Idaho and Utah, gradually wending their way to St. George, where—after a day of arguing about Jerry and their future—they scraped together the last of the money for a motel room that overlooked a plush green golf course carved into the barren desert. He picked up the discussion with Colette while she was in the shower, then trailed her across the room as she dried herself and shook water from her ears. Each logical approach to the problem was stymied by Colette's ambivalence about a reunion with Jerry. Kevin believed the most sensible arrangement would be for him to visit his father alone; but she was insulted by this solution, and accused him of being ashamed of her. When he countered by offering that she join him, she refused, explaining that Jerry obviously hated her far too much. Kevin sensed that there was no winning this argument, so he focused on the idea of a final scam.

"I figure to start a good respectable life, you need something in the high five figures, minimum."

"Kevin, don't be ridiculous," she said, climbing into a T-shirt. "If your father is trying to get you involved in some ludicrous scheme, I guarantee you it's a trick. I bet he just wants to get me back."

"Get you back?"

She sat on the bed and began reeling up her jeans. "I mean, in the sense of revenge. Not the other sense."

Neither sense sat well with Kevin, and during the final leg of the drive through Nevada and the Mojave Desert, his jaw ached from tension and his fingers hurt from gripping the wheel. An hour outside Barstow, while she was lying back in the reclined shotgun seat, her arms crossed tightly over her chest, her eyes closed, Colette said, as if at the climax of a long, paranoid meditation, "Whatever happens with this, Kevin, just remember we had a wonderful year."

Jerry had rented a bungalow outside Los Angeles, just below the smog-obscured contours of the San Gabriel Mountains.

When Kevin and Colette first arrived that warm winter night, Melody greeted them at the door. Seeing her again was dreamlike. She appeared to have aged on an accelerated timeline, a sweet shrunken-apple quality to her cheeks and her complexion now the dingy color of cigarette smoke. Her mouth had wrinkled around capped teeth, shiny and improbably white; and her carrot-colored hair was chopped into a little girl's design, bangs framing an old face to create an effect of cheerful dementia.

Jerry was out buying groceries for a barbecue, and Melody led them into the front room. She gave Colette an emphatic Parisian kiss, then hugged Kevin, whose arms remained listless beneath the tight squeeze. They sat in an arrangement of stained white chairs around a bowl of bright orange tortilla chips, and she talked with a cult member's voice about all of the great progress Jerry had made since his release. She seemed to have no suspicions whatsoever about his ongoing scams and no inkling of Colette's place in the family history. Instead she talked about how Jerry was now attending church with her on Sundays, reading the New Testament, and beginning to make his own peace with God. Kevin felt the strain of performing for a mark; but Colette appeared charmed by the strange woman, as if she were a kitsch souvenir from Jerry's travels, part trucker's T-shirt, part Gideon's Bible. When Melody began describing her upcoming expansion of the party favor company, branching out from piñatas to gag fortune cookies, Colette said she was happy to meet a real entrepreneur.

"I just think fortune cookies are a big waste right now," said Melody. "I mean, that's space that could go to use, something that *everyone* reads. But they're all hogwash. It's because there just isn't enough incentive to say anything meaningful. So I came up with this idea to cross the cookie with a jigsaw puzzle. You take a bigger message, and you cut it up and put the pieces into a whole set of cookies. That way everybody gets involved."

"I think it's a wonderful idea," said Colette. "If you had a big enough dinner party, you could put a whole novel in there."

They sat together in the hot, close room, crunching chips and nodding politely, while Kevin thought that this harebrained business with the cookies must have been Jerry's reason for staying with her, some kind of front or money laundering scheme. Melody took Colette on a tour of the bungalow's four small rooms, while Kevin said he was happy in his chair. In the kitchen Melody claimed, "It'll do for now—though it's not quite ready to mass-produce."

Jerry arrived at the front door with a bag full of clanking beer bottles, cursing the torn toe band on his foam rubber sandals. Now with a beard, mostly white, and long slate-colored hair, a tanned, leathery texture to his face, he looked as if he had been lost at sea for several years. Kevin said, "What are you, some kind of wise man now?"

"Hey—holy shit. Look at you." He put down his groceries and they shared a brief hug, rapidly patting each other's backs. "Where'd you get the beauty mark?"

"France."

"Ooh la la. Melody give you the grand tour yet?"

"It's going on right now."

"Great. Let's avoid that. I'll get the grill started—come outside and we'll talk business."

"Dad? You want to say hi to—you know—to my wife?"

"Oh, Jesus Christ. Do I have to?"

Colette came to the threshold between rooms and tilted against the doorjamb. Although Kevin had visualized this reunion during recent restless nights, always assuming that the future would outshine the past, that a grudging forgiveness was possible and that uncomfortable memories could be stowed away, the moment he saw the real and deep antagonism on their faces, he marveled at his own powers of denial, and realized with certainty that he had just destroyed an entire volume of illusions. Jerry and Colette stared each other down like immovable foes. There was a fleeting hint of respect in Jerry's slanted mouth, and, in Colette's calmly blinking eyes, the resurfacing determination of a prodigal student.

"Does everybody know everybody?" asked Melody.

"It's nice to meet you, sir," said Colette. "I've heard a lot about you."

She put out her hand, and Jerry frowned at it like a wad of cash being flashed in broad daylight. Then he smiled a wide phony smile and, clasping her hand in his, replied, "Welcome to the *family*. Such as it is."

A few minutes later Kevin found Jerry out on the driveway furiously squirting gasoline onto the barbecue coals. He was mumbling to himself, and when he saw Kevin approaching in the darkness, he stood up straight and lit a match. The fire spread quickly across the pile, and they both stepped back as the flames rose and twisted and shed sparks precariously close to a row of dusty cypress trees. Kevin saw the silhouette of a rat crawling along a phone wire from the house.

"I know everything is complicated, Dad."

"Hey, if you can live with it—not my problem. I will tell you something though." He gestured the neck of his beer at the kitchen window. "She's the same woman. She's going to walk off with every cent."

"Dad, you said two words to each other. How do you know?"

"I got eyes. She's using you. That's just my opinion, there's no law that says you have to listen to me."

"How could she be *using* me? I don't have anything."

"Of course, there's probably no law that says you're really married either. That's Europe—they don't honor that shit over here."

"I've been dead broke for over a year, Dad. If she was going to scam somebody, there's a hell of a lot better catches than me."

"She knew. No, no, no—she knew you'd come across a big score like this sooner or later. I'm just looking out for you, Kev. But forget me. I'm just your father, I'm just your old man. What the fuck do I know about anything? Sooner or later, you'll see what I mean."

Jerry paced over to an ice cooler by the garage, triggering a motion-sensitive light. He opened another beer and handed it to Kevin.

"Dad—about this big score. I don't mean to sound skeptical, but—"

"Yeah, yeah, yeah, what am I doing in this dump? That just shows your ignorance right there. I got to keep everything quiet, man. Everything. I got my own marital situation going on in there and she's got Jesus ganging up on me now. I'm telling you, you put enough cocaine in a decent woman's nose and she turns into a freaking Jehovah's Witness. You should see all the ex-crackheads wandering around this neighborhood, handing out literature."

"Melody's going to put it all in fortune cookies."

As the women moved into the lighted kitchen, Jerry and Kevin watched the quiet scene: Melody was opening a bottle of wine, then elicited Colette's help when the cork broke in half. Jerry drew a last hard swig from his beer, then he whispered for Kevin to follow him into the garage.

When he turned on a fluorescent light, something crawled away in the far corner, hiding behind a row of water heaters and stacks of cedar paneling. Jerry explained that he was turning this garage into a sauna, but he said it in an exaggerated handyman's voice that seemed designed to fool his wife. "Anyway, she'll never come in here. We got a little rat problem, and she's got some kind of phobia about them." He held his empty beer with just his finger stuck into the opening. "You need to pay attention, Kev. This job *demands* your expertise." He scanned the dark opening of the garage, the waning fire and the catching coals, and he continued, "And you know what, somebody else is going to want in on this too."

Kevin groaned and said, "No, Dad. She doesn't want in on anything."

"When she hears it, yes, she will. You might as well explain it to her. She's going to get her hands on your share one way or the other."

"She doesn't want to do it anymore."

"If you say so."

The tired wrinkles around his eyes, the curling wavelets of gray hair, there was something mythical about Jerry now, and his anger seemed less like a mood than a permanent feature. Kevin wondered if he had always been like this in some subtler way, if he had always plotted his heists with the same wrathful intensity.

Kevin asked, "Is there some reason you *want* her to be in on this, Dad?"

"She could be helpful. She's good at reading people, always has been. Shit, I'd say she's practically a genius at that. Yeah, I'd like her on the team. I need the talent. Tell her we don't have to look at each other, we don't have to say a thing. But I need you, I need her. And this is business now. Let's try to grow up and be professional for once in our fucking lives."

"All right, Dad. Whatever the hell you've got going here, I'll pass it on."

Three hours later, Kevin and Colette lay together on Melody's foldout couch bed with painful springs beneath them. With their faces just a few inches apart, Kevin told her everything he had heard from his father. She listened, as if to a bedtime story, and he noticed how the prolonged whisper began to weaken his voice.

He summarized Jerry's time in prison, when after a brutal year in Lompoc, he was transferred to a minimum-security facility outside Baker, California, which he described as a "rough playground" filled with an amusing combination of armed robbers and terrified embezzlers. Jerry was a tough old man in that joint, and he sold protection to some of the "waterheads," one of whom was a white-collar crook named, for the sake of convenience, Herb.

"Was that his real name?" whispered Colette.

"I don't think so."

Herb had once worked inside one of the country's largest TRWs—Equifax—where he was caught copying credit reports and selling them for forty dollars apiece to a gang of carders. What distinguished Herb from other corrupt low-level frauds was his incredible sense of loyalty. Throughout the time he was leaking sensitive information, he had been working with a partner—call him Steve—whom he had never mentioned during the arrest or trial.

"Did your father come up with these aliases?"

"Right."

Normally white-collar criminals panic at the first show of a badge, turning in everyone they've ever known; but Herb earned Jerry's respect with this show of fortitude, and the two developed a strong friendship.

A year passed and apparently the problems seemed resolved at Equifax. When Jerry was released on parole that spring, Herb repaid him for the protection and friendship by putting him in touch with Steve.

Steve was a family man. He had a wife and three insatiable daughters and he sold the credit reports with the abject bitterness of a man who would never be able to satisfy their needs. Undaunted by his friend's arrest a year earlier, he began selling reports at the same price.

But Jerry had come out of prison feeling his age. A few years is enough to give an ex-con a sense of stepping outside and into the future. An entire new generation of con men had arisen. Jerry no longer had the energy to cultivate virgin credit and fence hot commodities; so he began peddling the stolen reports to his contacts around the West Coast.

Jerry was making an adequate return, selling thousands at a 50 percent profit; but he considered the work a temporary job while he fulfilled his parole obligations on a construction crew. His contacts grew, however, and one day he was introduced to a group of young thieves, in their twenties, he guessed, Colette's age, maybe even Kevin's age. They were techies. Hackers. Computer geeks. Jerry had never done business with the new breed of hustlers, and he thoroughly disliked them all. He foresaw a world in which the con man was replaced entirely by a robot. He dreamed of computers robbing other computers. He saw a lifetime of firm handshakes and phony smiles go down the tubes.

"What did they do?" asked Colette, smiling and wide-eyed at the bedtime tale.

"They wrote a very sophisticated computer program," Kevin whispered, his voice now hoarse. "It's impressive but—even to me—it definitely takes the fun out of the game. Sort of like hunting deer with automatic weapons."

The program was able to run through thousands of stolen credit card numbers in under an hour, using rotating merchant codes to charge a revolving $49 fee to every account. The cash was continually funneled into different bank accounts, removed, and used to purchase larger lists of stolen numbers. The mysterious charge on the credit card bill would appear either as a "telecommunications surcharge" or "an installation fee," and—to the credit card companies—would appear to be from a valid business.

"The reason it's even more disgusting," whispered Colette, "is that they're charging forty-nine."

"Right. Credit Card Fraud Act. Anything under fifty the cardholder has to pay. I think the basic idea is that the credit card companies won't pursue them as aggressively if they're not actually getting ripped off. I mean, there's so much big fraud, why waste resources chasing down forty bucks here and there."

"It's nasty though," said Colette, and her eyes shone in a pass of headlights turning through the room.

"It's exactly like a scam my dad used to run when I was a kid. But he'd set up real-looking stores to fool the investigators, and they'd use numbers they'd actually swindled themselves. This has a computer doing it at about a thousand times the rate. And there's no real store, but a bunch of phony services. They keep the program circulating, and over a few weeks it racks up hundreds of thousands of dollars."

Despite his growing rancor, Jerry had continued selling the information to them, noticing that the capacity of the program seemed to grow exponentially. "Like a woman's expectations."

"Did he actually *say that*?"

"He's not a happy man."

The three hackers cashed out every month, and they had accumulated a fortune. After a short hiatus, in which Jerry assumed they had been arrested, they returned suddenly to discuss a massive deal. They liked Jerry; they trusted him; they treated him like a harmless relic of a bygone age. Boasting that they couldn't feed in the numbers quickly enough, they bought him drinks and patted his shoulders and apologized for confusing his feeble mind. Even when 20 percent of the fraudulent transactions were caught, the kids seemed impervious. They must have migrated from basement to basement, through college computer labs and public networks. They were the mice in a sprawling system. But they were ready to make a splash: they wanted fifty thousand credit reports at a discount of twenty apiece.

Jerry talked them up to thirty.

"One point five mil," whispered Colette.

There was one problem: Steve and his wife and insatiable daughters were gone. One morning he had packed up the station wagon and left town, leaving an empty house on the market and a new internal investigation at Equifax.

"But the kids never knew anything about him," she whispered.

"Exactly. And Dad wants to sell them a briefcase full of garbage."

"Can we forge fifty thousand credit reports?"

"If we work around the clock, get the same computers, the same paper, the same everything—sure. They're easier than passports or cards or birth certificates."

"But these kids must check credit card numbers before they make the buy."

"Of course," Kevin whispered, running his hand along her side under the covers. "But I've got a formula. The checksum algorithm. I can make 'well-formed' numbers that will show up as valid on their verification software."

"All that stuff you've been doing," she said, deflecting his kiss. "You can do it now?"

"Right," he whispered and sank closer to her, burying his face along-side her neck.

"But what if they call VeriFone, or some other 800 number to check?"

With his voice buried between kisses, he explained, "We'll reroute the phones."

"A mobile phone," she said breathlessly as his hands roamed up under her T-shirt.

"Then we'll get a signal jammer. They're not much different than fuzz busters."

She tilted her head back and in the rustling of sheets breathed slowly and heavily through her nose. "All the technology," she whispered. "It's window dressing. It's just an old-fashioned robbery."

He traversed down the warm pocket of covers, uncovering the hot skin beneath her clothes. "That's right," he whispered.

"Shhh, Kevin—they might be listening. Not *here*, honey. It's too weird."

He was kissing around her navel, folding down the band of her sweatpants, and he mumbled, "I said you wouldn't be interested. It's just a way for us to score enough cash to get out of the whole game safely."

"Kevin? I need to know something and I don't want you doing that while I ask you."

He slid back up and faced her in the dimness of the room.

She asked, "Did your father *ask* to have me included in this?"

"Yes," said Kevin.

She clicked her tongue, and said to the ceiling, "All right then. I'm in."

THIRTY-SIX

Among the water heaters, rusted tools, and ice coolers, Jerry set up a makeshift office space in his garage. The printer scraped continuously for days off an Eagle computer with a screen that wavered whenever the main house received a phone call. Jerry, Kevin, and Colette lived on coffee and peanut butter sandwiches, which Melody left on a platter in the driveway, too afraid to approach the vermin-infested office. She complimented Jerry's new show of initiative, believing some fatuous story that he was starting a company that would repair and install used water heaters.

The three cautious partners worked late into the night. Past four in the morning, from the garage, Kevin watched Colette's cigarette flaring and fading across the dark yard. They had all fallen off the nicotine wagon, smoking like prisoners. When Kevin saw another orange light move toward her, like the beacon of a passing ship, he rushed out into the darkness to make sure she didn't have time to talk, fight, or plan anything with Jerry.

By the end of the third night forging reports for an entire fictional population, they were ragged and paranoid, hypnotized by the steady whir of the printer, light-headed from the smell of toner and copier exhaust. They drank cold coffee and watched the sun rise through phone wires and palm trees. Dogs bellowed, sprinklers bloomed on the empty lawns, a paperboy bombed the doorsteps. They each stood on the driveway with thinned lips and clenched fists.

"My favorite hour," said Jerry.

At fourteen thousand reports and counting, Jerry introduced the fourth member of the team. His name was Lenny Hutsinger, an old associate, and apparently Colette had known him during her worst months as a runaway in Los Angeles. He was a big, awkward man with a long ponytail and shaggy sideburns, whose sweaty T-shirts smelled like day-old pot smoke and who seemed, from his languid demeanor, to be in a constant mesmerized state.

For the most part, the past few days had been businesslike and uneventful, but something in the loaded silence between his father and Colette had made Kevin too vigilant to tolerate this new addition. He complained that Hutsinger threw off the dynamic; he accused his father of plotting to hide and funnel away the cash; and he asked Colette what her relationship had been with the overgrown hippie back in the early days.

"Kevin? I don't think I've ever hidden anything about that. I had a bad six months in my life. What do you want me to do? Magically turn into your little virgin?"

"See. Don't say something like *that*, because now my head is just all over the place—"

"I find it very distressing that with all of what's going on, you would fixate on that idiot."

"What are you saying?"

"I'm saying there are bigger things to worry about here."

"Oh, I'm *worrying* about those things too. I'm just heading up the foothills first, you know—before I climb fucking Mount Everest."

The only release for the crystallizing tension of the long hours was the daily meeting in the garage. While Jerry paced in front of a blackboard, the other three sat in foldout picnic chairs, showing off their skills and ideas. They surprised each other. Years on the grift had given each of them an effective and particular style. Kevin was the technical advisor; Colette was the psychological profiler; Jerry was the grumpy tactician. "All right—if that's a problem, then how do we solve it?"

"Let's trail them and see what kind of mobile phone they're using," said Colette.

"If it's something like an NMT 900, an Ericsson," added Kevin, "then it's basically a converted police radio. You can tune a scanner to the frequency and you've just tapped the phone."

"His Ukrainian girlfriend taught him that."

"She wasn't my girlfriend—she was just—"

"All right, all right," said Jerry, holding up his hand. "But in case that doesn't cue you soon enough, we should go with the earlier plan. I'll wear a wire. It'll make it seem more like a bust. You hear my cue—run up there and play FBI. The most important thing is we get these kids to shit their pants. It only needs to look authentic until someone panics."

"It wouldn't be the FBI," said Kevin. "It would be the Secret Service."

"Why?"

Kevin shrugged. "The Secret Service investigates computer crimes."

"We're not killing the president."

"It's just the way it is," said Kevin. "They do a lot of financial crimes."

"You can't show up and yell 'Secret Service.' Even if it's true, it doesn't sound right."

"Well, that's just who investigates computer fraud, Dad. I didn't make the rules."

"It's fine," said Colette. "The Secret Service wear better suits anyway."

"There you go. Got to keep the little woman happy," said Jerry, prompting Colette to bat her eyelashes sarcastically.

"The point is," Jerry continued, "everything technical, all these gizmos and doodads, it's just to get that money up into the room. Once it's there, we come in with a show of force, guns blazing, and get them to lose track."

Lenny raised his hand like a listless student in traffic school.

"Yes, Leonard?"

"Are we using real bullets?"

Colette shifted in her chair and replied, "With this group here, I'm going to cast my vote *against* live ammo."

On Thursday, Jerry had a preliminary meeting with the buyers in a coffee shop on Ventura Boulevard. Kevin and Colette sat beside each other at the far end of the counter, holding hands and carrying on a staged heartfelt conversation as atmosphere.

"It's not that I'm a jealous person," said Kevin, slurping his coffee, "I just don't want there to be too many secrets."

She stared ahead at the three young marks. Two of them were pasty kids who looked uncomfortable in direct sunlight. One of the two had a long black goatee, "like Lenin," said Colette, and the other was a doughy, heavyset man in his early twenties with a distinct asthmatic shortness to his breath.

"It's the tall one that's going to be trouble," she said.

When she pointed it out, one member of the team did seem more confident and poker-faced. He was tall and gaunt with a prominent Adam's apple, and a short haircut combed flat over his long forehead.

He had a long nose and aggressive eyes and watched Jerry with far more suspicion than his teammates.

"I think what's most important in any relationship is *trust*," said Kevin. "And I'm just having some problems, you know, figuring out where you are in all of this."

"I agree completely," she said, distractedly, then lowered her voice to add, "he's from a whole different background than the other two. He might have actually done some time before."

"I want you to know that if you ever had any doubts about us, it would be better to talk about them, than, you know, to do anything drastic."

"Of course, darling. You have my heart on a platter. Look at their faces. The other two don't respect Jerry at all, but the big one is really paying attention."

"I'm going to come right out and admit something."

"Kevin, no one is listening. You can quit the routine."

"I don't think it's too late for us to change our minds about this project. We could back out. Maybe we have some marketable skills, you know."

"Shhh, hold on."

He watched only her eyes, which were narrow and focused, as if she were a cat sneaking up on a bird.

"Your father just tells jokes, and the other two think he's some harmless clown. The fat one is trying to talk the price down. That's a good sign."

"Do you remember the story of the thief and two sharpers? I read it to you once when you were sick. From *The Arabian Nights*."

"God, what has the world come to when outlaws look like these kids? They couldn't run up a flight of stairs."

"These two thieves are going to rob a traveling merchant. They make their plans, agree to divide the loot."

"It's just a video game to the fat one."

"But on the night before the robbery, both of them decide to keep everything for themselves."

"You know, I bet he's never been laid."

"So they poison each other. The merchant wakes up the next day, heads off on his way, and he never knows the difference."

Without looking at Kevin, she smiled mischievously and said, "I hear you, honey. Poison is out. But I think your father will be disappointed if we don't each have a little contingency plan."

Sunday, two days before the scam, Kevin scouted the hotel alone.

It was an art deco tower, faded pink, looking like an ancient beach-front resort now stranded inland, as if the ocean had receded to leave a tidal flat of freeways and billboards. Jerry and Kevin had explored it together several times and Kevin already hated the decor, like the coffin in a gaudy funeral. The walls were a dilapidated burgundy faded to a bloody shade. The elevators were scuffed gold. The corridors were long, dim, windowless tunnels lined with pictures of old celebrity tenants, smiling desperately, all dead or forgotten.

Kevin assumed that the heart of this game, even if for mere pride, was to escape alone with the money. He found his own routes amid the old corridors and basement tunnels. When Kevin passed the front desk, he saw a young girl glancing at him with a fidgeting smile. She was either flirting or knew something—and either way he was curious. He talked to her for a while about her job, until she said, "How did you get the scar on your cheek?" reaching out and tracing it with her fingertip.

Kevin was studying her eyes closely, and he replied, "When was she in here?"

"Who?"

"The girl. My wife. About your height. Sandy-blond hair. Talks a mile a minute."

"I don't know who you're talking about."

"Yes, you do. She may be a good liar, but you're not. What did she offer you?"

"I don't have to tell you anything."

Kevin whipped out his wallet and flashed the phony Secret Service badge, then said, "You do if you want to avoid any jail time, honey. I'm Secret Service and I'm undercover in this operation. I need to know exactly what she told you."

The girl laughed and replied, "Do you want to know what *she* told me? Or what the old man said? Because *he* said you'd be too cheap to offer me any money; and she said you'd claim you were with the Secret Service."

"Were they together or did they come to you separately?"

"She also said you'd ask that. Separately. Oh yeah. She told me to say, 'Stop worrying so much.'"

The night before the scam, Kevin and Colette lay awake on the fold-out couch. Kevin couldn't imagine what was going through her mind. She lay still, her head against his chest, and they both pretended to be sleeping. She had agreed to accompany Jerry as his backup during the exchange in the hotel room. She was a liar, she was a daredevil. She had taken his father's bait—knowingly. But Kevin believed he was a more meticulous planner than the rest of them, and if this scam tomorrow was to become a test of skills, he believed that he could dazzle them both. In the past forty-eight hours he had studied the hotel's dumb-waiters, the service and regular elevators, the switchboard, the mainte-nance room, the underground parking. He had pored over blueprints at city hall, studying the drainage and sewage tunnels dug into bedrock beneath the hotel. He had determined to handcuff Lenny to the bed to subvert any plot between him and Jerry; and, searching the hotel reservation records, he found an extra room that he believed Colette had rented in a phony name, *Justine Case*. The name was so silly that Kevin thought she must have intended him to find it.

Tuesday morning all three of them were up before dawn, sharing a pot of coffee in the dark kitchen. They drove to the hotel in silence, then set about their separate errands. Kevin found Jerry's alternate getaway car by matching it with new parking permits issued through the front desk, and he disabled it by removing the distributor cap. Whatever his father wanted—to break up a marriage, pay back an ex-fling, reassert himself as the alpha thief—he'd see the real resourcefulness of his son. Jerry also had road flares in his car, and, because they seemed like suspicious props, Kevin stole them and burrowed them in the deep interior pockets of his coat.

As he entered the stairwell and headed upstairs, Kevin smiled at the thought of so many different plans converging on this one musty old hotel. If he was the winner, if he slipped out with the cash in hand, he wouldn't wait forever—maybe just a few hours, long enough to make them agonize. He wouldn't gloat. He wouldn't vanish. He would simply ask for his due. He might even pay his father a small commission, say, 10 percent. A finder's fee. A sin tax.

THIRTY-SEVEN

Two of the three marks arrived at the hotel a little before four o'clock in the afternoon. Believing that they were checking into a random room for the exchange, they were instead diverted to a prepared suite on the tenth floor by the sympathetic young woman at the front desk. While Jerry and Kevin tested the radio transmitter in another room on the seventh floor, the warning call came from the house phone in the lobby. Colette said that it was just the first two, without the money: the heavy-set kid with the strained breathing and the bodyguard with the jagged Adam's apple.

Hutsinger was complaining that his suit pants were too short for him. He had lost his phony badge. All afternoon they had made preparations in this one cramped room, now reeking with cigarette smoke and body odor, and Hutsinger had made himself too comfortable on the bed, eating sun-melted candy bars and surfing through TV channels.

A police scanner sat on the cabinet, broadcasting a sedate recitation of street names and other crimes in progress. Jerry secured a mike over his sternum with surgical tape, covering the brambles of gray chest hair. Buttoning his shirt and adjusting his blazer, he paced in the hallway and the stairwells and repeated, "Test, test," until he began singing a Johnny Cash song.

Kevin heard mostly the rustling of clothes, like a flag in the wind, and the faint squeal of feedback. He leaned into the hallway and whispered, "Dad, keep your mouth farther away from the mike."

When Colette joined them she was flushed from running up the stairs. She began fixing herself in the bathroom mirror, and Jerry called, "What do you think this is, the prom? Let's go."

"Hold on, Jerry. How does it look if I'm sweating?"

Jerry stalked across the room, kicking Hutsinger's legs out of his way, and dialed the room number on the tenth floor. "Yeah," he said. "They didn't give me the room number, kid, I'm down in the lobby. All right, give me two minutes, I'll be right up. Oh—and you know I've got backup with me. She's checked out. Don't worry."

He put down the phone and clapped his hands together. "Okay, you bunch of sorry losers—let's get this done."

Just before they stepped out the door together, Jerry and Colette waited, smiling at each other with the nervous resolve of a circus act, and Kevin felt suddenly bitter about having to remain stranded in the room. As they crossed the hall and rode the clattering elevator, Kevin cupped his palm over the earpiece and listened to their conversation as if through a seashell. They spoke in hushed voices, most of the words lost in the movements of Jerry's shirt.

"That's pathetic," said Colette.

From the breathing and scrambling sounds, Kevin figured they were crossing the long hallway.

Maybe they were waiting to steel their nerves, because clearly Kevin heard his father say, ". . . but you were the best thief I ever knew."

"Don't turn back into Svengali on me now, Jerry. Especially with Kevin listening."

Jerry asked her something that was lost, and Colette, her voice in the midst of high-pitched frequencies, like a whale's songs, replied, "If you even *try* to distract me with that, Jerry, the whole thing is off."

"Just answer the question."

"You're completely different people. There isn't any comparison."

". . . from the start . . . weren't you? I know you kids were."

"Oh, my God, Jerry. Why are you still thinking about this?"

". . . not happy and you'll never be happy, and he's not either . . ."

"Not *now*, Jerry. We're working." Jerry's shirt rustled loudly again, and Kevin panicked that it might be some physical contact. But he was relieved to hear Colette laugh and, in a wave of diminishing static, say, "Kevin, honey—if you're listening. Your father is still a pig."

Finally they entered the room and the fragments of conversation took on a businesslike tone. Jerry was bantering with the kids. It sounded from the rustling that the bodyguard was frisking Jerry and Colette. The other said, "Throw her into the deal, homes."

". . . gallantly than that," said Colette.

Readjusting the scanner frequency, Kevin tapped into the phone call for the third mark, who sounded like he was pacing beside a busy street. It would be a few more minutes while they checked numbers. Through Jerry's transmitter Kevin heard a modem connection, and he waited patiently through the muted conversation, hearing as numbers were fed through the verification software.

"So far so good," said someone.

Hutsinger was falling asleep on the bed, one limp arm hanging down. In the earpiece, Kevin heard, "Looks good, old man!"

Kevin pulled one set of handcuffs from his belt line and abruptly cuffed Hutsinger to the bedpost. After two feckless tugs on the chain, Hutsinger gave up, eyeing Kevin with a look of mere annoyance. "You're just like your old man, kid. You people always got to make this shit complicated."

"Just shut up and keep eating your candy bars."

He tuned the scanner and heard the swimming, scattered frequencies of the phone call: "We're good." Through the earpiece he caught the wheezing kid announcing that the money was on the way up. Kevin checked his gun, loaded with blanks; he hung his counterfeit badge from his coat pocket; and he followed closely along the walls to the stairwell.

Thinking out loud, he whispered, "Which way are you coming up, kid? Stairwell, stairwell." But on the earpiece he heard the third mark enter the room. Kevin shouted, "Fuck!" The money must have been somewhere close by, maybe on the roof.

Everything was fine, he repeated to himself: there were still a dozen other options in his plan. As he was moving up the stairs, holding his ear, listening as the money was checked, Jerry said, in a blast of hot air, "Now that's a fucking *nest egg*." He said it so loudly that a squeal of feedback trailed his voice. The screeching sound made Kevin throw the piece from his ear.

Kevin stood still on the landing of the ninth floor. He was lathered with sweat and his heartbeat pulsed in his temples. He tilted his head back and said, "Oh, *no*—Dad!"

Three muffled gunshots came from the floor above.

Kevin sprinted upstairs and pushed through the fire door and onto the faded red carpet. He crouched down against the wall, sliding ahead toward the room. The door was already open. Someone had fled in the other direction, toward the service elevator. But, as if the sequence of deafening sounds in his ear had cleared his mind, Kevin lost track of his plans and escape routes and could only think of the ongoing catastrophe. Every plan seemed a stupid piece of vanity now, pointless showboating; and he wanted nothing more than to torch the entire room while dragging out his father and Colette.

He knelt in the doorway and peeked inside the suite's main room, making out the disarray of overturned armchairs and the scorched smell of gunpowder. From a momentary glimpse he tried to reconstruct the layout in his mind: at the base of chintz curtains there was a black piano, which faced the sturdy enclosure of a wet bar, lined with shattered decanters. Off to the left was the bedroom with salmon-colored walls. With his back pressed against the wall, Kevin rose up, then held the badge into the doorway. "Secret Service—this a bust! We've got backup on the way. Let's get down on the floor."

A gunshot burst at him, taking a chunk from the doorjamb. He dropped back down, breathing rapidly, and tried to figure out where it had come from.

He glanced around the door again, then fell back, fishing out his gun. There was the fireplace facade, a television playing a commercial without sound in the center of the carpet. Kevin's ears were still numbed by the shot.

"Kevin?" Colette called from the bedroom. "Kevin?"

The fact that she would break out of character and use his real name was more alarming to him than the series of gunshots. He ducked down and scrambled into the room, diving into a spot behind the white couch. From behind the wet bar, someone fired another shot, which struck the piano in a dissonant crash of notes. Across the white carpet Kevin now saw a trail of sprayed blood.

"Kevin? Kevin, honey?"

"This is Secret Service—we've got LAPD backing us up on the stairs. Let's put the guns down."

After a long silence, a nasal voice came from behind the bar: "Yeah, *right*."

As Kevin retreated into the cornered bedroom, in a crossfire, two, maybe three shots came from the bar and the bathroom. He slid across the carpet, behind the wall, where Colette was perched behind the cabinet with her gun drawn. The mirror of the closet door was angled so that she could see into the main room. Her face was red and her hair unraveled; she blew a strand out of her face and said, "Don't fire too much or they'll figure out we're using blanks."

"Where the fuck is my dad?"

"He did it. He got exactly what he wanted, Kevin—the piece of shit. I swear to God if we get out of this I'm going to cut him up and feed him to the fucking seagulls."

A rapid series of gunshots blew apart the wall beside them, thudding into plaster like wet sand, ringing off door hinges and fireplace irons, blowing the television apart like cheap fireworks, until there came a pause filled with the sound of reloading clips.

Colette said, "It's a hell of a trick. But he didn't expect these punks to be so heavily armed."

"What *happened*, Colette?"

She fired one blank shot into the room, the sound echoing, then she fell back, wiped her forehead, and said, "The bodyguard—the big Adam's apple. I knew it, I knew there was something wrong with that kid. He was Jerry's *plant*. They obviously had a deal worked out together. When everybody heard the reverb on the mike, the bodyguard just popped up like he expected it—took out a gun and in some ridiculous struggle dragged Jerry and the cash out of the room. It was a joke,

Kevin. It couldn't have fooled anybody but these two idiots. And they think they're in a fucking video game."

Kevin fired another meaningless shot through the doorway, then asked, "Well, what was your plan then?"

"Oh, for God's sake, Kevin. Will you look around for a second?"

A bullet whistled through the doorway and shattered a lamp across the room.

"I mean it," said Kevin. "What were you going to do? Were you leaving me?"

Suddenly her face grew slack and her eyes looked sad. She touched him on the face and said, "No, honey, I wasn't. What do I have to do to earn a little bit of faith here?" She fired two deafening shots through the open door.

He sagged against the wall and took a relieved breath of air, checking the cylinders on his revolver. "All right," he said. "Then I don't care about anything else. I'm through. I'm going to learn carpentry. Go to night school. I'm going to get my fucking GED."

From outside there came the first distant sirens, and within moments, a helicopter traversed the sky. Kevin shouted at the main room, "All right—congratulations. You figured it out. We're not cops and we all got ripped off. Hear me? So let's stop firing and we can all walk out of here."

"Fuck you," yelled the kid in the bathroom, with the hysterical sound of tears in his voice. "You fucking liars."

"This is all my fault," said Colette. "That son of a bitch has been wanting to get back at me for years, and I let him distract me with all kinds of father-figure bullshit, and I'll just never forgive myself."

"Okay, I don't want to talk about *that* right now, Colette."

It was fifteen strides across the suite to the front door, and Kevin didn't see how they could make it. To test his theory, he grabbed a pillow from the bed and hurled it into the main room. Both gunmen fired wildly, shredding the case and blowing goose feathers across the room.

"All right—we have to climb over the balcony."

They moved across the bedroom and quietly slid open the glass door. The sun had fallen to just above the hills, glaring off the windows around them. A police helicopter now circled the building, and, farther out, news choppers were drifting inward from the pink and orange haze on the horizon.

The neighboring balcony was separated by about six feet, with a straight drop into traffic below; so Kevin nodded to the balcony overhead. "Okay," he said. "You want to go up or down?"

"You've got to be kidding me."

"Up is safer. If the sliding glass door is locked, just bust through. We don't have time. Now get on my shoulders."

"This isn't a trapeze act, Kevin."

"Now!"

He stooped down as if for a game of leapfrog, and she kicked off her shoes. She climbed onto his shoulders and grabbed his hands, and—in a wobbling, precarious motion—he raised her upward. "Get both hands on the bars." He could barely keep his balance as she stood upright, her heels wedged into his shoulders. Suddenly he felt her stabilize them by grabbing the rungs, and her feet lifted off him. When he looked up, she had wedged one bare foot between the bars and was hauling herself upward under a fray of drifting hair and hanging clothes. "I'm going to fucking kill that man!"

At last she was upright against the railing, as the helicopter sank downward behind them. She hung her hands down and he waved them away. "I'm going in the other direction."

Over the din of rotor blades she called down, "Kevin? I have a room downstairs and an escape route."

"I know! *Just in case.*"

She smiled and reached down to touch his outstretched fingers a last time, pulling away as the loudspeaker on the chopper began to call them with a muffled voice. When Kevin looked ahead at the closed portion of the glass door, he saw—behind his own reflection—the shadow of another man.

A shot punctured the glass, sending weblike cracks outward and changing the angle of light so that he could see the mark, standing just a few feet away. He was about Kevin's age. His face was broad and flabby, his hair long and unwashed. He was an unlikely gunman, with his doughy arms and his asthma inhaler, but something in his black, lifeless eyes seemed less open to negotiation than any of the villains of his lifetime; for unlike them, he lacked even the simplest mercenary look of self-awareness. He watched Kevin only with curiosity; he savored the spectacle he had created. He grinned, raising his pistol, and, as if there were no other possible conclusion, pulled back the hammer. Kevin said, "You're not going to last."

He aimed the muzzle sideways, like a casual movie gangster, pulled the trigger, and with a sudden, violent kick, fired and missed from point-blank range.

Kevin gave a sharp bark of stunned laughter, then stepped over the balcony railing. The helicopter was drifting closer. Just as Kevin began shimmying downward, the second mark ran into the bedroom firing wildly. A rattle of bullets came from the chopper and the room simultaneously, and Kevin slipped off the railing just as he had swung his momentum inward toward the hotel.

In the chaos, Kevin first had no idea if he had fallen one floor or ten. Gradually he realized that his trajectory had flung him over the next balcony: he had dropped, struck the railing, and splashed off through a glass table. He was bleeding. The back of his head had struck the baluster. Something was burning in his side; worse than pain, it was like a crippling weight, and he thought it must be glass from the table. He climbed to his feet and, with the world bowed and spinning, he stumbled through the open sliding glass door and threw up a stomach full of coffee onto the floor.

When he looked up he saw three terrified children sitting on the bed, loud cartoon sounds on the television behind him. He touched his jacket and it was wet; his hand was smeared with blood. To the children he said, "No, no—don't be scared. I'm not—I'm not—I'm okay. *I love you all*—I would never hurt you." He could scarcely tell where his own voice was coming from.

He was cold, and he took a coat off a hook in the entryway. He struggled ahead, heard someone screaming behind him, and soon he was out of the room and into the hall, moving ahead with such determination that it seemed an entirely new country. Doors peeked open along his path, clicking shut again as they saw him. Yes, he was hit; it was more than glass from the table. His leg wouldn't bend and every breath was like a stab in the lungs. Had he been hit from the front or the back? Was it the mark or the police? He felt a physical wave of sadness that he might never know who was responsible for killing him.

As he reached the stairs, an alarm system went off throughout the hotel. He clambered down three flights, throwing up again through the steel mesh, and on the sixth floor he wandered out to find Colette, repeating the room number like a mantra, until it was a meaningless sound.

She was there in the hall. She grabbed him and led him into the room, whispering, "No, no, no, no—just walk. Just walk. You're hurt."

Inside the dim room, the curtains drawn and glowing with the last captured light, Colette had assembled housekeeping and bellhop uniforms, luggage racks and room service trays. He reacted to the sight as if it were some unexpected trick, and began fighting her, thrashing against her arms. She grabbed him, her palms around his face, and kissed him hard on the mouth. "You're delirious, Kevin—you have to listen to me. The police are all over the place. But we're going to get out of here and get you to a hospital."

"The laundry room," said Kevin. "Go to the laundry room."

He thought an insect was buzzing rhythmically under his collar, tickling his skin, but he soon realized it was the earpiece, playing the distant indecipherable static of his father's voice. Colette was guiding him to the service elevator, where she used her copy of the key. Inside, the bodyguard lay in a heap on the steel floor. Colette checked his pulse and said, "He's alive. At least your father isn't a murderer yet."

The alarm was howling on the basement floor as Colette helped Kevin forward, moving under the fluttering lights. She said that her plan was to go out with the dry cleaning, but Kevin, choking on his words, said, "No—they'll grab us." He pointed to a square drainage grate in the floor.

"I can't tell how clearly you're thinking right now," said Colette.

He swallowed, tasting blood. For a moment he felt warm and calm with satisfaction. "My plan was *better*."

"Jesus, I can't believe you're going to be competitive with me right now. Let's go then. Let's get down in the trash where we belong."

She patted around his coat and found a road flare and matches, raising her eyebrows at the discovery. She pried up the rusted steel grate, which gave way easily, then spit into the darkness, hearing the faint plink in the water below. "I might need a minute here."

Kevin went first. With a deep, keening pain down his side, he lowered himself into the darkness, hanging, slipping, and finally splashing into shin-deep water. Mildew and bleach fumes, chlorine and sewage, the smell was frightening, and when Colette dropped into the stream behind him, she made a horrified gasp.

She lit the flare, holding it upward like a torch. They were in a narrow drainage tunnel, filtering downhill toward a chewed grate in the distance, the steel walls in a pattern of rust and moss. He saw diluted blood running from the lining of his coat. When he looked down into the murky water, a slick rat swam past his legs. There was a frothy edge to the water, where, caught among shoals of scum, there floated chains of forgotten things: a doll's head, clots of newspaper pages, patterns of socks and dryer lint. Colette was trudging forward, grimacing. "Okay," she whispered. "Okay. We're right under the cops. Do you know where we can come up?" She paused, reared back from something in the water, then said, "I am so fucking scared right now."

There were sweeps of childlike graffiti on the concave walls, lost blankets and cardboard boxes, what looked to Kevin like the desperate washed-out homes of children and fugitives. He was dizzy and numb in his teeth. "Somebody lives here," he said. Police cars gusted overhead, their sirens echoing below, rumbling in the concrete, giving way finally to the swirling, breathing sounds of the tunnel itself.

She kept struggling ahead beside him, the flare shedding sparks into the muck at their feet.

"Don't touch anything, Kevin. You'll die from the infection."

The shrinking light of the torch crossed over pillows and papers, barricades of milk cartons and grocery bags.

"Keep going," he said. "We need to be under the next alley."

He felt a sudden shock in his chest, and thought it might be a final seizure—but it was the battery pack and the earpiece, shorting out with dampness. He peeled it off and hurled it to the side, then once again felt the wild throbbing of the bullet in his side. The shock seemed to be wearing off in stages, and he felt the first sobering intensity of terminal pain. Above them now was a cluster of massive pipes, leading toward a recess in the low ceiling. "That's a ladder," whispered Colette. "Are we going to come up in the middle of the street?"

"I'm dying, I think."

She grabbed him and helped him forward, and he lay against her, smelling a pocket of her sweet shampoo in the midst of all the rank water. "You must honestly love me," he said.

"I must."

In another fifty steps, they were ascending a steel ladder with so much moss grown over the rungs that it seemed built of short, bristling hairs. Colette fought against a heavy manhole cover overhead, finally pushing it to the side to reveal a circle of late evening sky. She helped him upward by the arm, the last steps, and they emerged onto a dim alley beside the boulevard.

A sports car sat beside a lit doorway, from which poured the smells of a restaurant, and Colette drew her gun and waited beside it. Kevin sagged against the car and set off the alarm. When the man rushed outside, Colette pushed the gun against the back of his head, and hissed, "Give me the keys or your fucking brains are all over the pavement."

In the growing shadows, the man stood still and quietly dangled his keys from an extended finger. She took them, ordered Kevin into the car. As she turned the ignition and dropped the clutch, they hiccuped forward into rush-hour traffic.

She was gasping, her mouth open, trying to figure out the manual transmission. "I don't ever want a gun in my hand again. Real bullets or not," she said with her voice shaking. "There just wasn't enough time to be classy about it."

For blocks she didn't look at Kevin, but he knew they were both following the same thought: it was a disaster beyond what anyone had ever dreamed, and Jerry was out there somewhere, oblivious.

The car phone rang and they waited in silence, while Colette twisted her head to find the helicopters in the sky.

"And by the way, I'm going to murder your father. I'm going to make it my life's purpose."

She reached across the car and touched his face, "Don't give up on me, baby."

He felt no anger, no bitterness, no anxiety, no regrets, only an intense, searing pain that reduced his life to a flickering of memories and images. It was a slide show passing out his window, darkening with each frame. He looked out the window and for some reason recognized each alley and street corner as if it were his childhood home. He wanted to recount everything decent and real he had ever known along these streets; but instead he could only sputter, "Look where we are. We were kids—"

"Shhh, honey. Try not to talk."

AN OVERNIGHT DRIVE

In the hospital corridor he moved with a clawing pain in his ribs, finding the package and clipboard, ducking in and out of rooms as he approached the elevators, and leaping inside at the last minute with a group of patients. He was sweating and trembling and an old woman asked him if he was all right.

"I'm just afraid of hospitals, ma'am. I had a bad experience in one."

As the doors opened for the lobby, he stepped out into the crowds, full of faith. He had no idea how any of this would work, but he moved ahead, and didn't question. He recognized the feeling, distantly, as when he'd first fled with his father and driven off into the night. Winded, he moved through the momentary clutter of a changing shift, then rested against a large semicircular desk lined with black-and-white TV monitors underneath, where the night security guard was just arriving and hastily getting organized.

The guard was an old man with a scowl that looked permanently etched into his face, and, instead of Kevin's eyes, he looked at the urgent package.

"Ah, Jesus Christ," said the guard. He fumbled around rapidly through papers, then looked back at the clipboard, moving his face very close and lifting off his glasses. "You're telling me Eddie just signed this and sent you upstairs."

"Guess so."

"No, no, *no*. Look at the address here—you got to get over to wing C. Hurry. What the hell is in that thing, anyway?"

Kevin shrugged.

"Fastest way is right outside, straight across to that building over there."

Kevin pointed, mimicking the guard's actions.

"And Jesus, hurry up."

When Kevin reached the main door, he was out of breath. He saluted the guard, pushed out backward, and moved into the balmy, breezy night. The skies were pink with captured streetlights and the air was alive with the ambient hum of the nearby boulevard. Kevin walked across the plaza, through saw palmettos, down a grassy slope to the curb. Sirens rose and faded all around the city, just a lonely sound on a warm night.

In a row of parked cars, a pair of headlights flashed on, shining across him like a searchlight. As the car pulled forward, Kevin saw his father behind the wheel.

He got quietly into the backseat of the car, and as they sped off with the windows down, he felt the thoughtless pleasure of the wind blowing across him. His father was panicked by his injuries, alternating between vehement apologies, sudden fits of anger about the three hackers, and pleading that Kevin would heal into his former athletic self. Every now and then something sounded too rehearsed, like an uncertain prayer or a nervous eulogy, but he knew that his father didn't mean to deceive him again. He simply didn't have words for the truth.

Kevin was in pain, but because he believed he would survive, he could tolerate it now.

Colette sat in the backseat with Kevin, reaching over to touch him and sitting upright again when he seemed more comfortable in his own stream of wind. They grew superstitiously quiet. Across freeway interchanges and under winding tunnels, they moved outward through ringlets of hills, into the San Gabriel Valley, where the air smelled like baked concrete.

"Your father still has the money," said Colette. Her hair was trailing wildly around her, and she fought away the loose strands, holding it off her face.

But, speaking as if under some anesthesia that loosened his tongue, he said, "There's no fucking money anymore."

"Yes, there is, Kev. I promise you. I meant to teach your little wife some humility back there, but I never meant to cut you two out of the deal. It's all there. My fifty percent and yours."

"Oh, fifty percent between the two of us!" said Colette, laughing.

"Don't start fucking arguing the numbers on me now, baby—we've just brought Kevin back from the dead."

"And you're going to nickel-and-dime us to the bitter end."

They arrived at Jerry's rented house in a dust storm, wind devils forming on the dead lawn, trash cans lying overturned, and plumes of mist rising off the sprinklers from a nearby yard.

"Are they staking out the house?"

"Not anymore," said Jerry. "Last car left after they searched the place and didn't find anything. But we got to be quick."

He led them out to the garage, raising the door to reveal a clutter of shadows in the dark. Everyone was startled by the dark configurations inside, but when Jerry turned on the lights, it was only Melody's decorations. She had made up the room as if for a party, with streamers that read, "Welcome home," hanging piñatas, hula skirts, and a mannequin in a Hawaiian shirt. Jerry looked seasick for a moment, then said, "I guess she got over the rats."

Nothing else remained but overturned water heaters, cedar boards, and reams of torn-up paper. Jerry took out a screwdriver and a crowbar and began taking apart one of the water heaters, while Colette sat on a foldout chair, wearing a party hat and exhaling into a blowout horn that unraveled and retracted like a frog's tongue. Paper buckets were filled with candy; balloons were tethered to every exposed electrical conduit. Colette began blowing her horn over and over at Kevin, laughing at his exasperated face.

"It's here," said Jerry.

Finally he pried his way into the water tank, cursing as he hurt his hand. Out of the water heater spilled hundreds of fortune cookies, the farthest few tumbling and resting at Kevin's feet.

Jerry looked back and forth between the cookies and his team, then rose up suddenly, shouting and stomping on them like a swarm of fire ants. "That whore. That back-stabbing lying bitch. I'm going to find her and I'm going to fucking kneecap her."

Colette started laughing, so hard and hysterically that her feet ran in place and her cheeks turned red. "You have a gift with women, Jerry."

He threw himself into the cedar boards and slumped down, flabbergasted and as limp as a scarecrow. Kevin picked up a shred of paper and read it aloud: ". . . which may be all you truly deserve . . ."

"Yeah, yeah," said Jerry from his slumped position. "She's an idiot. She thought people would sit around at parties trying to piece together some stupid message in a bunch of cookies."

Colette found one and read: "Elizabeth, I'm sorry I couldn't get to know you . . ." She sniffled, recovering from laughter, and said, "God, Jerry. It's a letter to us."

So for a solemn half hour the three partners moved on their hands and knees, piecing together a long message on the floor. At times they almost forgot their catastrophe, cooperating like children around a jigsaw puzzle. When the message lay completed, beginning in the middle of the garage and swirling outward in the shape of a whirlpool, they took turns reading it aloud:

Dear Jerry, Kevin, and Elizabeth, a.k.a. Daniel, Douglas, and Esther:

Congratulations on gaining and losing a fortune that would make any group of common thieves proud. I had my doubts, but I'm pleased to see that you've finally met your potential. It's particularly touching that you would all reunite for this occasion, so please enjoy my special pecan fudge birthday cake, along with many other consolation prizes. You have much to celebrate. Aside from each other—which may be all that you *truly* deserve—you have years of fond memories and a wonderful unexplored future. I have relieved you of the money, and in exchange I offer you sole proprietorship of my up-and-coming business venture. May you bring others as much joy and amusement as you've brought me. Jerry, you are a masterful teacher; Kevin, you are a spirited young crook. As for you, Elizabeth, I'm sorry I couldn't get to know you better, but I hope that you will enjoy the macaroons I've left on the table. As for your eternal souls, consider this exchange to be your first step toward a great involuntary redemption. Zero is a liberating number. And—for your own salvation—this money will be used for great purposes: feeding the hungry, nursing the sick, or whatever floats your boat. I will see to it that no dollar is wasted. Christ hung on the cross between two thieves, one good and one evil. I have always considered myself that good thief, and I am looking forward to embracing Him with all of my newfound riches.

Sincerely,

Melody

P.S. At dawn I intend to leave an anonymous tip with the police. Now might be a good time to begin your new lives.

The three thieves stood in a circle, staring down. Colette reached out and held Kevin's hand, while she patted Jerry on his sunken shoulder.

"You have to admire her craftsmanship," she said. "She's a goddamn Scheherazade."

An hour later, Kevin sat in the front seat while Colette drove them beyond the last streetlights, out into the desert where the skies opened and the air smelled rich with dust and creosote. Jerry lay down in the backseat, facing the ceiling, moaning that he had never been so angry and miserable in his entire life. If he lived a thousand years he would never trust another woman. In a passing fit, he raged and kicked the upholstery until finally, like an infant, he exhausted himself and was pacified by the rocking over uneven roads.

Kevin thought he could read Colette's thoughts from the way she fluctuated on the gas pedal. She was hesitant through the mountains, uncertain through the empty trench of highway along Barstow; but once they hit the open stretch toward the dark horizon, she began to accelerate unknowingly, as if toward some distant lingering belief. He could tell by the determination on her face that she was still brave enough to expect something better on the other side of this road; and he knew for the first time, seeing the landscape and perceiving the vastness of what lay ahead, that he was finally tough enough and patient enough to find it. Kevin leaned back and savored the rolling pain in his chest, a souvenir, a burning trinket, a brand on his bones that he might feel forever, until it took on the certainty and comfort of a ritual. He sat up straight in the seat, dug the last crumpled bills out of the glove compartment, and said, "Get us to Vegas by sunrise, honey. And I'll cover breakfast."